ALL HE WANTED
WAS TO TOUCH HER

She served him, gracefully and from her knees with her legs folded under her—the shy, unassuming maiden offering him anything he cared to take. The choice was entirely his.

"Would you like a piece of seed cake now?" Her soft voice caused every nerve ending in his body to tingle. "It's very good."

"I'm hungry," he heard his own voice say as he shifted closer to her on the blanket, "but not for seed cake." His hand went to the back of her neck and drew her close. He tasted her lips, gently, carefully. The sensation was so exquisite that he moaned. Such soft, full lips, warm with vital life, shyly kissing him back.

She was his, everything about her said so. And he was finding it impossible to disagree . . .

Silken Dreams

SHARON GREEN

AVON BOOKS ◆ NEW YORK

SILKEN DREAMS is an original publication of Avon Books. This work has never before appeared in book form. This work is a novel. Any similarity to actual persons or events is purely coincidental.

AVON BOOKS
A division of
The Hearst Corporation
1350 Avenue of the Americas
New York, New York 10019

Copyright © 1994 by Sharon Green
Inside cover author photograph by Olan Mills
Published by arrangement with the author
Library of Congress Catalog Card Number: 94-94345
ISBN: 0-380-77393-7

First Avon Books Printing: December 1994

AVON TRADEMARK REG. U.S. PAT. OFF. AND IN OTHER COUNTRIES, MARCA REGISTRADA, HECHO EN U.S.A.

Printed in the U.S.A.

RA   10   9   8   7   6   5   4   3   2   1

My thanks go, in alphabetical order, to the following people:

To Charles L. Fontenay, for generously supplying the necessary words in the Chinese language;

To the marvelous Anne McCaffrey, for the phrase, "Lady Mine";

To David Shockley and Kevin Ward, artists and friends, without whom the first love scene couldn't have been written nearly as well;

To the late Robert van Gulik, for the incomparable "Judge Dee" mysteries set in ancient China.

Chapter 1

England, 1751

Amanda Edmunds stood at the rail of the ship, watching the docking excitedly. After all the years of dreaming about this moment, it was finally coming true. She would be in England, and not just in England, but in London itself.

"Good morning, Miss Edmunds," she heard a pleasant voice say, and Amanda glanced up to see Colonel Ebersham to her left. "I expected the two of us to be the only ones watching the docking. The others are still undoubtedly recovering from last night's farewell revels."

"I don't understand how they can bear to miss their actual homecoming," Amanda said, eyes still glued to the slow but steady approach of their vessel to the dock. "Don't they realize what a marvelous occasion it is?"

"It's only marvelous to the likes of us, child," Colonel Ebersham replied with a chuckle. He was a pleasant man just beyond middle years, with a bushy brown mustache that was showing the first signs of gray. His carriage was always militarily erect despite the permanent limp he'd acquired in the line of duty, and although he often barked out orders to those around him, he'd never done so with Amanda.

"You see, my dear, you and I are able to appreciate what being away from England for an extended period of time can mean." His words were to the point, but Amanda

1

knew he was also watching the docking closely. "You left England as an infant, and I as a soldier. Neither of us was free to return whenever the whim struck us, so finally managing it has special meaning. All the others come and go as they please."

"I can't decide if I envy them or pity them," Amanda said thoughtfully after a moment. "I had to lose my father before I was able to make this journey, but I also regained the land of my birth. The others were spared the grief of loss, but they also missed gaining anything. The wise men were right when they said that a life without loss is very difficult to enrich. Achieving something means less when you don't have a *lack* of achievement with which to compare it."

"It continually amazes me how wise a girl you keep proving yourself to be despite your youth," the colonel responded warmly. "It must be your upbringing in the Orient that accounts for it, as none of the other young ladies aboard show signs of the same. Not to mention a spark of your bubbling charm. You *are* being met at the dock, I trust?"

"Of course." Amanda's small laugh was one of delighted anticipation. "My half brother Richard will be here, and I can't wait to meet him. I'm sure he's just as wonderful as his letters have been."

"That would be your mother's son from her first marriage," Colonel Ebersham recalled aloud. "You told me that he inherited from his late father when still quite young, and for that reason he was left to be raised here in England. I believe you said your mother returned once a year to visit?"

"Until two years before her death." Amanda's nod was heavy with the sadness of the memory. "She'd meant to start taking *me* back with her, but fell ill before she could. She fought to stay alive as long as possible, to keep from deserting *two* children was the way she put it. In the end death won, but not easily. Even at the age of ten I was able to appreciate how hard she fought to make things come out *her* way. I'll always admire her courage and determination."

"As well you should," the colonel agreed gruffly, the unsteadiness in his voice showing how touched he felt. "A woman with that much heart is a rarity in this modern day of ours, and had I met such a woman myself I would not have remained unmarried. And I must say I'll miss *your* company when we part, and not only because you made me and this blasted walking stick less conspicuous. Are you certain you're strong enough to debark on your own?"

For a moment Amanda didn't understand, and then she remembered what she'd said about the four-foot length of bamboo she usually had with her. It had taken everyone's immediate attention, and she had to come up with a tale about needing the staff to lean on during the times when she suddenly felt weak. If those about her didn't know what the staff was really for, it would be foolish to tell them. And how marvelously useful it was that young ladies were *supposed* to be subject to the sudden onset of the vapors.

"Please don't concern yourself with me, Colonel," she said, turning to give him a sincerely warm smile. "I'll be fine during debarkation, and I won't be alone. My companion Pei is with me, you know."

"Ah, yes, the slender and silent Miss Han," Colonel Ebersham said with a nod. "She's kept so much to herself during the voyage, I'd nearly forgotten about her. The language difference must be something of a difficulty for her."

"Not really," Amanda returned with private amusement. "Pei speaks English even better than I speak *her* dialect. My father felt his studies of China would be nonexistent if he didn't learn the local language, and even Mother knew some words and phrases. The learning was easiest for me, as I grew up with the various languages, as did Pei. When we were children, we practiced together."

"Her mode of dress is rather exotic," the colonel observed with a small frown of memory. "A long, straight

gown over loose trousers. Your gowns, however, appear to
be quite up-to-date and proper. I've wondered how you
managed that."

"Mother was the one who managed it," Amanda told
him, glancing back to see that the ship was now completely docked. "Father's modest income was a veritable
fortune in China, so Mother used part of it to have gowns
in the newest fashion made and sent to her once a year.
Those times were between her visits home, so she had new
gowns twice a year. Before she died, she changed the arrangement so that *I* would have the proper gowns. And
now I really must ask you to excuse me. Pei and I are all
packed, and as soon as the gangway is in place we'll be
debarking. It's been a pleasure to know you, Colonel."

"And twice the pleasure for me, dear lady," he responded, taking her hand and bending over it. "Perhaps
I'll be fortunate enough that we'll meet again someday."

· Amanda simply smiled at that, then left him at the railing. Colonel Ebersham was a really nice man, but finding
a husband for her was her brother's job. Mother had made
sure she understood that from the time she was very
young. Father was too wrapped up in his studies—not to
mention hardly in a position to know who was and wasn't
eligible and acceptable—and her brother Richard had long
since accepted the duty. He would make sure she was as
well matched as possible, and Amanda was really looking
forward to the time courting began.

But right now she was looking forward even more to
being off that ship and beginning her new life. She held up
the skirts of her dark green traveling gown as she hurried
to her cabin. She already wore her hat, but still had to get
her gloves and reticule—not to mention the staff of bamboo. Pei was sitting in a chair reading when Amanda entered the cabin, but looked up immediately.

"Are we finally there?" Pei asked in almost accentless
English. "I mean *really* there, not just coming close?"

"It's no longer 'there' but 'here,' " Amanda answered
with a laugh. "We are *here,* so why are you just sitting

there? By the time we get back to the deck, the gangway should be in place."

"It will probably take them longer than that, but I'd rather be waiting in the fresh air," Pei said, rising to put the book in one of her cases. "That's what I've missed most on this trip, I think, the smell of green growing things."

"I'm afraid you'll continue to miss it for a while," Amanda said, gathering together the items she wanted. "There are a lot of smells up there, but green growing things isn't among them. Not that *I* care. First I want to meet my brother, and then I intend to find out what happened to Mr. Lichfield."

"Which you will," Pei said with an amused smile. "*Ssu Te Lung* is never denied."

Amanda laughed softly at the name Pei had called her by. It meant Silken Dragon, and had been given to her by Miles Lichfield, her father's long-time secretary. After Amanda's mother died, Mr. Lichfield had been there for her much more often than her father. Professor George Edmunds had loved his daughter, but the obsession of his work usually kept him from showing it. Mr. Lichfield had become both mother and father to his employer's child, and she had come to love him like the daughter he'd never had. Now he was missing, but Amanda had no intentions of letting that situation continue.

Amanda led Pei back up to the deck, and Pei's earlier guess turned out to be right. "Rot," Amanda muttered. "The gangway *isn't* in place yet, and the other passengers obviously knew it wouldn't be. Even Colonel Ebersham is no longer on deck."

Amanda's impatience flared, but she wasn't dressed to jump from the ship even if she decided to go that far. Waiting seemed to be the only option . . . along with keeping alert for anything she might find it possible to do.

Miss Han Pei stood on the deck beside her best friend, working hard not to wrinkle her nose against what seemed like hundreds of aromas, all of them combining into one large foul stench. The docks at Po San where they'd boarded the ship hadn't been this bad, but there also hadn't been so many buildings and people, or so much bustling activity. After growing up in Kiyang Province, England would have a lot of things to which she'd have to adjust.

But that went primarily for her. Amanda stood there all but glowing, despite the flaring impatience Pei could see so clearly. Her friend was a girl who greeted everything new and strange with bubbling delight, who dived in to investigate without a moment's hesitation. That penchant had nearly gotten her into trouble more than once, but it still hadn't taught her caution and restraint.

Pei sighed, wondering if anything ever would teach Amanda not to dive headlong into things. It seemed highly unlikely, especially as Amanda also expected to be victorious in any and all encounters. To look at her, one would never suspect . . . only a touch taller than average for European females, they'd been told by her father, with shining dark brown hair, bright blue eyes, a merry smile usually on her pretty face, an excellent figure in those odd English gowns—so innocent looking, and so guileless. . . .

But Pei knew better than that, and so did anyone else who knew Amanda. It was the reason Mr. Lichfield had nicknamed her Silken Dragon, looking as soft and gentle as she did, while hiding the unyielding remorselessness of a flaming dragon within. Amanda *always* got what she wanted, whether or not others were willing to give it to her.

And now what she wanted was to find Mr. Lichfield. The wonderful older man had come ahead to England after his employer's death, to settle Professor Edmunds's small estate and to make arrangements for Amanda's arrival. Amanda had stayed with Pei's family, but when the third packet had docked at Po San without word from Mr. Lichfield, Amanda became convinced something had happened to him. She'd immediately begun to try to find a way to make her own arrangements for going to England, but then the letter from her brother arrived. He'd heard about her father's death and had quickly arranged her passage.

Which meant, apparently, passage for two. Young English ladies never traveled alone, it seemed, and after learning what dressing entailed for them, Pei wasn't surprised. Amanda had had a maid in her father's house, a girl from the village who was sweet but not terribly bright. The idea of traveling to the land of foreign devils had terrified the girl, and she had run home after tearfully refusing to accompany Amanda and had not returned.

But that had given Pei her chance. Her father was the largest and most well-known merchant in Kiyang Province, not to mention the wealthiest. The women's compound of his house held his four wives, his two concubines, and his three daughters, as well as the younger children. The rest of his grown children were sons, a total of twelve in all, his being able to afford all of them easily another mark of his high position.

"So I don't understand why he won't let me go with you," Pei had complained to Amanda after speaking to her father. They had used Pei's rooms for the meeting, which meant they'd had to keep their voices low. "I know three daughters aren't many, but some people consider daughters so unimportant that they sell theirs to brothels. Why does *my* father have to be a man who loves and values his?"

"I seriously doubt if you're complaining about *that* part of it," Amanda had responded with amusement. "I agree that his loving you makes things inconvenient, but we should be able to work around it. Find out when *I* can talk to him."

Pei had been delighted with Amanda's offer to help and had arranged the meeting as quickly as possible. She had accompanied her friend, but had stayed quietly to one side of the room.

"This unworthy one thanks the honorable Mr. Han for seeing her," Amanda had said in Chinese with a bow when

Pei's father had looked up from the document on his desk. "This one has come to apologize for having presumed far too much."

"In what way have you presumed, child?" Mr. Han had asked with puzzlement, putting aside his writing brush. "I have always found you an extremely suitable companion for my daughter Pei; one who not only knows of our ways, but follows them."

"It has been this one's honor and pleasure to do so," Amanda had replied with another bow, this one of thanks. "Perhaps it was for this reason that I presumed. This village is the only home I have ever known, and I love it with all my heart. Now, however, I must depart for alien places, and my fear and reluctance to go are considerable. Also, the thought of leaving Pei behind is extremely painful to me. She and I have grown to be like sisters, and parting from her for all time . . . I had thought to borrow her strength to sustain me in this time of leavetaking, and to put off having to bid her farewell forever—"

Amanda's words had broken off then with a catch in her throat, and Pei had caught a glimpse of the tears on her cheeks before Amanda bent her head. Pei's father had looked seriously touched, not to mention troubled.

"I am able to see your deep concern, child, and truly share your sadness," he'd answered gently. "To leave one's home is no easy thing, but far easier than to leave one who has become like one's own blood. That you must now do both is a tragedy, and yet I cannot see a way to assist you. If you were relieved of the need to travel alone by having Pei accompany you, then *she* would be faced with the very same need when the time came to return. You certainly would not wish to cause her to be in such a position."

"Certainly not," Amanda had responded, raising her face to him again. "And I must apologize for that as well. Although my brother would surely find a companion to accompany her on the return voyage and pay all expenses both going and coming, there was little reason to disaccommodate you. Your need for Pei to remain here is surely greater than mine for her to accompany me."

After saying that, Amanda had simply gazed at him sadly. But also appealingly, something that couldn't possibly be considered a waste with a man whose household contained six women for his pleasure. Pei's father had sat stroking his long black beard, his gaze lost in deep thought, and at last he had sighed.

"Perhaps I was overhasty in my original decision," he had allowed, smiling fondly at Amanda. "I had not considered the bond between you two, and how painful the severing of such a bond must be. Pei will travel with you, with my permission, but she *must* be properly companioned on the return voyage."

Amanda had solemnly given her word that it would be done even if *she* had to pay the cost, the two of them had taken their leave, and so Pei had embarked on the adventure she'd dreamed of all her life. Not specifically a trip to another land, but something marvelous and different. She expected to marry and settle down someday, but the thought of spending the rest of her life in the women's compound of some man's household without memories to sustain her . . . that would be a doom too horrible to bear.

"Oh, how good of you, Captain," Pei heard, and looked up to see that Amanda's drippingly sweet words were addressed to the captain of their vessel. "It's so delightful for a lady to find herself among gallant gentlemen."

That particular gallant gentleman, roughly dressed and unshaven, bowed like one of the dandies among the other passengers and hurried away to shout orders at the men rushing around the deck. Amanda waited until the man was out of earshot, then turned to Pei with a very tiny smile.

"It seems we've docked slightly ahead of schedule, and the captain saw no reason to lower the gangway before beginning to unload the cargo." Her murmur was very soft and carried to no one but Pei. "Now, however, he seems to have discovered a reason, which means we'll be ashore in just a few minutes. I wonder if all European men are as easy to twist as this?"

Pei was even more amused than Amanda, but a proper upbringing in her country included learning how not to show it. "Inscrutable" was the way Professor Edmunds had put it, but her people considered it simple intelligence. Why give things away to those you dealt with, thereby increasing the strength of their position?

But the point Amanda had brought up was a good one. Women in Pei's land were taught to defer to men, but also how to flatter and cajole them in order to get what they wanted. The men had grown used to treatment like that and rarely came around at the first shy drop of a gaze or deferential stance. If the men in *this* land *weren't* used to such treatment, the possibilities were virtually limitless. . . .

With the captain shouting at his crew, it wasn't long before the men had set the rope-railed gangway into position. Pei watched as the captain took his cap off and bowed as Amanda swept past him with a dazzling smile of thanks. And he didn't even glance in her direction as she followed quietly in her friend's wake. Amanda had once despaired over the fact that she would never be one of the world's great beauties, but Pei couldn't see that it was making much of a difference. Her inner glow seemed to make her more than beautiful in the eyes of men, an advantage she wasn't hesitating to use.

Once again victorious, the Silken Dragon led the way to the dock proper, and once Pei had joined her Amanda began to look around in earnest. Pei found the area was terribly crowded with wagons and waiting people and bales and sacks, leaving very little room for the new people who began to arrive. Their attention on the ship said they were there to meet passengers or take delivery of cargo, and the whole place began to take on the semblance of one of the Taoist hells: people running every which way, as though pursued by invisible devils.

"Richard will never find us in this madhouse," Amanda

said over the mounting noise. "Let's see if we can find some place more peaceful to wait."

And then she led off at once, giving Pei no chance to point out that it might not be wise to leave the vicinity of the ship. Pei followed with a sigh, wishing for the hundredth time that Amanda wasn't quite so fearless. It had a lot to do with what Amanda had learned from Master Ma, the most famous instructor in Chinese boxing of his time. Master Ma had his compound in their village, and as children she and Amanda had often gone there secretly to watch the fighters learn and practice.

But where Pei had just watched, Amanda had begun to learn, and later practiced what she'd learned. That might not have been so bad, but the day finally came when Master Ma calmly approached the place they'd thought was so secret, and announced it was time they showed him what they'd learned. Pei hadn't been able to do anything but touch her head to the ground in apology for the intrusion, but not so Amanda.

The Silken Dragon had calmly gotten to her feet, bowed respectfully to Master Ma, and then had shown him what she'd practiced. Master Ma told her in detail how bad her form was and how many mistakes she'd made, and then had ordered her to try again. That had been the beginning of her lessons, and when Mr. Lichfield had found out about it, he'd even given her the copper cash to pay Master Ma. She hadn't been taught *everything* the male students were, but what she did learn she was rather good at. Unfortunately.

"There," Amanda said, recapturing Pei's attention. "That small alleyway looks empty, and we'll be able to see people arriving without being trampled by them. Let's wait in there."

"You sound as if you expect to recognize your brother," Pei pointed out as she followed again. "Since you've never seen him, how do you mean to do that?"

"He's certain to be the most handsome man who arrives," Amanda replied with a laugh to show she was only joking. "But beyond that, he'll be carrying the small length of bamboo I sent him. How many other men are likely to be carrying bamboo around here?"

Pei granted the point with a silent nod, paying more attention to where she put her slippered feet than to the conversation. The dock wasn't as clean as it might have been, and there was a real possibility of stepping in something unpleasant. The closer they got to the alleyway, though, the better it became. That probably meant the alleyway wasn't used much.

"Having so many tall buildings all around is going to take getting used to," Amanda said as she stopped just inside the mouth of the alleyway. "I thought Mr. Feng's warehouse was huge, but most of these are twice the size."

Pei had thought the same and was about to say so, but never got the chance. She'd stopped beside Amanda, both of them facing toward the ship, and suddenly there were hands grasping her arms from behind. She cried out as she was yanked backward, toward the dimness of the alleyway where the rising sun hadn't yet reached.

"Yell all ye like, girlie, none'll hear ye through the noise," a coarse voice chortled, turning Pei's fear to terror. "Us 'n you two's 'bout t' have some fun."

A large body brushed past her, obviously heading for Amanda, and then everything began to happen at once. Pei had only just started to struggle when there was a cry of pain, but it did *not* originate with Amanda. The man who had tried to seize Amanda collapsed to the ground, and then the Silken Dragon was going after a second man. This one put up an arm to fend off the swinging bamboo, but it did him little good. Amanda used the bottom of her staff to strike lower, and when he clutched at himself with a choked sound of agony, the top of the staff struck his head hard enough to put him beyond pain for a while.

After that the man holding Pei seemed the only one left, and when Amanda started toward *him* with the dragon look in her eyes, he decided against making any useless gestures. The staff in Amanda's hands was still being held at the ready, and he wisely turned and ran before he ended up joining his friends on the ground. Amanda wasn't the best staff fighter Master Ma had ever trained, but neither was she the worst.

"Pei, are you all right?" Amanda asked with concern as soon as it was clear the third man was gone for good. "Did he hurt you?"

"Only if you consider being frightened half to death as being hurt," Pei answered, trying to calm the thundering of her heart. "This was almost as bad as when that tiger came down out of the hills during our outing that time."

Amanda smiled with a nod, undoubtedly remembering the time as clearly as Pei did. They'd just been children with their families, but luckily the magistrate and his tribunal officers had joined them for the outing. The magistrate's two lieutenants had used spears from horseback to drive the tiger away, and later had led the hunt for it.

"I think I've changed my mind about how good a place this is to wait," Amanda said, putting an arm around Pei's shoulders. "Let's find another before those two wake up."

"Weren't *you* frightened, even a little?" Pei demanded as Amanda urged her around the two unconscious men. "You sound as though this was nothing more than a routine exercise set you by Master Ma, and I find that extremely annoying."

"But Pei, I didn't have *time* to be frightened," Amanda countered with a grin. "I turned when I heard you cry out, and then those men took turns coming at me. When they were both down I was able to see the one holding you, and that made me mad. He had no right to touch you, and I was about to teach him that when he ran. By then there was nothing left to be frightened *about.*"

Pei made a sound of continued annoyance, but let the subject drop. Amanda would always be Amanda, with nothing likely to change that.

They moved far enough away from the alleyway to be sure they couldn't be reached a second time, and then Amanda looked around again. Pei was certain her friend was trying to decide between returning to the ship and taking a chance on finding another place to wait, but the problem was solved for her. A male voice called out Amanda's name, and then a pleasant-looking and dignified man was hurrying over to them.

As soon as Amanda heard her name being called, she knew her brother was finally there. She turned to see a rather handsome man striding toward them, brown-haired and blue-eyed like herself. He was fairly tall and quite nicely dressed in dark blue breeches and coat, white shirt, and pearl-gray vest, but his smile was the least bit on the formal side. He was, however, carrying the short length of bamboo she'd sent, so there was really no doubt about who he was.

"You *must* be Richard," she said with a smile as the man approached her and Pei. "I knew my brother would be the most handsome man in England."

"But I didn't expect my sister to be the most outrageous flatterer," Richard answered with an honest laugh. "Or quite so presentable a young lady. Welcome home, sister. I've waited years to be able to say that."

And then he opened his arms to her, and Amanda hurried into them to return his hug. It was almost like being hugged by their mother again, which brought tears of happiness to Amanda's eyes.

"Oh, Richard, now I do feel as if I've come home," she said with a teary smile. "And you needn't worry. I'll never make you sorry you opened your home to me."

"*That* I'm quite sure of, little sister," he answered with a matching smile, minus the tears. "Mother always told me what a sweet young lady you were growing to be, and how proud of you she was. From what I can see she had every right to be proud, and now it's time to take you the rest of the way home. I've two of my house men with me, and they'll see to your luggage."

"Oh, you haven't yet met Pei," Amanda suddenly remembered, then turned to gesture her friend closer. "Richard, this is my good friend Miss Han Pei, who agreed to be my companion for the journey here. Her father is the most respected merchant in our entire district, and was very difficult to convince about letting her come along. Pei, allow me to finally present my brother Richard Lavering, Lord Pembroke."

"Lord Pembroke," Pei said in acknowledgment with a curteous bow. "Amanda has spoken of you constantly, and it's a pleasure to finally meet you."

"Miss—Pei?" Richard faltered, looking toward Amanda. "The pleasure is mine, young lady, but I'm afraid I've missed something in regard to your name. Amanda, why are you calling your friend by her surname?"

"Richard, Han is her surname," Amanda told him, delighted to be able to play the part of tutor. "Her personal name is Pei, which follows rather than precedes her family name. In China, family names always come first."

"I see," Richard said in tones of revelation, then smiled at both of them. "I've always enjoyed learning new things, which means I'm now even more delighted that you're here. Once you ladies have rested, you must certainly tell me all about China. And as well as Miss . . . Han speaks English, I'm certain that won't pose any problems at all."

He and Pei exchanged smiles and Pei bowed again, and then Richard led them off the dock to his carriage. Three men waited nearby with a wagon, and when Richard nodded, two of them headed toward the dock. To fetch her and Pei's trunks, Amanda knew, and how lucky they'd brought a wagon. Pei would be returning to China, but Amanda had taken her every possession with her.

It felt the least bit odd to Amanda to be handed into a vehicle pulled by horses rather than into a palanquin carried by bearers, and Pei's lack of expression said she probably felt the same way. Once the three of them were settled their driver got the horses moving, and in a little while they'd left the docks far behind. By then Amanda was wide-eyed and open-mouthed, having seen nothing like London in her entire life.

The buildings' walls seemed to be made of brick or wood rather than glazed paper and enameled tile, and rather than being built wide with separate courts, they'd been built tall. And they were so close together! More like the poorest district in the village they'd left, but the buildings didn't look ill-kept, nor did the people in and around them. They looked quite prosperous, as a matter of fact, and the number of other carriages and similar vehicles—*all* pulled by horses—was almost dizzying.

"You seem rather impressed by the city, sister," Richard said, sounding very amused. "Surely you were told all about it, if not by your father or his secretary, then by Mother."

"Of course I was *told,* Richard," Amanda said with faint exasperation. "I was told about a lot of things including dragons, but that doesn't mean I *believed.* But even if I had, hearing about all this isn't anything like actually seeing it. But now that you've reminded me, I have a question to ask: Have you learned yet what became of Mr. Lichfield?"

"I learned that he did indeed reach the city," Richard told her, no longer amused. "In fact he saw to the transfer of your father's estate, naming me as trustee of your interests. After that he seems to have fallen off the edge of the world, as one morning he left the rooms he'd taken but never returned to them. He has relatives in the village he came from, but there's no reason to believe he went there without his possessions. I have inquiries out, of course, and as soon as I hear something I'll be certain to inform you."

Richard then began to point things out to her and Pei, but Amanda was no longer listening. She couldn't have cared less about the best shopping district, or which way the Thames was, or a promised visit to one of the royal palaces. Richard was a dear, but as long as Mr. Lichfield had seen to his duty before disappearing, Richard was no longer concerned about him.

But Amanda was, and if Richard's "inquiries" weren't

answered rather quickly, she'd have to look into the matter herself. How she was going to do that in a giant metropolis like London she had no idea, but something would come to her. Even if she knew nothing about the place including where to start, she'd find *some* way. . . .

". . . and tomorrow night happens to be the time for that ball," Richard was saying, drawing back her attention. "Claire and I were hoping you would arrive on time, and so had your dressmakers produce an appropriate gown. You will be quite lovely in it, and all of the eligible bachelors in our circle will be completely taken with you. You'll be married so fast you won't have time to settle into *my* house, more's the pity. I was hoping you'd be plain enough to let us get to know one another."

Richard grinned to show he was only joking, and that warmed Amanda. Both her father and Mr. Lichfield had been serious nearly to the point of solemnity, leading Amanda to suspect that all Englishmen were the same. She was pleased to find they weren't, and was also looking forward to meeting Richard's wife Claire. Not to mention the men to whom Richard had referred. One of them would become her husband, and could even conceivably turn out to be *him*. . . .

Amanda laughed at herself silently, amused that that old daydream had popped up in her thoughts again. About five years earlier, a stranger had one day shown up at Master Ma's compound. He was the first *young* Englishman Amanda had ever seen, and he was so handsome that she'd fallen immediately in love with him. He, however, had been interested in nothing but studying with Master Ma, and had even brought an introduction from the Provincial Governor.

Gossip traveled rather quickly among Master Ma's students, so Amanda learned that the stranger had come to the Provincial Governor with an introduction from his own government as well as with the permission of the Imperial Family in the capital. He had been sent to Master Ma because he was far from being a novice in Chinese boxing, his instructor having been a Chinese servant in his own country. He had come to polish his skill, but not to mention his name. For the entire year he stayed there and studied, no one ever called him anything but *Chin Te Quei*, meaning Golden Devil. He paid for his lessons in gold, something no other student did, and he fought like a devil.

And during that year, he'd never once noticed Amanda. She'd managed to get in his path once or twice, trying to force him into noticing her, but all he'd done was continue on his way after patting her on the head. He'd treated her like a child, obviously blind to the woman she was in the process of becoming, and that had annoyed her almost to the bursting point. But it hadn't stopped her from daydreaming about him, even after he left and never returned.

What a silly little fantasy, she thought with an inner smile, listening with half an ear to the polite conversation between Pei and Richard. *In a city the size of this one, you and he could live out very long lives and still never meet. Assuming he was* in *the city to begin with, which is even less likely. And don't forget that he's certainly old by now, so if you did meet him again you'd surely be sorry. If you want to think about men, think about the one you'll eventually marry.*

Amanda would have been willing to do that, but she didn't yet know who Richard had in mind for her. Anticipating one sort of man and then getting another sort would be extremely disappointing, so she thought instead about how she might go about looking for Mr. Lichfield. She hadn't gotten anywhere at all when the carriage slowed, then turned into a small circular drive.

"Well, ladies, this will be home to you for the next few months," Richard announced. "I think you'll be comfortable."

Amanda exchanged a quick glance with Pei, who sat opposite to her, the two of them apparently thinking the same thing. Richard's house stood alone with some grounds around it and looked large, but it was also tall and seemed to have nothing in the way of compounds. The air around them was cooler than what Amanda was used to, but the sight of all that brick rather than oiled rice paper gave her the feeling of stiffness. She and Pei would certainly *try* to be comfortable, but as far as achieving it went ... well, Amanda knew she'd better get used to it. From that moment on she'd be in England for the rest of her life.

"How lovely to see and smell green growing things again," Pei said to Richard as the carriage pulled up in front of the large, heavy house. "My father's gardens never fail to impress visitors, and we're all very fond of them. Yours seem to be just as lovely, Lord Pembroke, and just as carefully kept."

"I appreciate your saying so, Miss Han, but you really must see the gardens of my estate in the country." Richard was obviously pleased by Pei's compliment, and smiled as he opened the carriage door and stepped out. "My wife and I will have to take you two down for a few days, once Amanda has been properly introduced around. Taking a young lady out of the immediate reach of any ardent suitors for a while usually turns them even more ardent."

His smile showed amusement again as he helped them from the carriage, leading Amanda to believe that he was delighted with the duty their mother had imposed on him. Amanda was pleased to see that, as she hadn't wanted to be a burden to this stranger she shared blood with, this brother whom she had only just met. She would do exactly as Richard wanted her to—as soon as she discovered the whereabouts of Mr. Lichfield.

With that thought warming her, she and Pei followed Richard inside to meet his wife Claire.

Chapter 2

⌒◯◯⌒

The man known as Jack Michaels strolled out of the gaming room of his favorite club, feeling and looking very pleased with himself. A bearded man he knew relaxed in a chair to the left of the sitting room, reading a book rather than the newspaper folded on his lap. Jack took note of the arrangement, but gave no indication that it meant something very specific. Instead of going over to the man or even nodding in his direction, Jack gave a silver penny to the servant who brought his hat, and then he went whistling out into the night.

Trowbridge Street had more than one club, but the hour was so late there wasn't much in the way of traffic. Jack turned right along Trowbridge and strolled to Essex Street, where he turned right a second time. Essex had even fewer people and carriages, which meant none at all. Jack made sure of that before he slipped through the entryway of number 21, silently closing the door behind him. He walked along the worn hall and climbed the rickety stairs almost as silently to the first floor, where he opened the second door on the left without a key.

That no one had stopped him didn't mean no one knew he was there, of that Jack was certain. Number 21 Essex Street was always under the watchful eyes of his associates, which was what made it such a safe place to meet people. Jack poured himself a whiskey and sat in one of the curtained room's comfortable chairs, and about fifteen minutes later Sir Charles Kerry entered the room.

"And what were *you* looking so pleased about?" Sir Charles asked as soon as he'd closed the door behind himself. He was a big man who nevertheless carried himself easily, with reddish blond hair and a red, bushy beard. His usual good humor and easygoing ways often kept people from noticing the sharp intelligence in his dark blue eyes, which was just the way Sir Charles wanted it. "I mean, what were you looking so pleased about when you came out of the gaming room?" he added.

"Winning usually pleases me, but tonight's was especially sweet," Jack answered with a grin. "That fool Caruthers was in, and just after my father told me how the man had gloated over the 'useless wastrel' of a son my father had. I can't quite say I cleaned him out, not with *his* fortune, but Father will have trouble being properly condemning when Caruthers complains about his losses."

"Serves the boor right," Sir Charles rumbled as he took a chair with his own glass of whiskey. "If your father thought you really were a wastrel instead of knowing you're an agent of the Crown, he would have found the man's comments very painful. And now I'd like a final report on that matter involving Bryan Machlin."

"The fish has been gaffed without one of ours needing to get too openly involved," Jack said, his satisfaction turning grim. "Earlier tonight we went to Ranelagh Pleasure Gardens for the masquerade, where Bryan stopped his quarry from kidnapping his wife Rianne. Luckily we had substituted our own people for half of Ranelagh's tray servants."

"It's a good thing *you* thought to do it, you mean," Sir Charles corrected gruffly. "Another man in your place, knowing he would be there himself, would have insisted on handling it alone. Did Machlin or anyone else suspect you're something other than what you claim to be?"

"Happily, no," Jack replied with a fond smile after sipping at his whiskey. "Bryan hates the idea that I'm making no attempt to put my many talents to some good use, but he's too much of a gentleman to try to convert me. Robert

Creighton, the new Lord Redstone, happened to catch a glimpse of my—'efficient' fighting style and later tried to talk me into buying a commission in the army, but I was able to laugh the idea off. Decent man, Creighton. He even offered to lend me the money to buy the commission."

"Someday I'm going to engage a team of scholars to study how you keep everyone in the dark," Sir Charles said, staring at him with fascination. "No matter what you do, everyone sees something else entirely, and I don't understand how you manage it."

"There's no mystery to it, my friend," Jack answered with a laugh, thoroughly amused. "It's never what you do and say, only *how* you do and say it. It's all a game, and once you understand that, you can make the game turn out as you please."

"So you simply deny your gambling wins?" Sir Charles asked, a peculiar expression now on his bearded face. "I suppose that would do it. . . ."

"No, no, no," Jack corrected with a sigh. "The rules of the game are clear in that if you deny something, everyone will be most uncooperative and will immediately believe it instead. What you have to do is *tell* everyone that you win, but you say it in such a way that it *sounds* like a tall story. And if the person you're speaking to happens to have been there for one of your wins, you quickly remind him about the time. That makes him believe you're spinning tall tales based on a long-ago reality, which makes him even more convinced that you're lying. The game is quite easy, really, as long as you thoroughly understand all the rules."

"And treat it *as* a game," Sir Charles said, back to studying Jack with an odd expression. "Most of our people don't seem able to do that, which may be why they're so much less successful than you. But none of that is why I arranged this meeting. Something has come up, and I'd like you to look into it."

"I was supposed to have some time to visit with my family," Jack reminded him, no longer amused. It had been so long since he'd been home, so long since he'd been able to do more than have brief, secret meetings with his father . . .

"There really is no one else I can send, John," Sir Charles said gently, his tone apologetic but completely firm. And when he said John rather than Jack, the matter always *was* urgent . . . "If you insist I'll have to send someone completely inappropriate, but I'd rather not do that. This one concerns one of our own."

"Who?" Jack asked, his frown something he could feel. If one of his brother agents was in peril, honor would demand that he stay and help.

"Two days ago, Cyril Hughes got this letter," Sir Charles told him, reaching inside his coat to produce the document. "When he returned to his rooms he found it on the floor, obviously having been pushed under his door. Neither his landlady nor any of his neighbors admitted to seeing a stranger either in the house or outside of it. Whoever left it knows how to turn invisible."

Jack took the envelope and examined it briefly before turning his attention to the letter inside. The paper was cream colored and of excellent quality, expensive but not of exclusive design or weave. The red sealing wax had been broken, but it hadn't contained anyone's crest or sigil. The paper matched the envelope, but the handwriting didn't.

"This printing has been deliberately made to look childish," he commented, then began to read the letter aloud. " 'Dear Mr. Hughes, I regret the intrusion of this missive, but I am in desperate need of your help. Had I not known that you were an agent of the Crown I would not have dreamed of involving you, but since you are I've been given no choice. Please be at the Ashford's ball in three days' time, and I will contact you in person. Until then, I remain, a desperate acquaintance.' "

"So you see," Sir Charles commented in turn. "Hughes has no clue about who could possibly have spotted him, and we don't have any idea if it's a man or a woman. Even beyond that, something feels . . . *wrong* about that letter.

Hughes spotted it first and I quite agree with him, although neither of us can put the feeling into words."

"But I believe I can," Jack responded thoughtfully. "If you were going to ask someone for their help in something important to you and were using the threat of revealing a secret of theirs, would you put that secret into writing? What would have happened if this letter had fallen into the wrong hands? And what will happen when Hughes finds out who the author of it is? They could not only *not* get his help, but might conceivably be arrested for treason. Threatening to reveal a Crown secret *is* treason, and this letter is proof of it."

"Which means if the letter-writer were serious, he or she would have simply approached Hughes and mentioned his or her knowledge in casual conversation." Sir Charles nodded as he spoke, now seeing the point clearly. "The writer has something else in mind, then, which has nothing to do with favors or self-introductions. What we still don't know is what it *does* concern."

"And that's why you want me at the ball tomorrow night," Jack said, also nodding. "To keep an eye on Hughes and watch to see who approaches him. I'm certainly willing, of course, but what excuse will I give for being there? The Ashfords are a far cry from the crowd I usually hang about with."

"We've arranged for the perfect excuse, but not for the purpose you just mentioned." Sir Charles's words surprised him. "I don't want you there to keep an eye on Hughes, since Sellars will be there for that purpose. Those two are good friends of long standing, and Sellars insisted. What I want *you* there for is to watch everyone else, to see who doesn't belong or who might be acting strangely. I haven't another man who can do that as well as you while being completely visible."

"You mean while making a complete fool of himself," Jack muttered, then waved a hand to forestall Sir Charles's comment. "Sorry about that, I'm just tired tonight. Once I've been able to rest awhile, the game will have my full enjoyment again. For the moment . . . just ignore me, and I'll be very grateful. So what perfect excuse have you arranged for me to be at a party that would bore my public character to tears?"

"I took the liberty of speaking to your father," Sir Charles said, and suddenly he seemed more diffident than assured. "I'd—ah—heard about what Caruthers had said to him, you see, and it all fit so well. You have my word, John, that if I'd had any idea the arrangement would embarrass you—"

Jack groaned silently when Sir Charles's words broke off, noting that the man was as close to flustered as Jack had ever seen him. Whatever he'd arranged must be downright raw. . . .

"Just tell me straight out," Jack said with a sigh, already braced for the worst. "Have I been betrothed to a giggling matron who has already buried three husbands? I warn you now, I won't go through with something like that even for king and country."

"Really, Jack, it's nothing *that* extreme," Sir Charles remonstrated, now faintly put out. "His Grace your father is a fair man, and would never agree to betraying a woman's hopes in such a cavalier manner, nor would I. We've simply let it be known that your father would be extremely grateful if you were included on the Ashfords' guest list from now on, in the hopes that associating with decent, straight-living people will bring you around to the straight and narrow. Of course it won't, but we needn't tell *them* that."

"Of course not," Jack agreed, trying not to sound depressed clear to the ground. When he was very tired he grew to despise the character he'd built, hating the man's refusal to do anything really productive, or to commit himself to anybody or thing of any importance. That man slouched and strolled, told inane stories, smirked at the thought of settling down . . . He had all the women he could possibly want, but never *one* woman. He had hundreds of acquaintances, but no true friends. Jack knew the man's every lack and flaw, but when he was tired he hated most the fact that the man was himself.

"I think it's time we both went searching for our beds," Sir Charles said after a brief silence, his tone gentle as he stirred in his chair. "I promise you, Jack, as soon as this one is over you'll be on holiday, and that no matter *what* comes up. It shouldn't take very long at all, you know, so you *will* be all right, won't you?"

"I'll be fine, Sir Charles," Jack forced himself to say with a smile after emptying his glass in a single swallow. "And your idea about searching for beds is a smashing one, especially since mine will be empty. What I need now is sleep, and happily I can get as much as I like. There are benefits as well as drawbacks to having a reputation like mine."

Jack stood to perform a casual and mocking bow, then left the room to a seriously troubled man. Sir Charles leaned back in his chair again, realized he still held an untasted glass of whiskey, and slowly put it aside. He'd known Jack Michaels for many years, since the time he was a boy, in fact, and for the first time he found himself truly worried about the young man.

"Too many people believe his game," Sir Charles muttered to himself, unable to stop fretting. "Everyone now sees him the same, and the capable, upright man behind the mask is beginning to be embarrassed and hurt by the deception. But he can't announce the truth, not when king and country are depending on him to keep silent and simply carry on. He can't continue on for much longer as he is, and he can't change things. I wish I knew what in blazes he *can* do."

Another few minutes of prodding at the question produced the same lack of results, so Sir Charles forced himself to his feet and also went toward the door. He was beginning to be too old for late-night excursions such as these, especially since he did have to be up rather early. But at least it wasn't an empty bed he was heading for, unlike poor Jack. He had a loving, understanding wife wait-

ing, one who would scold him for pushing himself so
hard.

A pity Jack would never ask a woman to share the shal-
low life he'd built, not when his shame would then be hers
as well. Jack was too much like his father, Edward, Duke
of Norland, both men filled with iron pride and an unshakable sense of duty. But then, that was what made Jack so
excellent an agent of the Crown.

Shaking his head sadly, Sir Charles left the private
meeting room on Essex Street.

Chapter 3

Amanda stood in front of the full-length mirror, finding it impossible to stop staring at the exquisite gown she wore. It was blue silk to match her eyes, trimmed with silver lace just about everywhere. She felt like a princess in it, and loved Richard and Claire even more for having had it made for her.

"The gentlemen will certainly notice you in *that*," Pei said from a chair, amusement in her voice. "My father would have a fit if I ever put on something that came down so low on top, but it doesn't bother me because I would never look the way you do in it. If I did, I'd be willing to risk it even if my father had three fits."

"And Richard won't have even one because he and his wife bought this for me." Amanda was still getting used to such an alien way of thinking, along with other unusual concepts like stairways and a special time to have tea. Not that the English didn't drink tea at other times. They drank it whenever they pleased, but still apparently needed a time that was specifically for tea!

"Your brother's wife Claire is a lovely woman," Pei said, "but I'm afraid I shocked her this morning. I mentioned I was my father's daughter by his second wife, and she said something commiserating about his loss of his first wife. Without thinking, I assured her that his first wife was perfectly fine, as were his third and fourth wives. If I hadn't seen the color drain from her face, I probably would have mentioned his concubines as well. Have you found out yet why England is so uncivilized that men are allowed only a single wife at a time?"

"No, but I *have* thought of something else," Amanda replied, finally turning away from the mirror. "If a man can have more than one wife in China, why can't a woman have more than one husband? I mean, it can't be a matter of supporting them, because it's men who *do* the supporting. And isn't it common knowledge that women can enjoy a large number of men, while most men need help to enjoy more than one or two women? It seems to me . . ."

"Amanda, please!" Pei protested, and this time *she* was the one who looked pale. "If anyone heard you talking like that—! The idea is completely outrageous, and if you don't know why, then I can't explain it. Let's find something else to discuss."

Amanda agreed with a graceful nod of her head and a serene expression, but on the inside she was laughing. She hadn't been serious about what she'd said, but had seen that her friend needed a small lesson in comparatives. Pei considered herself sophisticated and cultured, and tended to look down on occidental barbarians with unconscious superiority. Both the Chinese culture and the British were the same in that each considered *its* way of doing things the only proper way for *anyone* to behave, and Mr. Lichfield had explained the situation to Amanda many years earlier.

"You'd like to know which one is right?" he'd echoed Amanda's question, amusement in his dark and gentle eyes. "The only possible answer, child, is that they are each, *in their own place,* perfectly and fittingly right. As long as there are even so few as two people who do things differently, each method is right and proper for that individual. If their methods cause harm to no one, they may properly be condemned by an equal no one."

"Richard still has no word about Mr. Lichfield," Amanda, no longer amused, told Pei. "His people are still supposed to be looking, but I have the distinct feeling that if they are, they're simply going through the motions. They don't care why an unimportant man has dropped out of sight, but I do."

"Your caring doesn't seem to be the issue here," Pei pointed out gently. "Even if you knew this city, I can't quite imagine your brother letting you run all over it as you please. And since you *don't* know it, even complete freedom would be of little help. Frankly, I can't imagine what *would* be useful."

"Oh, that part of it is easy," Amanda said, waving one hand to dismiss the entire list of difficulties. "What I need is an accomplice, someone who knows this city and is also willing to help me. What I don't yet know is who the accomplice will be, but I *will* find someone. I refuse to consider the possibility that I won't."

"I think I'm going to be very glad I decided against going to that ball with you tonight," Pei said with a sigh as she rose from her chair. "The sight of men being helplessly attacked upsets me, but that's obviously what you intend doing. Does your brother Richard know what your nickname is?"

"No, and he doesn't *need* to know," Amanda responded firmly but with a laugh. "He'll be introducing me to gentlemen for *his* purposes, and I'll be eagerly meeting them for my own. Since the two aren't mutually exclusive, where can the harm possibly be?"

"I refuse to discuss that or *any* arguable matter with you," Pei announced just as firmly. "In the years I've known you, it's become perfectly clear that even Master Confucius would probably have trouble winning against you with an opposing point of view. That, of course, doesn't mean you're right, only that you're too stubborn to admit when you're wrong, and now I believe your family is probably waiting for you."

"Which pronouncement ends our discussion on *your* terms," Amanda pointed out, amused rather than annoyed. "But since you're probably right, I'll let the point pass.

And tomorrow I'll tell you about everything that happens tonight."

"Aside from the gory details, I'm looking forward to it," Pei said with the bland expression that told Amanda she was laughing on the inside. "You go ahead now and have a good time."

Amanda paused to exchange a hug with Pei, and then she did leave to see if the others were ready. She would have been much happier if Pei had been going along, but Pei was too wise in the way of people's behavior to want to intrude on what was supposed to be Amanda's night. She would let people flock around the "exotic stranger" some other time, specifically sometime *after* Amanda had had her introductions. Not everyone would have considered that, or let it stop them from being the center of attention even if they had; it was one of the reasons why Pei was Amanda's best friend.

Even wearing flat-soled slippers, going down the stairs was tricky for Amanda. Climbing them wasn't nearly as hard, but she found that going down, especially in a wide-skirted gown, took concentration. When she reached the ground floor she breathed a sigh of relief, but before she had the chance to start looking around for her brother and his wife, she heard a sound from above. Then Claire came down the stairs a lot more confidently than Amanda had.

"Oh, Amanda, you look marvelous!" Claire enthused, inspecting her husband's sister even as she descended. "I *knew* that gown would be perfect for you, and everyone else will think so, too. You can be sure that if some man doesn't insist on meeting you tonight, he'll either be married or very nearsighted."

Claire was a very beautiful woman in Amanda's opinion, but hadn't seemed to let that beauty spoil her personality. Blond-haired and blue-eyed and usually smiling, Claire had welcomed Amanda and Pei into her home without the least reluctance. Amanda knew her presence was, to a great extent, an intrusion, but Claire refused to see it that way.

"And," came Richard's voice from behind Amanda, "if any of the married ones try to come over anyway, *I'll* be there to take care of it. Claire is quite right, little sister. You do look marvelous."

Richard had come out of the small room Amanda had been told was his study, and his smile was just as true and warm as Claire's. Amanda looked at both of them, and then reached out to touch their hands.

"You two have to be the most wonderful people in all of England," she said with a smile, meaning the words sincerely. "Maybe even in the entire British Empire. I promise I'll be out from under foot as soon as you find someone suitable for me to marry, but I won't ever forget your kindness. If someday I can repay it . . ."

"Nonsense, my dear, nonsense," Richard interrupted with a pleased smile of his own as he patted her hand affectionately. "Claire and I are delighted to have you here, and I'm even more delighted that you aren't filled with this modern nonsense too many young ladies these days have been spouting. Can you imagine that some of them have actually tried to refuse to marry the man chosen for them? What they think they're about I have no idea, nor do I care. And now, ladies, our carriage is waiting."

Claire had come down in a bright green cloak which covered and matched her green velvet gown, and a gray cloak was quickly produced for Amanda. Richard wore brown brocade with golden buckles and buttons, with a white shirt, hose, and cravat, and seemed quite resplendent in his own right. Once he had his hat, they all went out to the carriage.

The trip to the Ashford house was only a matter of a few blocks, and other guests arrived all around them. Once inside and in the ballroom, Amanda was introduced first to Lord and Lady Ashford, who said they were delighted to meet Richard's sister. Their welcome was somewhat on the restrained side, but Amanda was too dazzled to notice or mind. All those candles glowing on the magnificent crystal chandelier, all the people already dancing to the marvelous music being played by the orchestra, all the laughing, and talking, and movement—Amanda had never seen anything like it. She had just enough time to hope that the dancing her mother had taught her wasn't too far out of date when the men began to descend on them. . . .

Jack Michaels stood on the outskirts of the large but very restrained crowd in Lord and Lady Ashford's ballroom. Having anticipated that most of the guests in attendance tonight would know him well enough to conclude he didn't belong in their crowd, Jack had decided that any attempt to remain unobtrusive would be a complete waste of time.

So he'd chosen instead to be as visible as possible. He was a sighing martyr decked out in golden brocade and a sky-blue vest, a blindingly white shirt and a cravat dripping with golden ruffles, white hose, and golden buckles. Just by looking at him, every guest there should assume that his quarterly allowance had been threatened, otherwise he would certainly be in what he considered more congenial surroundings.

After a short while he publicly allowed himself to spot Sellars, who was a member of Jack's usual crowd. He immediately made his way over to where the other man had positioned himself, a vantage point that let him see everyone who approached Hughes.

"I say, Sellars, how good to see a familiar face," Jack burbled, shaking the other man's hand more than enthusiastically. "Thought I was exiled from home and country completely, but here you are. Let's have some champagne to celebrate my relief."

"Sorry, old son, but I'm afraid I must pass," Sellers said quickly as he disengaged his hand. He'd been told Jack would greet him like a long-lost brother, and they'd worked out a response together. "I'm here for a—ah—delicate reason, and three's a crowd, you know. Delighted to see you and all that, but you really must toddle along. And not come back."

"Oh, well, certainly," Jack agreed, projecting disappointment and hurt. "Do have a smashing time and all that. . . ."

Backing off slowly gave Sellars a chance to think better of the stiff rebuff and invite Jack to stay with him after all, but of course Sellars didn't, so Jack finally left him to the solitude he'd demanded. He also now had a solid reason not to return or speak to Sellars again, and it should have been clear to anyone watching that Jack wasn't there by choice and that he had no idea Sellars was there for anything but to meet a woman. Since Sellars was unknown to the writers of the letter, he and Sellars would likely have no need of the sham, but there was no sense in taking chances.

Jack took a glass of champagne from the tray of a passing servant and sipped it as he glanced casually around. He was there to look over the other guests, to see if he could spot the one who had sent Hughes that note, but he didn't expect to get very far. People who suggested specific meeting places usually did so because they were familiar places in which they were comfortable. They became indistinct in a sea of faces. . . .

A tinkle of gentle and delighted laughter arose from another corner of the room, and Jack realized he'd heard the pleasant sound more than once that night. One of Lord Ashford's personal friends had brought his sister tonight, Jack had learned when they first arrived, and the eligible gentlemen present were apparently rather impressed. They'd stood in line to be introduced, and now each attempted to monopolize the attention of the newcomer.

And that was something Jack could easily understand. He'd seen the girl when she'd first walked in, and he'd almost joined the throng heading for her. Not that she was the most beautiful woman there, because she wasn't. But there was something about her, the way she moved and gestured and smiled and laughed. . . . It had made him want to join her in doing all those things, especially the smiling and laughing.

But that had been a fleeting fancy. The sight of dark hair and light eyes and a sensational figure in a gown of floating dreams was captivating, but a distraction of that sort was one he could ill afford. Unfortunately.

And even beyond that, he'd somehow gotten the idea that if Hughes was approached, it would be by a woman. If that turned out to be true, he had to be free to do some approaching of his own. Not that he would be that blatant about it, but he'd dutifully built a less-than-honorable reputation for just such a situation. His attention turned toward a tall blonde standing across the room from him. There had been any number of conversations going on around her, but she hadn't participated in any of them— nor had she even seemed to be listening. Now might be a good time to ask her to dance . . . *before* Hughes was approached by anyone at all. . . .

Amanda was having a wonderful time, and it seemed that everyone around her knew it. Her dancing hadn't been all that far behind the times, but on the occasions when it was, her partner of the moment always graciously guided her. She'd been taught many of the newest steps, and everyone seemed very impressed with how quickly she learned those that were unfamiliar. She hadn't mentioned how much easier this was than learning the forms taught by Master Ma, especially when Master Ma wasn't known for his patience with slow learners.

"That was smashing, dear girl, just smashing," her current partner, Albert Hofern, raved as the dance ended. "And to think I nearly stayed home tonight! I shall certainly thank Mother for insisting that I attend, to deliver her and Father's apologies if nothing else. Father's a bit under the weather, d'you see. It must have been that beastly hunt out in the country wilds, Mother is certain of it. . . ."

Albert burbled on and on, but Amanda had stopped listening. He was certainly a pleasant enough young man, but the key word was "young." The man was years older than

Amanda, but she couldn't shake the impression that he was still more of a little boy. He'd mentioned any number of times how much money he had in his own right, as though that was an adequate substitute for maturity. If Albert proposed and Richard accepted his petition, Amanda would have to marry him. But not very happily, not happily at all. . . .

"Aha, the honor is now mine," declared Thomas Attenborough, who pounced on Amanda as soon as Albert escorted her back to the sidelines. Where Albert was tall and slender, Thomas was tall and husky—and rather dashingly handsome. He took Amanda's arm from Albert and kissed her hand, but before they could return to the dance floor there was an interruption.

"I do hope you'll excuse me a moment's intrusion, Attenborough," Richard said, an unfamiliar girl standing beside him. "Miss Simmons expressed a desire to meet my sister, so I'm here to perform the introductions. Miss Margaret Simmons, allow me to present my sister, Miss Amanda Edmunds."

"Edmunds rather than Lavering, Lord Pembroke?" the girl asked, ignoring Amanda completely. "I don't—ah, yes, I see now. You meant sister of the spirit rather than of the blood. How generous of you to adopt a familyless waif."

The girl, slightly younger than Amanda, smiled at Richard in a superior way as she continued to ignore Amanda. She was slightly taller than average, very fair-haired, and light-eyed, which gave her a washed-out look to go with her boyish build. Amanda hadn't been in England long, but she recognized the ploy the girl used from having grown up in a culture that considered indirect insults an art form. Richard didn't seem prepared to answer, but Amanda was.

"How sweet of you to be so understanding, Miss Simmons," she said at once, "especially when there's no need for it. Richard and I share the same mother, which does make us brother and sister. When you get home, I'm sure your nurse will be able to explain the matter to you."

Most of the men standing around chuckled. The girl's obvious scheme to suggest that Amanda was a common interloper, unworthy of the men's interest, had caused her embarrassment instead. She uttered a mortified "Oh!" as she colored, and then she fled back to the group from which she'd come. Richard shook his head then, after sending Amanda an apologetic glance, followed after Miss Simmons.

"That won't have gained you any popularity among the ladies," Thomas said, looking down at her fondly. "Not that you had much to begin with. You're too lovely a vision for them to have greeted you with open arms, but mine have been welcoming since the instant I saw you. Shall we join the others on the dance floor?"

Amanda answered his gallant bow with a gracious nod, then let him guide her out onto the floor. Thomas's compliments were a pleasant change from Albert's aimless chattering, but her mother had once said that sometimes when a man used lavish flattery while courting, he ran short after the marriage ceremony was over. Amanda had the impression that Thomas would be one of those, but that wasn't her main concern. None of the men she'd met so far would make the sort of accomplice she needed, and the night wasn't growing any younger.

Since they came to the dance floor late, the music ended only a moment or two after they stepped out. "Ha, I knew this would happen," Thomas said, faintly annoyed but also determined. "That little scene delayed us just long enough for most of the dance to be wasted. Well, no matter. We'll simply have to have the next one as well."

"Of course," Amanda agreed politely. And since she really did agree, she stood beside Thomas, waiting for the music to begin again. She used her fan idly during the time, looking around at the people she hadn't been introduced to yet, and then a glint of gold caught her eye. It took a moment before she realized it was a man dressed in gold brocade, which struck her as rather odd. Most of the other men there wore dark blue, or brown, or dark gray. . . .

And then Amanda's jaw almost dropped. The man in gold brocade . . . he was tall and broad-shouldered, handsome, with long brown hair and dark eyes, obviously attempting to charm the slender blond woman with whom he spoke. He was the Englishman who had attended Master Ma's school for a year, the one the other students had called the Golden Devil because he'd been so good, and his face hadn't changed a bit! She would have sworn there was no chance of their ever meeting again, and yet there he was!

"Miss Edmunds, are you all right?" Thomas asked, now sounding concerned. "Don't you realize that the music has started again?"

"Forgive me, Mr. Attenborough, I'm a terrible dreamer," Amanda apologized with a quick smile. "And to tell the truth, I was wondering who that man in gold is. No other man here seems to be dressed in quite the same manner, and I can't recall that Richard has introduced me to him."

"I should certainly hope he has not," Thomas replied, the words stiff and disapproving. "That man calls himself Jack Michaels, just as if everyone didn't know his father is Edward, Duke of Norland. He's been forbidden to use the family name, of course, in an effort to keep his escapades from causing too much scandal. Duke Edward asked Lord Ashford to extend an invitation to Michaels, in an effort to expose the man to decent influences, but I can't see that the attempt has been in any way successful. Michaels seems to be making every effort to stand out like a sore thumb."

Amanda was amazed to hear that, and even as she began the slow, courtly steps and curtsies of the dance, her mind worked furiously. The man she'd known only as the Golden Devil had certainly not been one to engage in "escapades," not when he'd devoted his entire being to his lessons. And he'd come to Master Ma with an introduction from the Imperial Family, an introduction requested by the Englishman's own government. That wasn't the same man Thomas had described, and an important question suddenly occurred to her.

"Poor Duke Edward," she murmured to Thomas when the dance brought them temporarily together. "Imagine having a son who starts out making you proud, and then turns into such a disappointment."

"Happily His Grace never had *that* burden to bear," Thomas murmured back with a snort. "The way I hear it, Michaels never *was* the sort of son you brag about at the club. The man has never taken *anything* seriously, least of all the dignity of his family position. A lesser man than Duke Edward would have disowned him years ago."

And then they separated again in another figure, which allowed Amanda to go back to thinking—and making certain guesses. Thomas had said, "The way *I* heard it." That meant he didn't know about this Jack Michaels from personal experience, and chances were excellent that few others did either. They all "knew" what a disreputable character the man was, and yet his father, a man in a high enough position to be embarrassed by almost anything, still hadn't disowned him. According to what Amanda's mother had said, that wasn't the way it was usually done, not when face meant almost as much to the English as it did to the Chinese.

So there was more than one fact that didn't add up. Amanda smiled at her dancing partner as her mind raced to piece together this information. If Jack Michaels was so ignominious, how had he gotten an introduction to the Imperial Family from his own government? The only reasonable possibility was that it was all a hoax, and the man was only pretending to be irresponsible. If true, it meant he might well be working for the British government, in a position no one wanted to have known.

Amanda realized she was jumping to conclusions. As she curtsied low to the last strains of the music, she knew her theories were useless if the man Jack Michaels proved to be other than the man she thought she remembered. Years had passed, after all, and she'd been a child at the time . . . Well, the only thing for it was to test her theory. If he turned out to be the man she believed he was, she'd have the best possible accomplice for locating Mr. Lichfield.

"Miss Edmunds, you dance like a dream," Thomas said as soon as the music ended, once again bowing over her hand. "Perhaps later you'll honor me again?"

"The honor will be mine, Mr. Attenborough," Amanda answered with the smile the men seemed to like so well. "At the moment, however, I wonder if I might ask a favor. I'm simply parched, and would prefer not to dance again until I've quenched my thirst with a cup of fruit juice. May I wait for you over there, away from the other gentlemen, until you've found one for me?"

"Dear lady, that would be a pleasure rather than a favor," the man answered with a delighted grin. "And if the others fail to find us by the time you've had your drink, perhaps *I'll* have that second dance sooner rather than later. Stay right here, and I'll return as quickly as possible."

He guided Amanda to a place hidden from the view of the other men, then bowed and went off looking for a servant with fruit juice. Amanda had noticed that there was more champagne being offered than juice, so with luck she would have just enough time to accomplish her aim. Almost as soon as Thomas Attenborough turned away, Amanda began to move through the crowd.

The man called Jack Michaels wasn't all that far off, and the slender blond woman had apparently been claimed by another man for a dance. The Golden Devil—if that was indeed who he was—stood alone in his own crowd of one, and very briefly Amanda felt her heart ache for him. These people really didn't like him, and they made no effort to keep that feeling secret. The thought almost made her hesitate in her plan, but then she remembered how *he'd* treated *her* so long ago: like a silly little child who didn't matter at all, just as though she had no feelings. Well, now was the time to return the gesture.

"Ninhao-a," she greeted him politely in Chinese, a language no one else present was likely to know. Luckily, the man was apparently distracted; without thinking, he began, *"Hen Hao—"* which was the proper response to the greeting as he turned toward her, and then he quickly cut it off.

"I beg your pardon, but did you say something?" he tried instead, flashing her one of those dazzling smiles she remembered so well. "If you did I'm afraid I didn't quite catch it, and I don't believe I've had the pleasure of an introduction."

"Our first introduction was about five years ago, in the province of Kiyang," Amanda said with a smile of her own, just as though they were exchanging ordinary pleasantries. "If you don't want me to *'accidentally'* mention that meeting to everyone I speak with from now on, come calling tomorrow at my brother's house and convince him to let you take me for a drive. I'll explain everything then, and don't forget that your government is undoubtedly counting on your discretion. Do as I ask, and they'll be able to count on mine as well. Good evening, Mr. Michaels."

The man's expression was priceless as Amanda turned and walked away, and it was all *she* could do not to laugh aloud. Jack Michaels was furious, but it served him right. She'd teach him to ignore a girl who was terribly in love with him. This time she'd made sure he couldn't ignore her, and he was certainly smart enough to realize that she wasn't bluffing. If *she* didn't get the help she needed to find Mr. Lichfield, she would not grant Jack Michaels the silence *he* needed.

Amanda returned so quickly to the place where Thomas had left her that she needed to wait a few moments for him. No one seemed to have noticed that she'd wandered off and spoken to Jack Michaels, and that was the way Amanda wanted it. Richard would certainly not care to have her associating publicly with someone like the "black sheep," which led her to wonder how the man would manage to take her driving the next day. Ah, well, that was his problem, and a true hero would solve it easily.

When Thomas reappeared, fruit drink in hand, Amanda daintily sipped the refreshment before joining Thomas for the second dance she'd promised him. After that they returned to the small group that was still waiting, and the next gentleman claimed his turn. Amanda couldn't quite remember his name, but he was another really nice "boy." The one after him was quite mature, in fact the man was one step away from being elderly. He was a widower who had grown lonely for the company of young people, he told her, but also neglected to repeat his name. He seemed to think she should know who he was, which had to mean he had position as well as money.

Having concluded her dance with this almost-elderly gentleman, Amanda waited patiently while the last two men who hadn't had a dance with her yet argued politely about which of them would have the honor next. Suddenly Richard showed up again, but it wasn't another young lady he had with him. This time he'd brought Jack Michaels!

"Amanda, child, I've been asked a favor by our host, Lord Ashford," Richard said, his complete lack of expression showing how unhappy he was. "This—gentleman would like to be introduced to you, so I've come along to do it properly. My dear, this is Mr. John Michaels, who doesn't usually move in our circles. Mr. Michaels, my sister, Miss Amanda Edmunds."

"Miss Edmunds, how delightful to meet you at last," Jack said with that incredible charm of his as he bent over her hand. "As your brother, Lord Pembroke, pointed out, until now I've foolishly spent my time in other places and with other people. Now that I've seen the light of your glorious presence, however, I can assure you that that will change. May I have the honor of this next dance?"

He positioned his hand in the middle of her back before Amanda had the chance to say a word, and then he "guided" her toward the dance floor. He wasn't rough, only determined, but she felt it was clearly time to rein him back a little.

"Stop pushing me, or your too-abrupt 'courtesy' will make me *stumble,*" she murmured, certain he'd know what she meant. All of Master Ma's students knew how to fall if the situation called for it, but if *she* "fell" *there* because of Jack Michaels, he'd be lucky if he wasn't hanged from the chandelier. "And what do you think you're doing? You're supposed to call on me tomorrow."

"And how do you suppose I would have gotten past your brother tomorrow?" he countered, his voice low, his expression easy and unconcerned. "Tonight I had Lord Ashford to intercede for me, so I took advantage of it. And now I want to know what this is all about. You seem to believe you know me, but I'm sure there's been some mix-up. I've never heard of whatever place that was you mentioned earlier."

By then they were out on the dance floor, and he stood slightly behind her. She held her arms partially raised so that he might reach around her and take hold of her hands. The body that brushed against hers was hard and trim, and the hands holding hers were large and strong, the way a man's hands should be. Amanda found herself comparing this man with all the others she'd danced with this evening, and quickly stopped the thought before the others suffered by comparison. Jack Michaels would be completely unacceptable to her brother, and she was annoyed that he was trying to lie his way out of being caught.

"Really, Mr. Michaels, I expected you to come up with a more imaginative argument than, 'I don't know what you're talking about,'" Amanda murmured as the music began. "Not only isn't it original, it isn't even *slightly* logical. You do see that, don't you?"

"No, Miss Edmunds, I must confess I don't," he responded, the words so very even that Amanda wished she could catch more than an occasional glimpse of his expression. "Truth does have a habit of being unimaginative, much as it would please me to delight you with fabrication. And as far as logic goes . . . I'm forced to admit, dear lady, that that doesn't happen to be one of my strong suits. If you say I've been less than logical, I must bow to your greater wisdom without having any idea of what you mean."

Glancing in his direction, Amanda saw the laconic smile of an ordinary, not-very-bright scion of the wealthy. Jack Michaels was displaying a protective mask, but this time it wasn't going to help him.

"What I mean is very simple," she answered, giving him her own I'm-just-a-poor-little-female smile. "When I spoke to you in Chinese, you not only responded but did so *properly*. Until then I wasn't sure you were the one who had studied at Master Ma's school five years ago, but now I'm absolutely certain. I saw you there myself, and I'm willing to say so."

"You seem to believe that someone would care," he replied, still acting the distantly amused dabbler. "Even if what you said was true, people would yawn when you told them, then would quickly change the subject to one that was interesting. Where I go and what I do is of interest only to myself and my debtors."

"Really!" Amanda responded in tones of revelation. "I hadn't realized that. Then you're sure other people won't want to know that you were called the Golden Devil, and that you came to China with an introduction from your government? Now that's odd. If it were me hearing it, I'd at least want to know where and how someone with *your* reputation got that introduction."

This time there was no smooth and easy rejoinder, and a second glance at the man's face showed his expression to be unreadable again. But his dark eyes weren't the same, not with all that barely controlled anger flashing from them. Jack Michaels was caught, but not yet willing to admit it.

"You know, Mr. Michaels, you may be right about people not caring what I have to say," Amanda pressed, still with that empty-headed smile. "I've learned that men usually *are* right, and that I'm just a silly girl, but I usually have to find that out the hard way—by trying what I've been advised not to. I doubt if this time will be any different from the others, but as long as I know *you* don't mind, there won't be any harm done. Will there?"

His stare came to her face, and the smile he saw seemed to add to his anger. Then the dance called for him to bow to her, and when he straightened again he'd regained control of himself.

"For a silly girl, you're unbelievably persuasive, Miss Edmunds," he said, those eyes watching her every move. "Just what is it that you want?"

"I need the help of someone capable, and familiar with this city, to find someone," Amanda answered, distantly wondering why his stare made her feel so odd. She'd thought herself madly in love with the man once, but that was when she'd been a child. It was probably nothing more than a lingering shadow of her former feelings. . . . "Do you want to know who the man is now, or would you prefer to save that for tomorrow?"

Since the dance was ending, the question was more than just for form's sake. They executed the final curtsey and bow, and then Jack Michaels offered her his arm.

"Allow me to escort you back to your friends, Miss Edmunds," he said, smiling easily, and then answered her question obliquely. "Most likely I'm overstepping myself, but I do hope you won't mind if I call on you tomorrow to go driving with me. As I said earlier, I find myself quite taken with you. I shall have to have a word with your brother first, of course, but two gentlemen will surely be able to come to some sort of accommodation. Until tomorrow, then."

By then they were back among her small group of admirers, and as soon as he'd bowed over her hand he left. Amanda turned away before Jack Michaels was completely out of sight, pretending that she'd already dismissed him from her thoughts. The truth was that she couldn't wait for tomorrow, and finding Mr. Lichfield had only a little to do with it. This time the Golden Devil couldn't *afford* to ignore her, even if the truth was that her own sense of the proper would never have let her expose him. But he didn't need to know that, and if her plans worked properly he never would.

Thoroughly satisfied with the way things had gone, Amanda let the next tedious man lead her out to the dance floor.

Jack Michaels was furious, and even more furious that he couldn't show his anger. He'd spent years creating his public character, and now a slip of a girl was threatening to turn it all into wasted effort! And who the devil was she? He didn't remember any English girls at Master Ma's school. . . .

The strolling pace he'd been forcing himself to keep suddenly became easier as a long-forgotten memory surfaced. A small face and dark hair surrounding enormous blue eyes . . . he'd thought the child was Chinese, until she'd put herself right in his way that time. Then he'd seen she was occidental, but he still hadn't known what she wanted. To spar with the Golden Devil? She'd been skilled for a child and a girl, but he couldn't have sparred with a girl even if she'd been a full student and at his own level. To ask him something about England? He'd paused for a moment back then, waiting to see what she had to say.

But she hadn't said *anything,* doing nothing more than stare up at him, and so he'd gone on his way. The chances of them ever meeting again had been at least a million to one, especially at a party he would normally never have attended. All that luck he usually had at gaming—was he now destined to pay for it in the worst way possible?

Jack took a glass of champagne from a passing servant's tray, then forced himself to sip it slowly as he looked around. Hughes was still keeping himself unentangled so that the letter writer might approach him, and Sellars was pretending to have a conversation with that blond and slender young lady who had had no trouble resisting the Jack Michaels charm. Jack noticed she seemed to have considerably more interest in Sellars than she'd had in him, actually appearing to listen to the man rather than all but yawning in his face as she'd done with him. If he didn't have other things to worry about, he might wonder if he were losing his touch. . . .

That thought lightened his mood enough to let him grin to himself. "Jack Michaels," the renowned rogue, might worry about losing his touch, but *he* was usually too busy to pay attention to things like that. And besides, wasn't he being forced to satisfy the desires of a very attractive young lady? Possibly not in the way he would have preferred to satisfy her, but who knew where their drive tomorrow might lead?

This time Jack laughed at himself, but with only a touch of amusement. The young lady in question apparently knew all about his public reputation, and had flatly refused to argue her brother's opinion of him. *He* was the one who had to get around her brother, and once he did he could then help her do whatever it was she felt she had to do. She wasn't interested in *him,* only in his knowledge, ability, skills, and contacts.

Another sip of champagne let Jack swallow the disappointment he'd never quite managed to get used to. He'd had more than his share of females—companions—who enjoyed his company, but no woman he might have gotten serious about had ever looked at him twice. That was hardly unexpected, but it had continued to be painful. Maybe someday . . .

But right now he had a job to do, one in addition to his original reason for being there. He'd have to find Lord Ashford, and burble out his enthusiasm over the "lovely young lady" he'd just met. He'd also have to drop very broad hints about how grateful his father would be if his irresponsible offspring became involved with a woman who would succeed in making him settle down to the responsible life. If *that* didn't get Ashford to convince the girl's brother to permit him to come calling, nothing would.

And he'd have to stop thinking of her as "the girl." Her name was Amanda, he'd been told, a sweet and lovely name. Helping her do her chore shouldn't take too long, and then he'd revert to his old, unacceptable habits which would certainly get him barred from her company. That shouldn't prove too hard to take, especially not with a female blackmailer. Whatever could have made him forget she wasn't really the "nice girl" she pretended to be?

Well, he wasn't likely to forget again. And serious involvements weren't for him anyway, so what was the difference? Jack couldn't answer that, and actually didn't want to. He surreptitiously checked on Hughes again, then went to find Lord Ashford.

Much of the night went by with nothing in the way of positive results to show for it, and Jack found himself weary as well as bored. He decided on a moment or two of fresh air to wake him up and so stepped out onto the terrace, but once outside he received a surprise. Miss Edmunds sat on a metal bench to the right, looking almost as weary as he felt. Jack knew he ought to turn around and go back inside, but something made him approach her instead.

"Well, Miss Edmunds, hello again," he said with a bow, drawing her startled attention. "I hadn't expected to find you alone tonight, nor to have the opportunity to speak to you until tomorrow, when we go for our drive."

"I take it that my brother has agreed, then," she responded, no longer looking weary. "I congratulate you, Mr. Michaels, for having accomplished what you set out to do. Truth to tell, however, if ladies were permitted to come and go as they pleased, I might have been out driving alone tomorrow rather than in your company."

"But then, dear lady, I would have been left bereft," he protested, surprised to find that there was a good deal of truth in the automatic gallantry. Some part of him *was* looking forward to tomorrow, even though she'd just said she would have gone alone if that were possible. "And even beyond that, there's your safety to consider. Where would the world be, if ladies went forth as they pleased and exposed themselves to danger?"

"Danger can be found anywhere, Mr. Michaels, even in one's own home," she replied comfortably with a smile. "Remaining at home is therefore less of a path to safety than learning to cope with danger as it comes. But, then, I'm sure a man of your wide experience already knows that."

Jack bowed to show his agreement, amused in spite of himself. She'd reminded him that they'd both had lessons in taking the danger out of wandering about alone, but hadn't said it in any words the people standing not far away would understand if they overheard her. It was delightful to meet a woman who was almost as good as himself at dissembling.

"I still find it difficult to believe that you've been abandoned," he said, returning to the point that really did surprise him. "Has some catastrophe occurred, that all the men who clamored for your attention earlier are no longer about?"

"I begged a few solitary moments in the night air to refresh myself," she answered, still wearing the smile that turned her more than simply pretty. "I'm told that ladies in this country find the night air harmful in some way, but my having grown up elsewhere means I don't consider it the same. The stars are so very lovely, and at what other time is it possible to see them?"

"You have an excellent point," Jack conceded, turning to look up at the stars just as she was doing. Actually, though, it was a picture of *her* that his mind saw, that and her enjoyment of so simple a thing as stars. The women he knew were usually more concerned with their own beauty than with the beauty around them, an outlook Jack found tedious and off-putting.

"I should someday love to attend a ball held outdoors,"

Jack continued, turning from the stars to the more attractive sight of Miss Edmunds. "The uncertainty of English weather usually makes the idea extremely impractical, but nevertheless the concept fascinates me."

"There would have to be candles rather than torches, so the stars might be fully appreciated," the girl said, immediately adopting the idea. "Paper lanterns would do, as they're used in China, with their many colors adding to the festive air of the occasion. A large canopy might be erected in case of rain, but otherwise everyone would dance and sit out under the wide, dark sky."

"And stroll through the grass and near the flowers," Jack contributed, amazed at how much pleasure the conversation was giving him. "The dancing would continue on until dawn, and then everyone would pause to watch the sunrise before sitting down—still outdoors—to a lavish breakfast."

The girl continued, "And then everyone would—" but her words were interrupted by the arrival of four or five men, all of them pushing their way between Jack and her.

"My dear Miss Edmunds, we've come to rescue you," the man who had been pointed out to Jack as Thomas Attenborough said to Amanda. "This night air is *so* awful for a delicate young lady such as yourself, and we've sorely missed your presence. You must return inside with us now, and settle the argument as to which of us has the honor of the next dance. We . . ."

Attenborough's voice faded as the group moved back indoors with Amanda in their midst, giving Jack no chance to say even a single word more to the girl. Anger and frustration flared in Jack, along with an irrational urge to call Attenborough out, but that was impossible. Jack was there on official business, after all, not to pay court to a young lady or to bring himself to the serious attention of the people around him. He had to be careful of what he said and did.

It took two or three turns around the terrace before Jack had control of his temper again, and it was certainly about time. How could he have forgotten that Amanda Edmunds had blackmailed him into helping her? He would be calling on her tomorrow because he had to, not because he wanted to do so. With that thought planted firmly in mind he went back into the ballroom to attend to the real reason he was there, deliberately refusing to remember how incredibly different—and wonderful—their brief conversation had been.

Chapter 4

"**I** can't believe you threatened the Golden Devil," Pei said for the hundredth time, still staring wide-eyed at Amanda. "There were only two fighters at Master Ma's school who were better than him, and one of them was Master Ma himself. What if he decides to kill you to keep you quiet?"

"Pei, this is England, not some backward place like the colonies," Amanda reminded her with a laugh, reaching again for her teacup. They were sharing a pot of tea in Amanda's sitting room while they waited for Amanda's "young man" to call for her. "If a woman was murdered in China, wouldn't the district magistrate work his people day and night to find out who the murderer was? It's done the same way here, and besides, I can't imagine that Jack Michaels would ever harm a woman. Not that he isn't probably wishing he could."

"You obviously find the idea of his anger amusing," Pei observed, reaching for her own teacup. "If *I* ever inspire murderous thoughts in a man, you can be sure I won't find it funny. And you really think he'll help you to find Mr. Lichfield? What if he just goes about his own business, then comes back after a while and tells you there's no trace of the man?"

"That's one of the reasons I intend to go with him while he does his looking," Amanda answered, realizing she hadn't said anything to reassure Pei that she'd be safe with Jack Michaels. She had decided not to reveal her suspicion

52

that Jack Michaels worked for the British government, although that would imply he was a man of honor no matter what his reputation. Moreover, Amanda could *feel* his strength, and strong men helped women, they didn't abuse them.

"And Richard agreed to let you go poking about with a strange man?" Pei asked, her brows raised in surprise. "I hadn't thought he would agree to something like that."

"Pei, Richard doesn't know anything about this arrangement," Amanda quickly told her. "I thought you understood that, or I would have discussed it sooner. You should have heard him this morning, when he told me what a busy day I have ahead of me. He started with the fact that Thomas Attenborough will be taking me to the theater tonight, and then began to list all of Thomas's attributes. When he was finished, he paused and cleared his throat."

"Which let you know he wanted to discuss something delicate or distasteful," Pei said with a nod, showing how much she'd learned from the master merchant who was her father. "I certainly hope you didn't laugh the way you sometimes do."

"Richard is a dear, and he can't help being obvious," Amanda said, glancing at the mantel clock. It was still too early for Jack Michaels to be there, but she felt as if the morning had been at least a sennight long. "I stood there solemnly and listened while Richard explained that a . . . 'gentleman'—*his* pause and stress—was going to be taking me driving this afternoon. He said I was to be courteous and polite, but to take whatever was said to me with an entire sackful of salt. The gentleman's intentions *might* be sincere and honorable, and if they were, I would have a nice, pleasant time seeing the sights."

"With a man who's dreaming sweet thoughts of murder?" Pei asked with a grin. "Is that another old English custom?"

"Well, you have to remember Richard doesn't know about that part of it," Amanda said with her own grin. "As far as he knows, Mr. Michaels has become suddenly smitten with me and might even turn over a new leaf if he decides he can't live without me. That wasn't *exactly* the way Richard put it, but it's what he meant. I can't tell you how hard it was to keep my face straight, especially during the warning."

"Oh, this I have to hear," Pei said, leaning forward in her chair. "What were you warned about that you haven't known since my father's favorite concubine sat us down as little girls?"

"I was warned that some men are vile, and will lie to a girl just so they can steal a kiss!" Amanda whispered with her eyes wide, trying to look shocked to the bone. "That doesn't mean that they love her, or intend to offer honorable marriage. It usually means just the opposite, and a girl who lets a cad kiss her without protest becomes known as a very foolish girl. If Mr. Michaels tries to kiss me, I'm to tell Richard immediately and *he'll* take care of it."

"If Mr. Michaels tries to kiss you, you'll probably discover that he's suffering from a fever," Pei corrected dryly. "And if the man has such a terrible reputation that you need to be warned against him, I still don't understand why your brother would let him take you driving in the first place. The wise men say it takes more than good intentions to change one who has strayed from the true path, especially if the intentions aren't *his.*"

"The matter seems to have more to do with Mr. Michaels's father than with him," Amanda admitted, bothered by that part herself. "His father is a very wealthy and important man in this country, and Richard has been asked to let Mr. Michaels come calling because of that. His father is supposed to be hoping for a sudden character change in Mr. Michaels, but Richard doesn't put much faith in its happening. Although if it ever did, Mr. Michaels's father would be very grateful to—and generous with—the woman who caused the change. Hearing that made me glad Mr. Michaels isn't seriously interested in courting me. If I ever married him under conditions like those, I'd feel—bought and dirty."

"Girls *are* bought and sold in China, but I think I know what you mean," Pei said, now obviously sharing Amanda's darker mood. "If my father ever gave me in marriage to someone simply because the man offered an enormous price for me . . . but he'd never do that, and not simply because he doesn't need the gold. He's most interested in doing what's best for *me,* and I'm sure Richard feels the same way about you."

"You're right, of course," Amanda agreed, deliberately pulling herself away from the shadow of disappointment she felt. "It's more than likely I simply misunderstood Richard's point, especially since I'm to tell him at once if the man tries to 'kiss' me. I wonder what I'm supposed to do if he tries to make love to me without first starting with a kiss?"

Amanda joined in as Pei giggled, but Pei wasn't given the chance to answer or comment. A knock came at the sitting room door, and then a housemaid entered.

"Beggin' yer pardon, ma'am, but th' gentleman is here t'take you drivin'," the girl said with a curtsey. Amanda felt the urge to get immediately to her feet, but instead merely nodded.

"Please tell the gentleman that I'm still dressing, and that I'll be down in a few moments," she said. When the girl curtsied again and left, Pei waited only until the door had closed.

"Why did you do that?" she demanded, nearly outraged. "I thought you were in a hurry to search for Mr. Lichfield, and that's the only reason Mr. Michaels is here. Are you deliberately trying to get him angry again?"

"Don't we both know that an angry man is never fully in control of himself or the world around him?" Amanda countered after finishing her tea. "I have the feeling that if I give Mr. Michaels the chance, he'll find a way to avoid helping me. If I keep him angry instead he won't have the chance to find that way, at least not until we've located Mr. Lichfield."

"Or until he decides to murder you after all," Pei said sourly as Amanda stood. "If it happens, don't say I didn't warn you."

Amanda laughed as she went to the mirror to put on her hat. Because Pei was so cautious, she missed out on half the fun to be had. Amanda wouldn't allow herself to do that, but there was a reason for keeping Jack Michaels angry that Amanda hadn't mentioned, one that was solely for *her* benefit. She found Jack Michaels much too attractive, and that wasn't good. If the man was continually angry and annoyed, he wouldn't be likely to consider any attraction to *her*. They would find Mr. Lichfield together, and then each would go his or her own separate way.

Which will be best for both of us, Amanda thought as she went to collect the rest of her accessories. *I might not want to believe that now, but when the time comes I will. I know I will. . . .*

Jack Michaels maintained an easygoing and uncaring expression, but inside he was fuming. The housemaid had told him that Miss Edmunds wasn't ready yet, and *that* he hadn't expected. The girl had all but put a pistol to his head to get him there, and now she was making him wait? Talk about your bare-faced gall. . . .

Jack forcibly kept himself from pacing by concentrating on unpleasant memories. Like the reaction he'd had from Sir Charles the night before, after breaking the news about his sudden involvement with a woman, and what it really meant. He and Hughes and Sellars had made their individual ways to the Essex Street rooms to meet Sir Charles, and first they'd discussed Hughes's situation.

"Nothing but another note," Hughes had said in disgust, handing the envelope to Sir Charles. "I don't know what game they're playing, but I really don't care for it."

Hughes shook his handsome, blond-haired head in disgust, but Jack knew him well enough to realize that he was also worried. *Something* was going on, and until they knew what it was they would none of them rest easy.

" 'My dear Mr. Hughes,' " Sir Charles read aloud after first glancing over the note. " 'I really meant to contact you in person tonight, but my courage has failed me. My need for your help continues to be just as desperate, but fortune has blessed me with a brief respite. With more time now at my disposal, I'll work at bracing up my courage before I make another attempt to meet you face-to-face. The time will not be long, and when we do meet, my appreciation will be substantial. Once again, my thanks for your willingness to cooperate. Yours, etc. etc.' Have you any idea who sent it?"

"I tried to look into that part of it when I saw the servant delivering the note," Sellars said, running a weary hand through his black hair. "The servant had no idea where the note came from, only that it was lying on the tray that was left for him to circulate with. He assumed he was meant to deliver it, and so he did."

"There's something else about this note that I'm sure you've all noticed," Jack said after Sir Charles passed it to him and he'd had a chance to examine it. "This printing looks identical to that of the first note, but it hasn't been hastily scrawled. It's been all but drawn, which means it was prepared beforehand. Our mystery writer brought the second note along tonight, which also means he or she never intended to contact Hughes in person."

"Did you see anyone who looked in the least suspicious?" Sir Charles asked him. "Someone who definitely didn't belong, or who found too great an interest in Hughes?"

"I had my suspicions about one of the ladies there, but she turned out to have more interest in Sellars than in Hughes," Jack answered with a grin. "My own charm was a bit too much for her, so naturally she turned to a man with a good deal less of it."

"In other words, he bored her to tears," Sellars corrected with a laugh. "Miss Justine Landers was delighted to find a gentleman there who was capable of intelligent conversation, she said, not like some she could name. She didn't *do* any naming, of course, but I think we all know whose name would be first on the list."

"And *you* weren't approached by anyone who aroused your suspicions?" Sir Charles asked Hughes, ignoring the banter. "Not even someone who seemed the least bit odd?"

"I had my ear bent by an old man calling himself Sir Guy Falkening," Hughes answered after thinking for a moment. "His name was unfamiliar to me, which apparently made me the perfect victim to hear of his extensive travel adventures. It took some effort to escape him, but you can't call the incident odd or even unusual. There are different versions of the man at any party you go to, and no one else did more than briefly exchange amenities with me."

"So we keep the man in mind, but otherwise have no choice but to wait for your correspondent's next move," Sir Charles said with a sigh. "If we had even a hint of what they might be after. . . . Well, patience is a virtue, I'm told, and we could all do with an extra bit of that. If none of you has anything else to add, I'm for home before my wife forgets what I look like."

"Sir Charles," Jack said, keeping the man from rising from his chair. "There's another matter I need to speak to you about, if you can spare just a few minutes longer."

"That sounds like you don't need *us,*" Hughes commented as he and Sellars rose from their own chairs. "If that's the case we'll leave first, and I'll be in touch the moment I hear anything else."

Sir Charles nodded, watched Hughes leave, and waited the five minutes before Sellars did the same. Only then did he turn his attention back to his last remaining agent.

"All right, Jack, let's have it," he said, dark blue eyes concerned. "I recognize the tone of voice you used, but I can't remember ever hearing it from *you* before."

"That's probably because I've never been caught out before," Jack admitted wryly as he shifted in his chair.

"There was a young lady at the Ashford's tonight, the half sister of Richard Lavering, whom you may know as Lord Pembroke. She—caught me in a distracted moment and spoke to me in Chinese, and without stopping to think, I answered in the same way."

"The young lady speaks Chinese?" Sir Charles asked with brows high. "How odd. But I fail to see your problem. Haven't you said you're prepared to claim to have learned the language from your father's Chinese manservant?"

"If it was just a matter of the language, I would have done exactly that," Jack returned glumly. "The problem arose when the young lady announced that she'd recognized me from Master Ma's school, and that everyone at the school knew I'd come to China with an introduction from the British government."

"Oh, dear," Sir Charles said, an understatement if ever Jack had heard one. "And she spoke to you in Chinese in order to confirm that it really was you she remembered. That doesn't sound at all heartening. What did you do to make her believe she was mistaken?"

For the first time in many years, Jack felt the urge to squirm like a schoolboy. "I—told her it didn't matter *who* knew I'd been to China because no one would care, and that was when *she* told *me* that bit about the introduction. Then she said that if no one would care, I shouldn't mind if she 'accidentally' told everyone in sight about it. At that point I asked her what she wanted."

"I'm almost afraid to hear what her reply was," Sir Charles muttered with a sigh. "A man is never so helpless as when he's at the mercy of a woman."

"She apparently needs help in locating someone," Jack supplied, fighting the feeling that he was an abysmal failure. "At first I considered it too much of a coincidence that someone would ask for *my* help in almost the same way Hughes had been asked for his, but after thinking about it, I've decided it really is a coincidence. The girl approached me herself, made no effort to beat about the bush, and didn't even look at Hughes. I took advantage of that story you used on Lord Ashford, told the man I'd gone dotty over this girl I'd just met, and had him intercede with Lavering on my behalf. After a good deal of resistance on Lavering's part, he agreed to let me take his sister driving tomorrow."

"He must be seriously fond of the girl," Sir Charles commented, now eyeing Jack speculatively. "Considering who your father is, *you* have to be thought of as a catch, but not for an innocent young girl. Not unless you change your lifestyle. When exactly did you meet the young lady?"

"We never met, not in the way you mean it," Jack grumbled, rubbing his face with one hand. "As best as I can remember, I came face-to-face with a solemn-eyed little girl just once during my year in China. At first glance I'd thought she was Chinese, but closer inspection revealed that she was definitely European. Tomorrow, I'll find out how she happened to be there."

"While you're at it, don't forget to find out how far her discretion extends," Sir Charles suggested, the words dry. "It would be rather unpleasant if she linked you more solidly with the British government, and then gossiped about it."

Jack had nodded in silent agreement, too embarrassed to mention just how solidly she'd already linked him to the government. And now he stood in her brother's hall, cooling his heels while the impertinent snip took her own sweet time.

"Ninhao-a, Chin Te Quei," Jack heard suddenly behind him. The words meant, approximately, "Hello, Golden Devil," and there was no doubt who uttered them. This time, however, Jack was forewarned about speaking without thinking, so he put on a faintly surprised smile and turned.

"Ah, it *is* you, Miss Edmunds," he exclaimed with a delight he wasn't quite feeling. "I've been waiting so anx-

iously, but the wait was definitely worth it. And I do beg
your pardon, but what was that you said?"

"I merely said hello, Mr. Michaels," she replied with an
easy smile of her own, secret devilment dancing in her
light and beautiful eyes. "How nice to see you again."

"Lady mine, all pleasure is in *my* possession," Jack responded smoothly as he took her hand and bent over it. It
was the sort of thing he usually said to women, an automatic comment as he fought a sudden and very unexpected
feeling. He *was* enjoying seeing her again, and that despite
the circumstances. What could he be thinking of. . . .?

"Shall we go?" she suggested when he released her
hand, the look of amusement still strong in her eyes. "It's
such a lovely day, I can't wait to be out in it."

Jack bowed in acquiescence and offered his arm, and
when she took it he began to lead her toward the door. She
really did look lovely in a day gown of pale gray embroidered all over with tiny designs in orange and crimson. The
designs were, of course, Chinese pictograph writing, but
Jack was only able to recognize it, not read it. The matching gray of her hat, slippers, reticule and gloves seemed to
emphasize the quiet gaity of the gown.

And of the girl herself. Her dark and glorious hair was
carefully swept up, but that merely emphasized the round-
cheeked girlishness of her face. Not that she looked like a
child, quite the contrary. Her features were those of a
woman, but with her light blue eyes and sweetly curved
lips, she couldn't be described as anything but adorable.
An adorable woman with dancing eyes and a body that
made a man want to see more of it. . . .

"I've hired this carriage and driver for the entire afternoon," Jack said after clearing his throat, the carriage in
question now in front of them in the drive. He also silently
cursed himself for letting his mind wander, especially to so
impossible a topic. "Is there anything in particular you'd
like to see?"

"How nice of you to ask," the girl commented with a
brighter smile as Jack handed her into the carriage. "As a

matter of fact there *does* happen to be a place I'd like to see, specifically for the unusual architecture of the building. I've been told that the Office of Registry for legal documents or some such is almost unique in one aspect or its design, and I would dearly love to see it for myself."

The bland look she gave him, along with her preposterous request, told Jack two things. The first was that she'd picked up immediately on the fact that they couldn't speak freely in the hearing of their driver, something he'd hoped she'd understand. He hadn't expected her to be *that* quick, though, nor had he expected to feel so pleased over the sharpness of her mind. As he seated himself in the carriage beside her, he silently ordered himself to stop the nonsense. Amanda Edmunds was too dangerous to play around with, a point confirmed by the second thing he'd noticed: she played her own games and was having a marvelous time doing it.

"The Registry Office?" Jack finally echoed, raising his brows. "And you say there's something unique about its architecture? Well, that I certainly do have to see for myself as well. Driver, the Registry Office on Crawford Street, please."

Their driver made an affirmative sound and flicked his reins, and the fine pair of matched bays responded immediately. Jack meant to question the girl more thoroughly once they had some privacy, but for the moment he had questions he could ask openly.

"I understand, Miss Edmunds, that you come from China," he said as he turned to the girl. "How on earth did a lovely English lady end up in a heathen place like *that?*"

"The answer is quite simple, Mr. Michaels," she said mildly, the amusement in her eyes easily apparent. "I was taken to China as an infant by my parents, which means it happened *before* I became a lovely English lady. My father was a scholar who devoted his life to studying China and her people, and we all very much enjoyed living there."

"I'm sure you did," Jack responded, unreasonably annoyed that she'd made fun of his compliment rather than accepting it. "You must have had some unusual experiences there, doing things a young lady raised in England would never dream of," he said, trying again to find out how she'd happened to be at Master Ma's school. "I'd love to hear about some of them."

"Oh, there weren't *that* many things," she protested, but with that same look of devilment in her eyes. She knew what he wanted to hear, all right, but whether or not she would give it to him still remained to be seen. "There were the early summer picnics, of course, given by the wealthy and influential men of the district, and attended by the entire village," she mused. "Those weren't unusual, except for the time the tiger came down out of the hills to join us."

"Tiger?" Jack blinked, trying to picture something he'd never personally seen, and then he understood. "Oh, you mean symbolically. I've heard the Chinese are big on using tigers and dragons as symbols of things for good luck."

"That tiger was no symbol," she denied with a grin. "And it certainly wasn't good luck, not even for itself. It almost got one of the children before some of the men frightened it away, and then the district Magistrate sent members of his tribunal out to hunt it down. It was a male who had been ejected from his family group because of old age, they said, and for the same reason had trouble hunting his usual prey, so he had to find something slower to eat. Humans are slower, but they're also a good deal more dangerous. Which that poor tiger quickly found out."

"Yes. Indeed." Jack cleared his throat, not quite knowing what to say next. Very few English girls were threatened by tigers in their childhood. What else had she experienced?

"Let's see, what else was there," she mused, tapping a finger on her chin, virtually reading his mind. "Well, it was always interesting to entertain one of the important men of the district. Usually they sent a servant ahead with their large, square calling cards to make an appointment, and then at the appointed time *they* showed up. If it was a business occasion the man would come to the gate of your compound alone in his palanquin, his guards accompanying him on foot or on horseback."

"Palanquin?" Jack interrupted to ask, not because he didn't know, but because he would be *expected* not to know. Their driver *was* listening, even though he certainly couldn't hear the whole of the conversation.

"A palanquin is a one- or two-person carriage that's carried on the shoulders of men rather than wheeled and pulled by horses," Amanda said, groping for the proper words of description. A flash of annoyance in her expression told Jack she probably wanted to say, "Oh, you know!" but couldn't. "The thing is rather small and has four poles, two sticking out the front, two out the back. The four bearers are always the same approximate size, since each one lifts a pole and rests it on his shoulder. The palanquin itself is a covered and windowed box of sorts with a seat—or two seats facing each other—and only wide enough for the shoulder width of a man. They come equipped with privacy curtains, of course, which are usually put down if a woman is inside."

"Fascinating," Jack acknowledged with a smile and a nod, pleased that he'd accidently managed to irritate *her* for once. "Do go on."

"As I said, if it was business, the man came alone," she continued, obviously trying to shed her annoyance. "If it was a social occasion, the man usually brought one or more of his wives in one or more other palanquins. Sometimes he even brought his concubines."

"Wives, *plural?*" Jack was forced to blurt out in shock, which immediately rekindled her amusement. "And—concubines? Oh, I say!"

"Really, Mr. Michaels, the practice is quite common throughout history," the chit told him with such smirking condescension that Jack would have enjoyed tearing something dangerous apart with his bare hands. But not her, definitely not her. He wanted to do something more—lingering—to *her.* She'd maneuvered him into having to look and sound the fool, while she sat back and enjoyed his discomfort. Yes, he'd definitely have to find something lingering to do. . . .

"And even beyond that, Mr. Lichfield put the whole matter into perspective for me," she continued blandly. "Mr. Lichfield was my father's secretary, and he made it his business to look after me when my mother passed away. Mr. Lichfield said that the best way to get along in the world was to understand that different people have different customs. If you wasted your time trying to figure out who was right and who was wrong, you'd soon get to the end of your life without having thought about anything but opinions. The best thing to do is to say, 'This is *their* custom, and this other one is mine,' and then get on with your life. That way you can also learn to appreciate people without a cloud of criticism getting in the way."

"This Mr. Lichfield of yours sounds like quite a man," Jack remarked, now diverted from his anger. The amusement in her demeanor had left Amanda when she spoke about Lichfield . . . was he the one she wanted to find? Maybe there was a way to find out. "Perhaps one day you'll introduce me to the gentleman. Did he accompany you on the journey here?"

"Mr. Lichfield left a number of months before I did," she answered, and the direct way she looked at Jack told him this *was* the objective of her game. "He's here in England now, and as soon as I discover exactly where, I'll be glad to introduce you."

Jack nodded casually to show he'd gotten the message, then took a moment to think about it. If the man had been so close to Amanda, he would hardly have gone off on his own without first making certain she reached England safely. The girl was probably right to be worried about him, so at least Jack would not find the episode a complete waste of time. Amanda did need his help, but first she needed a little taking down.

"You know, now that I think about it, it *is* best to accept strange people and their customs," he commented after a moment. "And you're quite right in saying history has shown us many men who held concubines. They were men who had the strength to take what women they pleased, and the women were undoubtedly terrified to have it so. The men of today find it preferable to be gentlemen, which must be quite a relief to the ladies. Can you imagine what it must have been like for them, being forced to the pleasure of a man?"

Jack's tone of voice had been carefully disapproving, but the way he looked at the girl was meant to send a different message: he'd spent a year in China, and when a man spends that long among strangers, some of their outlooks may begin to rub off on him. Taking any woman you cared to wasn't any more legal in China than it was in England, but they did have their strong men, the warlords, who lived in mountain fortresses and were a law unto themselves. Jack wanted the girl to remember that he was only pretending to be a dandy—and possibly grow a bit nervous at the thought, and then refrain from prodding at him. She, however, proved to be just as cooperative as he was beginning to expect her to be.

"Oh, Mr. Michaels, I'm sure you can't be *that* naive," she chided, her vast amusement showing. Their conversation was very nearly improper, and the pedantic tone she used must have been her way of continuing it. "Certainly there were women who were terrified to be taken captive by strong men, but there were also ones who were delighted by the whole thing—as well as ones who simply got angry. Those last were the ones *men* had to worry about, you know. It doesn't matter *how* strong a man is, if he's foolish enough to fall asleep after abusing an angry woman. And what man is strong enough to stay awake forever?"

Her question was bland and easy, but the look in her light eyes more than matched the one Jack had been trying to show. Miss Amanda Edmunds *was* more dangerous than she appeared to be at first glance. He'd tried to teach her not to push so hard, and she'd countered with a nice example of the veiled threat: If any man ever abused her, she'd kill him even if she had to do it while he slept. Jack didn't doubt her for a minute, but why did he have to feel so blasted pleased by her spirit?

He spent some time in silence trying to answer that question, but hadn't come to any satisfactory conclusion when they pulled up in front of the Registry Office on Crawford Street. The area wasn't as full of people as it might have been, which was one bit of luck. If he could get the girl inside and somewhere private . . .

"I'm sorry, Miss Edmunds, but I don't seem to see any architectural marvels," he said, gesturing toward the building while he pretended to study it. "Columns, buttresses, and stone, but no marvels."

"Of course not, Mr. Michaels," she answered with a light laugh, taking the opening he'd given her. "The unique feature I was told about is inside. Do you think we might go in and walk about?"

"I am completely and entirely at your service, lady mine," Jack returned at his most charming, then stepped out of the carriage and turned. "Allow me to assist you to the ground."

"How nice of you, Mr. Michaels," she murmured as she took his hand with a smile, pretending she needed the help. Despite the awkwardness of a gown, Jack seriously doubted if she needed help doing anything. But her slender hand felt uncomfortably good in his, and that in spite of her glove. With that in mind, Jack let her go as soon as she was standing beside him, then turned to the driver.

"I've no idea *how* long we'll be, Higgins," he said, playing the happy and idle scion of wealth. "If anyone official dislikes your being here, take a slow turn or two around the block."

"As ye say, sor," the man agreed, touching a hand to his hat. "Stay 'ere till I'm chased, an' then around th' block."

"Excellent man, Higgins," Jack said jovially, then turned back to Amanda to offer his arm. "Shall we, lady mine?"

The girl took his arm with a silent smile, and they climbed the steps up to the building and then entered it. The place was large and old and looked like it had been someone's unofficial palace once, but now it was given over to unending sets of offices. Jack waited until they reached a large column with no one in sight, then quickly drew the girl behind it.

"All right, now tell me the real reason we're here," he said, looking down at her. "Your Mr. Lichfield must have been by to file whatever papers he had, but the clerk who helped him isn't likely to know where he went afterward—or even to remember him."

"I know that, but I still intend to ask," she said, determination replacing the amusement in those blue eyes. "Once I'm *certain* that part of it is a dead end, we'll go and see Mr. Harold Melton in the pensions department. Mr. Lichfield was an old friend of his and intended to stop in and see him while he was here, but I don't know if he visited or took care of business first. Knowing Mr. Lichfield, it was probably the latter, but assuming things without checking to be certain usually means you're wasting your time."

"And you'd rather waste other people's time rather than your own," Jack returned dryly. "And while we're discussing time, how long do you intend to drag me around as your supposed escort? I *do* have other things waiting for my attention."

"But surely none of them are as important as pleasing the new lady in your life?" she countered, that look of devilment back. "Don't worry, Mr. Michaels, I haven't captured you forever. As soon as I have what I want from you, you'll be free to go your own way again—Oh, dear, perhaps I put that badly. I do hope you're not offended."

The hell she hoped he wasn't offended. Jack felt the fury rising in him again, and all because of what she'd said. She'd deliberately made it sound as if she were going to take pleasure from him before tossing him out again the way some men did with women. She was still coming back at him for what he'd tried in the carriage, and he'd had more than enough.

"All right, I think it's time to spell out the rules of this little game," he growled, which finally got rid of the smirk on her face. "To begin with, you don't have as much leverage with me as you seem to believe. I'm humoring you now by going along with your demands, but I can just as easily have you arrested for interfering with the actions of a government official, not to mention blackmail. The instant I decide that this is more trouble than it's worth, that's exactly what I *will* do. Is that clear?"

She parted her lips to say something, then wisely changed her mind and simply nodded. He wasn't joking or bluffing, and she seemed to know it.

"If it's clear, then you'd better remember it," he said, pressing the point as hard as possible. "You will especially remember it when talking to me in public, where my choice in response is necessarily limited. And in case you don't know it, it isn't *proper* for a young lady to discuss subjects like concubines. If you do it again I'll tell your brother, and also mention how well a sound spanking does in teaching a girl some manners."

"You wouldn't!" she blurted, for an instant looking as trapped as he'd been feeling. "My brother has nothing to do with this, so you *can't* bring him into it!"

"Try me," he offered flatly, needing to let her know where he stood. "You've had a merry old time walking all over me, but that stops right now. I don't take well to being walked over, and if I have to I'll teach that lesson the hard way. I've agreed to help you find Mr. Lichfield so I will, but there will be *no more* taking advantage. Do you understand me?"

By now she looked down at her hands rather than up at him, and she wordlessly nodded her head. For a moment her very obvious misery made him feel like a complete cad, but he purposefully pushed the feeling away. He'd only said what needed to be voiced, especially since he couldn't bear to look the fool in front of her. There would be enough of that once he reverted to his public character.

"All right, now we can get on with your investigation," he said, his tone softer than his previous one. "We'll do it in the way *you* want it done, but I'll be the one accomplishing it. I have the experience, after all, and it would be silly to waste it."

She nodded obediently again, then took his arm when he offered it. Jack sighed to himself as he led the way to the records office that handled vital statistics, but he made no effort to apologize for hurting the girl's feelings. It was something that had had to be done, and as soon as he located her Mr. Lichfield he'd be out of her life again. Something that ought to make *her* happy enough. . . .

Chapter 5

Amanda managed a glance at the face of the man whose arm she held, and then sighed silently with relief. She'd almost pushed Jack Michaels *too* far, but luckily he'd chosen to scold her rather than turn around and walk away. If he only knew how experienced she was at looking contrite during a scolding. . . .

But he didn't know, so everything ought to be all right now. Amanda was tempted to chuckle over how quickly he'd believed her "desperate" attempt to keep Richard out of the matter. She'd learned that being desperate about *something* usually made her pretended regret seem more real, but Jack Michaels had been faster than most to accept the ploy. Apparently he hadn't realized that Richard would be much more apt to believe *her* side of any presented disagreement, especially after she embroidered her version a bit. Embroidery *was* a woman's skill, after all.

But the main point was that the Golden Devil still worked on her behalf. He'd tried to escape her capture, but hadn't noticed it when his own strength had been used against him. For someone who knew Chinese boxing so well—much of which was *based* on using an opponent's strength against him—he *should* have noticed, but Amanda wasn't about to complain. His attempt at being masterful had been delightful, but only because it hadn't been successful. She'd have to be more careful from now on.

"Ah, here we are," he said in the tone of voice that announced he was back in his part of the dandy. Amanda

71

looked up to see a door with the words, "Bureau of Vital Statistics" painted on it, just before Jack opened it. She entered first, of course, to see a chest-high wooden counter dividing the large room. Four people stood in front of it, three of them busy writing. Behind the counter were a number of desks with four men sitting at them, all of whom were apparently too busy to look up. A fifth clerk stood at the counter, looking thoroughly bored and uninterested.

"Ah, there's someone who should be able to help us," Jack announced lazily as he gestured toward the standing clerk. "Fine chaps, these, doing their duty with such excellent diligence. I say, my man, I wonder if we might have a moment of your valuable time."

The clerk looked to Amanda as though most of his pleasure in life came from ignoring the people he was supposed to be there to help, but he wasn't stupid. When Jack had said "valuable" he'd also put his hand on the counter, and the soft clink of a coin just about made the clerk's ears perk up.

"Good day, sir, and may I be of some service?" he said, moving over to stand directly in front of Jack. His accent was odd, not at all like the ones Amanda was used to, but the words were clear enough.

"You certainly may be of service," Jack told the man lightly, his hand still over the coin. "Some months ago a man visited here to register the death of one George Edmunds. I wonder if you would be so good as to find the necessary paperwork."

The man had Jack spell the full name, and then he disappeared through a doorway into another room. They waited in silence, but not for long. The clerk reappeared quickly, now holding some papers.

"It's all right here, sir," he announced, waving the papers. "Everything perfectly in order and properly done."

"Oh, I don't doubt it," Jack hastened to assure the man, his smile full of calming support. "What I wanted to know was who handled the matter here in your office. I would like to see how good his memory is."

At that point Jack slid his hand away from the silver coin it had been covering, and the clerk quickly put his own hand over it. When he also slid his hand away the coin went with it, and now the clerk was smiling.

"The man you want is Reggie Nichols. Over there." He nodded toward one of the seated men. "Hoy, Reggie, over here a tick. Gentleman wants a word with ya."

Reggie Nichols was on the thin side with a nervous tick in his cheek, the sort of man Amanda would never have trusted behind her back. He looked as though he wanted to ignore the summons, but with everyone's eyes on him he stood and slowly walked over. He made no effort to meet anyone's gaze, and when he reached the side of the first clerk he stood there in sullen silence.

"Mr. Nichols, how good of you to take the time to help us," Jack said with all of his considerable charm, his hand on the counter again. Nichols should have heard the clink and seen the renewed gleam of silver, but he made no effort to look up. "I understand you handled the matter of registering the death of George Edmunds," Jack went on. "I would like to know what you remember of the man who registered the death."

"I don't remember anything," the man said at once, the words sullen but perfectly firm. He also had an educated accent, not something one would expect from looking at him. "I don't pay any attention to the people who come in here, so to me they're all the same. You're best off keeping your money, as I know nothing of any value."

"What a pity," Jack said mournfully, taking his coin back. Then his hand returned to the counter, and this time there was the gleam of gold. "Are you certain you remember nothing at all?"

The first clerk drew his breath in softly, which, if Nichols hadn't noticed himself, certainly must have told him that the reward had been increased. Amanda was sure the man realized he was refusing gold, but again it wasn't possible to tell simply by looking at him.

"I've already said I don't remember anything," he maintained, stubbornly still not looking up. "And I haven't the time to stand here gossiping all day."

With that he took himself off, but not back to his desk. He left the room entirely, with the first clerk staring incredulously at his retreating back.

"Well, that's that, I would say," Jack commented, taking back the gold coin. "If the man is *that* certain, there's no room for argument."

The first clerk looked as though he wanted to do *something* to keep the gold from leaving, but since it wasn't possible for him to offer any information himself, he was forced to keep silent. Amanda and her escort did the same until they were back out in the hall, but once she saw there was no one else nearby, she quickly turned to Jack.

"That man Nichols was lying," she stated, not in the least unsure. "Anyone else in his place would have at least tried to remember *something,* simply in an effort to get the cash."

"Money," Jack corrected in a murmur as he looked idly around. "It's called cash in China, especially when it's copper, but here it's generally called money. And of course he was lying. He didn't even look at the paperwork to see if there was something unusual involved, like a foreign death certificate. I daresay they don't have so many people dying in China that they'd fail to remember one who did."

"So what are you going to do about it?" Amanda demanded, ready to have a "private" talk with the man herself. "If he's lying then he does know something, and probably more than a little. Let's have the city Magistrate arrest him, then question him under torture."

"My dear girl, that sort of thing is frowned on in the British Empire," he answered with a grin as he took her arm and started to walk. "Magistrates aren't permitted to question *anyone* under torture, even if they're absolutely positive the man is hiding pertinent information. You must make an effort to remember that this isn't China."

"Then I wish it were," Amanda huffed, suddenly seeing the land of her birth as the backward, provincial outpost Pei undoubtedly considered it. "A Chinese Magistrate can't question just anyone under torture, he has to be absolutely certain that the person is guilty. And even so, if the person dies without confessing the crime, then the *Magistrate* usually faces the same thing in punishment: death by torture. What better way is there to make certain the practice isn't abused?"

"Miss Edmunds, it so happens I agree with you," Jack said in a very low voice. "I did the same sort of comparing when I first got back to England, wondering why *we* couldn't be as cultured and wise. I finally came to two conclusions, which are as follows: one, the Chinese people have had thousands of years more practice at it, so this country needs to be given a chance to grow and mature. And two, this is what we have to work with, so why waste time and energy wishing it wasn't so? The wishing won't change anything."

"I suppose you're right," Amanda admitted grudgingly, accepting the philosophy rather than the conclusion. "But does that mean we're just going to let him get away with it?"

"Not at all," Jack denied with a laugh, guiding her hand to his arm again. "Right now we're going to work around him by seeing that man in the Pensions department. If that doesn't help, well, then we'll have to consider our options."

Amanda simply nodded, momentarily willing to allow Nichols to get away with lying. If they found themselves at a complete dead end, though, she would be back to see the uncooperative Mr. Nichols. He might refuse silver and gold, but she knew there were things he would find it impossible to refuse. Amanda was convinced that Mr. Lichfield was depending on her, and she was *not* about to disappoint him.

The Pensions office was in another part of that very large building, but they eventually found it. Opening the door this time showed only three men behind a counter, but all three were attending those who had come there for help. They were also somewhat older men who appeared to be a good deal more pleasant than the ones in Vital Statistics, and as soon as one of the three clerks became available, he approached Amanda and Jack where they stood at the counter.

"Good afternoon, sir and madam," the man said with a smoother accent than that other clerk. "May I be of assistance to you?"

"Indeed you may," Jack answered just as pleasantly, his hand—and a coin—on the counter again. "We would like a few words with Mr. Harold Melton."

"Our Mr. Melton is just over there, helping someone," the clerk responded with an amused glance for the coin Jack had produced. "If you'll excuse me, I'll go and take over for him so that he can come and speak to you."

The man nodded amiably and walked away, leaving Jack with his brows raised. Amanda gathered that sort of behavior wasn't very common, and then another man came to stand in front of them. This one was fairly tall, with a distinguished look about him that was increased by the presence of graying hair and an air of calm authority. He was plainly but impeccably dressed, and smiled at his two visitors.

"I am Harold Melton," he said in a rich, cultured voice. "May I help you?"

"Mr. Melton, I'm Jack Michaels and this lady is Miss Amanda Edmunds," Jack said, and when Amanda glanced at him she noticed that he'd put the coin away again. "We do apologize for calling on you here, but Miss Edmunds is trying to locate someone whom we believe is a friend of yours."

"Mr. Miles Lichfield," Amanda supplied when she realized that Jack didn't know the full name. "He was secretary to my late father, Professor Edmunds, in China, and returned to England ahead of me. Since then he seems to have dropped out of sight, but he did mention that he meant to call on you. Have you seen him?"

"Yes, it so happens I have," Mr. Melton answered, an oddly disturbed look now in his eyes. "Just a moment, please."

He went over and spoke to the clerk who had called him, and that man nodded with a pleasant smile. With business apparently taken care of, Mr. Melton returned to open the end of the counter into a short door.

"Please come this way," he invited. "There's a room where we can speak more comfortably."

Amanda stepped through and waited for Mr. Melton to close the counter again behind Jack, then she followed the gentleman into the next room. There were wooden cabinets with drawers along every wall of the room except where there was another door, and in the middle was a small table with three chairs.

"We often take turns lunching in here," Mr. Melton said with a smile as he held one of the chairs for Amanda. "Or we take a few moments for a cup of hot tea in the winter. To answer your question again, Miss Edmunds, I did see my friend Mr. Lichfield a few months ago, when he came to the building on business, but I'm afraid I haven't seen him since."

"Did he by any chance tell you where he meant to go next?" Amanda asked as he and Jack took their own chairs. "I haven't had a word from him since he left China, and that isn't like Mr. Lichfield."

"In point of fact, he said he was returning to the rooms he'd taken in Marsden Mews," Mr. Melton replied. "He refused to interrupt me here in the office, you see, and so we arranged to attend the theater together that night, and afterward spend time catching each other up. I called for him promptly at the appointed hour, and only then learned from his landlady that he hadn't yet returned from the afternoon."

"Surely you informed the authorities about his disappearance," Jack said while Amanda felt the clutch of fear around her heart. "What were *they* able to discover?"

"Absolutely nothing," Mr. Melton answered, his disgust obvious. "First they suggested he'd stopped for a 'quick one' and lost track of the time. After he'd been missing for a full day, they suggested he was 'making up for lost time among the heathens.' You'll forgive me, I hope, Miss Edmunds, for not explaining that comment, but I'm certain Mr. Michaels understands. When I told them that was absurd, that even if it were true Mr. Lichfield would not have also arranged to attend the theater with me, they laughed. He probably came across an opportunity he hadn't expected and couldn't pass up, they insisted. He'd soon be in touch, they assured me, as soon as 'business' was taken care of."

The man now spoke primarily to Jack, and Amanda pretended she *didn't* understand the references, but of course she did. And Mr. Melton was quite correct. Mr. Lichfield wasn't too old to be interested in women, but he would never have made an appointment and then missed it because of one.

"And what did they say after days had passed and he still hadn't shown up?" Jack asked, obviously working to keep from being angry.

"They had me view all the most recent corpses that hadn't been identified," the older man replied, an illness now in his eyes. "They sent for me every two or three days for weeks, until I simply couldn't bear to go back again. Forgive me for mentioning so distasteful a subject, but I would like to have you understand that I really did try."

"Of course you did," Amanda told him firmly, patting his hand. "It was vile of them to put you through that, but it did prove one thing: Mr. Lichfield may be missing, but he isn't dead. If he'd been killed, there would have been no reason to go to the trouble of hiding his body."

"As far as we know," Jack murmured, which annoyed Amanda, then he continued in a louder voice. "Mr. Melton, was there *anything* Mr. Lichfield said to you while he was here in your office that might point to his possible whereabouts? Please think about it for a moment before you answer.''

Mr. Melton did think about it, and then he said, ''Now that you've put the question, there *was* one other thing he said. When he first came in and greeted me, he remarked, 'And yours is the second familiar face I've run into today.' I agreed that that was a remarkable coincidence, since he never did know many people in London, and then we made arrangements for that night.''

''Miss Edmunds, can you think of anything else you'd care to ask?'' Jack said, and when Amanda shook her head he turned to the older man again. ''Mr. Melton, you've been a great deal of help and we give you our thanks. Mr. Lichfield has a true friend in you.''

''Thank you, Mr. Michaels,'' the older man said with a quiet smile, standing to shake hands with Jack. ''I truly wish I were able to do more, and in fact would ask the favor of your return if it should turn out that I *can* do more. Please be assured that you have only to ask.''

Amanda added her thanks to Jack's as they both promised to call again if it became necessary, and then Mr. Melton let them out the second door Amanda had noticed when they entered the room. They found themselves in a different corridor than the one through which they had reached the office, but they spotted a small sign on the wall that indicated the way out.

''So whatever happened to Mr. Lichfield happened between here and his rooms,'' Amanda said as she and Jack made their way back to the building entrance. All that marble made Amanda very uncomfortable, and she couldn't wait to be outside again. ''I wonder if he hired a carriage, and if so, would the driver remember him?''

''I seriously doubt if he hired a carriage,'' Jack murmured, glancing around in a bored way. ''Marsden Mews is only a short distance from here through the park. It's also not all that far from the docks, which probably means

Mr. Lichfield meant to be handy when *you* arrived. The area of the Mews isn't the best of neighborhoods, but it's reasonably inexpensive and the worst it can be called is shabby. Do you know the number of his address?"

"Number fifty-three," Amanda replied promptly. "I got that from Richard, or rather from his investigator's report. They never did learn about Mr. Melton, so I wasn't terribly impressed. I'd like to see the park you just mentioned, although we aren't likely to find a clue after this long a time. We can visit Mr. Lichfield's rooms tomorrow."

"What's wrong with this afternoon?" Jack asked, for an instant letting annoyance show through his supposed boredom. "I thought you understood that I really can't make a career of this investigation."

"I have to get home because I'm going to the theater tonight," Amanda said, trying out an apologetic smile. "Richard is really working very hard to find me a suitable husband, and it would be unforgivable of me to make the job any harder. But as close as we are to a dead end, you certainly won't be involved in this much longer, Mr. Michaels. Another day or so, and then you'll be rid of me."

"Yes, that's very true," Jack replied after an odd hesitation Amanda didn't understand. "All right, we can ride through the park on the way to taking you home."

He was about to lead her to the steps that would take them out of the building, but Amanda felt there was something else that needed saying.

"Mr. Michaels, just a moment please," she said, halting him where he was. "Before we go to the carriage, there's something I'd like to tell you. You've been more than ordinarily decent about helping me with a problem that isn't in any way yours, and I'd like to take this opportunity to thank you."

"You're *thanking* me?" he echoed with brows high, looking honestly surprised. "Have you forgotten that being here wasn't a free choice on my part? People usually save their thanks for those who act voluntarily, not for the conscripted."

"But that's exactly the reason why I'm thanking you," Amanda explained. "Someone else in your place would have made minimal effort, but you haven't done that. You gave me your agreement to help, and you've fully honored the pledge. I have no idea how many men would have done the same, but I'm certain the number isn't large."

"Nonsense," he muttered, for some reason looking uncomfortable rather than pleased. "Any gentleman would have done exactly the same, since honor is inseparable from gentility. Surely you're aware of that fact?"

"If you say so," Amanda murmured, deciding not to pursue what was apparently a delicate subject. A man who felt uncomfortable with thanks was better off being spared them, no matter how well deserved those thanks were. Besides, Amanda thought it was adorable that the Golden Devil was shy on the point. Such a big, strong man, afraid of a few small thanks; who would have imagined . . .?

With that finally settled they left the building in silence, but when they reached the bottom of the steps their carriage was nowhere to be seen.

"Dash it all, Higgins must have been chased," Jack said pettishly, back in character. "That's rather an annoyance, but I say, why don't we have a short stroll in yonder park while we wait? There must be flowers in there somewhere, and lovely ladies always adore flowers."

"I consider flowers pleasant," Amanda allowed with a small nod of her head. "Very well, Mr. Michaels, a short stroll through the park, and then I really must be getting home."

"Which I shall see to the instant my carriage returns," Jack promised grandly with a bow, then offered his arm again. "Until then, your company is happily all mine."

"What park is that?" Amanda asked as they cautiously crossed the street. "Is it a famous one I might have heard about?"

"Actually, dear lady, most people in the city have never heard of it," Jack said, gesturing with one hand. "That sign calls it Winthrop Park, but I haven't the foggiest for whom it's named. And I daresay it's not very big, but we shouldn't let any of that spoil our enjoyment of it."

By then they were moving into the park proper, and although Amanda didn't say so aloud, she *was* enjoying the stroll. Jack Michaels's arm felt so strong through his coat sleeve, so supportive and so good. As a girl she'd dreamed of walking with him like this, a sweet garden scent all around, the sounds of the world fading into the distance behind them. There weren't many people present in the small park, and those who were there seemed more intent on treating it as an uninteresting shortcut.

Which just about turned the park into their own private place. Amanda knew nothing could come of her attraction to Jack, but that didn't stop her from fantasizing. That area just ahead, for instance. Once they rounded the curve into the deeper privacy of those tall hedges, Jack might stop and take her in his arms. Then he would kiss her with all of the interest he was hiding behind his wall of professional patience. He would show he wanted her just as much as she wanted him, and then—

And then he could take her home so that another man might escort her to the theater. Amanda's sigh was silent, but deep for all of that. The longer she stayed in Jack Michaels's company, the more she wanted her old daydreams to come true. She wanted to lie in his arms while he made love to her, giving her the pleasure that Green Jade, Pei's father's favorite concubine, had described to Pei and herself. Even if she couldn't marry him, she longed to have the memory of his lovemaking to keep forever.

But they'd already turned into the hedged walk, and Jack Michaels continued to stay firmly in character. He chattered about something or other, nothing at all important, his free hand gesturing at the same nothing. No desire-filled smile, no arms around her, no kiss, and certainly no lovemaking. Amanda felt like screaming in vexation, or possibly even hitting him with something hard. Couldn't he see she wanted him?

And then, suddenly, there was only one thing for both of them to see. Four sloppily dressed men had followed them into the privacy of the hedges, and with no one else in sight they came after their chosen victims at a run with only one shout as warning. She and Jack Michaels were being attacked!

Chapter 6

Amanda had lied to Pei about not being frightened when those men on the dock had tried to attack them. Amanda's heart had pounded like mad, and only years of training had let her respond properly with the weapon she'd held. Now, though, with Jack Michaels beside her, she really wasn't afraid. He was the Golden Devil, and those four would never have a chance against—

"Oh, I say!" Jack exclaimed, then began to bounce around like a clumsy novice, threatening the oncoming men with foolishly waving fists. "Never fear, lady mine, I'll see to these ruffians!"

Amanda's groan was covered by the laughter of their attackers, who obviously thought Jack was too funny for words. He clearly intended to keep to the part he was playing unless it became plain that their lives were at stake. Since the four men had empty hands, that time might never come.

"Folks as go where they don't belong ends up bashed," one of the men announced, showing bad teeth along with his grin. "An' they gets t'pay fer th' bashin' t'boot! Fork it over, gov, an' if ya gives us enough, maybe it won't be s'bad."

"You'll not find *me* paying tribute!" Jack announced, still dancing around and waving his arms. "Come ahead and see what you get for your efforts, villains! The lady and I will not be harmed!"

"Let's see, then," the apparent leader of the group said,

84

and all four of them began to slowly close in on Jack. The men were all still smiling, but Amanda knew the attack was no joke.

Which meant it was time to take precautionary measures, just to be on the safe side. Jack supposedly knew what he was doing, but in case something went wrong, Amanda wasn't completely unarmed. She'd gotten back that short section of bamboo she'd given Richard, and now slipped it out of her reticule. The four men were big and burly, and if she had to face any of them she didn't want it to be barehanded.

The four men were obviously trying to surround Jack completely before closing with him, but Jack, who was bouncing around in what looked like a completely random way, was skillfully outmaneuvering his opponents. After repeatedly failing to encircle Jack, the men had lost their amusement, and then one also lost his patience. He stalked close without waiting for his friends, and threw an oversized fist directly at Jack's face.

Amanda might have gasped with worry if she'd had the time, but Jack moved too fast. As though afraid of his burly attacker Jack threw both arms up in front of himself in defense, and one of them just "happened" to block and divert the burly man's punch. At the same time one of his dancing feet "accidentally" kicked the man in the leg, making the ruffian howl with true pain. Amanda knew the man's leg could well be broken, a theory supported by the way he hopped back before falling to the ground.

There were three attackers left, but the survivors were more annoyed than wary over the downfall of their fourth. Because of that they all rushed their helpless victim together, forgetting their strategy in their desire to pound him flat. Fists swung in anger with speed and strength behind, the force of which should have brought the helpless, foolish victim down.

But the helpless, foolish victim appeared to be too frightened to stand his ground. He yelped and ducked, and one of those thrown fists smashed into the wrong face.

The attacker on the receiving end went down and stayed there, unconscious and out of the fight. In the interim between the blow and the fall, the man who had thrown the punch was misfortunate enough to run into their victim's elbow. Since chance caused it to strike him in the throat, his own collapse came only seconds after that of the man he'd hit.

And that left only a single attacker, the one who had done all the talking. The man was furious, but mostly with his disabled and unconscious cohorts. After all, *Jack* hadn't done anything to them, so their pitiful condition had to be all their own fault. Amanda wanted to laugh in delight, but it wasn't yet over with.

"And so, villain, you see what a man of pure heart can accomplish!" Jack crowed, adding to the last man's fury. "Be wise and retire from the field, else the same will happen to you."

Amanda thought that was overplaying it a bit, and apparently the remaining man thought the same. He snarled and went for the silly dandy with both hands raised, seemingly intending to tear his victim apart. His victim, abruptly no longer as sure of himself, squeaked and jumped aside at the last instant. As luck would have it he also happened to trip his attacker, but jumped the wrong way as the man went down. His lurching jump put a sharply kicked foot in the falling man's face, and that took care of the last of the four.

Amanda quietly slipped the short length of bamboo back in her reticule while Jack continued to bounce around for a moment, very obviously looking for more opponents. After the moment he let himself notice that the first man was still conscious, but curled up on the ground whimpering as he held his broken leg. All the others were unconscious, and Jack stood victorious.

"And let that be a lesson to you," he announced grandly to the unconscious men, then strutted over to Amanda and bowed with a flourish. "Lady mine, the deed is done and your honor and person safe. Shall we continue our stroll?"

"As the hour grows late, I think it best that we return to your carriage," Amanda replied as she took his proffered arm with a smile. "Perhaps we'll stroll again another day."

Amanda was doing what she considered her part by giving them a reason to leave the park, but Jack didn't seem as pleased as he should have been. The expression in his eyes flickered before he bowed again in agreement, and their walk back to the park entrance was a silent one. The carriage was just coming around the block as they reached the street, and the driver saw them immediately. Moments later they were in the carriage, and the drive home didn't take long.

Jack mentioned every landmark and point of interest they passed, but there was no real conversation between them until they reached Richard's house. After helping her out of the carriage Jack asked if he might see her again the next day, and she solemnly agreed not to chase him off with a broom. He escorted her inside, bent over her hand, said something flowery about seeing her the next day, and then left. Amanda stood staring at the door until Richard came out of his study.

"Amanda, are you all right?" Richard demanded as he moved closer. "Michaels didn't—insult you in any way, did he?"

"No, Richard, quite the contrary," Amanda replied, making sure her disappointment over that didn't show in her voice. "Mr. Michaels was attentive and charming, but above all he was a gentleman at all times. And he's invited me to go driving again tomorrow."

"Well, that's all right, then," Richard said, grudgingly pleased, then he put a hand to her arm. "But if everything went so well, why do you seem so—odd?"

"I was just wondering why *Mr. Michaels* seemed so odd," she answered, telling the complete truth. "He definitely seemed to be—holding himself back in some way. The word 'restrained' comes to mind, but that's really much too mild."

"Ah, now I see," Richard said with a smile, all worry

vanishing. "It's clear you don't know much about men, dear sister, but that's just as it should be. I would venture to say that Michaels is now even more entranced with you than he was last evening, and is therefore striving anxiously to do nothing wrong. He wants to impress you favorably, dear, and may be worrying that he hasn't managed it. It's a good sign, and you really should be pleased."

"If you say so, Richard," Amanda returned doubtfully, privately doing more than doubting her brother. Jack Michaels wasn't worrying about impressing her; he barely knew she existed. What he was most interested in was finishing her investigation and relieving himself of her company. So that still left the question of what could possibly be bothering him.

"I do say so, dear, so don't worry your pretty head about it," Richard told her with a chuckle. "Enjoy your time with Michaels, but don't consider him the best you're likely to find. He's only a younger son, after all, and in two nights' time we'll be taking you to the party at Lord and Lady Maydew's. Not all younger sons earn the sort of reputation that Jack Michaels has, and you'll likely find yourself pleased with the difference—as well as possibly finding yourself attracting someone who isn't merely a younger son."

Amanda said something polite in agreement, then excused herself to go to her rooms. She already knew there would be a difference between Jack Michaels and any other man she met, but it wasn't one that *was* likely to please her. If only she could make him feel the way *she* did! But that was *very* unlikely, despite her eagerness for the next day to arrive. Rather than looking forward to it, Jack Michaels was probably dreading it. . . .

Jack Michaels dismissed the carriage for the day in front of one of his clubs, but didn't go inside. He stood fiddling with one of his coat cuffs until the carriage was gone, and then he made his way on foot to the rooms on Essex

Street. When he walked in Sir Charles Kerry was waiting for him and sipping tea, and the older man immediately raised his brows.

"Did it go *that* badly?" Sir Charles asked, returning his cup to its saucer. "You look ready to commit violent murder."

"At the moment I would enjoy committing violent murder," Jack confirmed, then began to pace back and forth. Sitting quietly in one place would have been impossible in his present state; he had never felt so absolutely vile ... "Miss Edmunds and I will be continuing our inquiries tomorrow, when I take her driving again."

"Do you really think you ought to be spending so much time on this?" Sir Charles asked quietly. "Especially considering the state it puts you in? The lady's brother does have a man looking into the matter, after all, and he hasn't found a thing. After so long a time, you're not likely to do any better."

"We've already done better, and this is no longer something that can be dismissed," Jack said, stopping long enough to pour himself a whiskey. "The lady and I visited the Registry Office building, and afterward walked a short way into the park Lichfield must have crossed on his way home. Only minutes after we got into the park, we were set upon by four men."

"My dear Jack!" Sir Charles exclaimed, sitting up. "What a horrible experience. But surely it was no more than a coincidence."

"It was anything *but* a coincidence," Jack corrected, then related all the details of their visits to both bureaus. "Lichfield stopped to visit his friend as well, made an engagement for that night, then should have gone directly home. That he never *reached* home means he was intercepted, most likely in that park. And since no body has been found, chances are good that the man is still alive. That park isn't big enough to hide a body indefinitely, and carrying it away would have been unnecessarily risky. No, the man is still alive, but for what reason God only knows."

"If he's alive, then he may well have disappeared of his own volition," Sir Charles pointed out, stroking his beard thoughtfully. "Despite Miss Edmunds's determination, he may not *want* to be found."

"I still haven't told you what those four in the park said before trying to close with me," Jack disagreed, pausing to look down at the older man. "I was informed that those who go poking where they don't belong get 'bashed,' and I would also pay for the privilege by first handing over my money. I'm fairly certain the Edmunds girl thought the man was referring to our being in the park, which is what she was meant to think. We would consider the neighborhood 'too dangerous,' and never go back."

"But you don't believe that, and I can see why," Sir Charles said with a frown. "You ask questions of someone who refuses to answer even for gold, and a short while later you're warned against 'poking' around. That *is* too large a coincidence to swallow easily, and suggests there's more to the matter than simply the disappearance of one man. How the Bureau of Vital Statistics can be used to harm the empire I can't imagine, so perhaps you'd best look into the matter to be certain it can't be."

Jack nodded, already having known Sir Charles would come to that decision, and then he drained his glass. If his sense of duty had been even slightly less intense, he would have kept the incident to himself and happily let the matter be dropped. Now, though . . .

"All right, John, tell me what the real problem is," Sir Charles said with a sigh. "Now that I've agreed with your conclusions, you seem even more disturbed than you were. What haven't I yet seen in all of this?"

Jack wavered, feeling foolish as well as stupid, but he did need someone to speak to. Maybe it would prove possible to talk him out of the nonsense.

"It was the fight I had with the four who came to warn me off," Jack admitted, finally going to a chair and dropping into it. "Since they were unarmed I had no reason to kill them, which meant they would still be alive at the end of the fight. That in turn meant I had to stay in character, specifically in the bumbling dandy aspect I worked out for situations like that. It went so well that the fourth man clearly blamed his friends for what had happened to them—until he was too deeply unconscious to blame anyone about anything."

"Then why are you so unhappy?" Sir Charles asked gently. "If it all went the way it was supposed to— Ah! Yes, now I see. Miss Edmunds was there to witness the whole thing. I take it she didn't appreciate your performance?"

"You have to remember she knows what I can do," Jack mumbled as he leaned forward, staring down into his empty glass. "When those four first came at us, a glance at her face told me she was anticipating the Golden Devil going into action. When she got Jack the Bouncing Braggart instead, she actually went so far as to bring out a short length of bamboo she carried in her reticule. She didn't believe I'd be able to protect her, you see."

"So she armed herself with a small piece of wood?" Sir Charles said with a snort of ridicule. "What could she possibly have done with it even if the need arose?"

"She could have given those fools more of a surprise than *I* gave them," Jack returned with his own note of ridicule. "A two inch diameter staff of bamboo will stop a sword strike, and even a short length like hers can be devastating in the hands of someone who knows how to use it. And I don't doubt that she knows how."

"But surely her opinion changed once the fight was over," Sir Charles tried, ignoring how morose Jack had now become. "Your attackers were down and the danger was over. That means you won no matter *how* you accomplished it, so she had no reason to scorn you."

"Well, she didn't, not in so many words," Jack admitted, feeling not in the least better. "Her expression was completely neutral, just the way they all do it in China.

But when I suggested we continue our stroll, *she* suggested I take her home instead. She has an engagement to go to the theater tonight."

"She does," Sir Charles murmured, and when Jack looked up he saw he was being studied carefully. "But if you're seeing the young lady only because she forced you into it, I don't understand why any of that should trouble you. Does it matter *what* she thinks of you—or where she goes with other men?"

Jack didn't answer, at least not aloud. He sat back in the chair again as he tried to tell himself it *didn't* matter, but himself wasn't agreeing. When she'd first told him about going to the theater tonight, and that her brother was working diligently to marry her off—For God's sake, he'd known about her brother's intentions, so why had he felt as though someone had jabbed him hard in the middle? And then she'd thanked him for helping her, in a way that no other woman—and damned few men—would have done. How was he supposed to forget *that* . . .?

"John, are you seriously finding this girl attractive?" Sir Charles asked gently. "I know you've only just barely met, but there are times when a man needs no more. Is that what's happening here?"

"It can't be," Jack denied, working to make the words believable to both of them. "We both know I can't drop my public character, and once I revert to my old ways her brother won't let me near her. Not that I'd ever drag her down with me even if her brother *didn't* have me thrown out. Nothing could ever develop between us, so what's the point in lying to myself?"

"Well, they do say the one person you should never lie to is yourself," Sir Charles commented. "If we remember that, life does become simplified, and now I believe it's time to change the subject. Hughes has received another letter."

"So soon?" Jack said, forcing himself to be diverted by the new development. "Why didn't they just say what they had to in the letter delivered last night?"

"Possibly because they hadn't yet made the decision?" Sir Charles suggested. "The actual reason could be almost anything, so we'll put that question aside for now. The thing was brought to Hughes by an urchin, who said some 'bloke' gave it to him to deliver. He was also given a silver penny, and promised another when the note was delivered. Hughes paid over the penny, but the only information he got for it was that the 'bloke' had a thick, bushy black beard, with matching eyebrows. The rest of the man was completely ordinary."

"Meaning that because of the beard and eyebrows, the urchin didn't notice the rest of the man," Jack said with a nod. "What was in the letter?"

"More apologies, of course," Sir Charles said with a grimace. "And a request that he show up at Lord and Lady Maydew's party two nights from now. Hughes has no choice about going, but Sellars won't be there again to watch him. If he did show up again our letter writer would certainly notice, so this time I'm sending Rawson. But I do want *you* to be there again."

"That will take more than a little doing," Jack said, frowning thoughtfully. "You may not know it, but the previous Lord Maydew and my father didn't get along. Asking the son to do a favor for a man his father didn't like . . . I doubt if it will work."

"And even if it did, it would be in poor taste," Sir Charles agreed with a sigh. "But we'll have to think of something else, since you *must* be there. The longer this goes on the more uneasy I become, so I want it ended as soon as possible. If it isn't, I have a very strong, very unpleasant premonition . . ."

Sir Charles didn't finish his sentence, but he didn't have to. Over the years, all the men who worked with him had learned to respect his premonitions. Anytime they ignored one, they ended up wishing they hadn't. So Jack would have to find a way to be invited to the party, even though partying was the last thing he wanted to do. Partying, going to the theater, having a good time of any sort—it all made him think of the woman with whom he wanted to share that good time. Not to mention other things he wanted to share with her. . . .

But he wasn't meant to share things with her, especially in view of the way she now undoubtedly saw him. He was a buffoon to the woman he most wanted to be a hero to . . . Jack abruptly left his chair to refill his whiskey glass. One more drink and he'd go home to the only thing that awaited him: an empty house. He might even let himself dream a little, as long as he fully understood it was a dream, and he only did it a little. A man in his position couldn't allow himself to dream more than that . . .

". . . and he was absolutely incredible," Amanda said to Pei with remembered delight. Once again she sat drinking tea and waiting for Jack Michaels, but that was the first opportunity she'd had to speak privately with Pei since yesterday afternoon. "Those four didn't have a chance against him, and he was only playing. Can you imagine what he would have done to them if he'd decided to fight them seriously?"

"I don't have to imagine," Pei returned with amusement. "That was me next to you while you watched him practice at Master Ma's. But all you've talked about so far is Jack Michaels. What about your time at the theater last night? Did you enjoy yourself?"

"The play was fine," Amanda answered with a shrug after sipping her tea. "Mr. Attenborough was very attentive, and we had a nice time. He wanted to take me somewhere again tonight, but I begged off. Since there's another party tomorrow night, I need at least one night to myself. I told him I wasn't used to being so active every day."

"And I'm sure he believed it, since he doesn't know what Master Ma had you doing every day." Pei was even more amused, but there was also a gleam in her dark eyes. "Do you really want tonight for resting, or do you intend to spend it with Jack Michaels? Will he come by to help you sneak out after you've supposedly gone to bed, or will he simply sneak in to join you there?"

"Whichever books you're reading, I'd appreciate it if you would lend them to Mr. Michaels," Amanda came back sourly. "He seems to need *something* to give him ideas, since he's been nothing but a perfect gentleman at all times. Pei, do you think it's possible that he doesn't find me in the least attractive?"

"It's possible, but not very likely," Pei assured her, sounding really certain. "I watched from the top of the stairs when you joined him in the hall yesterday afternoon. He was so deep in thought that he didn't notice you until you spoke, but then he *really* noticed you. It was only for a moment until he had control of himself again, but for that moment he wore the same expression I've seen on my father when he's alone and looking at his women. I'd say Mr. Michaels definitely wants you, but why he isn't showing it more I have no idea."

"Probably because he knows as well as I do that nothing can ever come of it," Amanda said, now feeling frustrated. "I'm sure he'll go back to being a notorious black sheep once he finishes helping me find Mr. Lichfield, and once he does Richard won't let me see him again. But I want more of him to remember than just his assistance, especially since my future husband won't know the difference."

"Oh, yes, I'd almost forgotten what Green Jade told you," Pei said slowly, sipping her own tea. "All that very strenuous exercise you went through for so long at Master Ma's— She said you probably no longer had an intact maidenhead, and if that was so you would need to tell whoever would be arranging your marriage. Men are often understanding if the matter is explained to them beforehand."

"*Chinese* men," Amanda qualified, wondering what she would have done all those years without the wise council of Pei's father's favorite concubine. "I still don't know how English men look at it, but Green Jade was perfectly correct. She and I discovered that my maidenhead *is* no longer intact, and I've already told Claire about it. If I ever told Richard directly, he'd most likely die of embarrassment."

"We have to remember he comes from a country that's still very young," Pei said encouragingly, but nevertheless sounded like an Imperial grandmother. "But that means you can do as you please with Mr. Michaels—*if* you can get him to cooperate."

"I'll find a way," Amanda vowed, replacing her cup in its saucer. "One way or another I *will* find it. If I have to spend the rest of my life dying of boredom, I *will* have at least one exciting memory to look back on."

"The Silken Dragon looks out of your eyes again," Pei observed with a faint smile. "But I know exactly how you feel, so maybe I can be of help. You see—"

Her words broke off at the knock on the door, and then a housemaid was entering.

"Beggin' yer pardon, ma'am, but Mr. Michaels is downstairs," the girl said. "He said t'say he hopes yer ready."

"I think that today I *will* be ready," Amanda decided aloud, standing to smooth the skirt of her gown. "If nothing else, it should confuse him. Pei, I'll see you later."

Amanda barely noticed her friend's calm nod of agreement, so involved was she with thoughts of the man who now waited for her downstairs. He was there for a reason and an important one, but it wouldn't have mattered to her if there was no reason at all. She *had* to bring him to the point of wanting her as much as she wanted him, she just had to. And recalling some of the things Green Jade had taught Pei and herself, she suddenly realized there just might be a way. . . .

Chapter 7

This time Jack Michaels watched Amanda Edmunds
come down the stairs. He'd been ready for the same
sort of wait he'd faced the day before, and didn't understand why today she'd chosen to appear so promptly. The
calm and unhurried way she walked said there was no
emergency or new information she couldn't wait to tell
him about, and she appeared so graceful she almost
seemed to be floating. Today she wore a gown of green
trimmed with white, a gentle green that emphasized her
dark hair and light eyes.

And also emphasized her lush figure and lovely face.
Jack didn't need to be reminded about how attractive she
was, but every time he saw her it was as though someone
invisible stood beside him, whispering in his ear, insisting
that he notice her all over again. That adorable, good-
natured expression on her face made her seem so innocent.
It would be criminal to take the least advantage of her, especially knowing he would never be able to do the honorable thing afterward.

"Mr. Michaels, how nice to see you again," she said as
soon as she reached the bottom of the stairs, offering her
hand with a smile that went through him like a flash of
blazing sunlight. "I've been looking forward to our drive."

"Not half as much as I've been looking forward to it,
Miss Edmunds," he returned, taking her hand and bending
over it. Jack had learned that it was possible to tell the absolute truth in such a way that it came out sounding like

gallantry instead, and right now he needed the help of that technique desperately. The way she had looked at him, with vibrant blue eyes that lowered demurely when he tried to meet them . . .

"And how nice that we've been given another lovely day," she observed, her warm hand ever so gentle and light in his larger one. He hadn't been able to resist touching his lips to the glove that covered her soft hand, but she hadn't withdrawn it. Obviously she hadn't been paying close enough attention to have noticed the breach in etiquette.

"That lovely day awaits us along with my carriage," Jack told her, offering his arm with a smile that usually meant nothing. He was about to add something inane about leaving, but suddenly lost the words. Her hand had come to his arm, sliding around and over in a slow path he could feel even through his coat sleeve. As though she caressed and invited him rather than simply taking his arm. . . .

Jack cleared his throat and all but shook his head hard, fighting to rid himself of that ridiculous notion. The girl was *not* caressing and inviting him, that was his lust making him think otherwise. Amanda Edmunds needed him for only one thing, and that had nothing to do with slowly removing clothes in a dim and secret place for two . . . *Damn it, man, get a grip on yourself!*

Getting the grip came close to making Jack sweat, but he did manage to compose himself as he guided the girl outside. The house man who held the door for them apparently noticed nothing out of the ordinary, which reassured Jack that he'd been successful in hiding his feelings. His association with Amanda Edmunds was difficult enough without making the girl think she might have to protect herself from him.

Jack handed her into the carriage and then followed, and once they were settled a flick of the driver's reins set the horses to moving. The driver had already been told where they were going, and hadn't needed directions to Marsden Mews.

"Oh, look at that lovely house," Amanda said suddenly, leaning toward Jack in an effort to see more of the house as they passed it. "I wonder who lives there."

"That house belongs to Bryan Machlin, a friend of mine," Jack answered automatically. With her that close and actually leaning against him, he suddenly found it very difficult to breathe freely. The girl had no idea what she was doing to him, of course, so she made no effort to move back again.

"And those others?" she asked, looking at every house as they passed it. "Do you know the people who own them as well?"

"Some—some of them," Jack got out, then made himself come up with the names he knew without stumbling over the pronunciations. Her question had made her sound utterly impressed with him, and it wasn't just the fact that he seldom impressed people that had thrown him off-stride. Part of him stood tall and straight in the glow of her admiration, grinning and enjoying it. The rest of him groaned in pain, then fought to dismiss what that first part felt. He could *not* afford to get serious about this woman, he simply could *not!*

Jack discovered there was a big difference between making that decision and sticking to it. Once they were out of the St. James district Amanda leaned back, but she seemed to be in the mood for sightseeing today. Every time they passed something that took her interest, her hand came to his arm or hand before she pointed out the object of her curiosity. Jack managed to identify everything properly, but by the time they got to Marsden Mews he was one step short of twitching.

Number 53 Marsden Mews was attached seamlessly to its neighbors, one anonymous door in a row of others just the same. Or almost the same. Number 53 was blue, while the door to the left was red and the one to the right, orange. The doors clearly hadn't been painted recently, but they seemed to be kept fairly clean. There was no step up to the door, nor was there grass in front of any of the houses. Marsden Mews wasn't the sort of neighborhood where grass was encouraged to thrive.

"All brick and utterly plain," Amanda murmured once the carriage stopped, obviously less than pleased with the look of the place. "And this is where Mr. Lichfield was forced to live."

"I doubt if forced is the proper word," Jack responded, resisting the urge to give her hand a comforting pat. "There are neighborhoods a good deal worse than this in London, and I'm sure your Mr. Lichfield knew it. There may not be any gardens and private drives, but there also aren't any robbers, drunks, or bodies in every other doorway."

Jack's comment left Amanda expressionless, but he felt sure she was shocked. He'd been deliberately trying to shock her, of course, in an effort to expose her to the ugly world he was sometimes forced to move through, in the hopes that she would pull back from him completely. No woman would want to associate with a man who came in contact with *that*, not even accidentally. If there was any interest at all on her part, Jack wanted to be certain it disappeared.

When it was clear Amanda would not be commenting again, Jack stepped out of the carriage, turned to help her down, then led the way to Number 53. He had to knock twice before the door was opened, and the woman who appeared looked them over with very little approval.

"Don't rent no rooms fer only a hour," the woman stated through compressed lips. "There's them about 'ere who do, but *my* 'ouse's r'spectable. Find some place else fer—"

"Excuse me, madam, but that's not what we're here for," Jack hastily interrupted, closer to being embarrassed than he'd thought was possible. "We understand Mr. Miles Lichfield had rooms here. This lady is the daughter of Mr. Lichfield's late employer, and she's concerned about his disappearance."

"Oh, Lord a me," the woman exclaimed, taking over

Jack's embarrassment. "I do beg yer pardon, sor, but there's them as come 'ere lookin' fer— Oh, do come inside. Can I be offerin' tea, 'r . . .?"

"Please don't put yourself out, madam," Jack said soothingly as he and Amanda stepped inside. "We've just come by to assure ourselves that no stone has been left unturned in the search for the man. You *have* spoken to those who came looking before us?"

"That I 'ave," the woman agreed, trying to smooth back graying hair. Her clothing was neither new nor expensive, but it was clean and in good repair. Judging by the tiny hall they stood in and the one room they could see through an open doorway, the house was also neat and well kept. The woman did seem to be as respectable as she claimed, and knowing why they were there had also turned her sympathetic.

"Poor Mr. Lichfield never did go off on 'is own," she stated, not in the least uncertain. " 'E was a gentleman, 'e was, an' treated a lady proper even if she *din't* wear silks nor talk fancy— Beggin' yer pardon, m'lady, I don't mean t'be insultin' t'nobody, but there's them as says different. Never laid eyes on th' gentleman, but they knows 'em better'n them who 'ave—"

"I know exactly what you mean," Amanda interrupted, reaching out to touch the woman's agitated hands. "I was told the same foolishness about why he disappeared, but didn't believe it for a minute. Mr. Lichfield all but raised me himself, so no one can tell me stories about him. I happen to believe he's still alive, and that means we have to find him as quickly as possible. Is there anything you can tell us that might help us do that?"

"Lord a me," the woman muttered, wrinkling her brow in thought. "Don't know more'n I already said. Mr. Lichfield, 'e was nearly set t'go visitin' some kin in a place called Tarin' Poole. Was a small village near Braxton Meadows, wherever that might be. Meant t'keep 'is rooms, 'e did, said 'e'd be needin' 'em again when 'e got back. 'Ad the feelin' 'e din't mean t'stay away long."

"And we know he expected to be home the night of the day he disappeared," Jack said with a nod. "He'd made definite plans, and would hardly have abandoned them all for a momentary whim. Are his personal possessions still in his rooms?"

"Couldn't keep th' rooms unlet past th' time 'e paid fer 'em," the woman said, sad rather than defensive. "Packed it all up meself, an' put it in th' back parlor. Don't use th' room fer more'n storage, an' there waren't much. Nobody else ast t'see it."

"Well, *we'd* like to see it, if you don't mind," Amanda said, obviously sensing the woman's hesitation just as Jack had. "Mr. Lichfield would certainly thank you for guarding the privacy of his possessions, but we need to see the daily journal he kept. There might be something in it that could help us."

"You mean that writin' he done each night when I took up his last cup a tea." The woman wasn't asking a question, and her eyes rested shrewdly on Amanda. "Din't nobody else know 'bout that. Back parlor's this way."

Once the woman turned away, Jack glanced at Amanda approvingly. She'd handled the situation exactly right, and now they were going to see something none of the other investigators had. If she'd been a man, Jack wouldn't have hesitated to recommend her to Sir Charles. And if she'd been a man, *his* life would have been a good deal more simple. . . .

Jack brought up the end of the parade into the back parlor, a small, airless room with no windows. Once a lamp was lit it was possible to see the old furniture and stacks of anonymous boxes, but the room wasn't dusty or dirty. The lady of the house led them to a corner where three large cases lay, then excused herself. There were things to be done about the house, she said, but Jack had the feeling she couldn't bear to look at the missing man's possessions again.

"She really cared for Mr. Lichfield," Amanda murmured

after the woman was gone, staring back through the open doorway. "I'll have to tell him that when we find him."

Then she turned her attention to the cases, leaving Jack to consider her in silence. Not *if* we find him, but *when* was what she'd said. Determined was too weak a word to describe Amanda Edmunds, and Jack sighed at the thought. He hadn't been at all worried when those four men had tried to attack him in the park, but now . . . If it was possible to work out a routine to keep a man safe during attack, why wasn't it possible to do the same against a woman's determination? Especially when their newest lead was most likely to become the same dead end that everything else had.

Jack stood back and let Amanda go through the cases, but he watched closely enough to be certain nothing important was overlooked. The top case held the man's clothes, conservatively cut and soberly colored. The second held personal items and books, all of them carefully kept but obviously well used. The third held small items hidden in thick woolen wrapping, which showed they must be breakable or valuable. Also in that case were two stacks of slender, leather-bound volumes, each one with a different year stamped in gold on its front. Amanda lifted out the topmost of the stack on the right, and ran her fingers over the embossed date.

"These were specially made for Mr. Lichfield, courtesy of the man he worked for before Father," she said. "Each volume represents a year, and the first five were presented by the man himself. He died about halfway through the fifth year, but to Mr. Lichfield's surprise he'd left instructions in his will. All Mr. Lichfield had to do was let the book company know where he was, and every five years another five volumes were delivered to him. He said receiving them made him feel as though the next five years of his life were guaranteed. After all, it was completely against his nature to waste things, so he *had* to live long enough to fill the volumes—"

Her voice broke off as she bent her head over the book

she held, and Jack quickly stepped forward to put a comforting arm about her shoulders. He knew she'd been raised in a land where people were taught not to show their innermost feelings, but he tended to forget that when she spoke so matter-of-factly about the missing man. The girl must be frantic and worried sick, but this was the first clear indication he'd had of it.

"If Mr. Lichfield were here now, he'd probably tell you to brace up," Jack said, lamely trying to comfort a woman rather than charm her, which was where his strength lay. "You're doing everything possible to find him, and one or two things that never would have occurred to anyone else. Let's see if there's anything useful to be found in his journal."

She raised her head and nodded, making no effort to look at him. *Trying to dry her tears from the inside,* Jack thought as he patted her arm in approval. Amanda Edmunds clearly had more control of herself than most of the *men* Jack knew. She cleared her throat and took a deep breath, and then was back to the way she'd been. Which meant Jack hastily withdrew his arm. What *was* there about the woman that made him so aware of her that a simple arm around the shoulders was well-nigh painful?

There was no easy or immediate answer to that question, so he simply stood there brooding while Amanda looked through the journal. Over her shoulder he could see page after page of small, neat writing, not a single mistake or crossing-out marring any of it. There weren't even inadvertent blots of ink. Lichfield had been the perfect secretary: meticulous, conscientious, and efficient.

"There's nothing here," Amanda said with a sigh after another few minutes, closing the book. "He wrote about how nice Mrs. Harger was to him—that must be the woman whose house this is—and about his plans to visit Taring Poole just as soon as he'd arranged my passage to this country. He couldn't do that until the funds became available, and if it took too long he was going to speak to Richard. The last page talks about seeing his friend Harold

Melton again, and his hope that the man still worked where he had a year ago, the last time they'd corresponded. After that—nothing."

"Which is hardly surprising," Jack felt compelled to point out. "Whatever caused his disappearance happened after he visited the Registry Office and before he was able to return here. Since he updated his journal at night, he hadn't the opportunity to put down anything at all."

"So where does that leave us?" she demanded, turning her head to pin him with those very blue eyes. "The trail *can't* stop dead, not when we haven't yet found him. There has to be a side trail we missed simply because we walked past it."

"You point it out, and I'll be glad to help follow it," Jack said, indecently relieved that it looked like he was about to be out from under his commitment. Part of him was disappointed rather than relieved, but he firmly ignored that part.

"I'll have to think about it first," Amanda said after a short hesitation, obviously unable to offer a suggestion on the spot. "If I haven't found anything by the time you come by tomorrow, you'll be able to—go back to what you usually do."

Jack simply bowed his agreement, his mixed emotions refusing to let him say anything coherent on the subject. He didn't *want* the next day to be the last he saw of Amanda Edmunds, but his life demanded that he leave her behind without a backward glance. But that would not be happening until the following day, so there was every reason to take advantage of the time he had left.

"Since there's nothing more for us here, let's continue our drive," he suggested. "If we return too early your brother might become suspicious—unless you'll be going out again tonight. I would certainly hate to come between you and your . . . admirers."

He hadn't meant to add that last, and certainly not in the dryly disapproving tone he had. The girl looked at him quickly, her pretty face expressionless, and then she nodded with that sideways turn of the head that was so very Oriental.

"You're quite right, Mr. Michaels," she conceded, glancing at him rather than meeting his gaze. "We shouldn't return this early, so by all means let's do continue our drive. It so happens I'll be staying in tonight, to rest for tomorrow night's party. Richard is quite looking forward to taking me there, since Lord and Lady Maydew have a rather large circle of friends."

She turned away then to replace the book in its case and then put the other cases back where they'd been, leaving Jack to the sourness of his thoughts. The size of the circle of friends the Maydews had had nothing to do with her brother's eagerness to get her to their party. It was the number of eligible bachelors they would find that interested Richard Lavering the most, and was the very point that most grated on Jack Michaels. He foolishly didn't want Amanda introduced to other men, not when he wasn't free to compete with them.

And then the point he'd missed finally came through. The Laverings and Amanda would be going to the very party to which he was supposed to gain entry. If that wasn't fate nothing else would ever come close, and he simply had to take advantage of it. *After all,* he thought with a private grin, *if I don't, Sir Charles will never forgive me. So my time with Miss Amanda Edmunds has just been extended, and my conscientious side will just have to live with the necessity.*

Once Amanda finished fixing the cases, Jack turned the lamp down and followed her out. His mood had improved to the point where he was almost too foolishly pleasant to Mrs. Harger when they thanked her. He *would* have to part company with Amanda eventually, and he had to keep that firmly in mind despite the struggle it had become. He'd had to stop calling her "lady mine," a phrase that no longer qualified merely as a charming way to speak to a woman. If he also had to stop seeing her before it was absolutely necessary— No, better to watch what he said and did, to make the time last as long as possible.

Jack escorted Amanda back to the carriage and helped her in, a sudden thought sobering him. He needed to go to that party tomorrow night with her, but the only one who would enjoy their shared company would be himself. He'd remembered about yesterday afternoon in the park, and the clod Amanda must now consider him. *From elation to depression in one easy step,* he thought as he settled himself in the carriage and gestured to the driver to drive anywhere. *The sooner I'm out of this girl's life, the better off she'll be. . . .*

Amanda let Jack Michaels help her into the carriage, knowing the serene expression on her face showed nothing of the glee she felt inside. So the Golden Devil *did* find her of interest, much more so than he'd been trying to pretend. What he'd said about the possibility of her going out again tonight—he'd seemed to hate the idea, hopefully because she would be with another man. Maybe he *did* want her, fully as much as she wanted him.

And the way he'd reacted to her earlier ploys . . . thinking about that made Amanda wish she could laugh aloud. The little tricks Green Jade had taught her—touching a man gently in passing, as though by accident; briefly leaning against him in the same way; drawing his gaze and then shyly being unable to meet it—Jack Michaels had nearly burst trying to pretend he was unaffected, obviously thinking she had no idea what she was doing. If she could have gotten him alone—*really* alone—she might already have what she wanted from him.

But with this silly pretense of courting, she never would have that opportunity. Amanda sighed, no longer as amused as she'd been. Nothing was working right today, not with Jack and not with her search for Mr. Lichfield. It was as though the earth had opened and swallowed the man up, and she couldn't even discover where it had opened. Why was an even more difficult question, but happily needn't be answered immediately.

Jack shifted in his seat, and Amanda's glance showed her that his thoughts seemed to be far away. He'd appeared to be in high spirits before they left Mr. Lichfield's lodgings, but now he was all but brooding. Amanda was close to sharing that mood, but certainly not for the same reason. If nothing happened to change matters, tomorrow would be the last time she saw Jack. She would have to give up both the man and the search, two awful defeats in the same blow. There had to be a way to avoid that double fate, there just had to be.

Amanda's thoughts also drifted away, so that details of the drive disappeared behind the demands of her mind. For some reason she kept returning to the question of *why* Mr. Lichfield had been made to disappear. What finally recaptured her attention was the slowing down and stopping of the carriage, but not in front of her brother's house. They seemed to have entered a park, and not the one they'd been in the day before. This one appeared to be much larger, and even contained a lake.

"I thought you might like to stroll around a bit," Jack said quietly when she looked at him questioningly. "It's quite proper, as long as we stay on the public walks. Which we certainly shall."

Since he didn't seem to be joking, Amanda decided with a sigh that he simply wanted to talk to her in private. He was back to being coolly distant and absolutely proper, leading her to wonder if it would be possible to "accidentally" kick him. That was the least he deserved for being so very uncooperative.

They left the carriage in a graveled area with two other carriages, and began to take their stroll. It was a lovely day so they weren't the only ones out, but as Amanda held onto Jack's arm a very strange feeling slid through her. Those other men and women who walked along in the same way—their laughter and enjoyment of each other was actually painful to watch. She still loved the man who had captured her girlhood dreams, but it would never be possible for her to belong to him. What did it matter that he'd seemed momentarily jealous of any other man she might see? He was hardly likely to continue to feel that way for long, and even if a miracle happened and he did—No, it wasn't even worth thinking about. Her brother would find her a proper man to marry, and she'd never see Jack Michaels again.

"Miss Edmunds, I find I must ask a favor." Jack's voice brought Amanda out of painful thought again, and it seemed to her that his tone was faintly odd.

"It's rather an important favor," he continued, "and I hope you won't consider me too bold. I should be crushed if you ever thought *that* of me."

Amanda suddenly realized he was playing to the people around them, telling everyone who happened to overhear him that he was nothing but a silly man flirting with the woman he escorted. For a moment Amanda ached for the man behind the silliness, for the pain his sense of duty surely forced him to endure. But then she remembered that he'd chosen that life, and that he would eventually choose it even over her. Well, if that's what he wanted, that's what he would get.

"Why, Mr. Michaels," she exclaimed, meeting his gaze long enough to bat long, dark lashes at him. "I find it astonishing that you believe I would *ever* think you too bold. Other men may be bold, but you? Never!"

"How nice of you to say so, Miss Edmunds," he muttered, a glance showing Amanda how far from pleased he was. Her shot had hit the mark, and his silliness had been turned back on him. "Yes, delightfully nice," he muttered even lower, then continued after clearing his throat. "What I meant to say was, the favor I'm after is the honor of being your escort to Lord and Lady Maydew's tomorrow night. If you agree, I'll be the happiest man in London."

He seemed to be hovering as he waited for her answer, but Amanda was suddenly too alert to reply without thinking. Jack Michaels was playing his public role, but his re-

quest had been far from idle. The way he held
himself—tension behind outward ease—the way he spoke
to a definite point despite the nonsense, the way he
watched her carefully amid the artfully obvious anxiety: it
all said her answer was important for something other than
his happiness, and Amanda wanted to know what that
something else was.

"But, Mr. Michaels, I don't see how I can grant your favor," she protested after a very brief moment. "I'll be going to the party with my brother and his wife for the
purpose of meeting eligible gentlemen. That purpose
would be nullified if I appeared with an escort, would it
not?"

Frustration flashed in his dark eyes, and a glance around
showed him a large tree not far from the walk and closer
to the lake. Since no one was near that tree he led her to
it and stopped, within sight of everyone but out of easy
earshot.

"Amanda, I need to be at that party," he said softly
while his expression announced to the world that he discussed trivialities. "I can't tell you why, but it happens to
be important."

"I thought that might be the case, Jack," Amanda murmured, pleased to have her guess confirmed. "But that
doesn't change the fact that my objection was valid. You
know you aren't seriously courting me, so how can I ruin
Richard's plans for nothing? Not to mention the fact that
he might refuse to allow it."

"But it wouldn't *be* for nothing," he objected, now
clearly controlling himself carefully. "It's for the good of
the empire you mean to make your home in, which means
it's ultimately for the good of you and all your family. I
know how strong your sense of duty is, so I can't believe
you'll refuse me."

"Let me think for a moment, Jack," she asked, ignoring
the strong sense of pleasure that saying his personal name
brought her. He'd used the word "duty," and that was a
word that did *not* give her pleasure. But an idea had come

to her, and she realized there was a way to accomplish both of her major aims at the same time. In fact, it was Jack who had just given her the weapon to make it happen.

"You know, Jack, you're absolutely right," she said slowly at last. "I do have certain duties I take very seriously, so I think we can come to an accommodation. I've thought of another path to pursue in my search for Mr. Lichfield."

"Why am I suddenly very suspicious?" he asked, a question to which he clearly expected no answer. "I've already agreed to follow any side trail that we missed, and I don't believe for a moment that you've forgotten that fact. If you're now talking about coming to an 'accommodation,' you have to have something more than simple investigation in mind. Something, in fact, that you're sure I won't like, so how about telling me what it is."

"How very perceptive you are," Amanda said with a delighted smile, meaning every word of the compliment. "Most men would have missed that, but you . . . Well, you needn't worry. I'm not going to ask for the impossible, just the somewhat difficult and unusual. Do you remember that man in the Bureau of Vital Statistics? The one who refused to answer your questions even for gold?"

"What about him?" Jack asked, for some reason looking even more suspicious. Amanda didn't know why he would, but right now that wasn't the point.

"I think we agree that that man knows something important," she continued. "It's also fairly obvious he won't speak to us, so we'll have to try to get his help without his knowing about it. If he's involved in something secret, which is extremely likely, he just may have visitors in the dead of night. Last night they would have stayed away because the man had been questioned only a few hours earlier, but tonight will be another matter. If he does have visitors they'll be his accomplices, and learning who they are would give us a new lead to follow."

"That's a very good idea," Jack said, all suspicion gone

behind serious consideration. "If I arrange to have the man watched, we could well find out what he's up to. Without his realizing it, he would be all but marking anyone he came in serious contact with."

"Exactly," Amanda agreed, but only with the general idea. The details would *not* be Jack's to arrange. "The man needs to be watched, but tonight *I* want to be one of those doing it. Not only is it my idea, but this is also my investigation. If nothing happens I don't want to be told about it, I want to know it for a fact. And if you're going to say something about it not being safe, don't bother. If anything comes up that *you* can't handle, I'll be glad to take care of it."

Jack had opened his mouth, probably to spout the usual danger warnings she'd heard so often, but the last of her words silenced him again. An odd expression came and went across his face, and then his silence ended.

"If that's what you call merely difficult and unusual, I'd hate to see what you do consider impossible," he stated, his dark eyes hard. "You not only expect me to follow the clerk to where he lives, you then want me to show up at your brother's house and convince him to let me keep you out for most of the night. If the clerk doesn't discover me behind him and suddenly decide to shoot me, your brother will happily take care of the matter *for* him. The whole thing's impossible, and it can't be done."

"Of course it can," Amanda corrected with a faint smile. "You take care of following the clerk, and I'll take care of my brother. He doesn't need to know anything at all about the outing, so you'll simply come to our *house* at dark, not to the front door. I'll come out and meet you—but that reminds me. You'll also have to find a comfortable and private place for us to stay while we're watching the clerk's lodgings. If someone sees us watching, we'll be wasting our time."

"Perish the thought," he muttered, still staring down at her darkly. "We'd never want to waste our time. What happens if you *can't* get out of your brother's house without getting caught?"

"Then the problem will be mine and none of yours," Amanda answered blandly. "Besides, we don't have to worry about ruining *your* reputation, now do we? If this works out properly tonight, tomorrow night you get to be my escort to the party. Richard will fuss, I'm sure, but I'll think of something to tell him. Is it a deal?"

"What choice do I have?" he countered, his tone sour. "All I can hope is that your brother does catch you trying to sneak out, and paddles your bottom to teach you a lesson. A sound paddling would do you no end of good."

"Finding Mr. Lichfield will do me no end of good," she corrected, privately amused by Jack's helpless anger. "Shall we stroll closer to the lake now?"

"Now we'll stroll back to the carriage," Jack said, taking his turn at correcting her. "With the sort of schedule you've laid out for me, I'll have to get started as soon as I take you home. My arm, Miss Edmunds."

"Thank you, Mr. Michaels," Amanda answered, taking the offered arm with a private smile. If everything went well tonight, by tomorrow she'd have a new lead to follow on the road to finding Mr. Lichfield—and a memory to keep her warm during the following years of her life. Jack Michaels had to be even more eager now to be out of her company permanently, but that was all right. Since she'd never expected anything else, where was the loss?

She tried to smile to herself again, but awareness of the strong arm under her hand refused to let her do it. There would be loss, all right, possibly more than could be balanced against any amount of gain. But that wasn't something she would let herself think about, especially not now. . . .

Chapter 8

Jack Michaels had the carriage return him to his small house before he dismissed it, and once he was alone he discovered he was muttering to himself. And daydreaming, definitely daydreaming. On the ride back to her brother's house the girl hadn't done any of the things she had on the way out, but she'd sat *much* too close to him. He'd started to picture himself pulling her even closer, tasting those lips that drew him with the strength of a team of horses—

"Stop that, damn it!" he growled at himself, pausing in the middle of changing his clothes. "Bounder would be too good a word for you if you ever took advantage of that innocent girl. Even if she *has* been running you like her personal servant."

And that was another sore point with Jack: a major sore point. Amanda Edmunds was a perfect lady—sweet, gentle, demure—until she decided she wanted something. Then it was like dealing with the king's privy council; you listened, said "yes sir" or "no sir" as circumstances required, then left to carry out your orders. At no time did you argue or even try to disagree; if what you were being asked to do seemed impossible, your first job was to *make* it possible.

And it was also necessary to admit that the idea she'd had was a good one. He really ought to have thought of it himself, and if he hadn't been so distracted he might have, but he certainly would *not* have suggested he share that

114

night's watch with a woman he was beginning to want very, very badly.

Jack sighed and went on with getting out of his clothes. He'd sworn to himself that he would *not* touch the girl, and he intended to keep to that. He was already anticipating seeing her that night, but for nothing more than enjoying her nearness. At least he would have that to remember when the time came to leave her behind: a sweet memory rather than a regret. Even though there was one order he *wished* she would give him. . . .

Jack growled again as he went to his private wardrobe and began to pull out clothing, now determined to think only about what he meant to do. He couldn't very well follow the clerk Nichols dressed as a gentleman, not if he hoped to go unnoticed. But it had been necessary for Jack to be inconspicuous on other occasions, and he had put together outfits to suit each particular need. His beggar disguise was best when it was the upper class that had to be dealt with, but Nichols fell into another category.

For that reason Jack took out the brown breeches and coat that were never cleaned, the unevenly faded shirt, and the hose with runs and holes. Once he was dressed he added the scuffed brown shoes that no longer had buckles, and the tricorn that was as crushed and dusty as his coat. He also had to use soot on his face to pretend that he wasn't clean-shaven, but hopefully Nichols would stay far enough ahead that he'd never notice. Once he took the ribbon off his hair and tousled it, he retied it with a thin strip of leather and then was ready to go.

The greatest benefit to the house Jack lived in was the unadvertised door in the cellar, which opened on a rough passageway that led to the cellar of a wine shop in the next street. The shop was owned by a retired king's man, who never took notice of comings and goings through his cellar and premises. Jack wasn't the first to indulge in those private comings and goings, nor would he be the last. He simply waited in the back room until the shop was empty, then shuffled out into the street.

He had to walk to Crawford Street, but still managed to get there before the offices let out for the day. Going around to the back of the building let him find the employees' entrance, and a handy pillar let him slouch in the shadows while he waited. If Reggie Nichols, unbribable clerk, left by a different egress, Jack's neck would be on the block and no mistaking it. He not only had his orders from Miss Amanda Edmunds, he was certain she would not let him escort her tomorrow night to Lord and Lady Maydew's if she didn't get to watch a house tonight. If he happened to miss Nichols, he might have to simply pick a house and tell her that was the one they wanted.

But the Fates seemed to have taken pity on Jack. Nichols was one of the first clerks out the door, and he paid no attention to anything around him but the fastest way to the street. Jack half-expected the man to cross the street to the park, but he turned right instead and strode off up the street. Nichols was walking home and making no effort to see if anyone followed.

Jack shuffled along behind the man, for the most part keeping the clerk in sight only out of the corner of his eye. It was just possible Nichols had a friend or two watching to be sure he wasn't being followed, and that was why he seemed so unconcerned. Jack saw no one who might fit that description, but there was no sense in taking chances. He stayed in his role of a man down on his luck, one who walked the streets because he had nothing better to do with his time.

Nichols led Jack to a neighborhood that had small houses standing on tiny plots of ground, some with miniscule gardens, some without. A few of the houses looked shabby but the rest were unfinished, and here and there was an empty piece of ground. The shadows were really deepening by then, so Jack stepped into the cover of the darkness and watched Nichols casually enter his house. A minute or two later a lamp glowed to life, and Nichols could be seen passing a window.

Jack spent a few moments more in the shadows, making

certain there wasn't anyone else around except those who were coming home at the end of the day. There weren't many street lamps in the neighborhood, but the few that were there were already being lit. Time to go back and make a few preparations before going for Amanda. But first he had to find that "comfortable" watch post she'd requested. Out of sight was more to the point than comfortable, but he might as well look for both.

And luck was really with him. Right across the street from Nichols's house was one of the unfinished houses Jack had noticed earlier, the one to its right, where the side door was, looking temporarily empty. Jack approached the unfinished house from that side, and discovered there wasn't yet a lock on the side door. Since there also wasn't any glass in the windows, putting a lock on would have been useless.

Inside was the smell of freshly cut wood, suggesting someone had been working on the house earlier today, but happily the place was now empty. The nearest street lamps were too far away to illuminate the interior once it was completely dark, so watching through the front window ought to keep them well out of sight. Jack looked around one last time and then left, staying in the shadows until he was far enough away from the Nichols house. He still had some preparations to make, and then—

His thoughts broke off suddenly as he realized that five men had materialized out of the gloom to surround him. The neighborhood wasn't a good one, but the shabby way he looked should have kept something like this from happening. It didn't make sense to rob someone who obviously had nothing worth taking, but then Jack got an unexpected answer to the puzzle.

"Nice ring yer sportin', buff," one of the five drawled, gesturing to Jack's left hand. "Seen it when ya come through b'fore, but din't have me mates handy. Got 'em now, though, so give it over. Lots better things t'do wiv a ring like that 'n wear it."

The man's gap-toothed grin wasn't matched by his

friends, showing just how seriously they took their robberies. Jack silently cursed himself for a damned fool, and knowing it wasn't entirely his fault didn't help. He'd been thinking about Amanda while he changed his clothes, which made him forget completely about the ring he wore. Associating with that woman was becoming really dangerous, and her problem was actually the least of it.

"C'mon, c'mon, give it 'ere," the man repeated without a grin, snapping his fingers impatiently. "Trash like you don't d'serve that ring, an' like as not ya stole it. Gotta give ya a beatin' fer it, t'teach ya not t'do it agin. Give it over *now*."

This time a couple of the others showed their teeth in eager anticipation of the beating Jack was to be given, but Jack outgrinned them. He'd been trying to talk himself into handing over the ring in an effort to avoid more trouble, but now he knew that wasn't necessary. If they planned to beat up on him anyway, he might as well keep the ring. And there wasn't anyone around who could recognize him even if they did happen to see what he did.

"Sure an' ya don't really want t'take things from a poor man like me," Jack said with an Irish brogue that covered his upper-class accent. "Be a bunch of good little fellers now, an' step out o' me way. Got a colleen waitin' who'll give me m'head if I show up late. Wouldn't want that t'happen, so I'd best be on me way."

None of them had liked being called "good little fellers," and when Jack started to walk around the spokesman they reacted as expected. Two of them growled and reached for his arms, while the one behind him came forward fast. That one obviously meant to hit him with something, and when Jack quickly half-turned to kick out behind himself, he saw that the something was a length of wood. The man holding the stave raised up high, gasped at the impact of Jack's kick and dropped his improvised weapon, but Jack didn't have time to watch him fold to the ground.

By then the two to either side of him had solid grips on his arms, which gave one of the remaining two the courage to come forward. He was the one who had done all the talking, his face now twisted into a grotesque mask of snarls and darkness. A distant street lamp glittered off the knife the man held in his fist, a knife he meant to bury in Jack's flesh. He was a vicious one, all right, more than willing to take advantage of the helpless.

But this time his victim wasn't helpless. Jack kicked the knife out of the man's hand, then immediately brought a crescent kick around to the side of the man's face. The kick was so powerful it broke the man's neck, but Jack didn't get the chance to do the same to the ones holding his arms. The one on his right screamed low and released him, then turned and ran. The one on his left had a fist ready to throw at him, but the man's reflexes were too slow. Jack body-punched him to free his left arm, then slammed the edge of his hand against the back of the man's neck to put him down.

That made only three down, but that's all there were. The fifth man had run away with the one who'd been on Jack's right, and Jack wasn't about to chase either of them. Instead he quickly removed his ring and put it in a pocket, then got out of there. After a block or two he ducked into a doorway to make doubly sure he wasn't being followed, but his last two attackers apparently had no interest in finding out the identity of the man who had done such a thorough job on their band. Once he was certain of that, he left the dark doorway and continued on his way.

"Pesky woman," he muttered as he walked, his mood blacker than it had been. "Not only does she make me forget to take the fool ring off, she isn't even here to see me *really* fight."

And now he had to finish his preparations and go and get her, in order to spend the night with her. But not the way he *wanted* to spend the night with her. If he had to go through much more of this he would probably lose what was left of his mind, so it was undoubtedly a good thing it was nearly over.

"But I can't think of it as a good thing no matter how

hard I try," he muttered, seeing very little of the street ahead of him. "I don't want to let her go, but I must. For her sake even more than mine. I positively must."

Jack squared his shoulders and walked faster, but he didn't miss the fact that he hadn't convinced himself of anything.

Richard was waiting for Amanda when she got home, but once she'd assured him Jack Michaels was still being the perfect gentleman, he went back to his study. Amanda was then free to go looking for Pei, who happened to be in her own rooms reading. As soon as Pei closed the bed-chamber door behind her, Amanda pulled her hat off and turned to her friend with all the frustration that had been building inside her.

"I've done it," Amanda announced softly so they wouldn't be overheard. "I thought of a way to get him all alone tonight, while we try to find a new lead to Mr. Lichfield. The only problem is, I don't think getting him alone will do what I want it to."

"I'm not in the least surprised that you've succeeded," Pei answered with a smile, leading Amanda to a pair of chairs arranged for conversation. "I'm also sure you'll get around whatever the problem is. Tell me how the Silken Dragon managed to get her way *this* time."

"It wasn't very hard," Amanda replied with a shrug as she put aside her hat, gloves, and reticule and then sat down. "We went to Mr. Lichfield's lodgings and looked through his possessions, but there was nothing among them to give us any help. I kept trying to figure out *why* it had been Mr. Lichfield who had been taken, and it finally came to me that it had to be because he recognized someone in the Bureau of Vital Statistics. He said as much to his friend Mr. Melton, and that along with the fact that the bureau clerk we'd first tried to question had refused to tell us anything means the clerk was involved in some way."

"I wonder if that clerk could have had anything to do

with the men who tried to attack you in the park," Pei said thoughtfully. "It seems to be too much of a coincidence that the attack came right after you and Mr. Michaels were asking questions."

"You know, I never thought of that," Amanda said slowly, seeing the chain of events falling into place. "But I'll bet you're right, Pei. That clerk left his office after refusing to speak to us, and we didn't leave immediately. We stopped to speak to Mr. Melton, just the way Mr. Lichfield did, so the clerk would have had more than enough time to arrange for us to be waylaid. Now I'm doubly glad that we'll be keeping an eye on him."

"The 'we' being you and Mr. Michaels," Pei said with a nod. "Unless he's insisted on bringing along someone else, I don't understand your problem."

"My problem is that he won't take advantage of me even to get a favor he really needs," Amanda returned sourly. "After looking through Mr. Lichfield's possessions it was too early for Jack to take me home, so he took me to some park instead. While we were there he said he needed a favor, which turned out to be wanting to escort me to the party at Lord and Lady Maydew's tomorrow night. I used that to bargain for the chance to get him alone *tonight*, but on the drive home I realized I might well be wasting my time."

Pei raised her brows without saying anything, but words weren't necessary to show that she still didn't understand.

"Pei, he had an important favor to ask, and we were alone while we went through Mr. Lichfield's possessions," Amanda explained more fully. "If he were prepared to take advantage of me, he would have at least kissed me while we were alone—especially when, on the ride over there, I used some of those techniques Green Jade taught us. That he didn't means he intends to continue being the perfect gentleman, maybe even forever. I'll be spending hours alone with him tonight, but I'm afraid nothing will happen."

"Then it's a good thing for you that *I* had a problem before I left home," Pei said with a gleeful smile. "I tried to tell you about it this morning, but you were in too much of a hurry to see your Golden Devil."

"Now I'm the one who doesn't understand," Amanda said, but hope began to fill her. "Are you saying you have a way around my problem?"

"Of course." Pei's answer included a laugh filled with amused anticipation. "You mentioned those techniques Green Jade taught us, but she has other—practices—she never discussed. About a year ago I happened to see her putting something into a cup of tea, and then she took the cup and a pot on a tray to my father, who was busy work-ing. He'd been busy working for weeks at the time, and even his women hadn't seen much of him. I expected Green Jade to deliver the tea and then leave him alone again, but she didn't. Through the open door I could see her massaging his shoulders while he drank, and a few minutes later he had her close the door—from the inside. I crept up to the door and listened for a moment, and then I left. My father was making love to her."

"And whatever she put into his cup was able to take his mind off business?" Amanda asked, all but disbelieving. "I would have sworn *nothing* could do that with your father, especially during his busy times. I take it you asked her later what it was that she'd added to his tea?"

"I had to wait until I could get her alone, but I certainly did," Pei confirmed. "A woman has to think about the time she'll be married, after all, and what it's possible to do to make the time less boring. Green Jade told me the powder was called Claws of the Tiger, but I wasn't to speak of it to anyone else in the household. My father would have been furious if he ever found out she'd used it on him, which is why those women who use it do so se-cretly. She also said no man was able to resist its urgings."

"Or taste it in his tea," Amanda decided. "If it had any-thing like a distinctive flavor, *some* of the men it was used on would certainly have noticed. But what good does that do me? Green Jade and her powder are too far away for me to borrow some."

"But I'm not too far away, and I have a supply of the powder with me," Pei countered, then laughed when Amanda stared at her with brows raised. "You have to understand that I wanted to be prepared, since my father could have given me in marriage at any time and with very little warning. I would have found buying the powder difficult or impossible while waiting to be married—*you* know how much there is to do, and how closely everyone watches the prospective bride—so I got some from the old woman Green Jade told me she bought it from. I couldn't very well leave it behind when I came on this trip with you, not when *anybody* could have gone through my possessions while I was away, so—"

"So it's here and available to solve my problem!" Amanda exclaimed, then got up to go and hug Pei. "You are definitely the best friend anyone ever had, and I promise I'll find *some* way to thank you. Now all we have to do is think of how I can take the tea with me tonight."

Amanda straightened in front of Pei's chair, frowning in thought. She was so close there *had* to be a way, and if there wasn't, she'd invent one. Jack Michaels was a fool to think of nothing but being a gentleman. He'd made no effort to find out if that was what *she* wanted, so he deserved whatever she did to him. One fool in a relationship was more than enough, even if there was no real relationship to be considered. It was better to have warm memories than cold regrets, it was said, and Amanda firmly believed that.

"I wonder if Richard ever goes hunting?" Amanda said at last when the idea finally came to her. "When the men of our district went hunting, they took waterskins filled with drinks that weren't always water or even tea. If Richard hunts, he should certainly have something of the same."

"Why don't we look around while pretending to explore the house?" Pei suggested. "And we also need to see about getting you some food to take along—unless I'm mistaken and you do plan to be here for dinner."

"You're not mistaken, so you're right," Amanda said, going to the table to gather up her belongings. "Jack will be here just after dark, so I'm going to have to be too ill to go to dinner. I'll take my things back to my rooms, and then we'll go exploring and foraging. And then we'll order up a nice big pot of tea."

"Two pots of tea," Pei corrected as she rose to her feet. "Or at least two waterskins. You don't want to drink the same tea he does, not if you're already eager for him. Just make sure you don't get the two mixed up."

Amanda didn't like how complicated this was beginning to sound, but with forgetting the whole thing being her only other option, she would simply have to accept the complications and work around them. And if it became possible to simplify things, she would certainly do it. The important thing right now was to get started.

Finding what she needed turned out to be a good deal easier than Amanda had expected. She and Pei wandered around for a while, looking behind closed doors, until they found what seemed to be a small armory. There were spears, swords and bows, glaives and morning stars, daggers, maces, chain mail and shields. There were also modern weapons such as flintlock rifles and pistols as well as the gunpowder and balls for them, but the true treasure was the two small waterskins hanging from a wall peg near the pistols.

"These pouches are lined with something, but I don't know what," Pei said after peering into one of the waterskins. "The outside also feels waxy, so they ought to be useable. How will you explain having two waterskins?"

"Why would I want to explain anything, when keeping one of them out of sight will be so much easier?" Amanda countered. "I'll be wearing a cloak, after all, so keeping a skin hidden under it should be no trouble at all. Let's take those things back to my rooms now, and then we'll try our luck in the kitchens."

By the time they came downstairs again, Amanda had worked out a plan of attack. It was her job to walk around looking for something to "settle her roiling stomach," and while the kitchen staff all made suggestions and tried to help, Pei was able to fill her sleeves with edibles. It was strange how Europeans never seemed to realize that Oriental sleeves were meant to hold more than the arm going through each of them, but that blindness worked to their benefit.

Amanda finally decided on a pot of tea and some light seed cakes, then left the kitchens after asking to have them brought to her rooms. She had also laid the foundations of the "illness" that would keep her from coming down to dinner later, something else Pei would help with.

"I'll just tell your brother that I'll sleep in your sitting room to be certain you're all right," Pei said once they were back in Amanda's bedchamber. "I've already told him what good, close friends we are, and how grateful I am for the opportunity you provided by letting me travel to England with you."

"I love Richard dearly, but there seem to be certain things he's close-minded about," Amanda said with a sigh. "I have the feeling he considers you more my servant than my friend, but we should disabuse him of that notion when he hears my plans for tomorrow night."

"More plans?" Pei asked, raising one brow as she continued to empty her sleeves. There was bread, meat, cheese, and fruit, just enough for two. "What are you after now?"

"Just a way to satisfy everyone," Amanda said, having given quite a lot of thought to the problem. "I promised to let Jack escort me to the party tomorrow night, but if I do that I'll be ruining Richard's plans. I had no idea how to get around that until I realized that *you* haven't really been anywhere yet. If we let Jack escort you instead of me, you get to go to a party, Jack gets into the party, and Richard will still be able to introduce me around. Unless you'd prefer to stay here, and I mean *really* prefer it."

Pei stood thinking for a moment, then looked at Amanda with a faint smile.

"If I were as wise as the ancients, I'd certainly stay here," she said, definitely amused. "Since I'm more curious than wise, though—not to mention restless—I'll accept your very kind offer. Assuming, that is, we can get your brother to also accept the arrangement. He and his wife have been kind to me, and returning dismay for hospitality isn't very nice."

"Just leave Richard to me, and everything should work out perfectly," Amanda assured her, then headed for the chamber door. "We'd better wait for the tea and cakes in my sitting room. I don't want any of the maids in here with our loot right out in the open, but refusing to let the girl in will look suspicious. We'll share a cup of tea once she's gone, and then I'll start to get everything ready."

"And I'll go for the powder," Pei said, following her. "It doesn't take a lot to do the job, but we'll be putting it in more than a single cup of tea. No sense in doing it if we don't do it right."

Amanda smiled at that, realizing again how good an accomplice Pei made. The merchant's daughter would have denied that, since she seemed to prefer to think of herself as involuntarily caught up in Amanda's whirlwind. Amanda knew better than that, had known it for years. If Pei hadn't been her spiritual twin, she never would have accompanied Amanda all the way to England.

They only had to wait a short while for the tea to be brought, and Amanda played sick while the housemaid was there. Pei took over with a smoothness that made Amanda laugh to herself on the inside, and once the maid was gone the two of them had a cup of tea. There was enough left in the large silver pot to fill both waterskins with some left over, so there was no reason to deny themselves.

"I'm curious," Pei announced after a moment or two. "What did you intend to do tonight before this thing with

Mr. Michaels came up? Did you really mean to stay home and rest?"

"I meant to stay home and exercise," Amanda answered, pulling her mind away from thoughts of what still needed to be done. "I've been spending a few minutes at it each morning and before bed, but I feel the need for a heavier workout. If I don't get to it soon, my body will forget all the proper responses."

"The ancients say that when a man and a woman first come together, they learn to play the music of the soul." Pei's words were soft and her face expressionless, which meant she was in the process of teasing Amanda. "Tonight you should be learning new responses rather than practicing old ones. I hope your soul is prepared for that sort of music. A sour note would ruin the entire melody."

"The only possible sour note will come from him," Amanda said, suddenly needing to talk about her deepest and truest feelings. "Pei, do you think I'm wrong to do this to him? I fell in love with him when I was still a child, and I suppose I expected to discover it was infatuation rather than love once I got to know him. But the more I'm with him the stronger that love grows, until now I find it hard to think about anything else. I know I'll never be able to marry him, so is it all that wrong to want him to make love to me just once?"

"How can it be wrong to want the love of the man *you* love?" Pei asked, and now her voice and expression were gentle with understanding. "Especially when he wants you as well, but is too honorable to borrow what he can never own? You have no hope of convincing him of his error with words, and the powder will not steal what he's unwilling to give. If he truly has no interest in you, the powder will simply make him uncomfortable. The old woman who sold it to me explained that."

"But if he really does want me, he'll respond," Amanda said, now feeling a good deal better. "I'm glad you told me that, Pei, since I was beginning to feel guilty about forcing him. I wouldn't want to be forced, but it's much too easy to say it's different with a man. I wonder how long it will take?"

"It didn't take long with my father, but he wasn't fighting to stay a gentleman," Pei pointed out, both hands on her teacup. "But have you considered what you'll do if it works so well that he removes your clothes? How will you ever get into them again without a maid to help?"

"That's an easy one," Amanda said with a grin after finishing her tea. "I'll be wearing my *chih fu,* which I brought from Master Ma's to wear when I practice. I don't need help getting into *that,* but I won't refuse some help getting out of it."

They both giggled at that, but Amanda also felt a flush of embarrassment at the thought. She'd never admit it to Pei, but she seemed to be almost as nervous as she was excited. Jack was a man of experience while she was a virgin; would she be able to do well enough to satisfy him? It was something to think about, but hopefully she would soon have the answers to *all* her questions.

Happily there were still too many things to do for Amanda to have the time to develop a case of fluttering nerves. She'd also begun to picture herself naked in front of Jack Michaels, and the image made her blush all over. She wasn't quite as adventurous as Pei gave her credit for, but she *was* determined. If she missed this chance, it was unlikely she'd get another.

Amanda wrapped up the food and made it ready to take with her. Pei went to get the powder, and when she returned Amanda paid a short visit to Claire. Spinning a tall tale about how all the activity since she arrived had exhausted her wasn't hard, and Claire agreed that she would be wise to take her upset stomach to bed early. With that done, Amanda hoped no one would try to get past Pei to see how she was feeling.

Once she was back in her own rooms, Amanda rang for a maid to help her undress. Pei waited in her sitting room, calling out that she would take her meal there, so if Amanda needed anything she would just be able to ask for it. Amanda was solemn and sincere in her thanks, and the maid never realized that the two young women were well-practiced in covering for each other. Amanda climbed into bed until the maid was gone, and then Pei rejoined her in her bedchamber.

"It's just about sundown, so I've got to hurry," Amanda said, throwing the covers aside and getting out of bed. "You keep watch at the hall door, and I'll whistle when I'm dressed. If anyone seems to be coming to see me, *you* whistle."

Pei nodded with a grin, then went to take up her watch post. Amanda knew all those plots and plans must look ridiculous to Pei, but she simply didn't care. She was frantic to be outside and waiting for Jack, and if she had to look ridiculous to accomplish it, so be it. There were times when there were more important things in life than dignity.

When Amanda was in her *chih fu* with the belt properly knotted, she whistled for Pei. She also wore slippers on her feet, but not quite the same slippers European women wore. *Her* slippers had ties across the top of her feet, so that if she had to fight someone a slipper would not go flying off with her first kick. Fighting half barefoot wasn't the problem; the unevenness produced in her stance would be the problem. Once your stance went wrong your balance followed, and thoughts of Jack were already doing far too much to ruin her balance.

At last it was time to fill the waterskins. Pei took a small packet of rice paper from her sleeve, and the two of them began to measure cups of tea into the first waterskin. It only held four cups' worth, but that was all right. Amanda didn't want Pei to use all the powder for her benefit and then be left with none for her own use.

"We'll only put a little more than two cups of tea in the second waterskin," Amanda decided aloud once the first had had its dose of Claws of the Tiger. "I'll make sure Jack drinks from the first skin, but if I have to pass this second one to him after I take my own drink, I don't want him wondering why it's still so full."

"You really have thought of everything, haven't you?" Pei said, and she definitely sounded impressed. "I never thought I'd pity the Golden Devil for being so helpless against someone stronger."

"But I'm not stronger," Amanda pointed out with a wry smile. "If I were, I'd be keeping my distance from him the way he's doing with me. I'm just a poor, weak-willed woman fighting against a lordly man as best she's able. How sad that they always prove to be stronger than us."

Pei giggled again at the patiently helpless expression Amanda had adopted, and then the two of them looked around one more time. Amanda had already put pillows and clothes in her bed to make it look as if someone slept in it, and once the lamps were out no one should be able to tell it wasn't her. Back in China she and Pei had used the ruse more than once, to sneak out and see things the adults around them hadn't wanted them to see. The only time they'd regretted it was the time they'd gone to see the dawn execution of that murderer. The Magistrate had had him pulled apart by four oxen—

Amanda quickly thrust away that memory, *knowing* this would not be another time like that. No screams, no horribly dead bodies, just pleasure between two people who would never be allowed to be together permanently. She slung the second waterskin over her left shoulder, put on her black cloak, then picked up the food bundle and the other waterskin.

"I'm ready," she announced unnecessarily to Pei. "Let's turn the lamps down, and then you can check out in the hall for me."

They did that, and when Pei gestured to her, Amanda slipped into the empty hall. Richard's house and staff were both fairly large, but there was one side door which was rarely used. It didn't make noise when it was opened— Amanda had made sure of that earlier, when she and Pei were exploring. Later, once everyone was asleep, Pei would go down and unlock the door and put out the latch string so Amanda would be able to get back in.

Amanda felt a thrill along her nerves as she slipped silently through the back hall, making as little noise as humanly possible. The servants should all be busy with preparing the family's dinner and eating their own, but it wasn't possible to know for certain whether or not she would run into anyone. For that reason she was very alert, which turned out to be a good thing. Just before she reached the back stairs, she heard someone coming up.

There was an alcove nearby with a suit of plate armor standing in it, and Amanda lost no time ducking into the dim recess. A moment later a housemaid appeared, her light step almost soundless in the quiet. Amanda's heart thudded until the girl was well past, and then she slipped out of the alcove and over to the stairs. The housegirl had made no effort to look back, but Amanda was already hurrying down the stairs.

There were no more close calls, a fact Amanda stopped to appreciate once she was outside. She paused in the darkness until her breathing quieted down, and then she pulled her cloak close against the chill and began to make her way around to the front of the house. Somewhere out in the night Jack Michaels waited for her, and *she* couldn't wait until they were together again. She had a gift to give him as he gave one to her, and he *would* want it, he *would!*

Chapter 9

I t had been full dark for a while before Jack made it to Richard Lavering's house. He hadn't wanted Amanda to stand out in the dark alone for long, so he'd hurried as quickly as possible. And he had no doubt that the girl would be waiting, none whatsoever. It was very difficult to imagine a poor, ordinary man like Richard Lavering being able to keep Amanda from doing anything she pleased.

Which wasn't a terribly comforting thought. Jack frowned into the darkness as he silently moved through it, wondering what would become of Amanda when she married a man as ordinary as her brother. She would certainly continue to do exactly as she pleased, even if that doing turned out to be dangerous for her. What she really needed was—

"It's about time," a soft voice whispered from his left, the direction the house stood in. "Are you late because there was trouble?"

"I'm late because I had to follow the man on foot," Jack answered, turning to look at the shadow of her form, still mostly hidden by other shadows. "Then I had to walk back again and make certain arrangements. Are you all ready to go?"

"Of course," her voice answered, sounding light and amused. "Did you expect me to wait until you got here before remembering all sorts of things I'd forgotten?"

"Women have been known to do that from time to time," he returned, forcing himself to sound patronizing as well as equally amused. If he could just manage to insult her without letting her know he was doing it on purpose, there was a good chance she would pull back far enough from him to let him think clearly again. He desperately needed to come to his senses, but with her so very close . . .

"If a woman suddenly remembers something she's forgotten until you showed up, she's playing a game," Amanda's soft voice came again, still sounding amused. "When she makes you wait she thinks she's in control, but that's silly. When you really are in control, you don't have to do things to prove it."

"But *you* do all sorts of things," Jack pointed out lazily, still hoping to reach her with insult. "That must mean you're trying to prove something."

"If that's the way you want to look at it, it's perfectly all right with me," she countered, the words easy and twined about with laughter. "I usually do things simply because I want to do them, but if you think I'm trying to prove something, you'll first have to tell me what it is you think I'm trying to prove."

Jack knew the girl wasn't trying to prove anything because she knew she didn't have to, and with every word and action she let everyone else know it, too.

"Let's save this discussion for when we get where we're going," Jack temporized, hoping the respite would give him time to think of something. "I left my carriage over in the next street."

"Carriage?" she echoed, following along as he turned back in the direction from which he'd come. "You can't mean the same carriage and driver we had this afternoon?"

"Of course not," Jack replied with a snort. "This is a very small carriage being driven by an—associate—of mine. He'll let us off a short distance from the clerk's house and wait there for us, just in case we happen to need a carriage. If someone does show up tonight, they might not be on foot."

"That's very true," she agreed, clearly seeing his point.

"It would be a crime to lose a new lead simply through not being prepared. And it also saves me from having to lug our provisions the entire distance on foot. I haven't practiced in so long, I must be in horrible shape."

"What provisions?" Jack asked, only just keeping himself from commenting on how *un*horrible her shape was. "You sound as though you expect us to stay on watch for the next month or more."

"Oh, were you able to stop for dinner?" she asked, glancing up at him from under the hood of a black cloak. Now that they were closer to a street lamp, he was able to see the package and waterskin she carried. "I couldn't very well ask for an early supper tray because I meant to sneak out, so I had to bring along a make-do meal. I brought enough for two just in case, but if you've already eaten . . ."

"No," he answered her question, for some reason feeling bothered. "I wasn't able to stop, and it didn't occur to me to pick up anything. It looks like it's a good thing you thought of it."

She gave him a smile and a graceful nod of her head, but nothing in the way of words. Almost any other woman in her place would have mentioned how impractical men were, and that was part of what bothered him. She also hadn't pointed out that he was thinking only of himself when he criticized her about the food, and that was perfectly true. He hadn't stopped to realize that she wouldn't have had time to eat, and that made him feel low and worthless. It didn't matter that this was the first time he'd shared a watch with a woman; his lack of consideration only proved how fortunate it was that the girl would never have to put up with him.

It wasn't far to the next street where the carriage waited, but even in that short a time Jack's black mood had deepened. Being unwilling to involve a woman in your life is not the same as feeling unworthy of that woman, a truth Jack had just had forced on him. Alfred Carver, the retired agent of the Crown who ran the wineshop Jack used as a back exit to his house, sat all bundled up on the driver's

seat of the carriage. It was recognition rather than the cold
Alfie had bundled up against, and he remained silent even
when his two passengers climbed aboard. Once they were
settled he shook the reins, and they were on their way.

"The trip will take a short while, even by carriage,"
Jack said from his place to Amanda's right. "If you like,
we can use the time to reduce the contents of that food
package. I myself brought blankets, for sitting on and
wrapping up in. Before the night is over we'll probably
feel chilled to the bone."

"Now we're even," Amanda said with an odd little
laugh. "I never thought of blankets, which makes me feel
foolish. But if you don't mind, I'd rather wait until we get
where we're going before we eat. I'm not used to dining
early, and I'd hate to find myself hungry again before our
vigil is over."

"As you like," Jack agreed, suddenly aware of how bad
an idea a small carriage was. The two of them were
shoulder-to-shoulder, and he was able to feel the press of
her arm against his even through her cloak and his rag-
gedy coat sleeve. She shifted just a little and then her thigh
was also pressed against his, somehow burning even
through layers of cloth. If Jack had known where to move
to he would have moved, but the little box of a carriage
was made for quick and private trips, not as a model of
spaciousness. He was stuck where he was until the trip
was over.

And it wasn't over nearly fast enough. Listening to their
horse clip-clop over the cobbles didn't do a thing to help
Jack forget who it was who sat so close beside him. For
some stupid reason he'd expected her to be in a gown, but
her cloak had opened far enough that passing a street lamp
showed the truth. It was a *chih fu* that she wore, golden
silk with what looked like part of a dragon embroidered in
red on the tunic. The long, loose trousers were also golden
silk, but her belt was as red as the dragon. If she'd also
worn a sword at her side, Jack wouldn't have been in the
least surprised.

And it was too bad that she didn't have a sword, because if he didn't get control of himself fast she would need it. Jack put a finger in his collar and tried to loosen it, hoping that more air would also mean more control. Since the collar was already loose he didn't accomplish a thing, except to wish that he hadn't washed his hands and face while Alfie was getting the carriage. Maybe if he still looked as disreputable as he had earlier, she would have put more space between them. His own efforts had gotten him nowhere, except to the point of needing to clench his teeth.

Their destination was three streets away from Nichols's house, and by the time they got there Jack's jaw ached. He'd also noticed that Amanda wore the faintest of scents, something that seemed calculated to draw a man closer just so that he might catch more of the elusive but delicately delightful odor. Jack's mouth was dry with the effort of keeping himself from doing that, and when the carriage stopped he all but flew out the door. He definitely stumbled, which made him realize how lucky it was that Amanda *hadn't* been there earlier for his fight. If she had been, he might not have survived.

"Here are the blankets," his nemesis's voice said softly from within the carriage, and he turned in time to see a pile of dark material being thrust at him. Alfie had stopped in the darkest place on the street, of course, which to Jack's mind was a blessing. If Sir Charles ever heard about how his valued and fearless agent was behaving . . . Jack took the bundle of cloth, then stepped back to let Amanda leave the carriage.

Which she did with a lot less difficulty than he'd had. She floated like dark smoke to the street beside him, her cloak pulled close once more, her features hidden in the shadow of the hood. Jack wanted to say something to her, possibly to tell her how much better off she would be if she returned to her brother's house. The problem was the words refused to come; if he warned her off he would be admitting defeat in the matter of controlling himself, and he didn't want to lose this time in her company. After tomorrow night he'd probably never see her again, so how could he justify denying himself the opportunity? After all, he would let himself enjoy no more of her than her presence and conversation.

"Follow me carefully," he said to her softly, then began to lead the way around the corner. The house they wanted was only a few short streets away, but they had to get there without being seen.

And that turned out to be a good deal easier than Jack had been expecting. Amanda's slippers were absolutely silent on the street, and even her presence behind him was more like a shadow than a living being. At one point a man passed them no more than five feet away, going in the opposite direction, and he had no idea they stood in the darkness waiting for him to get farther away before they continued on. Jack had worked with *men* who weren't as good as Amanda Edmunds at blending into the night; he expected the thought to be shocking, but actually it was quite exhilarating.

When they finally reached the house he meant to keep watch from, Jack left Amanda and the blankets outside while he quickly checked inside. The small house was still empty, so they were soon inside and settling down in front of the window. Or in front of the window opening, which meant they had to keep their voices down.

"There are still lamps lit in most of the houses around us," Amanda observed quietly once they were sitting, each on their own blankets. Jack knew he was a fool, but not fool enough to get intimately close to her again. "Is that the clerk's house directly across the street?"

"Yes, and there goes Nichols now, passing in front of that window," Jack answered, pointing to the man. "From the way he's taking his time doing whatever he's doing, he's probably still alone."

"Then this would be a good time for us to have our meal," she said, brushing her hood back before looking at him with her head to one side. "Unless, of course, you would prefer that we wait."

"No, now would be fine," Jack said, looking forward to having the food take his mind off the fact that they were completely alone. "Have you brought an entire feast?"

"Of course," she replied with a laugh that lit her face even in the near-complete darkness—or was he seeing her with his memory rather than his eyes? "Who would ever come out to spend the night watching a man's house, and not bring a feast?"

"*I* certainly can't think of anyone," Jack returned, feeling his own face crease into a grin. "So what do we have in the first course?"

"A choice of fruit or cheese," she responded, leaning toward him as she unwrapped the package she'd brought. "The second course is cheese, meat, bread, or a combination of any two or three, and lastly is a choice of cheese, fruit or seed cake. Along with all of that we also have the finest vintage of English tea, properly cooled for long nighttime vigils. Hot tea at such a time is completely unacceptable."

"Well, of course," Jack answered in his haughtiest tone while still grinning. "Only a boor would have *hot* tea in these circumstances. I believe I'll begin with a piece of fruit. Won't you join me?"

Her head inclined in silent agreement, and they began their meal. She served him first, which meant giving him a choice of which apple he preferred, and then she cut up the meat, cheese, and bread with a small knife while he took a swallow of the tea in her waterskin. Jack's eyes had long since adjusted to the dark, so much so that he was able to follow the graceful movements of her hands with a great deal of pleasure. And there was no chattering. They each spoke when it was necessary, but the rest of the time maintained an intimate silence.

A *restful* silence, Jack quickly corrected himself, almost choking on the bread, cheese, and meat he ate together. The thought of intimacy had sent a flare of heat and light-

ning through his loins, a sensation he had to fight to push
away. Desperately he cast about for something to help the
fight, and finally settled on pedantic conversation.

"You know, I think it's a good thing we're here tonight
rather than last night," he remarked once he'd swallowed.
"Nichols must have been completely alert yesterday after
the way I tried to question him and would have been on
edge last night, thinking he'd been found out. And as you
said earlier, any associates of his would also have stayed
away, to see if anything came of yesterday's incident.
Since today was quiet and everything was apparently back
to normal, they should feel that tonight it's safe to resume
contact."

"That's supposing they contact the man on a regular basis," Amanda returned after swallowing a bite of her own.
"Although that isn't necessarily true, we do know they're
up to *something*, so they ought to keep in fairly frequent
touch. We can hope this is a night scheduled for keeping
in touch."

Jack managed to make a noise of agreement, but a hot,
slow fire had begun to burn in him. He'd had to open his
mouth and start a conversation, and now she'd twice said
the word "touch." That was what *he* wanted to do, touch
her, but he'd sworn to himself that he would not. He fum-
bled for the waterskin and tried to use a long swallow of
tea to douse the flames, and for a moment it seemed to
work.

But only for a moment. Almost immediately his mind
flashed back to the way the girl had served him, gracefully
and from her knees with her legs folded under her. She'd
removed her cloak and left it pooled on the floor beyond
her blanket, and the red dragon on her golden *chih fu*
moved when she did. All of her movements were so very
Oriental, the shy, unassuming maiden offering everything
to her lord and master. Everything, anything he cared to
take, the choice was entirely his. *She* was his, everything
about her said so.

And he was beginning to find it impossible to disagree.

He mopped at the sweat on his forehead with his coat sleeve, then struggled out of the coat. It was so hot in there, much hotter than it ought to be, making it hard for him to think. Hard. Now *there* was a word that fit with a vengeance, one that shouted at him to do something about it. Maybe if he did a *little* something, he'd be able to forget about the rest—

"Would you like a piece of seed cake now?" her soft voice came, tingling up and down every nerve ending in his body. "It's really good, and whatever we don't eat of the rest we can save for later. I'm sure we'll be hungry again later."

"I'm hungry right now," he heard his own voice say as his body shifted closer to her blanket. "But not for seed cake. My dessert will be the taste of your lips, the sweetest lips I've ever seen."

His hand went to the back of her neck to draw her closer, and only then did he realize that her hair hung loose and long down her back. He loved her hair and wanted to bury his hands in it, but not when those lips were so very close to his. He tasted them gently, carefully, and the sensation was so exquisite that he moaned. Such soft, full lips, warm with the warmth of vital life, shyly trying to kiss him back.

And that, her trying to return his kiss, snapped every last restraint he'd had on himself. He lifted her onto his lap and held her close, then gave her the sort of kiss he'd been dreaming about since the moment they met. Heat, sizzling, burning heat, searing through him and into her, then coming back again. His hands were able to feel her body through the silk of her *chih fu* tunic, but suddenly that wasn't enough. He wanted to feel the silk of her skin, and nothing could be allowed to stop him.

He got her belt open and pulled it away one-handed while their lips still fought hungrily, then he groped around until he found the tunic's outside tie. A single pull and it was open, and then he was able to brush past the front panel of the tunic to reach the inside tie on the op-

posite side. Only a woman's uniform had those ties, something he luckily knew about, and that second one, too, was
quickly opened. Then there was nothing between him and
her glorious flesh.

And—Oh, God!—she *was* made of silk! Jack's hand
stroked her while he moaned, needing the feel of her even
more than a drowning man needed dry land. His fingers
and palm found her breast, a large, soft mound with a cit-
adel of stone at its top. The stone hardened even more
when he captured it with his fingers and stroked it with his
thumb, and he knew he had to taste it. His lips left hers
and went to the warm, pulsing stone, and when his tongue
caressed its top it was her turn to moan.

But that didn't stop him. He found her other breast and
did the same, and the small, mewling sounds she made
while her slender hands buried themselves in his hair only
encouraged him to go on. While his tongue made a circle
around her rock-hard nipple, his hand found the string of
her *chih fu* trousers. Again a single pull opened the string,
and then the rest of her secret treasures were his to explore.

And *what* treasures! Her thighs were as smooth as pol-
ished jade, her belly flat and quivering, the curls beneath
calling his fingers to tangle themselves even as they
stroked lower. Her mewling grew faster and more breathless when he touched her womanhood, and she almost
squirmed out of his grip. But he wasn't about to let her get
away, not now, not when his hunger was so much more intense. She *had* brought him a feast, and he meant to swallow every last crumb of it.

Somewhere in the back of his mind he remembered that
he'd only meant to take a kiss, but the thought was faint
and easily dismissed. He'd had the kiss, and it had only
served to show him how much more there was to feast on.
The woman under his lips, tongue, and hand was writhing
hard now, showing just how ready she was, but it was best
to be certain. His fingers slid farther back between her

thighs to find the flow of moisture, hot and slippery and begging for his presence.

But there was no need for her to beg, not when his manhood throbbed with desire for her. He was so fully aroused it was painful, his body demanding what he hadn't yet allowed it to have. That demand filled him completely, excluding the possibility of any other thought, refusing to consider the least doubt. He loved this woman and he had to have her, had to show her just how great his love was. And he *would* show her, without another moment's delay.

Jack was vaguely aware of tearing his shirt off, then fumbling his breeches open. The cool touch of night air on his enflamed manhood did nothing to ease it, and he quickly pulled away the girl's trousers. He'd already put her to her back on his blanket, and as soon as her trousers were gone he covered her with his body. Her breath came so fast it was almost as though she'd been running, and he kissed her face and throat in an effort to calm her just a little. He would be a long time satisfying his desire, and he didn't want to leave her behind.

As he kissed her his manhood found its way between her thighs, coming to rest at the entrance to her deepest privacy. She whimpered and clutched at him, not in the least calmed, and he realized there was nothing more he could do. It was time to show her his love, more than time, and his desire could no longer wait.

His lips found hers again as his need began to fill her, some last thread of sanity keeping him from rushing brutishly ahead. He couldn't bear the thought of hurting her, but he also couldn't stop himself, so he entered her slowly but without hesitation. He held her in his arms, one fist tangled in her hair, their lips locked together, and she squirmed and mewled under him as he went deeper and deeper inside her. How tight she was, oh, God, how exquisitely tight! He'd never felt anything so good, never experienced a sensation like that, all over his body. And in his head, so much in his head!

And then Jack realized he was completely inside her,

and he just *had* to begin stroking. Slowly at first, quickly building up speed, faster and faster, until that was all the world contained. His body giving her his love, his lips giving her his kiss, his hands and arms holding her as if she were the last means of salvation. On and on it went, mindless sensation and movement, and when the explosion finally came it briefly destroyed the world.

When Jack finally collapsed beside her, half on the blanket and half on the rough wood floor, Amanda couldn't move. No, to be precise she didn't *want* to move, not when that might mean losing the last moments of the most incredible experience she'd ever had. Her body still tingled and throbbed, the final ghosts of an indescribable ecstasy that she hadn't wanted to end. It had been better than the previous times Jack had brought her to that state tonight, so much better that she'd wanted to scream at him not to stop. Happily she hadn't had the breath to scream with, and he *hadn't* stopped, not until the blinding eruption had struck them both.

At last Amanda took a deep breath and used both hands to push back her sweat-soaked hair. She still didn't want to move, but it was vital that she substitute the second waterskin for the one from which Jack had been drinking. She had no idea what another dose of the powder would do to him, even though she wouldn't have minded finding out. He'd been incredible, better than her most wildly fanciful dreams, and simply thinking about him made her want him all over again.

But that wouldn't have been fair, not to him and not to the reason they were there in the first place. Part of Amanda didn't care about fair play, but the rest of her was stronger and still enjoying the satisfaction she'd had. The satisfaction Jack had given her. She smiled as she sat up, and turned to look at him.

The poor man seemed absolutely exhausted, so much so that he might even have fallen asleep. Small sounds came from him to confirm that theory, but Amanda still didn't

take any chances. Rising to her feet, she purposefully put
her hand on the floor, her body blocking sight of the waterskin she picked up. She then moved away from the
blanket into the deeper shadows of the empty house,
groped around until she found a gap in the unfinished
walls, and dropped the waterskin into it. It reached the
bottom of its hiding place with a small scrape and gurgle,
and that took care of that.

Amanda went back to the blanket and replaced her *chih
fu* before she sat down again next to Jack. It was chilly
without his big body covering hers and filling her with
heat, and she touched his hair gently as she smiled with
the memory. It *was* a memory she would have forever, her
greatest treasure that no one would ever be able to steal.
She'd been right to want that from him, but she still
couldn't help wondering if he would have given the gift
without the urging of the powder.

Amanda sighed and took her hand from Jack's hair, then
moved to the other end of the blanket. The second waterskin was hidden under the pool of her cloak, so she pulled
it out and drank from it. The tea was cold and faintly bitter, not as strong as what she'd grown up drinking, and in
any event trying to think about tea didn't help. The faint
guilt she'd felt over feeding Jack the drugged tea had now
grown, refusing to be banished even with the memory of
what they'd shared. She'd taken something from the man
she loved without waiting for him to give it freely, which
wasn't what you were supposed to do to show your love.
What if he'd done that instead of her? How would she feel
about him when she found out?

It was getting very chilly in that house, so much so that
Amanda took her cloak and wrapped it around herself,
feeling bowed under the weight of her thoughts. If Jack
had done to her what she'd done to him, she'd never want
to see him again. Instead of loving him she'd hate him,
and he hadn't even started out loving her. What he would
feel for her now would be loathing, a hatred so strong that
he would never want to think about her again. And it

would all be her fault, the Silken Dragon, who refused to be denied what she wanted.

Amanda lay down on the very edge of the blanket, quiet tears running down her cheeks as she tried to pull the cloak even closer about herself. She'd told herself that there could never be anything permanent between her and the man called Jack Michaels, but in her dreams he'd always managed to find a way around the problem. He would somehow win her brother's approval, find her wherever she might be, and carry her off to live with him as his wife. The Golden Devil could do anything he cared to, and somehow he would make it happen. . . .

But now, after what she'd done, he'd hate ever having to see her again. He wouldn't want her for his wife, and someday she would see him together with a woman he did love. She would be with the man *she'd* had to marry, a sweet and gentle man who never did anything in the least exciting, and Jack would pass by with his love without even seeing her. Amanda knew she deserved a future like that, but she couldn't bear the thought of it. Jack forgetting all about her while she spent the rest of her life loving him hopelessly . . .

Quiet sobs shook Amanda while she silently called herself every kind of fool, but the deed was already done. It was too late to learn to be cautious rather than headstrong, too late to realize how much she had risked. It was all lost now, all gone—

And then a sound intruded on her grief, a sound that was out of place in the now quiet neighborhood. Amanda sat up and quickly wiped the tears from her eyes, and then she was able to see the carriage she'd only heard before. It was small and black, with a device of some sort on the door, and as she watched, someone left the coach through the opposite door. It seemed to be a man in a dark cloak, but with the carriage in the way she couldn't be sure.

Keeping low, she moved to the window opening but that didn't help much. All of the houses in sight were now dark, except Nichols's. The same lamp burned somewhere

inside, and when the figure from the carriage knocked
briefly, the door was answered almost immediately. This
was company the clerk was expecting, then, the exact kind
of company they'd been hoping he'd have.

Amanda knew she should wake Jack immediately, but
just as she was about to leave the window opening, she
heard a strange, strangled sound from the house across the
street. An instant later the figure from the carriage reappeared, left the house, and climbed back into the carriage,
which immediately began to move. Just as it did so a hand
touched her shoulder, which made her jump a foot and immediately go into fighting stance.

"No, please don't do that," Jack's uneven voice came,
calming the thundering of her heart. "I promise I won't
touch you again, so please don't think you have to fight.
I just wanted to tell you to stay here."

His shadowy form moved quickly toward the side door
then, and it finally dawned on Amanda that he was fully
dressed. She had no idea when he might have replaced his
clothes, but that wasn't her main concern. He'd told her to
stay inside, but she couldn't do that. Something had happened involving her last link to Mr. Lichfield's disappearance, and she needed to know what that was.

By the time Amanda got outside, Jack and the strange
carriage were both out of sight. Now it was possible to see
Nichols's house more easily, and the first thing she noticed
was that the door stood open. Amanda hesitated, but she
really had no choice. She had to go over there and see
whether this night would be the complete loss she already
suspected it was.

The whole neighborhood was so quiet that Amanda felt
as though she were the only living being in the entire
world. The nearest street lamp cast light only around its
own feet, so it was darkness she walked through to reach
the open door. Light spilled out of it in a warm and
friendly way, pretending to offer safety and refuge, but it
was just a lie. Directly inside the doorway, lying in a
spreading lake of blood, was Reggie Nichols. He'd been

stabbed in the chest, and no one would ever again expect him to tell them anything.

Amanda turned away from the grisly sight, and sank down into a crouch right there in the street. Nichols was dead, Mr. Lichfield was still missing, and she'd never be able to look Jack in the face again. She bent her head to her arms, resting on her knees, feeling so weary she wished she could die. She'd made a mess of everything, let down everyone who'd been counting on her, and now all she wanted was to go home. It was too bad she couldn't *really* go home, but there was nothing left for her in China now. She'd have to stay in England, no matter how painful it became, and it would be very painful . . . and lonely.

Especially lonely.

Chapter 10

J ack ran through the shadows after the disappearing carriage, and after a few minutes even more of the cobwebs began to clear from his mind. That happened just in time, as he was about to pass the street where Alfie waited with his carriage. He couldn't afford to stop, so he whistled and waved his arm as he crossed the street. If Alfie hadn't fallen asleep, he would see him and follow.

Fallen asleep. Jack himself felt as if he'd just come out of a deep sleep, one that had included a terrible nightmare. He'd heard her crying when he awoke, and that's when he'd known it had been no nightmare. He'd lost control of himself and had attacked her, and there was no possible excuse he could offer up to make the deed less monstrous. What an unspeakable way to show a woman that he found her compelling!

Jack wanted to close his eyes and shudder, but he couldn't afford to slow down, not to mention stop altogether. The carriage he followed was already too far ahead, its team of matched blood bays making it seem to fly. His own carriage was somewhat smaller and lighter, but there was also only one horse to pull it. If he lost sight of the carriage up ahead he'd never find it again, and he heard the sound of his own carriage clip-clopping up from behind him. He only had to keep running a little while longer.

And that, of course, was when the black carriage turned a corner, taking itself out of sight. Jack ran with every

ounce of speed he possessed, but when he reached the corner there was no sign of the carriage. It could have turned
off anywhere, in any direction, and trying to find it now
would be a complete waste of time.

Jack stood blowing like an overheated horse until Alfie
pulled up next to him, and once he had his wind back he
explained what had happened. He was sure Nichols was
dead, and that the man who had killed him was the one for
whom the clerk had been working. There had been a device on the carriage door that he'd seen but hadn't recognized, and if he couldn't find it in *some* heraldic register,
he'd never find the carriage's owner. It had been a terrible
night all around, something he could feel in his flesh as he
climbed into the carriage for the ride back to Nichols's
house.

And back to Amanda, he thought as he slumped in the
seat. What in the world could he say to her? What *was*
there to say to a woman you'd just brutalized? That you'd
never shared so much of yourself with a woman in your
entire adult life? That it had been an experience he'd remember forever? More to the point was that *she* would remember it forever, along with fear of and hatred for *him*.
If there had ever been the slightest chance that he would
one day be able to claim her for his own, that chance was
now gone.

And the way she'd cried! She'd been so distraught that
she hadn't even heard him come out of it and begin dressing. It was a measure of her concern for the vanished Mr.
Lichfield that she'd banished her tears when the carriage
appeared, but that only made Jack feel worse. She had
such heart, so much more courage than any woman he'd
ever met, and what had he done to show his admiration?
He deserved to be horsewhipped, and it was just too bad
that he couldn't afford to let that happen right now.

By the time the carriage got back to the clerk's house,
Jack had made some decisions. The first was that he
would not escort Amanda home again. She'd certainly had
more of his company than she could possibly have wanted,

and Alfie would be better for walking her to her brother's house after they reached her neighborhood. Jack would stay there and search Nichols's house, and then he'd go home and do some serious soul-searching. It wasn't possible to deny that he'd behaved like a bounder, and he needed to own up to it like a man. It would mean paying a terribly high price—the price of never having his name and honor cleared—but as a punishment it was very fitting.

Amanda crouched in front of Nichols's house, looking like a lost soul with her dark cloak spread out around her. She hadn't stayed in the house across the street the way Jack had told her to, but he couldn't blame her. The memories in that place had to be too fresh and painful. She looked up when the carriage approached, giving Jack something to be grateful for. That defensive stance she'd taken when he'd touched her shoulder in the house had nearly broken him; the poor thing was terrified of him, and he was glad he would not have to inflict his touch on her again.

When the carriage stopped he got out, but made sure to stay at least six feet away and waited until she'd stood. He didn't apologize, of course. There are some things it isn't possible to apologize for.

"My friend will take you home now," he told her quietly, finding the way she avoided his gaze painful. "He'll leave the carriage a street away from your brother's house, and wait until you're safely inside. I have to stay here, since—Nichols *is* dead, isn't he?"

"Yes, he's dead," she answered in a voice as lifeless as the man she spoke about. "He's been stabbed."

"Then I'll also have to let the authorities know," Jack said, reflecting that he'd do that through Sir Charles, as he had with the street attacker he'd killed earlier that day. "You'd better be on your way now."

She nodded at that, still not looking at him, and began to move toward the carriage. She'd almost reached it when abruptly she stopped again.

"We had a deal," she said, the words a whisper as she stared at the carriage. "If you'll come to my brother's house tomorrow night, I'll see to it that you get into the party at Lord and Lady Maydew's."

And then she climbed into the carriage and closed the door behind herself, which Alfie took as the signal to turn the carriage back the way they'd just come. Alfie would see to it that she got home safely, and in the meanwhile Jack could stand there in the street and curse himself in the vilest terms he knew. After everything that had happened, she was still prepared to honor the arrangement they'd made. She, a violated woman, was showing honor to a man who clearly had none of his own.

It was all Jack could do not to howl at the top of his lungs with self-hatred. Since he *was* an animal he ought to show that truth to the world, but a more vital truth was that he still had a job to do.

Jack finally turned and went into the dead man's house, closing the door behind him. He still had the house across the street to clean out, but maybe he could leave that for tomorrow or the next day. Sir Charles ought to be able to arrange something where no one was allowed inside until he got around to clearing it. The owners would be furious about being kept off their own property, but what was another person or two hating him? The most important person already hated him, and probably always would. Even if he finally managed to do something honorable. Or maybe especially if he did. . . .

Jack pushed all those thoughts away and got down to the business of searching the house. Later he would be able to think of nothing but what he intended to do, as soon as he decided what that would be. He glanced at the dead clerk before walking away, but didn't quite have the nerve to wish he could be that lucky. He didn't deserve the easy way out, and certainly wouldn't be getting it.

Amanda had no trouble getting back into her brother's house, and she made sure to lock the door properly before making her way upstairs. She wasn't as late getting back as she'd expected to be, but everyone still seemed to be asleep. Or at least in bed, which served the same purpose, so she reached her rooms without incident.

Pei was curled up asleep in a chair in her sitting room, and for a moment Amanda thought about not waking her. That would let her put off admitting what she'd done, but the admission couldn't be put off forever. Better to say it now, and let Pei know what a fool she had for a friend.

"Pei, wake up," she whispered, putting a hand to the girl's shoulder. "I'm back."

"Are you?" Pei mumbled, sitting up and rubbing her eyes. "What time is it?"

"I don't know," Amanda answered. "Somewhere around midnight, I think. Come into my bedchamber."

Amanda headed for the bedchamber without waiting for her friend, and by the time Pei got there she'd lit a lamp, was out of her cloak, and was sitting on her bed. She'd also removed the extra pillows and blankets, so it no longer looked like someone was asleep in the bed.

"Well, don't just sit there," Pei said indignantly as she closed the door behind herself. "How did it go? Did it work? Don't tell me it was a disappointment?"

"That's something I *can't* tell you," Amanda returned with a sigh. "Not only wasn't it a disappointment, it was more wonderful than I'd ever imagined. And he was so careful of me. Even with the powder raging in his blood, he was careful of me."

"Then what's wrong?" Pei asked, obviously having noticed how Amanda had bowed her head with shame. "If everything went the way you wanted it to, why do you look as if someone has died?"

"Aside from the fact that someone did die, I finally realized what a fool I'd been." Amanda looked down at the quilt beneath her folded legs, wishing she were hiding under it. "It came to me that I would hate anyone who forced themselves on me, so now Jack hates me for having done it to him. I love him so much, Pei, but now he'll never want to find a way for us to be together. He didn't even take me home."

"Oh, Amanda!" Pei exclaimed, putting an arm around her. "How horrible! But what's this about someone dying? *Who* died?"

"The man whose house we were watching," Amanda answered after taking a deep breath. "Someone came in a carriage, walked inside, and stabbed the man to death. Afterward he got away, taking with him my last chance to find Mr. Lichfield. Tonight has to have been the biggest disaster of my life, and I'll certainly end up regretting it for the rest of my days."

Pei made soothing, sympathetic noises while she hugged Amanda, but Amanda was beyond being soothed.

"You poor thing," Pei commiserated, gently patting Amanda's back. "All that trouble on a night that was supposed to have been so special. Tell me how he found out you'd put Claws of the Tiger in his tea. I thought it was almost impossible to detect. Unless you came right out and told him?"

"Of course I didn't tell him," Amanda said indignantly, leaning away from Pei. "It would have been stupid to go to so much trouble beforehand just to blurt out the truth once it had worked. I can assure you he didn't find out from me."

"Then how did he find out?" Pei pursued, her brow knit into a frown. "Did he notice something odd about the tea? This English tea *is* rather thin at times, so maybe there was an aftertaste. Did he tell you that he knew?"

"Well, not in so many words," Amanda was forced to admit, suddenly feeling even more uncomfortable. "It was mostly the way he acted, which was perfectly clear in the light of what I'd done. I couldn't very well blame him for—"

"Amanda," Pei interrupted, putting a hand to her arm. "Just how *did* he act?"

"Well, he said he wouldn't touch me again," Amanda told her, gesturing vaguely with one hand. "And the way he looked when he said it! As though he couldn't believe I'd done something so vile to him. After that he went out to try to catch up with the carriage of the man who killed the clerk, but he came back too soon to have done it. He stopped so far away it was clear he didn't want me anywhere near him, and that's when he said his driver would see me home. Oh, Pei, you should have heard how terrible he sounded. It was as though he'd lost faith in the entire human race simply because of what *I'd* done."

"And how did he look?" Pei pressed, refusing to let Amanda collapse in tears again the way she was so obviously desperate to do. "Europeans tend to show everything they feel in their expressions, so how did *his* look?"

"You think I had the nerve to look straight at him?" Amanda demanded in turn, beginning very faintly to be annoyed. "It was all I could do to keep from knocking my head on the ground in apology, something I thought I'd *never* want to do. I tell you, Pei—"

"No, Amanda, let me tell *you* something," Pei interrupted, and just because she didn't look or sound annoyed didn't mean she wasn't. "You've been insisting that Mr. Michaels now hates you, but that doesn't make any sense. He *might* hate you if he knew what you'd done, but you haven't told me anything to make me believe he could have found out."

"If that's true, then why did he act that way?" Amanda challenged, now more than just faintly annoyed herself. "There was no reason for him to keep me at a distance unless he hated me, so—"

"How do you know he was keeping *you* at a distance?" Pei interrupted again. "What if he was keeping himself at a distance, and only because he thought you wanted him to? Did you cry at any time where he might have seen you doing it?"

"Well . . . certainly I cried, when I realized how terrible it would be when he found out what I'd done." Amanda couldn't quite see where the conversation was going, but she needed to know what Pei was talking about. "But he couldn't have seen me crying, because he'd fallen asleep from exhaustion—and because of the powder, I'll bet. So what has that got to do with keeping himself at a distance?"

"Amanda, stop to think for a minute," Pei urged, leaning forward to emphasize her words. "Obviously it really bothered you to give him the Claws of the Tiger, which means you saw everything through eyes blinded by guilt. Try seeing the events through his eyes, and then tell me what the picture shows."

"I can't," Amanda admitted, suddenly too confused even to try. "All I can see is the terrible thing I did. What picture do you think he saw?"

"The more reasonable one," Pei answered gently, patting Amanda's shoulder. "The powder forced him to make love to you, but he still probably has no idea that was what you wanted. After doing it he fell asleep, and when he woke he remembered what he'd done. He probably did see you crying, and thought it was because he'd attacked you. No wonder he stayed so far away from you and didn't take you home. He probably believed he couldn't trust himself, and that *you* certainly *wouldn't* trust him. If he hates anyone now, it's most likely himself."

"Oh, good grief," Amanda breathed, closing her eyes and covering them with a hand. "It isn't as bad as I thought, it's worse. Not only did I take inexcusable advantage of him, I also made him think of himself as a criminal. *Now* what am I going to do?"

"Telling him the truth is absolutely out," Pei said flatly, just about reading Amanda's mind. "After what he has to be going through, he'll probably kill you. And me as well, for being too ignorant to think about what I was offering you. If only we'd had the time to think about it, but you Europeans are always in such a hurry. Children rushing around, rather than adults calmly considering the best possible—"

"Pei, not now," Amanda said just as flatly as Pei, her eyes open again. "I know you're a member of the oldest and wisest race in the world, but saying it again won't solve my problem. If I can't tell him the truth, what can I do?"

"Maybe you ought to forgive him," Pei suggested, only a little put out over what Amanda had said. "You'd have to think of a reason for forgiving him, but if it's good enough to make him believe it, it ought to work. Unless, of course, you'd rather say nothing and simply accept what you say you want."

"What are you talking about *now?*" Amanda almost wailed, afraid to hear what Pei's answer would be. "I know I'm not thinking at all clearly tonight, but I can't seem to catch up to what's happening. If this is what comes from making love to a man, I may never do it again for the rest of my life."

"It's what comes from letting your emotions rule you," Pei lectured gently as she patted Amanda's hand. "I'm able to see these things because I'm just an observer, not someone who is involved. What I'm talking about is the possibility that your Mr. Michaels really is a man of honor—and will come to your brother to ask for your hand in marriage. That *is* what you want, isn't it?"

For a moment Amanda was so delighted and thrilled that she couldn't answer. It had never occurred to her that what she'd done might end up getting her the man she loved, and she was speechless at the possibility. If only it could be, if only—

But then the moment was over, and Amanda found herself able to think again. Jack Michaels had never said anything about wanting to marry her; he hadn't even hinted at it. The only reason he was anywhere around her was because she'd forced him to be. He'd been nothing but honorable in all his dealings with her, and now she was supposed to force him into marriage? She couldn't do that, she simply couldn't.

"No, that's something I can't let happen," she told Pei quietly, so sad and disappointed she really did want to cry. "Forgiving him for doing something that wasn't his fault in the first place is ludicrous, but it's better than pulling him down through his own sense of honor. If I ever do marry him it will be because he really wants me, not because I trapped him into it."

"Very wise of you," Pei commented, her smile extremely faint. "It's easier living with a man you don't care about than with a man you love who doesn't love you. So what are we going to do about all this?"

"The first thing I'm going to do is think for a while before making any plans," Amanda replied very firmly. "We're being rushed again because Jack will be here tomorrow night—rather, *tonight*—to go to the party with us. I knew he needed to be there, so in effect I told him not to stay away because he hated me. Now, of course, I realize it wasn't me he hated, and he'll take what I said as proof that I want nothing to do with him. Maybe my luck will return, and he'll use that to talk himself out of asking Richard for me."

"If you count on that, I'll offer my condolences and congratulations together," Pei said dryly. "You'll want them both for when he talks to Richard."

"I don't want them at all," Amanda told her sourly. "I might be able to sway Richard if Jack talks to him, but depending on what Jack says I might not. He probably won't tell Richard about what happened tonight, not when that would do more to compromise me than put blame on himself. That means Richard won't feel compelled to agree, so I'll have to do something to make him tend toward disagreeing. God, what a horrible mess! I read a book once where one of the characters did something like what I did, but there wasn't even half the trouble."

"That's probably because the character was male," Pei said, now obviously amused. "I'm sure men do this sort of thing all the time, but they've been at it so long they know how to avoid the problems. Next time you should know the same."

"*Next* time?" Amanda echoed, suddenly feeling carved

out of indignation. "Pei, have you lost your mind? If I had
the choice, I'd change my mind about doing it *this* time."

"Then it really *must* have been a disappointment," Pei
said, her bland look telling Amanda she was back to teasing. "All that effort and preparation for something you
wish you could undo. What a shame."

"No, it wasn't a shame and it certainly wasn't a disappointment," Amanda told her with a sigh, then she lay
back on the bed to stretch out. "I would never discuss this
with another living soul, but—he was absolutely marvelous. He took his shirt off, and although I couldn't really
see him, nothing kept me from touching. His arms and
shoulders are like rock, Pei, and his chest—"

Amanda found it impossible to go on, especially when
she remembered the feel of Jack's lips on her breasts.
She'd started out eager for him, but what he'd done before
finally taking her! When the moment came for them to
merge, she'd wanted him desperately but had also been . . .
well, nervous. The feel of his raging desire in a place
where nothing and no one had ever touched her before—
If he hadn't driven her so insane with his lips and tongue
and hands, she might have demanded that he stop.

But he *had* driven her insane, and the words refused to
come out as he thrust within. By then she wanted to
scream at him to hurry, but his lips on hers had kept her
from giving him any command at all. He was in command, and she'd needed to obey him utterly. How incredibly large he'd felt inside her, a presence that seemed so
much like completion, and then he'd begun to stroke deep
and hard—

Amanda lost herself to wordless memory of that time,
and when it finally ended she looked around to find that
Pei had gone. Which was a fortunate thing, since Amanda
now had no need to explain the tears in her eyes that had
formed when she'd realized she'd probably never have the
same from Jack again. The tragedy of that was almost impossible to bear. She wanted so much to feel his arms

around her again, to hear him whisper, "Lady mine," and really mean it.

But that wasn't going to happen. He didn't *want* to marry her, and she loved him so much that his happiness was far more important than her own. Jack's work was vitally important to him, and he didn't want to change that work, didn't want a wife, didn't want *her*. That fact was agony inside her and caused the tears to roll down her cheeks, but Amanda was strong enough to accept it. The Silken Dragon would see to it that the man she loved got what he needed and wanted, and in place of him she would have her memories.

In place of him, but not to take his place. Amanda turned over and buried her face in the quilt to muffle her sobs. Nothing would ever take his place, nothing and no one . . . not ever . . . never. . . .

Chapter 11

Jack Michaels woke up rather late, but that was because he hadn't gotten to bed until the sun was nearly
up. It hadn't taken him long to search the house of the de-
ceased Reggie Nichols, which had yielded up nothing in
the way of a clue. Nichols hadn't been terribly neat, but
his house also hadn't had much that could be messed
up—or that could hide something secret and important.
Whatever knowledge the man had had would go to the
grave with him.

Jack had used the walk back to his house to compose
the report he needed to write to Sir Charles, and had seen
to that chore as soon as he got in. He'd gone out again
briefly to deliver the report to a nearby stables whose pro-
prietor was also one of theirs. If Sir Charles didn't have
the report to read with his breakfast, it would be the dark
side of a miracle.

And, with that thought in mind, Jack had gone back to
his house again to finally think about his own dark miracle. He'd only had a single whiskey to help him do his
thinking, but somehow it had been too much for him. He
remembered staggering to his bed, then falling into deep
sleep rather than deep thought.

Which meant he still had consideration of the ghastly
mess ahead of him. Jack groaned and put an arm over his
eyes when he realized that, but hiding didn't help. He had
to get straight in his mind what his options were, and then

he had to act. But first he had to pull himself together so that he'd be *able* to act.

Jack got out of bed, stripped off the filthy clothes he hadn't bothered with the night before—or, rather, this morning—put on a dressing gown, then rang for his man. Withers had been with him for years, and never asked an awkward question or gossiped about what he saw during the hours he spent in Jack's house. At night Withers went home to his wife and family, which made things easier for the both of them. Most of what would be considered Jack's oddest behavior happened at night, when Withers wasn't there to witness it.

Withers appeared promptly with Jack's breakfast on a tray, and accepted the order to heat bath water with a silent bow before leaving again. He would not enter Jack's bed-chamber without permission, so Jack had time to hide the clothes that he'd worn. He poured himself a cup of tea, decided he really had no appetite for the food, and sat back with the tea alone.

"All right, let's start with what happened," he muttered to himself after he'd taken a bracing sip. "You finally got what you've been wanting, and now you ought to be satisfied."

But he wasn't satisfied, and not only because of the *way* he'd gotten what he wanted. Even if Amanda had invited him and enjoyed what he'd done—and it wasn't hard to fool himself into believing the latter, at least—he still couldn't consider the matter over and done with. The more he had from that girl the more he wanted, and the thought of holding her in his arms again was exciting beyond belief. Every other woman he'd known had been of no more than passing interest, but Amanda—

Jack stared down into his tea, trying to picture how it would feel to come home to her. Knowing she waited for him would quicken his step as well as his pulse, and once he had reached her he would take her in his arms and kiss her hello. She would return his kiss, making him wish it were bedtime, and then she would listen with enjoyment and understanding to how his day had gone.

But that day would have to be the sort other men had, otherwise hearing about it would embarrass her terribly. Not that he could picture her saying so; Amanda Edmunds tried to change situations she didn't like, but if change was impossible she simply accepted them. But that wasn't likely to keep her from being bothered, and Jack didn't want her to be bothered, not by anything in general or by him in particular.

So now he knew where matters stood. Jack sighed, trying to see another way out, but there didn't seem to be one. Honor demanded that he make reparations for the terrible thing he'd done, but honor alone wasn't what moved him. He *wanted* to do the honorable thing, wanted the outcome that would end with the girl being his wife. But if he did that, he couldn't remain an agent of the Crown.

"Excuse me, Mr. Michaels." Withers interrupted his thoughts, somehow having entered the room without Jack's noticing. "Your bath water is nearly heated. Shall I simply keep it warm while you finish your breakfast?"

Jack smiled faintly, knowing Withers must have begun heating the bath water even before he brought up the breakfast tray. It was delightful how often Withers knew exactly what he would want even before he asked for it, but this time the man had miscalculated.

"No, Withers, I'd rather you kept the breakfast warm," Jack said, then finished his cup of tea before rising. "I'll come down now for the bath, and maybe later I'll be in the mood to eat. At the moment I'm not."

Withers simply bowed and reached for the tray, showing nothing of the surprise he must have felt. In years past, nothing had ever ruined Jack's appetite to the point where he bathed *before* eating. Today was the beginning of a new era, and Withers would have to get used to more than one change. And Jack would have to get used to caring what went on behind a mask of no expression.

Downstairs in the kitchen, Withers transferred the heated

water to the wooden tub in the corner, added cold water to produce the temperature Jack liked best, then helped Jack off with his dressing gown. Once that was done the man turned away to busy himself with other things, and Jack stepped into the tub and lowered himself into the water.

Though the warm water soothed his body, it did not ease his conscience. He had to resign himself to giving up working for his country in the way he'd been doing. That part of it hurt, but it was only fitting that a terrible deed have terrible consequences. Amanda Edmunds had not invited what he'd done to her, and her tears had said she also hadn't enjoyed it. A man who did something like that to a woman deserved to spend the rest of his life in obscure and boring respectability, never earning anything with his efforts but money for the support of his family. At least he would have the woman he loved as his wife. . . .

"If she agrees to marry me," Jack muttered with a frown, suddenly unsure about that point. "I only need her brother's consent, but Lavering does love her. If she tells him she's terrified of me, and more to the point *why* she's terrified, he may very well refuse to consider the match. Observing the proprieties are all well and good, but I'd never let a sister of mine be claimed by a man who had already savaged her once."

"Beg pardon, sir," Withers said, drawing Jack's attention. "Were you addressing *me?*"

"No, Withers, I wasn't," Jack answered, just short of snapping. "I happened to be talking to myself—"

Jack cut the words off, ashamed of himself for taking his foul mood out on an innocent man. And he could use some advice from a man who *had* a wife, not to mention three daughters.

"Withers, I'd like to ask you something of a personal nature," Jack said, bringing the older man's attention back to him. "If, that is, you don't mind my asking."

"Not at all, Mr. Michaels," Withers responded, his face showing nothing but its usual calm. "It has been my pleasure to serve you these last five years, during which period your generosity has been many times in evidence. If I may be of help to you in some unusual way, it will please me even more."

"You're a good man, Withers, and I'm incredibly lucky to have you," Jack assured him, but assurance slid back into ongoing worry. "Can you tell me—I mean, how much do you know about women? If a man does something really terrible to one, is there any chance she'll ever forgive him?"

"There is always the chance, sir," Withers replied, and for once he wore a frown. "Women are quite different from us, you know, and not simply in a physical way. Their minds work differently, sir, and at times there is no possibility of understanding those workings. What we consider trivial can be of overwhelming importance to them, and, of course, the opposite is also true. We may see a particular action as unforgivable, and yet the lady in question may consider it of no more than passing interest."

"Take my word for it, Withers," Jack informed him with a sigh, bringing a handful of warm water to his face. "The lady in question does *not* consider the matter trivial or unimportant. Does that mean she'll never be able to forgive it?"

"As I said, sir, women are so different," Withers evaded, now looking faintly uncomfortable. "One neighbor of mine committed a small indiscretion, and when his wife learned of it she turned the rest of his days into a living nightmare. She never spoke to him but screamed, never commented upon anything without making reference to his lapse in proper behavior. In a year's time he was driven to taking his own life, and none of us was able to blame him. He, however, may well have been more fortunate than a second neighbor."

"I'm almost afraid to ask," Jack said hollowly, fearing the worst. "What happened to that second poor devil?"

"He, too, committed an indiscretion, yet his wife loved him and therefore forgave him," Withers supplied, apparently trying not to flinch. "She continued to greet him each evening when he returned home and never even referred to the incident, but some inner part of her seemed to be fading away. Her husband tried everything possible to restore her to the sweet, loving woman she had been, but his efforts were in vain. The inner fading became an outer one, and she simply wasted away. When she passed on, her husband was inconsolable in his grief. One foolish moment, he declared over and over, and the love was forever gone out of his life. One day shortly thereafter he disappeared, and hasn't been heard from since."

"Good lord," Jack whispered, guilt now stabbing hard into his chest. Were some women really so fragile, that giving them unexpected hurt did that much damage? What he'd done to Amanda was far worse than betraying her with another woman; how would *she* feel now, once the initial shock had worn off? Would she be thirsting for his blood or, far worse, be prepared to forgive him? Oh, dear God, if only she wanted his blood ... !

"Mr. Michaels, are you all right?" Withers asked, the concern in his voice deeper than usual. "I do hope you will forgive my speaking of such matters, but—"

"But I did ask for it," Jack interrupted, one hand over his eyes. The darkness was lovely, and Jack could finally understand why some men went so far as to take their own lives. The promise of unending peace without decisions and complications was so very tempting ... "Thank you, Withers," he added. "I'll go back to bathing now."

"Yes, sir," Withers said, and a moment later there were small sounds indicating that the man had resumed his interrupted tasks. Jack kept his hand over his eyes for a short while, then resolutely took it away and began to wash. He had no idea what he would face when he called for Amanda tonight, but all planning and decisions would have to wait until he found out. He still wanted very much to marry the girl, and maybe it would be possible to work that out.

As soon as he took care of the business he had at the Maydews' party. Jack cursed under his breath, but there was no getting out of it. He *had* to finish what would probably be his last assignment from Sir Charles, but right after that he would settle his own life.

And one way or another it *would* be settled!

Amanda slept later than usual, but when she awoke she felt refreshed and even more determined. She'd gotten what she'd needed and wanted from Jack, and now it was his turn to be satisfied. She would not let him suffer simply because she'd taken advantage of him.

A maid helped her dress in a day gown of yellow and white cotton, and by the time she was presentable a house girl had brought a tray with a late breakfast. Amanda took the meal in her sitting room, wondering whether Pei was still asleep or perhaps out walking in the garden. She had just decided to wait until she finished eating before trying to find out, when a knock came at her door and Richard entered.

"Amanda, how are you feeling?" he asked at once, concern on his dear, handsome face. "I considered calling a physician, but Claire suggested that I wait until this morning. I must say, you do look quite well after a good night's sleep."

"What I got last night was exactly what I needed, my dear," Amanda replied with less of a grin than the one she felt on the inside. "This morning I've completely returned to myself, and I want to tell you how I handled a rather delicate situation yesterday. I think you'll be proud of me."

"I'm constantly proud of you, dear girl," Richard said with the warmest smile as he seated himself at the table. "But do tell me about this delicate situation."

"May I pour you a cup of tea, Richard?" Amanda asked first, pleased that an extra cup and saucer had already been provided. Richard's staff anticipated the possible needs of the household, which made them delightfully efficient. When Richard nodded, Amanda poured his tea, then she continued.

"As you know, I was out driving with Mr. Michaels again yesterday. He continues to be the perfect gentleman, but I fear he seems rather more taken with me than I find comfortable. I can't help but remember what you've said about him, and I quite agree that I certainly ought to meet other eligible gentlemen before you decide which one is best for me."

"You are the most marvelous girl," Richard said with another warm smile, leaning over to pat her hand. "Other men must contend with daughters and sisters who foolishly believe *they* should be allowed the choice of who they will marry, but I—I have been blessed with a sister who sensibly leaves the decision where it belongs. But you still haven't mentioned what the delicate situation was."

"I'm getting to it, dear," Amanda replied, returning his smile. "As I said, Mr. Michaels and his earnestness made me most uncomfortable, and then he asked a favor that made it worse. I'd foolishly mentioned the party we'll be attending tonight, and he asked if he might escort me. I was on the verge of refusing outright, when I remembered what you'd said about his father."

"Ah—yes, Duke Edward," Richard muttered, having stopped himself just as he was about to be incensed. "Quite right, dear girl, I'd nearly forgotten about His Grace the duke. No sense in making enemies in high places if it can be avoided. I'll think about the problem and find *some* solution."

"I believe I've already found one, Richard," Amanda said, showing nothing of the satisfaction she felt over how well the discussion was going. "We certainly can't disappoint Duke Edward, but my being escorted by Mr. Michaels will spoil *our* expectations. For that reason I told Mr. Michaels that he could attend the party with us, but said nothing about who he would escort."

"But my dear, who else *would* he escort but you?" Richard asked, his brow now wrinkled in confusion. "If I ask Claire to allow it, we'll look positively ridiculous, not to mention completely improper."

"No, Richard, not Claire," Amanda said with a laugh. "I know you've been delightful about not taking advantage of a special guest under your roof, but surely you'll be able to stand the envy and admiration of your friends for *one* night. Obviously no one else in your circle will ever be able to produce an Oriental aristocrat who also happens to be distantly related to the Imperial Family of her country, but they won't continue to talk about it for *very* long. Please, Richard, as a favor to me."

"You mean Miss Han," Richard said, his brows now raised in considerable surprise. "I had no idea the girl was that well connected, but those who have the position find it unnecessary to speak of it. And there *will* be considerable interest on the part of my friends, but you're quite right about them eventually getting over it. Do you believe Miss Han will agree to accompany us, not to mention allowing Michaels to escort her?"

"I mean to speak to her as soon as I have *your* permission, Richard," Amanda assured him with her most innocent look. "It would have been inappropriate to bring up the matter sooner, but I'm sure she'll do it. She and I are the best of friends, you know, and I'll tell her I'd rather not wait until Mr. Michaels does something outrageous— like insisting that you give me to him in marriage. I have the strangest feeling he means to do exactly that, and may even resort to extravagance if you refuse."

"Extravagance?" Richard echoed, his brows high again. "You're the most level-headed woman I know, Amanda, so I consider this—premonition—of yours something to be taken seriously. What do you feel Michaels might do?"

"I really don't know, Richard," Amanda responded, now trying to look as though she were in the midst of considering the matter seriously. "I dislike saying this, but if the man has become obsessed with me there's no telling *what* he'll do or say. The idea of continuing in his company isn't something I look forward to, but if *you* think I should, or even if you believe I should marry him—"

"Now, now, there's no need to consider those possibilities," Richard interrupted firmly, patting her hand again. "You've only just come home, and you're certainly not so homely or backward that I have to accept the only offer of marriage you're likely to get. I expect to have any number of offers for your hand, so Jack Michaels can look elsewhere for an object of obsession. My sister won't be available under any circumstances."

"Oh, Richard, how sweet and understanding you are," Amanda exclaimed, giving him a radiant smile. "I feel ever so much better now, and I'll speak to Pei as soon as I finish the marvelous food you've provided."

"If you think this is good, wait until you taste the offerings of our cook in Braxton," Richard said, finally sipping at his tea. "We'll be going up for a while in a little more than a sennight, and while we're there I'll show you your father's place. That's where he met Mother, you know, when they were both in Braxton at the same time after my father died. His place is rather modest, but the surrounding lands are impressively beautiful."

"Is that Braxton Meadows?" Amanda asked, taking care not to show how suddenly alert she was. "Near a village called Taring Poole?"

"Why, yes, it certainly is," Richard answered, again looking surprised. "The Meadows are rather extensive, and quite a lot of people have houses up there now. Taring Poole supplies part-time servants for those of us who don't keep their places open all year round. How did you hear of it?"

"Mr. Lichfield mentioned the village any number of times," Amanda lied smoothly, her mind working fast. "Apparently he has relatives there, which I now find unsurprising. If he was either living or visiting there when my father discovered a need for a secretary, he would have been right on the spot to take the job. Once I visit my father's house, I really must see if I can locate Mr. Lichfield's family. They should be told about what happened to him."

"And possibly they'll have some information about him that no one else has had," Richard added, showing how quick he could be. "A pity I didn't know about this sooner, but it isn't too late. I'll put my man on it immediately, and hopefully by the time we get up there he'll have learned something."

Amanda doubted that Richard's investigator would, but she smiled graciously and nodded without commenting. She would do her own investigating once she got up there, and it might even be possible to do that sooner than Richard planned to go. She'd watch for an opportunity, and grab it if one appeared.

Richard finished his tea while she did the same with her meal, and then they separated so that she could go looking for Pei. She found her out in the garden, sitting on a stone bench, and Amanda wasted no time in addressing her.

"Dearest friend, this unworthy one has a great favor to ask," Amanda said in Chinese, warning Pei as well as drawing her attention.

"You have a favor to ask?" Pei translated for the benefit of any of the gardeners who might be close enough to overhear them. "Of course, my dear friend, you know I'd never refuse you. And do speak in this language, so that I might better my poor command of it."

"Certainly," Amanda agreed as she also sat on the bench, keeping her amusement off her face. "The favor I need to ask is a great one, but my brother joins me in asking it." As she spoke, Amanda looked carefully around. Once she was certain no one was close enough to hear everything, she lowered her voice and added, "You have a party to go to tonight."

"I don't know how you talked your brother into it, but I'm not really surprised." Pei's voice was just as low, and her dark eyes sparkled with her own amusement. "The Silken Dragon strikes again."

"It's too bad we can't carry on these private-but-open conversations in Chinese," Amanda said, her amusement even greater now. "But if we did, people would think we were keeping secrets. And if anyone asks—which they probably will—you're an aristocrat in your country and distantly related to the Imperial Family. At least I know you won't have any trouble acting the part."

"Stop calling me a snob," Pei said with a small laugh. "I'm simply a civilized woman aware of the deficiencies in her present surroundings. So what have you arranged for Mr. Michaels—and what reason for it did you give your brother?"

"I was forced to tell Richard that I find the intense interest Mr. Michaels has expressed in me quite disconcerting," Amanda explained with a smile. "I warned him that I somehow had the feeling Mr. Michaels would ask for me in marriage, and if Richard refused, the man might do something outrageous. What that something might be I had no idea, but I was certain he *would* try something. I offered to continue seeing the man—or even to marry him—if Richard wanted me to, but it turned out that Richard wanted nothing of the sort."

"Imagine that," Pei commented, raising her brows to show how really surprised she was. "Your brother has decided all on his own to refuse to let you do something you don't want to do. How incredibly unexpected. And since I'll be going to the party tonight, Mr. Michaels will be my escort. How do you expect him to take that?"

"He won't be pleased, but we have to remember that it's for his own good," Amanda said, the words as firm as her belief in them. "He may have had a physical interest in me, but that's no reason to ruin his life. It wasn't his choice to do what he did, so I refuse to let him suffer for it. If he gets desperate and tells Richard what he did, I intend to be very embarrassed over the horrid lie—and then I'll remind Richard what I'd said about the man doing something outrageous."

"And what a shame he won't be able to prove his confession by having you physically examined," Pei said, nodding absently. "Since you've already told Claire what all that physical exercise did to you, she'll know an examination would be useless. Yes, poor Mr. Michaels will find himself completely outflanked."

"Not outflanked," Amanda corrected primly. "You know that men are right when they say women simply haven't got a head for anything military, especially tactics. We'll just say that Jack has been—hmmm. What would be a good word?"

"How about outnumbered and outthought?" Pei suggested with a grin. "Those two fit rather well, and you're absolutely correct. We women would never *think* to mount a campaign against a man, not when we know how badly we would lose."

"I have no intention of losing, not when the outcome is so important," Amanda said, and then all amusement disappeared behind her sigh. "I can't believe I'm actually working to *keep* from marrying the man of my dreams, but somehow life doesn't go the way dreams do. If that's because I'm doing something wrong, I hope someone comes by soon to point out what it is."

"If they do and I'm not there, don't forget to tell me what they say," Pei contributed with a sigh of her own. "At this point I would even enjoy some help with deciding what I want. I've been sitting here thinking how much I miss Po San, but I'm also reluctant to go back without . . . something I can't seem to define. At least you know what your aims and objectives are, so you can work toward them. For myself, I have no idea."

Amanda leaned forward to touch Pei's arm sympathetically, but there was nothing she could say. They both seemed to have problems that resisted solution, and on the inside Amanda felt no more successful than Pei. Yes, she knew what she wanted, but she wanted it only because it was necessary. What she *really* wanted—

But why think about that? Amanda knew it would never happen, so it wasn't worth wasting time on. Thinking about how she would act with Jack Michaels was more to the point, since he would be there in a matter of a few hours. Her heart jumped with that thought, but she ruthlessly suppressed her eager excitement. The object of the next game was to make Jack walk away in disgust, but she couldn't be too obvious about it. Maybe . . .

Chapter 12

Jack Michaels left his carriage and approached the Lavering house with more outward confidence than inward. He'd spent much of that day thinking and planning, but he didn't feel as ready as he should have. He kept getting the impression he was missing something as far as Amanda was concerned, but excitement over how soon he would be asking for her hand kept him from thinking straight. The more he thought about marrying her, the sooner he wanted it to happen.

A house man opened the door to Jack's knock, looking somewhat surprised when Jack walked in. That was because he was early, Jack knew, and the ladies would certainly not be ready yet.

"Please tell Lord Pembroke I'd like to speak to him," he said to the man once he'd handed over his hat. "And be sure to mention that I'd like the interview to be *before* we leave for the party."

"Lord Pembroke is in his study, sir," the man informed him with a bow. "If you will wait here just a moment?"

Jack nodded with only a small amount of his impatience showing, and the man was as good as his word. A moment later he stepped back out of the room that must be Lavering's study, and gestured that Jack could enter. Jack was quick to do that, and shook hands with his host while the house man closed the door and left them alone. Lavering had risen behind his desk to offer his hand, and

Jack took one of the chairs in front of it when the man re-seated himself.

"Is there something I can do for you?" Lavering asked when Jack found himself reaching for exactly the right words. "I was just doing some updating of records while waiting for the ladies to come down."

"It's one of the ladies that I want to talk to you about," Jack said, giving up on looking for the perfect words and settling for simply sounding lucid and sincere. "As you know, I found myself greatly attracted to your sister, Miss Edmunds, when I first met her. The more time I spend in her company, the more right my initial instincts prove to be. I've come early tonight in order to ask for her hand in marriage."

"Have you," Lavering murmured, leaning back in his chair to study Jack with a surprisingly *un*surprised expression. "You find her attractive, then?"

"More than attractive," Jack responded, trying not to frown. This interview wasn't going at all the way he'd expected. "Miss Edmunds is certainly a beautiful woman, but there's so much more to her that I'm completely captivated. If my former reputation is what disturbs you, please be assured that former is the most accurate word. Due to my affection for Miss Edmunds I'm now a re-formed man, and you have my word that I'll never do anything to embarrass or upset her."

"I'm sure you won't," Lavering commented, but not in a way that reassured Jack. "I appreciate your position in regard to my sister, Michaels, and I'll certainly give your proposal serious consideration. How about a drink while we wait for the ladies?"

"No, no drink," Jack protested, knowing he didn't dare drink in his frame of mind. "I don't understand what you're saying, Lavering. You can't be *refusing* my proposal."

"I would have preferred to discuss this at another time, but you're quite right," Lavering responded with a sigh, settling back in his chair again. "I *am* refusing your pro-

posal, which I happen to feel is in my sister's best interests. If you decide against accompanying us tonight, I'm
sure everyone will understand."

"Nonsense, of course I'll be going with you," Jack had
the presence of mind to say, even through raging disappointment and bewildered hurt. "If it *is* my reputation that
disturbs you, allow me to assure you that my father will
certainly stand bond for my good behavior. He's been at
me forever to get my life on the straight and narrow, and
any woman who helps me to accomplish that will never
regret having married me. I'm sure you know my father
can be extremely generous."

"I'm sure Duke Edward would be all of that and more,"
Lavering said with another sigh. "I, however, happen to be
the sort of man who considers other things in addition to
material advantage, specifically my sister's happiness. Can
you give me the same firm assurance that Amanda will be
happy with you?"

"Why . . . I'll certainly . . . *try* to make her happy," Jack
stumbled, the memory of quiet tears in last night's darkness keeping him from speaking what could conceivably
turn out to be a lie. "If you're looking for guarantees, man,
you may be a long time in finding anyone's proposal acceptable. How can anyone guarantee another's happiness?"

"They can't, but for some the condition is more likely
to come about than for others." Lavering's sincerity
couldn't be doubted, and that made Jack's heart sink. "Can
you deny that it would be in Amanda's best interests if we
concluded this discussion, at least for a time? Perhaps in
another few days we'll all be seeing matters a bit more
clearly."

Jack wanted to argue the stance, wanted to demand that
his petition be accepted, but again memory interfered. In
his mind's eye he could see a forlorn little figure, a girl
who was unable to meet his gaze and who whispered
rather than spoke. After what he'd done to her, *could* he
make her happy? He wanted to believe that the answer
was yes, but was the answer true? If he told Lavering what

he'd done the man could well change his mind completely, but *would* that be in Amanda's best interest?

"Good man," Lavering said with warm approval when Jack remained silent for a while. "We'll both take some time to think about this, and then perhaps we'll speak again. For now I believe some tea would do us nicely while we wait for the ladies."

Lavering rose to ring for the tea, and it was brought with very little delay. Jack accepted a cup, then drifted off morosely into his own thoughts. He would have to restructure his position a bit more thoroughly before he broached the subject of marrying Amanda again.

Jack's attention returned to the present when Lavering rose, and only then did he notice that a manservant stood by the opened study door. The ladies must be ready then, and it was time to go to the party. He left what tea remained in his cup and also rose, then followed Lavering out into the hall. He felt reluctant to face Amanda again, but he very much needed to know how she was—and he desperately wanted to be near her again. His current fantasy was to spend days, months, *years* in her company. . . .

And she looked even more wonderful than he'd been expecting. Her gown was a lacy confection of blue and cream, and the silver jewelry she wore sparkled like diamonds. Her dark hair was piled high in an elaborate arrangement, accenting her lovely blue eyes and pretty face. Jack was relieved to see that she also wore a confident smile, which was his main interest. There were other people in the hall, of course, but for the moment they didn't exist for him.

"Mr. Michaels, I don't believe you've met Miss Han Pei, my sister's companion," Lavering said, pulling Jack's attention away from Amanda. "Miss Han has agreed to accompany us tonight, and you will favor us, I hope, by agreeing to escort her. I believe you already know my wife, Lady Pembroke."

Claire Lavering, Lady Pembroke, was closest, so Jack acknowledged their acquaintanceship and bent over her hand, trying to hide his shock. Amanda's friend gave him a faint smile and a bow rather than her hand when he turned to her next, carrying Jack back momentarily to his time in China. He returned her bow as a European rather than an Oriental, and only then did his mind begin to function again—with a very pressing question.

This business of asking him to escort Miss Han—was that Amanda's way of getting him into the party without ruining her brother's plans, or simply her way of avoiding him completely? Even if the answer was the former, that didn't make Jack feel any better. He didn't *want* Amanda to go along with her brother's plans to find her a man to marry, not unless he was the man. He had to find out the truth about what was going on, but first he really did have to speak to the lady who patiently awaited his escort.

"Miss Han," he said after only a brief hesitation, "what a pleasure to meet you. You look lovely tonight, and escorting you will be an honor."

"Thank you, Mr. Michaels," the girl responded with a regal nod, her English very nearly accentless. "I'll confess I'm looking forward to seeing more of your fascinating culture."

The words were a very fitting backdrop for her own gown, which was a vibrant red silk with gold, green, and blue embroidery. It went all the way down to the girl's blue slippers, but that was the only thing it had in common with the gowns of the other ladies. Its high collar covered Miss Han to the throat, and its straight lines were very nearly scandalous. It reminded Jack of a similar gown worn to Ranelagh Pleasure Gardens only a short while ago when he'd been there on Bryan Machlin's behalf. But that other gown had obviously been a costume, while this one just as obviously was not.

"I'll certainly be the envy of every man at the party tonight," Jack said, wondering why there seemed to be amusement in the girl's dark eyes. "Would you excuse me for just one moment?"

Miss Han nodded politely, and Jack bowed his thanks.

When he approached Amanda, she looked at him with unreadable blue eyes.

"Good evening, Mr. Michaels," she said in a voice that
somehow sounded faintly impatient. "It was nice of you to
agree to escort my friend Miss Han to the party."

"I'm delighted to be able to do so," Jack replied automatically as he bent over her hand, then decided it was
past time for nothing more than reserved conversation. "I
would much rather have been *your* escort," he added in a
very soft voice, "even though our last time together
was . . . less than pleasant for you. I'm beyond shame over
doing such a terrible thing, and would like you to know
that I've already asked your brother for your hand."

"What a silly thing to do," she commented, looking and
sounding as though she discussed boringly unspectacular
weather. "I've already forgotten anything that might have
happened, so you ought to do the same. If you feel you
need more, then please be assured that I forgive you."

Jack was so appalled by her last three words that he
nearly shouted, "No, please, not *that!*" Only the last ves-
tige of good sense he possessed kept him quiet, and then
Richard Lavering was ushering all toward the door.

With Jack's carriage available, it wasn't necessary to
crowd everyone into the Lavering vehicle. The only problem with that was that it was Miss Han he escorted rather
than Amanda, so it was Miss Han who joined him in his
carriage. Jack handed her in and then followed, but didn't
realize the depth of his distraction until his companion
spoke.

"Are you all right, Mr. Michaels?" her soft voice asked
out of the darkness, bringing him back to the dim carriage.
"You seem—troubled."

"It so happens I am, Miss Han," Jack admitted, needing
to find out if he really did have reason to fear the worst.
"Did Miss Edmunds seem—different—to you today?
More quiet than usual, as though the life had gone out of
her?"

"I can't say I noticed anything like *that*," the girl an-

swered, the tone of her voice the least bit odd. "Why
would you expect her to feel that way?"

"She has reason to be very angry with me," Jack confessed with a sigh, needing to talk about the matter even
if it was obliquely. "I expected to see some evidence of
that anger, but instead she told me she forgave me. That
isn't what I wanted her to do, not if it means covering a
terrible hurt. Covered things sometimes make you fade
away to nothing. . . ."

Jack's voice trailed off on its own, his mind sending
him horrifying pictures of Amanda looking like a ghost of
herself. He'd never be able to live with himself if anything
like that happened to her, especially when it would be all
his fault.

"I really can't imagine Amanda—I mean Miss
Edmunds—covering up or fading away from *any* hurt,"
Miss Han said, and now the words sounded rather hurried
and concerned. "Please believe me when I say that *Ssu Te
Lung* is *much* stronger than that, so you have no reason to
worry, Mr. Michaels. She's just fine, and I fully expect her
to stay that way."

"I sincerely hope that you're right, Miss Han," Jack said
fervently, then registered something the girl had said. "You
called her 'Ssu Te Lung.' I picked up some Chinese from
one of my father's servants, and if memory serves, that
means 'Silken Dragon.' How in the world would Miss
Edmunds have gotten a nickname like *that?*"

"Oh, it was just a—silly joke," Miss Han replied, but
now Jack could detect a nervousness of some sort behind
the hesitant attempt at lightness in her tone. "I'm sure you
know how foolish young girls can be, giving themselves
and their friends nicknames that don't fit in the least. No
one who meets Amanda is ever able to see anything at all
dragonlike about her."

"Well, that's certainly true," Jack allowed, but the darkness luckily hid his frown. A name like Silken Dragon
would never be given to anyone who was *obviously*
dragonlike, but there did have to be a good deal of truth

to it. He'd been called the Golden Devil, but not only because he'd paid for his lessons in gold and most people had thought he fought like a devil. The clothes he'd worn had made him look as though he didn't even have copper cash, never mind gold, and he'd been so easygoing he hadn't seemed able to fight at all. . . .

"I hope you don't mind that I only know one or two of your dances," Miss Han commented after a very brief moment, her tone now smoothly apologetic. "Since I'm sure you know many more, I'll certainly expect you to have other partners."

"That's very generous of you, Miss Han," Jack said, but just as he was about to assure her he'd do nothing of the sort, he remembered why he was going to the party. It had nothing to do with showing how gentlemanly he was, which meant he needed to make a different answer.

"I very much appreciate your understanding," he finished instead. "I'll be certain you aren't left alone, but I may use the opportunity to dance with another woman."

"Good," came the well-satisfied response, and then they lapsed into silence again. But this time the silence was filled with thought rather than recriminations, although Jack wasn't sure about where his thoughts were taking him. He had somehow gotten the impression he didn't know nearly enough about Miss Amanda Edmunds, but also didn't know in which direction to search for more. If she was ever going to become his wife . . .

If he was ever going to *make* her his wife, he first needed to find out why a nickname like the Silken Dragon made him more suspicious than curious. What could there possibly be for him to be suspicious about?

Amanda wasn't terribly happy, but at least she was satisfied. By the time they arrived at Lord and Lady Maydew's house, Jack no longer looked as if he expected her to cry and accuse him of things. He'd looked really terrible in Richard's house, but now the sense of tragedy had lessened if not disappeared entirely. He was being attentive to Pei, which bothered Amanda in some strange way. She really did want Jack to be entirely free of guilt, but she also wanted to be the one on his arm. Logically, it was best that she wasn't, but that made no difference to her heart.

There were quite a lot of people in the Maydew entrance hall, and Richard had to make an effort to stay beside Claire. That put him at a distance from Amanda for a moment, and she used the opportunity to make her way over to Pei, who stood momentarily alone.

"How is it going?" Amanda asked softly when she reached Pei's side. "Nothing of an unpleasant nature happened, I hope."

"If you're asking whether he's contemplating suicide, the answer is, I hope not." Pei's murmur was very soft, but also somewhat sharp. "What we did to him was shameful, and I really feel sorry I ever suggested it. He intends to ask you to dance later, so don't you even *think* about refusing him."

Amanda was very surprised to hear Pei speak to her like that, but after an instant the surprise was gone, and she had a moment to consider Pei's words. Perhaps Jack did deserve at least that much consideration.

By that time Richard and Claire had rejoined them, and then Jack had done the same. Amanda was curious about where he'd gone, but since it most likely had to do with his work, she wouldn't dare ask. As they moved into the ballroom in a group, Jack hung back while she and Pei were introduced to their host and hostess. Such a fuss was made over them, especially over Pei, no one noticed that Jack was never formally introduced.

They eventually managed to move away from the entrance area, and Jack led Pei out on the floor to dance. Everyone noticed her immediately, of course, and quite a few of the guests came over to speak to Richard. A number of the women also gathered around Claire, which left Amanda with the problem of focusing her attention somewhere other than on the dance floor. She wanted to be the one dancing with Jack, but beyond the one dance she'd promised Pei to give him, she couldn't. It wouldn't have been good for *him,* and that was all that mattered—

"Good evening, lovely lady," a deep voice said, pulling Amanda away from thoughts of regret. "I tried to arrange for a proper introduction, but the crowds around Lord Pembroke are impossible to get through. Since the impatient admiration filling me also makes it impossible for me to wait, I've come over with an improper but very necessary *self*-introduction."

The man grinned then, his expression a perfect blend of shared amusement and natural charm. He was tall and blond and very handsome, and was dressed quite elegantly in blue with a gray vest and white ruffles.

"I'm not sure a self-introduction is legal," Amanda answered smoothly. "If it isn't you'll be wasting your time, and will have to start all over again anyway. What will your impatience say to that?"

"I'm certain my impatience never thought of that," he replied, his eyes twinkling with amusement. "It's definitely something to consider, though, so let's discuss it. Do you think it would be legal if I saved the introduction for when it can be properly done, and simply told you my name is Robert Blake?"

"Since that isn't an introduction, it just *might* be legal," Amanda granted him, enjoying the interplay in spite of herself. "But then we'd be left with a different problem. I'm not supposed to speak to anyone I haven't been properly introduced to, so what do we do about *that?*"

"That *is* a problem," he agreed, rubbing his face with one hand. "I'd never ask a lady to do something she wasn't supposed to; no true gentleman would. I suppose that leaves me nothing to do but stand and stare at you."

"But staring is impolite," Amanda pointed out at once. "Would a true gentleman do something that was impolite?"

"Oh, never," he confirmed with a headshake, green eyes

dancing mischievously. "But without that I have *nothing* to do. Are you able to give me any alternate suggestions?"

Amanda was about to say she'd have to consider that question for a while, but was saved from having to make the effort. Richard had finally broken away from his friends, and had come over to join them.

"I do beg your pardon, Blake," he said to the tall blond man, shaking hands with him. "I saw you trying to reach me, but had no idea why until I noticed you with Amanda. Introductions are in order, of course, so let me get straight to them. Robert Blake, Baron Delland, allow me to present my sister, Miss Amanda Edmunds."

"Miss Edmunds, how delightful to meet you at last," Robert Blake said, bending over her hand. "It feels as though I've spent forever admiring you from afar."

Amanda couldn't help laughing at that, and Blake immediately joined in. That was the answer the rogue had challenged *her* to come up with, that he could admire her from afar. Of course Richard had no idea what they were laughing at, and Blake realized it at once.

"I think I'd better explain," he said, now looking the least bit shamefaced. "I wasn't able to get your attention but still couldn't keep away from Miss Edmunds, and your sister was kind enough not to turn her back on me. We discussed how we might speak to each other without a proper introduction, and—well, you came along just in time."

The explanation trailed off lamely, but Amanda could see that Richard was amused even if he didn't understand.

"As long as I did come over just in time, then everything is fine," he said with a smile. "Now you two are free to dance, so why don't you go ahead?"

"That's a marvelous suggestion," Blake said, then turned to offer Amanda his arm. "Dear lady, will you do me the honor of joining me on the dance floor?"

Amanda managed to smile and agree, forcing herself to ignore the fact that she wished Blake were someone else.

Once out on the dance floor, Amanda paid attention to no one but her partner. Robert Blake was an excellent

dancer and a wonderful conversationalist, not to mention
an extremely attentive companion. They finished what was
left of that first dance and stayed for the next, and only
then did Blake escort her back to Richard. Amanda
dreaded that because of who else might be there, but to her
surprise he wasn't. Pei stood surrounded by people who
seemed very eager to speak to her, but Jack Michaels
wasn't anywhere to be seen.

"Amanda, my dear, Baron Delland will have to give up
monopolizing your time," Richard said as soon as they
were close enough. "There are other gentlemen here demanding introductions, and I'm afraid they might get frac-
tious if they're made to wait any longer."

A chorus of fervent agreement came from the five or six
men standing behind Richard, but Blake wasn't overly impressed.

"They may have their introductions, but just remember
I've had mine first," he pointed out with a grin. "That
means I'm free to monopolize the lady's time for as long
as I can get away with it, and also means I won't give up
without a fight—and maybe not even with one."

The waiting men weren't pleased to hear that, but it
didn't stop them from getting their introductions. After
that they took turns dancing with her, and Blake managed
to get more than his fair share. After everyone had had at
least one turn, Amanda called a temporary halt and asked
for a glass of fruit juice. Three of her admirers went off to
find her one, and she was finally able to simply stand there
for a moment. Blake, apparently sensing her need for a little quiet, stood silently beside her while her remaining admirers chattered on about nothing.

Finally she was able to wonder what had become of
Jack. Pei had said he meant to ask her to dance, but she
hadn't caught more than an occasional glimpse of him
since they'd arrived. She knew he was there because of his
work, but surely one dance with her wouldn't have—

Amanda's thoughts broke off in shock when she finally
located Jack Michaels—dancing with a blond woman and

paying very close attention to her. The blonde somehow looked familiar, and then Amanda had her placed. The very first party she'd gone to, where she'd first run into Jack, he'd been lavishing attention on the blonde.

The men around Amanda laughed politely at something, and she managed a smile despite her churning insides. Jack had said he needed to be there at the party tonight, but he hadn't given any specific reason for the need. He'd hinted it had to do with his work, but what if it really had to do with getting close to the blonde again? And Jack was supposed to be Pei's escort, so his spending time with another woman was *very* improper.

Sharp pain stabbed at Amanda as she looked away from the handsome couple on the dance floor, but there was anger burning within her as well. Earlier tonight that man had told her he'd asked for her hand in marriage, and she'd told him it wasn't necessary. Had he been so upset about being rejected that he'd immediately turned to another woman? But that wasn't just any woman, she was one he already knew and obviously admired . . . and how coincidentally lucky it was that she just happened to be there.

So. Amanda began to fan herself with a very deliberate motion. She'd known all along that Jack Michaels had no real interest in her, but proving it conclusively in such an open way had been totally unnecessary. Her anger was growing to monumental proportions, but the pain was still very much there. She would ignore it and continue on as if nothing at all had happened, pretending her girlhood dreams hadn't been callously murdered.

But if Jack Michaels ever came near her again, he'd need every ounce of the skill possessed by the Golden Devil to keep himself undamaged!

Chapter 13

J ack wasn't surprised by the number of people crowding around Miss Han as soon as he returned her to the Laverings. He'd heard Richard Lavering introduce her to their host and hostess as someone related to the Chinese Imperial Family, and that, added to the exotic look of her, was more than most people could resist. Jack let himself be crowded out of the way—exactly as he'd hoped he would be—and then he was free to go about his business.

Hughes stood chatting with a man Jack didn't know, a fairly tall man with a full but neatly trimmed black beard. Remembering the description of the "bloke" who had given that urchin the last note to deliver, Jack immediately looked at the bearded man's eyebrows. The street urchin had used the word "shaggy," but the bearded man's brows seemed completely normal. Of course, false shaggy brows might be added and then removed, but until something happened to prove otherwise, he'd assume Hughes hadn't yet been contacted.

Jack glanced around casually and finally located Rawson, who was specifically there to keep an eye on Hughes. Rawson stood to one side with a glass in his hand, but more of his attention was on Hughes than on the people with whom he stood. That wasn't the way Jack would have handled the task, but Rawson had a limited amount of creativity when it came to coping. He was a good man, stolid and reliable, but as far as inventiveness went . . .

Jack cursed himself silently but roundly, but that did no good at all. He *had* to look at Amanda again, even though the sight of her enjoying herself with another man tore him apart. Jack knew she was there for just such activities, but his opinion of that hadn't changed. And he *would* claim a dance with her—the whole world be damned if he didn't!

Suddenly finding it necessary to regain control of himself, Jack took a glass of fruit juice and then let himself be captured by two elderly ladies who wanted a young man to entertain them. He responded to them gallantly but automatically, forcing his mind back to the threat to Hughes's cover.

It still made absolutely no sense. Jack smiled at and flirted with each woman in turn, but his mind fought to break through the dense and meaningless fog. They'd started to investigate the matter concerning Hughes even before Jack had met Amanda, but they hadn't even made as much progress as the pitiful amount he and the girl had made looking for Lichfield. Watching that clerk's house had turned out to be personally disastrous, but only bad luck had kept the clerk from leading them to everyone he worked with. It was—

So suddenly did the idea come to him that Jack almost stopped speaking to the ladies in midsentence. It was perfectly obvious and so simple that it was a wonder none of them had thought of it sooner. He now knew why those notes were being sent to Hughes, and the game was almost over. He'd make sure they wrapped it up tonight, and then he'd be free to concentrate on his personal life.

Jack excused himself from the ladies, then began to stroll around. There was someone he hadn't yet seen but fully expected to, and it didn't take very many minutes before he found her. The blonde woman, Miss Justine Landers, who had been so interested in Sellars when Sellars was keeping an eye on Hughes. Tonight Jack would be watching Miss Landers, and if his theory was correct the young woman would eventually locate Rawson.

It took effort and a good bit of time for Jack to watch
the Landers woman without being seen himself, but his
persistence finally paid off. The Landers woman drifted
here and there, sometimes dancing, always looking at the
people who stood not far away from Hughes. Jack knew it
when she spotted Rawson, watched her watching *him* for
a while, and then felt grim satisfaction when she finally
approached Rawson. She had the man she wanted; now all
she needed to do was play available until Rawson couldn't
help but approach her.

It had been the thought of what he and Amanda had
tried to do with that clerk that had finally given Jack the
answer. Somehow Hughes had been discovered to be an
undisclosed agent of the Crown, but that in itself hadn't
been enough for those making the discovery. They'd obviously decided they'd do better with a *list* of undisclosed
agents, and set about making one. They'd known Hughes
would hardly be likely to appear at a rendezvous alone, so
they'd looked around to see who was watching him. The
first party had yielded them Sellars, and since no one
wanted the observation to be too obvious, this time the
watcher was Rawson. The Landers woman would entice
him over and find out exactly who he was, and then they
would know two additional agents.

Jack gave the woman time only until Rawson had taken
the bait, and then he ambled over. Rawson, clear on the
point that he wasn't supposed to know Jack, didn't acknowledge him, but Miss Landers had to swallow her
surprise.

"Dear lady, how delightful to see you again," Jack exclaimed, immediately bending over her hand. "This must
certainly be fate, so you cannot refuse to join me on the
dance floor. I'm sure this gentleman will understand."

"I say," Rawson began in protest, but the lady had her
own protest to make.

"My dear sir, you fluster me," she said, trying to act shy
and embarrassed. "I do believe I recall meeting you before, but—"

"Now, now, dear lady, no buts," Jack interrupted smoothly. "Join me for just a single dance, and then I'll return you to this gentleman. He'll then be responsible for protecting you for the rest of the night, a duty I'm certain he won't in any way shirk."

"Of course not," Rawson confirmed indignantly, as though his honor had been brought into question. "I will certainly see to that most pleasant of chores."

Rawson sounded like many an upper-class fool Jack had met in his life, which told Jack the man had immediately caught on to the fact that something was wrong. Being unimaginative isn't the same as being stupid, as Jack was happy to see Rawson prove.

And the idea he'd given the Landers woman had also gotten *her* attention. If she danced a single dance with Jack, the man she was after would "protect" her for the rest of the evening while she pumped him for information. Something like that was worth the investment of a few wasted minutes, and her slow smile acknowledged that before her words did.

"I believe, sir, that you have convinced me," she added unnecessarily, before she took his arm. "One dance, and thereafter I will be under the protection of this gentleman. Do let us proceed."

Jack bowed and led her out to the dance floor with a smile, then spent his time pretending to be very attentive. In reality he examined the people in the room, and in just a handful of moments he found someone who was very interested in the man dancing with Miss Landers. Unsurprisingly it was the gentleman with the black beard, who had stood talking to Hughes until just a few minutes earlier.

Even as Jack smiled and said something gallant to his partner, his mind was admiring the cleverness behind the scheme. Anyone who approached Hughes while he was waiting to be contacted had to be considered suspect, so those people would be studied carefully by the man watching Hughes. It was probably the way Sellars had been located, and tonight Rawson had been given the description

of a man in a beard as a possible suspect. They couldn't
have kept that game going forever, so Jack was certain
they had another plan all ready to use once the first no
longer worked. It would be interesting to find out what it
was.

The dance was a long, slow one, but when it was over
Jack returned Miss Landers to Rawson. Rawson thanked
Jack in a stiff and awkward way that said he was prepared
to be very alert and careful while dealing with the woman,
and that was all Jack could ask for the moment. He bowed
a final time and then walked away, and once the crowd hid
him from easy observation he found a place to watch the
bearded man. He needed to observe the man a while to see
if he and the woman had any other confederates attending
the party.

Jack kept most of his attention on the bearded man, but
he was compelled to glance in Amanda's direction every
few minutes. There were something like half a dozen men
vying for her attention, but it soon became clear there was
one out in front of the others. The fellow was tall and
blond and handsome—if you liked that sort of thing—and
Jack wasn't able to place him. He dressed rather less som-
berly than the rest of this crowd and laughed a lot. *With*
Amanda.

The man in the black beard stood with different groups
of people and pretended to listen to their conversations,
but his full attention seemed to be centered on Rawson
and the Landers woman. He made no effort to speak to or
signal to anyone else, which was a lucky thing. More and
more often Jack's attention went back to Amanda, who appeared to be enjoying herself immensely. And making no
effort to look around for *him*. That he'd disappeared
seemed to bother her not in the least.

The rest of the evening was hard on Jack, but at long
last people began to leave in earnest. The bearded man
slipped away while Jack watched Amanda join her blond
admirer in another dance, but was luckily spotted again on
his way to the left side of the ballroom. Jack watched the

man glance around casually before taking an envelope out of his coat and leaving it on a tray with glasses of champagne. The tray had been prepared for the servants circulating with refreshments, and would be taken by the first servant whose current tray was emptied.

If Jack had needed confirmation of his guesswork, that had to be it. The bearded man went back to his original place, nodded casually when the Landers woman just happened to be glancing in his direction, and then it was the woman's turn. She said something to Rawson that looked apologetic, he took her hand and bent over it, and then she headed out of the ballroom. A moment later the bearded man drifted out after her, and Jack waited only until the man was gone before he stepped up to Rawson.

"Get Hughes and follow me immediately," he murmured to Rawson, then headed out of the ballroom after the bearded man. Unless he was mistaken, the bearded man and the Landers woman would soon be together.

And he wasn't mistaken. Landers had obviously taken her time adjusting her cloak once it was brought to her, since she was only then leaving the house—with the bearded man directly behind her. Jack sauntered to the front door, and stood looking out of the decorative glass border around the door until Rawson and Hughes reached him a moment later.

"Just as I was leaving I was handed another note," Hughes began in a low voice, but Jack gestured the information away.

"I already know all about it," he returned, his gaze on the couple outside. "That bearded man left the envelope for you, and he and the Landers woman are about to leave in the same carriage. As soon as they start to pull away, get in your own carriage and make sure you don't lose them. I'll arrange for more help, and wait with them at Essex Street."

Hughes and Rawson were anxious to get to the bottom of that game, so they nodded, waited until the man and woman were in their carriage, and then they slipped out to

follow. Rawson had come to the party in a special
carriage—as lightweight as possible and pulled by a
matched pair with incredible heart and stamina—and so
the two agents should have no trouble keeping up with
their quarry.

The only trouble involved was Jack's, but he couldn't
see a way out of it. He stood silently dithering at the door,
knowing he had to be on his way to get more men together, and there wasn't time to go back and take a proper
leave of the people with whom he'd arrived. That would
do badly for his image in Lavering's eyes—not to mention
for his peace of mind, leaving Amanda with that preten-
tious blond man—but Jack simply had no choice.

Departing at that moment was one of the hardest things
he'd ever done, but his sense of duty tended to provide
strength in the face of necessity. Somehow he'd explain
everything away, Jack promised himself as he called his
carriage with a wave. Somehow he'd make it all right
when his mind was clear and his duty done, and then he'd
be able to think about nothing but Amanda. . . .

Jack had the necessary men gathered and Sir Charles
alerted by the time Rawson reached the rooms on Essex
Street. Hughes had stayed to watch the house where the
man and woman had both gotten out before dismissing
their carriage. They hadn't been able to tell if there were
any others in the house, but that question would be answered before very long.

They were just about to leave when Sir Charles arrived,
obviously having dressed in a hurry. Jack was surprised—
and not very pleased—to find himself ordered to stay behind, but a few minutes of thought after everyone was
gone gave him the probable reason. Hughes and Rawson
were already compromised, and if their raiding force happened to miss someone involved in the plot, the two men
would be no worse off than they already were. Jack was
still unknown, and Sir Charles wanted to keep him that
way.

Jack spent most of the waiting time pacing back and forth, silently demanding to know why Sir Charles hadn't simply kept him in the carriage from which he would be watching. Sir Charles Kerry may have been their superior, but he never involved himself directly with operations no matter how important they were.

It was at least three hours before Sir Charles returned, and he looked tired but well satisfied. He took off his hat and poured himself a drink, then turned to raise the glass to Jack.

"Here's to you, my boy, for a job extremely well done," Sir Charles said before sipping at his drink. "Ah, that tastes good and I've certainly earned it. Sending you along on this business was one of the best ideas I've ever had."

"Then why was I left here to cool my heels while everyone else got to finish the job?" Jack demanded, unimpressed by the compliment. "The least you could have done was let me sit in your carriage with you."

"You never would have stayed in my carriage," Sir Charles returned calmly as he took a chair. Jack remained standing in the middle of the room, but Sir Charles ignored that. "You seem unusually agitated tonight, John," he added. "I thought you might want to discuss whatever it is that's bothering you."

Jack hesitated, knowing he did have to speak to Sir Charles, but he wasn't yet ready to do it. "Tell me what happened first," he countered. "If I did such a good job, I deserve at least that."

"Yes, you certainly do," Sir Charles agreed after a moment's hesitation. "Thanks to you, we now have all three of them. The last member of the group was the father of the two people Hughes and Rawson followed, who turn out to be brother and sister. Their father was once in the employ of one of the wealthier families, but he took to petty pilfering and was finally caught at it and dismissed. But by then he didn't much mind, because he had gotten an idea for large-scale stealing."

"By taking advantage of foolish members of the upper

class," Jack said impatiently with a nod. "Yes, that was obvious as soon as you said the father had been a servant. The girl didn't speak or act like someone from the serving class, so she must have been coached to pretend to gentility. How did they get onto Hughes?"

"It was some months ago, while they were fleecing their latest lamb," Sir Charles replied, his expression telling Jack he was duly impressed by Jack's deductions. "Hughes was in the group trying to locate the chap who was helping himself to high-born ladies' trinkets, and he found the man. He got the culprit out of the house and handed over to waiting constables without any fuss or anyone noticing—or so he thought. Actually the brother and sister saw it all. They'd already spotted the man, and were staying away from him in an effort to keep clear of the trouble they knew was bound to come."

"So when they saw Hughes taking him out, they asked questions," Jack summed up with a glum nod as he dropped into a chair. "They discovered he supposedly had nothing to do with the constabulary or the magistrate's office, and probably became curious enough to dig deeper. As soon as they were certain what he was, they started their little game. What were they going to do with their list?"

"Sell it for a large amount of gold," Sir Charles said with a shrug. "There are any number of men in this city who would pay handsomely to find out which of their well-born and idle acquaintances it would be best to keep their secrets from. A list like that could be sold more than once, and every man on it would thereafter be useless to the Crown. Hughes told me afterward that at first they weren't at all alarmed to see him at their door with men at his back."

"Undoubtedly because they were certain they hadn't committed any crime," Jack said with a faint smile. "It would have been interesting to see their faces when the word 'treason' was mentioned."

"They always seem to miss the fact that working against

someone who works for the Crown is also working against the Crown," Sir Charles agreed after another sip of his drink. "The old man was crying when they took him away, and the young man and woman appeared to be in shock. What happens to them now is none of our business, but you and your problems are *my* business. Are you ready to talk about it yet?"

"No sense in putting it off any longer," Jack decided aloud after taking a deep breath. "I—have to tell you that I'll be submitting my resignation, effective immediately."

Jack studied the carpeting beyond his clasped hands rather than look at the man he addressed, and at first there was no response from Sir Charles. Then there was the sound of a sigh, followed by the sound of swallowing.

"I was afraid of that," Sir Charles said quietly then, the sigh still in his words. "That young lady who meant nothing to you has come to mean a good deal more than nothing. You're certain it's not simple infatuation?"

"It isn't infatuation, and it certainly isn't simple," Jack said hollowly, slumping back in the chair without looking up. "I'm mad about her, but I've run into something of a problem. I—did something reprehensible, but when I spoke to her brother earlier this evening he refused to allow my suit. I haven't mentioned what I did and don't really want to, but that may be the only way to get him to let me marry her. Whether or not she wants to, which she well might not. It isn't the kind of situation to which the British government should be even a distant party."

"Even if it were possible to understand what the situation *is*," Sir Charles muttered, and Jack finally looked up to see that his colleague was frowning. "John, I've never seen you so close to being incoherent. How much have you had to drink tonight?"

"I've swallowed an endless amount of tea and fruit juice," Jack told him with a sigh of his own. "I haven't dared touch anything stronger, and now I think you know why. I'm incoherent enough without it."

"And the proud possessor of a completely unintelligible

problem," Sir Charles said with a headshake. "Well, whatever the trouble is, I won't accept your resignation as yet. You're due some time to yourself, so take it now and see if you can resolve that incredible mass of confusion. You won't be leaving any duties unattended to—unless there's still something to do on the matter of that missing man Lichfield. Your report said you meant to look through some heraldry books."

"And I haven't yet done it," Jack said after cursing under his breath. "I'll try to draw the device so someone else can do the looking, but there's one chore I need to see to personally. That house I stayed in across the street from Nichols the night he was killed—I still haven't cleared my possessions out of it, but I'll do that tomorrow without fail."

"But not too early," Sir Charles said, the words definitely an order. "The owners of that house deserve to have it back, but a few hours more won't make that much of a difference to them. You need a good night's sleep to clear up some of that confusion, and then maybe you'll see the solution to your problem."

Jack couldn't imagine even a year's worth of sleep being of help, but he suddenly felt too tired to argue. He would get that good night's sleep, take care of the house and draw the heraldic device, and then—

And then he would take steps to settle his private life. He wanted Amanda to be part of that life, and somehow he would make it happen. Unless she hated him now, in which case he would first have to change her mind before making her his wife. And also get her brother to overlook the way he'd just walked away from them tonight. . . .

Jack wanted to groan out loud, but had just enough control left to wait until he got home to do it.

Amanda followed everyone else into the house, aware of how good a mood they were in and depressed that she couldn't share it. They'd all had a good time tonight including her, and that was the most depressing point.

"I must say our houseguest was a roaring social success," Richard announced jovially as he gave his hat to a servant. "Miss Han, you handled that crowd like a member of *our* royal family and did your people proud. I hope no one went so far as to insult you in any way?"

"Certainly not, Lord Pembroke," Pei answered with her usual faint smile. "Everyone was most polite, although one or two were a trifle more than curious. I was forced to ask that one woman if she demanded a detailed lineage from everyone she met, and if so, how soon she would be mature enough to realize how unsophisticated such actions were."

"That was Lady Montmeer," Claire supplied with a laugh when Richard raised his brows. "You were busy talking to someone at the time, but I was right there to enjoy it all. That woman has needed to be put in her place for quite a long time, and the rest of us were delighted when Miss Han did it with such lovely condescension. Lady Montmeer colored with embarrassment, and didn't say another word for the rest of the evening."

"I wish someone could accomplish that with her husband," Richard said, sharing Claire's amusement. "Montmeer is forever telling the rest of us how to manage our affairs, and we're heartily sick of it. He usually starts in on Blake and his barony as soon as he sees the man, but tonight Blake had an excellent excuse for absenting himself from our group. He seemed quite taken with you, Amanda, and somehow managed to account for more of your time than any of the others."

"He's a very amusing and attentive man," Amanda agreed, forcing herself to join the pleasant conversation. "I find him extremely attractive, and agreed that with your permission he might call on me to go driving or to the theater. The only problem is—Richard, do *all* men fall in and out of love so quickly?"

Amanda didn't have to work very hard to put a plaintive note in the question she'd asked so deliberately. Everything that had happened tonight had helped to further her plans, especially what Jack Michaels had done. She now had an excellent reason for being cautious about the men she met—even though she wished she didn't.

"You poor thing," Richard commiserated, knowing exactly what she meant as he came closer to put an arm about her shoulders. "I heard Michaels tell you he meant to marry you, and not two hours later he was gone off on his own without so much as a by your leave. His behavior was shameful, but it's not as if it wasn't expected. Blake is nothing like the same, and *his* interest certainly won't turn out to be as fleeting."

"I wish I could be sure of that," Amanda said with a sigh, putting her head on Richard's shoulder. "If it were possible for me to go away somewhere before Baron Delland has a chance to come calling ... I'd consider his intentions much more reliable if he had to come after me to do his courting."

"You know, that just might be possible," Richard said slowly, a touch of revelation in his voice. "Tomorrow I'll be sending off some of the household staff to Braxton Meadows, to open the house and ready it for our arrival. If Miss Han will accompany you, I see no reason why you can't go with them."

"Oh, Richard, that would be wonderful!" Amanda exclaimed, then turned to look at her friend. "Pei, do say you don't mind going with me. If you really don't want to I'll certainly understand, but—"

"Of course I'll go," Pei interrupted calmly, her amusement clear to no one but Amanda. "I've been longing for a taste of the countryside, so you'll be doing *me* a favor."

"That's settled then," Claire said with a smile of approval just like Richard's. "We'll miss you two, of course, but we'll be along in just a little while. Right now I think it's time for us all to go to bed."

No one felt it necessary to argue with that decision, so they all went upstairs. Amanda's maid was already waiting to help her undress, so it wasn't long before she was in a nightgown and ready for bed. When the maid left, Amanda poured a glass of water and sat down on her bed to wait. She knew she would have a visitor, and Pei didn't keep her waiting long. Not five minutes after the maid was gone, Pei slipped through the bedchamber door.

"All right, let's have it," Pei stated as she took the chair opposite Amanda's bed. "I'll bet anything you knew your brother was sending servants to the country tomorrow, so you took advantage of it. What I want details on is how and why."

"How is perfectly simple," Amanda replied with a shrug. "I happened to overhear two servants discussing the trip this afternoon. Why I did it is a little more complicated."

"Ah, now I see," Pei returned, suddenly looking sympathetic. "He didn't even try to dance with you, and I was so sure he would. Maybe he became too involved with business matters and couldn't break away."

"Yes, business matters in the person of a slim blonde he showed interest in once before," Amanda told her, anger returning to join the pain that hadn't yet left. "I know I wanted to chase him away for his own good, Pei, but he didn't have to cooperate that wholeheartedly. He could have at least waited until tomorrow."

"And in the carriage he seemed so worried about you," Pei said with a sigh. "I confess I don't understand European men, but at least you had that very handsome blond man to keep you from feeling rejected. I couldn't hear any of his conversation, but he certainly *looked* interested."

"Yes, I've definitely made a conquest," Amanda said glumly, staring down into her cup. "He's intelligent, funny, attentive, handsome—and I hope he *doesn't* follow me to Braxton Meadows. If he does and gets around to asking for me, Richard will probably agree."

"Oh, you poor thing," Pei said, all sympathy now gone from her voice. "Being forced to marry a man like that, and one who's a baron on top of it. However will you manage to stand it?"

Amanda didn't answer the sarcastic question, but not

because the answer was obvious. If she had to marry Robert Blake it *would* be hard on her, harder than she'd ever believed possible. It wasn't Blake's arms she wanted to have around her—even though if a certain someone else tried it again, she'd beat him over the head with something hard.

"He'd better not ever try to come near me again," Amanda muttered, and wasn't surprised when Pei didn't ask who she meant. There was only one "he," the one she was beginning to hate. "When he said he wanted to marry me, I felt—oh, like you'd expect to feel when all your dreams come true. It made my heart hammer with excitement, as if I were being held captive by a dragon, and he had just vowed to rescue me. I told him it wasn't necessary, hoping madly that he would disagree and insist, but instead he simply accepted it. He stood there without saying a word, and then—and then—"

"And then he walked away to dance with another woman, and never even came back to say good-bye." Pei's voice was very cold, not to mention angry. "I know it doesn't feel like it to you now, Amanda, but you're well rid of him. Tomorrow we'll be off to the country, so even if he changes his mind again and is foolish enough to come back, you won't be here to see it. And after a little while you'll be ready to marry a *decent* man."

"He won't come back," Amanda said, taking a deep breath. "I was a fool to believe there was a chance he really cared about me, but that's over with now. I got Richard to let me go early to Braxton Meadows for a different reason, one that involves Mr. Lichfield. I want to do some investigating up there, preferably before there's anyone around to see it. We'll have plenty of time for me to tell you about it tomorrow, on the way. Right now we'd better get some sleep."

"Yes, they'll be in early to pack our clothes," Pei said with a nod, rising from the chair. "You have a good night's sleep, and I'll see you tomorrow."

Amanda also nodded, but once Pei was gone she made

no effort to prepare to lie down. Instead she sat there sipping her water, seeing in her mind again what she'd seen
at the party. She'd glimpsed Jack more than once, and
each time he'd been staring at only one person in the
room. It hadn't been hard to see who that person was, and
when he'd ended up dancing with her—

It took almost more self-control than Amanda had to
keep from hurling her glass at the nearest wall. She hated
Jack Michaels, more than she'd ever hated any person or
thing, and she'd never forgive him for not loving her. That
was a ridiculous reason for hating someone, almost a mad
reason, and she was ashamed to admit it even to herself.
It wasn't *his* fault he didn't love her, but—

But if that was so, he should never have asked her to
marry him. He should have kept his discussion with Richard private and never raised her hopes. It was *that* cruelty
she really hated him for, and would pray every night that
she never saw him again. Especially not with *that* woman.

Amanda quickly finished the last of her water, then got
up to do some of the exercises she'd learned at Master
Ma's school. If she didn't work off some of her anger
she'd never get to sleep, and she and Pei had a trip ahead
of them tomorrow. Even if speaking to Mr. Lichfield's relatives was another dead end, at least she would be good
and far away from *him*.

Chapter 14

⟨━━━◗◖━━━⟩

J ack followed Sir Charles's orders about sleeping late
without really intending it. It hadn't been early when
he'd finally gotten to bed, and then he'd tossed and turned
for what had seemed like forever. He eventually fell
asleep, but only to dream about Amanda Edmunds. He
awoke holding his pillow tightly in his arms, kissing it and
wondering why it wasn't kissing him back. It *had* kissed
him back at *some* point. . . .

"Well, how nice to see that you're already beginning to
go mad," he muttered to himself in disgust as soon as he
awoke far enough to appreciate the idiocy of that last
thought. "Soon they'll put you away in a dark place where
there *are* no pillows, so you won't have to wonder whether
or not yours kissed you back."

Jack continued to mutter as he got out of bed, but he'd
stopped paying attention to whatever he was saying. There
were things he had to do today, and it was more than time
he got started.

Withers brought up his breakfast, and while Jack ate he
also did his best to sketch the heraldic device he'd
glimpsed on the door of the black carriage that had carried
the man who had killed Nichols. It had been an arrogant
thing for the man to do, using his own clearly marked carriage when he knew he'd be committing murder. He might
have been counting on no one from the lower classes being able—or willing—to identify him, or at least Jack
hoped that was the reason. A less pleasant possibility was

that the man was insane, and because of that believed he could do anything he pleased without getting caught. That sort was easier to find, but usually not until they'd left a horrible number of dead behind them.

When Jack finished the sketch, he wrote out a formal letter of resignation—undated, so that Sir Charles could use it when and how he felt necessary. Then he put both items in an envelope and sent Withers to deliver them to a shop where they would be quietly forwarded to Sir Charles. After that chore Withers would take the rest of the day off, leaving Jack free to come and go when—and how—he pleased. In order to go back to that house from which he and Amanda had watched Nichols, Jack would have to use his man-down-on-his-luck disguise again.

A constable was on guard in front of the house when Jack got there, and Jack paused to murmur Magistrate Fielding's name as a password before going in.

The inside of the house at half past one in the afternoon made him remember it in the darkness of night, and that, of course, brought back other memories. He stood there for a moment in the middle of the unfinished room, remembering the feel of silken skin under his hands and lips, and it took some effort to finally pull out of it.

"If you stop wasting time, you just might manage to *do* that again rather than just dream about it," he growled at himself. There was nothing wrong with a man losing his head and heart over a woman, as long as he didn't also lose his intelligence. Jack meant to tackle Lavering again as soon as he was through in the house, and the faster he finished his task the sooner that would be.

The blankets were just where they'd been left, as were the wrappings from the food package and the waterskin of tea. Jack folded the blankets into an easily carried bundle, then rolled the other items into them. He hadn't noticed two nights earlier in the dark, but the waterskin had a small replica of Lavering's crest burned into its leather. It was the possibility of that sort of thing that had made Jack ask to have the house guarded until he was able to return

and clean it up himself. Outsiders didn't need to think
Richard Lavering was something he wasn't, and his own
people didn't need to know who his companion had been
that night.

With the rolled bundle tucked under his arm, Jack took
a slow, last look around. He did want to be out of there
fast, but there was no sense in doing an incomplete job.
Overlooking something for other people to find would
be— Jack paused when his eye caught something odd, and
he walked closer to the unfinished left-hand wall to see
what it was.

Two strips of planking had been nailed across the middle of the wall, with another single strip lower down near
the floor. In between those two sections was nothing but
open, unfinished outer wall, and something that looked
like a thin piece of leather hung out over the bottom strip
of wood. Curious, Jack crouched and pulled at the piece of
leather, but it wasn't loose. It was attached to something
hidden by the bottom plank, and it took a second, stronger
pull before that something came free.

"What the devil?" Jack muttered when he saw the waterskin, an exact replica of the one he'd rolled into the
blankets. It even had a tiny Pembroke crest, and its presence was so odd that Jack unrolled the blankets to make
sure he really had put the waterskin inside them. "Yup,
right where it's supposed to be," he added in even greater
confusion. "There are definitely two of them."

But he only remembered seeing one waterskin, one he'd
shared with Amanda. If there had been two she would
have said so, and then they wouldn't have had to share.
But how likely was it that someone else had gotten a waterskin with the Pembroke crest, and then had hidden it in
that very house? And it *had* been hidden, or at least an attempt had been made to hide it. If that wall had been
planked all the way down . . .

Only it hadn't been planked all the way down, but
someone groping around in the dark might not have realized that. It had probably seemed the perfect hiding place,

but for what? What could that second skin possibly hold? Jack opened the skin and let some of its contents wet his finger, then he gingerly tasted the sample. Tea, stale and oddly bitter, but definitely tea. And the skin was only about half-full.

By then Jack's suspicions were fully aroused, even if he had no idea what, precisely, he should be questioning. He tested the contents of the skin he'd wrapped in the blankets, and found stale tea as well. It wasn't nearly as bitter as the tea in the hidden skin, and the container seemed to be slightly less full. Which also didn't make much sense, as Jack couldn't remember that much tea being consumed. He himself had finished about what was gone from the hidden skin, but Amanda hadn't had as much as what was gone from the other skin. Unless the other skin hadn't been completely full . . .

"I've got to think about this, but not here," Jack decided aloud, then packed both skins inside the blankets and left the house. The constable outside pretended he didn't see Jack, which was exactly what he was supposed to do.

The long walk back to the wineshop, through which Jack had to reenter his house, disappeared behind furious thinking. It was undeniable that Amanda had brought both waterskins of tea, but why she'd done it was beyond him. Considering the fact that the two teas hadn't tasted alike led Jack to wonder if she'd needed to put something special in her own tea, but that didn't make sense. Jack knew of no medication that couldn't have been taken before she left her house, and even if there was one it wouldn't explain the incorrect amounts of tea left. Amanda hadn't had enough to empty half of one of the skins, and Jack clearly remembered that the one he'd drunk from had been full to begin with. And the one with the bitter taste had been hidden away, supposedly completely out of sight. . . .

"So what am I expected to deduce from that?" he mumbled as he made his way through the wineshop toward the cellar door, adding to his characterization without realizing it. "That I was the one who drank from the skin which contained the adulterated tea, and she drank from the other? A second skin that had started out less than full to make it *look* as if its contents had been consumed? Why would she have added something in the first place?"

Banging his head against those unanswerable questions was making Jack dizzy, but simply shrugging them off wasn't possible. He washed and shaved and dressed while mentally toying with explanations, but nothing made sense. Jack's hired carriage waited outside when he finally left, and he rode to the Lavering house trying to rehearse apologies for the night before. Getting one of those apologies accepted was a necessary first step toward discussing Amanda again, but Jack's mind kept drifting back to the mystery of the second waterskin.

Once inside the Lavering house, Jack was left in the entrance hall a good deal longer than he'd been the day before. When he was finally summoned into Lavering's study his host again stood behind his desk, but without a smile or an offered handshake.

"Please, Lavering, you have a perfect right to be furious with me," Jack began as soon as he entered. "I've come now with my apologies and an explanation, and ask only that you hear me out."

Lavering hesitated, obviously trying to decide between hearing him out and throwing him out, but finally settled on the former. It was clear he'd realized Jack could always be thrown out later, and then no one could accuse him of having refused to listen to reason.

"I can give you five minutes," Lavering said grudgingly, gesturing to the servant at the door to leave. "Please be brief and then go."

"This is really decent of you," Jack enthused as he sat, playing the innocent who was incapable of noticing how cold the atmosphere was. "I was so afraid you'd refuse to see me at all. Yes, well, I can see you want me to get on with it, so I will. The way I disappeared last night was inexcusable, but I was given no choice. It was either help old Cobby, or have his father find out when Cobby made a spectacle of himself."

"Who are you talking about?" Lavering asked with a continuing frown. "And *what* are you talking about?"

"If you don't know Cobby by that name, I'm afraid it would be indiscreet of me to tell you who he is." Jack wore his apologetic look, but under it he was pleased and encouraged. Lavering was the decent sort, and because of that Jack knew he couldn't help but take the bait. "I *can* say he's an old friend of mine who has fallen for a young lady of—uncertain—reputation. She's been leading him on, pretending she's mad for him, but all she's really interested in are those gifts he's been spending everything he has on. He wanted to marry her, but he's only a younger son and she's after bigger fish."

"I say, what a nasty turn of events," Lavering exclaimed, and now his frown was for something other than Jack.

"More than nasty," Jack agreed solemnly. "He spent a good part of yesterday drinking, getting his courage up for the party. He knew he would see her, you understand, and was going to demand that she marry him. The rest of us knew she would laugh in his face, and then there would be the most awful scene, so *we* took matters in hand. We spent some time getting Cobby sobered up a bit, and then I had a talk with the young lady. There was a way out of that mess, but only if she cooperated."

"What was the way?" Lavering asked, leaning forward with intense interest. "I shouldn't think freeing a man from his own folly is all that easy."

"Oh, it isn't," Jack agreed, also leaning forward. "At first the young lady was prepared to laugh at *me,* but I made it quite clear that among the bunch of us who were Cobby's friends, we had quite a lot of push to swing about in the form of our fathers. My father, for instance, wouldn't have hesitated to help out in such a good cause, and then the young lady would have found life in London quite intolerable. She didn't much like hearing that, but once she understood I was neither joking nor bluffing, she agreed to go along with the story we'd prepared."

"Which was?" Lavering prompted, still deeply interested.

"Why, that she couldn't marry Cobby because she was already married," Jack explained with a wave of his hand. "It was the only excuse Cobby would have been able to accept, simply because he had no choice. She was to explain that her husband came from a good family, but an accident had crippled him right after he found out his family was impoverished because of his father's constant gaming. She'd taken to supporting herself and her husband on the gifts given to her by admirers, but she'd grown ashamed of the deception and was giving up the life to go home to the man she loved."

"And he believed that drivel?" Lavering demanded with a snort. "A woman who deceives a man *has* no conscience, so how can she be bothered by what isn't there?"

"If Cobby wasn't the sort to believe that, he never would have fallen into her hands to begin with," Jack pointed out. "He cried when she told him, and gave her every sovereign he had with him, but did accept that it was over. Half of us took Cobby home, and the other half accompanied the woman to be certain she packed up and left. A ship was departing for France on the morning tide, and we made sure she went with it."

"Well, you certainly had an eventful night," Lavering said as he leaned back in his chair again. "That Cobby fellow is more fortunate than he knows to have such good friends. It so happens I saw you dancing with the young lady in question, and discovered that no one seemed to know anything about her even though she appeared at parties on a regular basis. It's a relief to know she won't do so again."

Jack nodded his agreement, privately pleased he'd been able to put Miss Landers to such good use. No matter what the authorities decided to do about her and her family, allowing them to go back to their old ways wasn't likely to be one of the options. Jack had been certain he'd been seen dancing with the girl, so he'd been careful to come up with a story that covered the point.

"I'll confess I was more than annoyed over your behavior," Lavering continued, "but it isn't possible to blame a man for being loyal to a friend. I would have appreciated a quick word in explanation last night, but I can see where circumstances simply swept you along. Now that I know the truth, we'll forget the incident ever occurred."

"That's really decent of you, Lavering," Jack said quickly, sensing he was about to be dismissed. "I think you know how anxious I am to retain your good opinion of me, but I've done a lot of thinking since yesterday, and there's something I need to make a clean breast of. It involves Amanda—Miss Edmunds—of course, and—she's at home now, I trust?"

"No, as a matter of fact she isn't," Lavering answered, back to frowning at Jack. "What can you possibly have to make a clean breast about with my sister?"

"You must understand at the outset that it wasn't in any way her fault," Jack hastened to assure his host, no longer completely at ease while letting the lies flow as they willed. It was time for the truth, which always turned out to be harder for a man. "She is and has been a perfect lady, but I—am guilty of a—serious breech in gentlemanly behavior. In all truth, honor demands that I offer nothing less than marriage."

"Does it indeed," Lavering commented, once again leaning back in his chair. Jack couldn't help noticing that unexpectedly calm reaction, just as though he'd confessed to catching a glimpse of Amanda's ankle. As a matter of fact it was too mild a reaction even for ankle-glimpsing, and Jack was back to being very confused.

"So you've done something that requires you to marry my sister," Lavering continued in that same, unnaturally even manner. "I'd be interested to know just exactly what that was."

"Good God, man, are you asking for details?" Jack demanded in outrage and embarrassment. "This is your sister we're discussing, not some strumpet off the street! I—dishonored her, though it wasn't my intention to cause her harm. I must have lost my senses for a time, but now that I have them back I'm willing to do the honorable thing. You certainly can't refuse to allow *that.*"

"The word 'outrageous' comes most immediately to mind," Lavering murmured with an odd smile, almost as an aside, and then he raised his voice a bit. "I'm continually amazed at how often my sister's expectations prove to be correct. But let's get back to this—dishonoring—you did. Just when and where did it occur, and why do you suppose Amanda neglected to mention it to me?"

"Ah . . . when and where," Jack echoed lamely, suddenly aware of the box in which he found himself. He couldn't very well tell Lavering the truth about that, not when the following chain of questions and answers would lead back to why he'd had to help Amanda in the first place. The work he did for the Crown was not to be discussed under any circumstances, even if he left the position. He knew he'd have to come up with something other than the truth, but Jack's being unprepared to lie left his host to speak first.

"You seem to be having difficulty answering my questions, so allow me to answer them for you." Lavering's tone was no longer mild, and true anger blazed out of his eyes. "You're unable to tell me when and where you dishonored my sister for the same reason she made no mention of it: the situation never occurred. You've become obsessed with marrying a woman who finds herself uncomfortable in your presence, and when I refused your suit you came up with this ridiculous story. Just how gullible do you think I am, Michaels?"

That last was said with a good deal of heat, and Jack hadn't the first clue about how to answer the demand. Lavering had eagerly swallowed the tale made from whole cloth, and now balked at the absolute truth! If the situation hadn't been so damnably frustrating, Jack would have thrown his head back and laughed.

"And now, I think, this interview is over," Lavering said, rising to stand very straight behind his desk. "I believe you'll understand when I say I don't expect to ever see you in this house—or near my sister—again."

For an instant Jack felt the urge to argue, but it was perfectly clear how little good that would do. Instead he rose and gave his host a formal bow, then he turned and left. A moment later he was back in his carriage, completely out of ideas. His last chance had exploded in his face like a faulty pistol, and the worst part of it was that he didn't know *why*. He added that unanswered "why" to the others he'd collected, brooded for a moment, then gave his driver directions to his father's London house. Jack needed to speak to someone he could unburden himself to, and his father had always been the best one to fill that role.

When the servant who opened the door announced that Duke Edward had left for a fortnight in the country, Jack began to wonder why the Fates had suddenly turned against him. He stood there in the middle of the magnificent entry hall he'd always loved, feeling totally abandoned and equally unsure about what to do next. The servants would know to which country house his father had gone. Should he find out and follow, or stay where the source of his problem was?

"Why, Mr. Michaels, how nice to see you," a cool voice said, causing Jack to look up. "If you've come to speak to your father, I'm afraid you've missed him by two days."

Jack silently apologized to the Fates for having doubted their support. Despite the cool welcome, the man walking toward him was Soong Tao, the man who had been his closest friend for many years, who had encouraged him to take the position with the Crown he hadn't been sure he was worthy of. Tao was only a few years older than Jack, and had taught him Chinese boxing when Duke Edward had defied convention and taken a starving, barbaric foreigner into his employ. Tao was fiercely loyal to the man who had rescued him from the streets, and his high intelligence and ability had paid off for his patron time and time again.

"Tao, I'm surprised that you're still here," Jack returned just as coolly as he nodded to the man. "You're usually at my father's side, guarding him from every danger imaginable."

"One may do no more than one's best," Tao returned with a wry bow, privately but clearly enjoying the faint hostility and scorn they'd arranged to show each other in public. "For the moment it's been left to those I trained to guard your father, for I've been given a different task. I'm certain you're far too busy to be interested in the details."

"As a matter of fact, I've all the time in the world," Jack countered airily with a wave of his hand. "I can drink a cup or two of tea while you're making the effort to explain."

Tao bowed stiffly in agreement, pretending to be insulted while he asked the waiting servant to have tea brought to his office. He was also silent while he led Jack through the house and to that office, but as soon as he closed the door behind the two of them he turned with a grin and an outstretched hand.

"It's good to see you again, brother," he said warmly, clapping Jack's shoulder while they shook hands. "You don't come around nearly enough to suit me *or* His Grace."

"A reputation as a black sheep has to be carefully maintained, brother," Jack countered with a laugh, already feeling somewhat better. "I'm seriously in need of someone to talk to, and since my father isn't here you can consider yourself trapped. If you have the time, that is."

"At the moment I have all the time you need," Tao assured him, quickly sobering. "Your father left me here to finish up a business matter that refused to resolve itself quickly, but it's all settled now. I'd planned to leave tomorrow to rejoin him, but if you need my help I can easily put off leaving."

"It may not come to that, but I can't be sure," Jack said with a sigh, taking the chair in front of Tao's desk. Tao clearly noticed the weary way he sat, but said nothing as he took his own seat. "I suppose it all started about five years ago, at Master Ma's school, where *you* told me to go," Jack began, running a hand through his hair. "Life is always a series of full circles, I know, but I never realized how easy it is to get run over when one of those circles starts to close up behind you."

Jack spent the next few minutes telling Tao everything that had happened, interrupting the narrative only when the tea was brought. While the housemaid was in the room Jack wove tales of his female conquests and winnings at gambling, but as soon as she was gone he continued with the real story. Toward the end of the narrative his vast confusion showed through, turning the precise reconstruction into a sloppy fisherman's net with more holes than solid weaving.

"So that's where I am at the moment," Jack finished up, still feeling as if he were missing something important. "Not only don't I understand how *she* behaved, I'm completely at sea over the way her brother acted. If it was your sister someone told you he'd ruined, wouldn't you be at the very least bothered?"

"Not if I knew it wasn't the truth," Tao commented, his brows drawn together into a deep frown. "If the confession came out of the blue I would certainly wonder at least for a while, but if someone had warned me that I would be lied to I'd react just the way Lavering did. Give you just enough rope to hang yourself, and then throw you out."

"But that's not possible," Jack said with a small laugh of incredulity. "How could anyone have warned him about anything when even I wasn't sure about whether or not to confess? The one doing it would have to be a sorcerer."

"Or a dragon," Tao suggested, his face now impassive. "You *have* heard that dragons are supposed to have had magical powers?"

"That's even more ridiculous," Jack said with a snort. "We're discussing reality here, not fantasy. I—"

"Ah, I see you've just remembered," Tao said, the words smooth with satisfaction. "There does happen to be a dragon involved with your reality, even though she's only a silken one. My people have learned that a dragon doesn't have to have wings and scales in order to be a true dragon."

"Is that observation supposed to help me?" Jack demanded, more with frustration than anger. "You're suggesting all this strangeness is Amanda's doing, but that can't be true. She may have a stronger mind than many *men* I know but she rarely even argues with anyone, let alone starts trouble. And even beyond that Lavering may love her, but he'd never dream of letting her direct him."

"Then you're saying that what you told me isn't true," Tao pressed, leaning back to pin Jack with an unrelenting gaze. "She wasn't the one who recognized you, realized you had secrets, and used the threat of revealing those secrets to force you into doing her bidding. She wasn't the one who decided to launch her own investigation into the disappearance of that man, believing she would do a better job of it than those who had investigated before her. She wasn't even the one who forced you to take her with you to watch the clerk's house two nights ago—"

"All right, all right," Jack conceded with both hands raised. "Maybe I do keep forgetting how really capable she is. That happens to be one of my main reasons for being attracted to her, and— Wait a minute. I've just thought of something that probably proves you're right."

"And what is that?" Tao asked, for some reason looking less than pleased with Jack's capitulation.

"I must have hurt her deeply when I—lost control of myself," Jack explained, suddenly feeling worse than ever. "That she was there was her own fault, proving how wrong she'd been to trust me. She was too ashamed to tell her brother how big a mistake she'd made, so she must have told him she feared me and begged him to send me packing. She must have also warned him that I'd lie to him, and that's why he didn't believe me."

"My poor brother," Tao commented, his tone showing none of the supposed compassion of his words. "Falling in love has not only blinded him, it's also turned him stupid. If I didn't know how quick a mind you usually have, Jack, I'd be tempted to wonder why you weren't in the care of a keeper."

"What's *that* supposed to mean?" Jack asked, feeling a flush of embarrassment in his cheeks. Tao hadn't spoken to him like that since he was a boy, and it had usually meant he'd made a pure fool of himself.

"It means you're interpreting actions and motives without making them match that real world you're so fond of," Tao told him flatly. "There's also something you don't yet know, but let's take care of the misinterpretation first. Would you say Richard Lavering's first concern right now is to see his sister as well married as he can possibly arrange?"

"Of course," Jack agreed, wishing he could see where Tao was leading.

"It so happens I know Lord Pembroke," Tao continued, "not to speak to, but I've observed him with others. He's certainly a nice enough fellow, but when it comes to putting up with nonsense, his patience is nonexistent. Now tell me how good a catch *you're* considered to be, especially if you're willing to give up your—disreputable habits."

"I'd be considered a great catch," Jack responded with a frown. "Especially since my father has done his part by saying how grateful he would be to any woman who set me on the straight and narrow. Considering the wealth and influence my family has, a woman could do worse marrying a man with a title, even if I *am* only a younger son. That's why I don't understand . . ."

"Yes?" Tao prompted when Jack's words trailed off. "Were you about to say that's why you don't understand how Lavering could dismiss you like that? A minute ago you said it was because Miss Edmunds told him she feared you. Assuming she did exactly that, would he have been moved to agree?"

"No," Jack was forced to admit. "Young girls are often afraid of the man they're told to marry, but they usually get over it. Lavering might have tried to soothe her fears, but he would have paid little or no attention to them. That means she must have told him something else entirely."

"About time you saw that," Tao muttered, then raised his voice back to normal levels. "And please don't suggest again that she told him you would lie about having violated her. Anyone but a moron would immediately wonder why she would suggest something like that, and then the truth would come out. No, I'm certain she was considerably more subtle, which was why Lavering believed her. She strikes me as excellent proof that even barbarians can learn to be civilized if they're raised properly."

For once Jack didn't rise to the bait and insist that Tao was the barbarian. He was too busy seeing that Tao was right; Amanda had learned the roundabout but incredibly effective tactics of the Orient, all right, and he'd been fighting that blindfolded with his hands tied behind his back.

"But that still doesn't explain everything," he protested. "Even if she doesn't like me, her investigation isn't yet over so she still needs me. Why maneuver her brother into throwing me out when she could have remained safe by never again being completely alone with me? And how in the blazes did she know I would ask for her hand? Since she got Lavering to refuse she *did* know, but why would she expect a bounder to turn around and do the honorable thing?"

"Now *that's* the question you need more information in order to answer," Tao said, leaning his arm on the desk in front of him. "Let's start by discussing the possibility that she knew you *weren't* a bounder. In that event, would she have had any doubt that you would do the honorable thing?"

"I certainly hope not," Jack said with a snort, and then something else occurred to him. "But wait a minute. The only way she could have known I'd do the honorable thing is if she also knew I didn't mean to violate her, but that still leaves the question of how. Unless . . . those two waterskins with the tea . . . but how could she possibly have . . . ?"

"It was probably the substance called Claws of the Tiger," Tao said, watching him closely. "The men of my country learn about it early, since the women certainly do. Some men, having taken too many wives and concubines, pretend they don't know it's being used on them, but most consider it a slur on their manhood. What I can't understand is why the young lady would use it on *you*. You don't precisely have a reputation for being virtuous."

"I *was* being virtuous," Jack growled, now furious rather than upset. "I knew she was here to be married and that I couldn't marry her, so I kept my distance. Even though that was the last thing I wanted to— Damn it, she *raped* me! She forced me to her will just as surely as if she'd used greater strength, and I'll be *damned* if I let her get away with it!"

"What are you going to do?" Tao asked, watching as Jack got to his feet, strode to a bellcord and pulled. "If you make too much of a scene there will be repercussions, and that won't do you or your father any good."

"The only scene I'm going to make is with Miss Edmunds herself," Jack returned, still in a growl. The *nerve* of that—! "I can see now how hard she worked to get me alone, and how lucky it was that she wore her *chih fu* instead of a gown. If she'd been in a gown, I might have had too much trouble reaching her— Ah, Banders. Please send Jeremy in here. I have a chore I'd like him to see to."

The servant Banders, who had come in answer to the bell, bowed and left again, which told Jack that Jeremy was available. It hadn't occurred to him that the man might not be, not when he needed him so badly. Tao didn't ask his question again, but Jack knew it wasn't because he no longer wanted to know the scheme. After he heard what Jeremy was to do, he'd ask again if necessary.

A long moment passed while Jack paced silently, and then a knock brought Jeremy into the room. The young serving man had a round, open, and friendly face that matched his personality perfectly. People loved to talk to Jeremy and tell him things, especially people of the lower class, who generally knew all there was to know. Jack had found him invaluable the time or two he'd used Jeremy to help him unofficially, and Jeremy's quick intelligence had led Jack to recommend him to Sir Charles. He had no idea if anything had come of the recommendation, but right now that wasn't his concern.

"Jeremy, it's good to see you again," Jack said briskly as he headed for Tao's desk. "Tao, a sheet of blank paper and an envelope, if you please."

Tao handed them over without question, and once Jack had folded the blank paper and put it in the envelope, he wrote "Miss Amanda Edmunds" on the envelope's face and then turned back to Jeremy.

"My carriage is right outside," he told the man, handing over the envelope. "Have the driver take you to Miss Edmunds's house, but don't go in. What I want to know is when she'll be back, so finding out when she left and with whom might be helpful. If the question comes up, you *can't* leave the envelope for her. You've been told to put it into no one's hands but her own, and that's why you want to know when she'll return."

" 'Cause I got a girl o' me own, an' don't like keepin' 'er waitin'," Jeremy added with a grin as he took the envelope. "That 'un works every time. I'll get what ya need, Mr. Michaels, and—thanks fer *everythin'*."

The sober look he gave Jack before he left let Jack know that Sir Charles had taken his recommendation. Jeremy remained in his present employ, but he now had an unmentioned employer as well.

"Jeremy does have a talent for finding things out," Tao said as Jack turned away from the door. "That means you'll soon know when the girl is expected to return, so what do you intend to do after that?"

"Find a way to get her alone," Jack answered, dropping into his chair again. "I'm going to know why she did it, I'm going to have a real, sincere apology, and then I'm going to turn the tables on her. This time *she'll* be the one who's taken advantage of—even if she *has* decided she wants nothing more to do with me."

"And how have you come to *that* conclusion?" Tao asked, obviously having heard the words Jack had only muttered. "For a woman to do what she did usually indicates more than a passing interest, you know. Why should she go to such extremes only to decide she wants nothing to do with you?"

"How can we possibly understand the way a woman's mind works?" Jack countered with a shrug, reaching for his cup and its undoubtedly cold tea. "All I know is what I can see, and that includes the fact that her brother has thrown me out even though he shouldn't have. We've agreed that that has to be *her* doing, so what other conclusion can I come to? She's had me thrown out because she wants nothing more to do with me."

"The logic of that is difficult to argue," Tao admitted with a sigh. "But you were also right in saying we can't know the workings of the female mind. Be sure you know the real truth behind her actions before you punish her for them."

"Punishing is what she needs no matter what her reasons were," Jack told him sourly after finishing the cold tea in an unsatisfying gulp. "Anyone called the Silken Dragon has to have been getting her own way for a very long time, but she has to learn there are limits. You can't violate people and then simply shrug and walk away.... Well, let's talk about something else until Jeremy gets back. Am I right in assuming that my father has finally talked you into changing from guarding him to helping him handle business matters?"

"Duke Edward is a very persuasive man," Tao allowed with another sigh. "I tried to point out that putting a foreigner in charge of important matters would cause hard feelings among many of the Europeans who serve him, but he refused to accept that sound reasoning any longer. His last three secretaries have been walking disasters, without an ounce of business sense among them. If His Grace's interests weren't going to all fold up and die, I *had* to take the position."

"And you've been doing very well at it," Jack told him with a smile. "I know that from the way the household staff treats you. They're all extremely loyal to my father, and if they had reason to feel hostility toward you their lack of efficiency would show it. But they're very efficient in responding to you, so they must know you're helping your employer despite your reservations. They'd appreciate something like that—unless you've threatened them?"

"No, I haven't threatened them," Tao said with an involuntary grin. "They're good people whom I've known for years, and they do seem to know what a mess I was given to straighten out. That I succeeded seems to have made them proud of me, but they weren't the ones I expected to dislike my promotion. The people I anticipated hard feelings from haven't disappointed me."

"But you still can't let them bother you," Jack said, reaching over to pour himself more tea. "If they haven't gotten themselves a similar position, it's either because they're incompetent or because they aren't capable of loyalty. In either event, the fault is theirs rather than yours even if they won't admit it."

Tao shrugged and smiled his "inscrutable" smile—meaning he wasn't about to discuss that particular point—so they went on to talk about other things. Jack was definitely enjoying himself, but he was also very aware of the time passing. He expected it to be quite a while before Jeremy learned what he wanted to know, and was therefore taken by surprise when a knock brought the young serving man into the room in a very short amount of time.

"Good grief, man, you've barely had the time to get there and back," Jack told him as he rose. "Did something go wrong?"

"Not in th' way you're thinkin', Mr. Michaels," Jeremy

hastened to assure him. "It's just that th' luck was really wi' me, an' this pretty little thing was sweepin' th' entrance step at a house acrost th' street. She knowed all about Lord Pembroke's sister—includin' the' fact that th' girl left this mornin' f'r her brother's country house. Since th' lord an' his fam'ly will be followin' in about a sennight, it ain't likely th' young lady'll be back too soon."

"She's gone to Lavering's country house?" Jack echoed with a frown. "But that doesn't make any sense when her investigation isn't finished. Where is his country house?"

"Braxton Meadows," Tao supplied when Jeremy only shrugged. "I know because your father also has a house there, and Lord and Lady Pembroke were His Grace's guests the last time we were up there. These days everyone wants a house in the area, but there's only so much land to go around. And, by the way, that's where His Grace happens to be right now."

"I should have known," Jack muttered as he closed his eyes and rubbed them. "The hellion hasn't given up her investigation, she's just changed its location. And now she obviously expects to handle it alone—when there's someone involved who kills as casually as another man brushes away lint. If she's still alive when I get up there, *I'm* going to kill her."

"You'll be going up with me tomorrow, then?" Tao asked, also standing. "If so, I'll have to make arrangements—"

"No," Jack denied, already heading for the door. "I'm leaving as soon as I can pack a few things, which means I'll be up there tonight. Try to look surprised if I show up on my father's doorstep tomorrow. I doubt if I'll be in the mood for longwinded explanations."

Tao seemed to have something else to say, but Jack had no time to listen. He had a harebrained female to catch up to, one who had used him as badly as some men were said to use women. He had no idea what would happen when he saw her again, but *something* would, that he swore!

Chapter 15

Pei fell asleep during the trip to Braxton Meadows, but Amanda couldn't seem to do the same. It wasn't London or the English countryside that kept her attention, just the same thoughts that had been whirling through her mind since yesterday. Leaving London meant leaving Jack Michaels behind, and although most of her said "Good riddance!", the rest of her didn't agree. It would probably take quite a while before she forgot how much she loved that miserable man, and until it happened all she could do was ignore the pain. And it wasn't as though she didn't deserve it, after all. She'd known she meant nothing serious to him, so she should have simply kept away. But that hadn't given him the right to flaunt that disgusting blonde the way he had. . . .

Amanda took a number of deep breaths to calm herself again, something she'd had to do over and over during the trip. Her thoughts kept blazing around in the same circle, and it was a positive relief when the coach turned into a long drive. That should mean they'd arrived, somewhat behind the wagons that had started out hours earlier. The wagons contained provisions, furniture, clothing and servants, most of what was needed to ready the house for its owner's eventual arrival.

The wagons had apparently made good time, as everything had already been unloaded from them and a light lunch had been prepared for her and Pei. The cook from the village had also been sent for, Amanda was told, so dinner that night would be a much tastier and more sub-stantial affair. She and Pei took off their hats and cloaks and gloves and left them in the rooms being readied for them, ate their lunch, then went for a walk to look over the estate.

"It's truly lovely up here," Pei said after a while, the first real words either of them had spoken since they'd ar-rived. "I expect to enjoy this time, but you don't seem to feel the same. If you're that unhappy, why don't you re-turn to London?"

"And do what with myself?" Amanda countered without looking up from the grass underfoot. "Attend more parties where I'll meet even more uninteresting men? At least here I can talk to Mr. Lichfield's family, and try to learn something that will give me a lead to what's become of him. First thing tomorrow I'm going to walk to the village and see what I can find out."

"I'll walk with you, of course," Pei said, and then, after a brief hesitation, asked, "What will you do if that baron does follow you up here? With no one else coming calling, he'll be able to monopolize your time."

"What do you think I'll do?" Amanda growled, know-ing how—proddish—she sounded, but helpless to change it. "I'll greet him with a sweet smile and spend as much time in his company as he wants me to. By the time Rich-ard gets up here the baron ought to be ready to ask for my hand, which Richard will happily give him. Then all the nonsense will be over and done with, and I won't need to be bothered with courting again."

Pei started to say something but changed her mind, which Amanda considered very wise of her. The Silken Dragon had made up her mind that since she had to marry, any man would do. One would be as bad as any other, so why prolong the boredom looking for what she would never find? Amanda had started out looking forward to be-ing married, but it hadn't taken long to cure her of that foolishness.

"What will you do if Mr. Michaels decides not to give

up?" Pei finally ventured, apparently having chosen her words carefully. "Yesterday he seemed really determined, and that was *after* you told him to forget about marriage. What if *he* follows you up here?"

"How is he supposed to find out where I've gone?" Amanda asked sourly, walking over to a tree to study its bark. "You can be sure Richard won't tell him, which will save me the trouble of having the man thrown out myself. I never want to see him again, and I mean that with everything in me."

Pei seemed to know that Amanda had spoken the truth, and thereafter found nothing else to say. They walked around the grounds in silence for a while, then visited the garden Richard was so proud of until they needed to return inside for teatime. The garden *was* beautiful, but Amanda was in no mood to appreciate it.

Dinner continued the silence between Amanda and Pei, except when they were forced to comment about the quality of the cooking. The woman from the village beamed with pleasure when she was brought out to hear their compliments, but that was the highlight of the evening. They finally left the dining room to discover that it had started to rain, which ended the day perfectly.

"I think I'll go to my rooms and read for a while," Pei said as Amanda stood looking out of a window at the rain. "Unless you'd rather have someone to talk to."

Pei's words were almost plaintive, and Amanda just had to turn to her and take her hand.

"Pei, you're the best friend in the world, but tonight I'm not even as good as the worst," she said by way of apology. "I didn't sleep very well last night, and I didn't even nap coming up here. Tonight I mean to do better, so by tomorrow I ought to be fit to associate with again. Unless you really want to put up with more of what you went through today, going to your rooms to read is a very good idea."

"And you can use the time alone," Pei said with that faint smile that warmed Amanda so. "With the size of this house, the few servants your brother sent don't even begin to fill it. Have your time alone, and tomorrow we'll walk to the village together."

Pei squeezed Amanda's fingers encouragingly, and then she turned and left the large withdrawing room. Amanda thought for the thousandth time how good it was to have a friend who really understood her, and then the brooding took over again.

Amanda wandered around the large house for a while, but the emptiness somehow felt disturbing even though she needed to be alone. She eventually went to her rooms and called a maid to help her undress, but it took the girl an unusually long time to get there. Apparently the servants' quarters were on the other side of the house, and there weren't enough of them to have someone up and around until everyone in the house retired.

Once the girl was gone, Amanda opened her balcony doors and stood looking out at the rain. She was still unused to viewing the world from higher than ground level, but the deep silence—except for the sound of rain—was very soothing. She ought to be able to sleep tonight, without even a single candle flame or sound to disturb the silence and darkness. Pei's rooms were across the hall, which meant she might as well be in another world.

After a while Amanda felt chilly in her fragile, open-patterned lace nightgown, so she turned the lamp down, carried a candle to her bedside table, and got into bed. Not that she expected to fall asleep quickly, no matter what she'd told Pei. The mattress was comfortable and the quilts warm, but there were too many things disturbing her mind for her to relax. Especially the things about Jack Michaels. In the flickering light of the candle she could almost see him, and unsurprisingly her desire for him had increased. Amanda wanted him desperately, but would probably never even see him again.

At some point Amanda fell asleep, but that didn't keep Jack Michaels from her mind. He was so real to her it was as if he had appeared from nowhere and had gotten into bed beside her, his hard, beautiful body bare under the quilts. She reveled in the sensation of her hand brushing his chest and feeling the curly mat of hair. *What a wonderful dream,* she thought with a smile as he moved even closer to her, the smell of rain emanating from him. *I can not only see him, I can even feel him.*

And then she felt even more when his big right hand gently covered her left breast, stroking it as though he'd been aching to touch her. His dream fingers felt so odd through the lace, close and yet far away, intimate and at the same time distant. Amanda wasn't sure she liked the sensation, but her dream Jack was able to anticipate her. He moved the wide, loose sleeves all the way down her arms, then helped her free those arms one at a time from the confines of the nightgown. Her arms were now free and bare, as were her breasts.

And that, apparently, was what the dream Jack had been after. He stroked her breast one more time before lowering his face to it, and then her nipple was on fire; his lips and tongue seemed to be trying to ignite her soul. Amanda moaned and tried to move away, but his hands on her arms kept her where she was. After an almost unbearable moment he gave his attention to her right breast, but that was no help at all. The flame he'd ignited had begun to spread through her blood, heating and burning wherever it went.

Amanda wanted to touch her dream man as well, but in that respect he wasn't quite as cooperative. When she tried to free her arms his lips left her breast, and then they were on her lips and taking a kiss. And what a kiss! Not in the least hesitant, so passionate and unrefusable! It was the Golden Devil demanding what he wanted, and Amanda found it impossible to deny him—or herself. She returned his kiss with the same unchained passion, searching for his soul even as he discovered and appropriated hers.

Now a moan spread throughout Amanda's body along with the fire, especially when her dream Jack slid his hand under her nightgown and began to stroke it slowly up her thigh. That was when she discovered he now held her

arms above her head by the wrists with one hand, still refusing to let her touch him. The refusal made her furious
and she tried to fight her way free, but the Golden Devil
had no trouble keeping her right where he wanted her. His
lips stole the words of anger from hers even before they
were spoken, and his unavoidable hand explored her as it
willed.

By then Amanda wanted him inside her even more desperately than before, but all he did was tease her flesh to
glowing flames. It was almost as if he were punishing her
for what she'd done to him, but that was foolish. He was
only a dream, and even the real Jack didn't know what
she'd done. She whimpered as he touched her womanhood
with a thumb, tried to raise her hips and lure him to her,
but his big body held hers down, allowing free movement
only to his hand.

Ages went by before he stopped tormenting her.
Amanda came half out of the fever dream to realize that
his knees were between her thighs, and then his manhood
was probing at her desire, searching for the way to her fur-
nace of flames. For the briefest instant Amanda considered
refusing him as he had refused her for so long, but that
was impossible. She would have fought her way through
an entire flight of dragons to share lovemaking with Jack
Michaels, and now that he was ready to do the same she
was not about to deny herself.

Even if he *was* only a dream. Some distant part of her
mind remembered that and expected disappointment, but
instead was incredibly shocked. The manhood that thrust
into her was thick and hard, intent on reaching the core of
her heat! She tried to gasp but his mouth still retained possession of hers, and then she was drowned by an ocean of
no longer restrained motion. All rational thought became
impossible when the thrust was repeated over and over,
harder and harder, again and again. It was exactly what
she wanted, and she happily lost herself to it.

Time has no meaning in a land of pure sensation, only
satisfaction does. Amanda lost count of how many times

she fell from that glorious, breathless height of fulfillment, but after the last time she felt close to exhaustion. She lay still for quite a number of minutes, expecting to fall asleep once her breath returned, but it slowly came to her that that wasn't possible just yet. She may have been asleep when that time of unreality began, but now she was fully awake and wanted some answers.

Sitting up and looking to her right showed something other than the empty bed a dream would have left behind. Jack Michaels himself lay there, still covered in sweat and still breathing harder than usual. His eyes were closed as he worked to regather his strength, but he must have felt her stare. He opened beautiful dark eyes to look at her in the flickering candlelight, and Amanda had to repress the faint tendrils of a desire too ready to return.

"I thought you were a dream," she said, trying not to sound accusing but failing. "What are you doing in my bed?"

"Making love to you," he answered with a grin in those eyes, one finger reaching out to touch her still-bare right nipple. "I thought sure you'd noticed."

"That isn't funny!" she snapped, knocking his hand away and quickly squirming back into her nightgown. "You have no business being here at all, let alone being in my bed. How did you find me?"

"Did you really think you could hide from someone in my line of work?" he asked, his amusement increased. "I know you're used to getting your own way, *Ssu Te Lung,* but that's about to end."

Amanda dismissed whatever words she would have spoken, pulled up short by his calling her Silken Dragon. His knowing that could only be due to Pei's lack of discretion, but the most important question had become what else he knew.

"So your method of disallowing women their own way is to sneak into their bedchambers and ravish them," she said after her momentary pause, forcing her voice to sound toneless but wounded. If she could manage to wrap him in guilt, he might forget whatever it was he'd guessed. "I always knew there was the possibility of that, but I thought—"

Amanda broke off in midsentence to look down at her hands, giving Jack the chance to finish her sentence for himself with the suggestion that she'd thought she could trust him.

"If you're thinking of turning all this into *my* fault, you can forget about it," Jack said, all amusement now apparently gone. "I happen to know for certain that you're the one who started this game, so I'm fully within my rights to continue it. Which I mean to do at every opportunity, both before and after we're married."

"Married?" Amanda echoed, now even more shocked as she stared at his unsmiling face. "You know you don't really want to marry me—"

"At first I didn't, but I've since changed my mind," he drawled, moving possessive eyes over her body. "You'll do well enough for warming my bed, and having to marry me despite all your machinations should teach you an important lesson. I don't like being manipulated in any way, not directly and not through others, and in this instance I refuse to stand for it. When I'm your husband, we'll have regular discussions about the dangers of interfering with the wrong people."

If Amanda had felt chilled before, his expression now made her feel buried in ice. She'd been right about his not wanting her, but now he meant to marry her as a punishment. This wasn't the Jack Michaels she'd thought she knew, and tendrils of fear began to quiver through her body.

"And I think you've already started to learn an important lesson." While her gaze was caught in the swirls of the quilt, his voice came again, somehow not as hard and relentless as it had been. "Something you consider a lark can turn into a nightmare, and all through not having used the least amount of common sense and good judgment.

You've got to learn to think before you act, and sometimes not to act at all. You—"

"Just a minute!" Amanda interrupted sharply, now staring at him again where he lay raised up on one elbow. "You're lying there and lecturing me, talking about larks turning into nightmares? That means you weren't serious a minute ago. All that about marrying me just to hurt me— you were just trying to frighten me!"

"Accomplishing more than trying, I'd say," he returned dryly. "The way your face paled said you got the message, which shows you're finally beginning to be sensible. There are no guarantees in getting your own way, because there's always the possibility that tomorrow could bring you something you were neither expecting nor prepared for, and the nightmare would then become real. But there's something else we need to talk about, and now's—"

"Get out," Amanda interrupted hoarsely, so furious that even her voice was beyond her control. "Take your things and get out of here, or so help me God, I'll—"

"Calm down," he interrupted in turn, his tone sharper. "You deserved to be frightened at the very least, so you have nothing to complain about. What we have to discuss is the fact that I wasn't joking when I said I intend to marry you, so—"

"Marry me!" Amanda echoed again, only this time in a screech, rising to her knees. "I wouldn't marry you if *God* proposed on your behalf! I want you *out* of my bedchamber and *out* of my life! *Now!*"

He parted his lips to say something else, but Amanda was all through with listening. Of course he wanted to marry her. Despite the fact that he now seemed to know he wasn't responsible for ravishing her, his conscience probably still bothered him. Or maybe he'd decided to use her for appearances' sake while he snuck around enjoying himself with that blonde. Amanda didn't know his reasons but she also didn't care, not while she was filled with towering rage.

From her knees she threw a fist at the miserable man's

face, bringing it forward from belt level with every bit of her body weight behind it. If she'd connected she would have done a lot of damage, but the idiot yelped as he ducked aside, then rolled completely out of the way. He came up on his own knees on the other side of the bed, and pointed a finger at her.

"Stop that right now!" he ordered, trying to look stern. "We both know I'm the better fighter, so— No!"

Amanda had risen to her feet, and his second yelp came when she crossed the bed holding her nightgown high and launched a side kick at his face. He managed to avoid that second attack, too, but had to throw himself off the bed to do it. He landed on the floor with a carpet-muffled thump among his scattered clothes, and looked up at her angrily.

"All right!" he snapped, one hand up with his palm toward her. "My being better than you doesn't help when I can't make myself box with a woman. We'll continue this conversation at another time, but we *will* continue it. Get used to the idea, because I won't take no for an answer."

Amanda growled wordlessly and stepped closer to the edge of the bed, and he hastily got to his feet and began to get into his clothes. Once dressed he started toward the balcony doors, but stopped just at the threshold.

"And don't even *think* about carrying on your investigation alone," he said very flatly, just as though they'd been discussing the point and he had a right. "I know the idea of danger doesn't bother you, but that has to change. There's—"

When Amanda jumped off the bed and started toward him at a deliberate run, he broke off immediately and headed for the balcony railing. Throwing one leg over let him reach the trellis, but he was able to give her one final glare before his head disappeared below the railing. He'd known well enough that she meant to launch a double flying kick at him, and the only way he could have avoided it would have caused *her* to be hurt. Once he was gone Amanda slammed closed the balcony doors, drew the curtains, then stalked back to her bed.

"The *nerve* of that fool!" she fumed, bouncing down onto the bed and folding her arms. "The absolute *nerve* . . . !"

Amanda was so furious she could barely speak, and it was all *his* fault. The nerve of him to follow her there, frighten the life out of her, and then calmly announce that he intended to marry her! Was she supposed to forget about the blonde hussy whose company he'd chosen over hers at the party? Just because she was in love with him, was she supposed to pretend it had never happened?

"Not in *this* lifetime," she growled, also remembering the way he'd tried to order her around. Another man in his place would know she didn't take orders, but Jack Michaels wasn't bright enough to notice. He hadn't wanted to be involved in her investigation in the first place, and now that he was out of it she would see that he stayed out.

Amanda looked toward the curtained balcony doors, remembering how wonderful his lovemaking had been but refusing to let that sway her. No matter why Jack now wanted to marry her, it had to be the wrong reason. If he loved her he would have said so, but he hadn't. Pei had been right when she said it was easier to live with a man you don't care about than a man you love who doesn't love you back. There was nothing cherished or nourishing in a one-sided love; being entirely alone would be better, far less painful in the long run.

The bed linens were all wrinkled and mussed, but Amanda lay down without trying to straighten them and stretched her hand out. It must be her imagination that the linens still felt warm from his body, but the scent of him lingered, though faintly. For the briefest moment she'd thought he was a horrible monster rather than the strong, honorable man she'd really fallen in love with, and she'd never forgive Jack for making her think that. It would have hurt less if he'd hit her. . . .

But he never would hit her, not even to defend himself. In Amanda's opinion that was idiotic, but it was the sort of idiocy that made her love him even more. Even while she hated him. Everything that happened—everything he did—proved more and more that they would never get together in the right way, the only way she was willing to accept. He didn't love her, and she was wasting her time loving him. Admitting that wasn't likely to make her stop loving him, but at least it ought to make her stop glooming around. The sooner she was married to someone else, the sooner he would have to leave her alone.

Amanda looked at the crease in the pillow where his head had lain, feeling too defeated to stay angry. He must believe she didn't know about the blond woman, and so had come to make love to her and talk her into marrying him. Had he spent the previous night making love to his slender blonde? The idea of that was like a sharp knife plunged into her chest, more so because it was *proof* that he didn't love her. As if she needed any more . . .

She blew out the bedside candle and pulled the quilts up to her chin, suddenly so sleepy that she couldn't think. But tomorrow the feeling of defeat would be gone, and she would think long and hard, making certain that there wasn't a single way left open that Jack could use to make good on his boast. He would *not* marry her, not if she had anything to say about it. He would learn that you don't try to take advantage of dragons, not even silken ones.

Jack had to concentrate while climbing down the rain-wet trellis to keep from slipping off and killing himself, so by the time he reached the ground most of his anger was gone. He moved away from the house through the downpour until he reached the nearest trees, then turned to look back at the windows he'd just left. They were closed and curtained now, but even as he watched, the faint candle-light that had drawn him to the windows in the first place abruptly disappeared.

"Well, *that* went nicely," he muttered, wishing he were still up there in that dry, warm bed, holding Amanda in his arms. "But it would be nicer still if you managed to make up your blasted mind. You went there to use her the way you were used, and to frighten the tar out of her. When did that change to deciding you were going to marry her after all?"

Jack sighed, knowing how bad off a man had to be when he took to lying to himself. He didn't decide this evening to marry Amanda; he'd never given up on the idea in the first place. What he'd intended to do was find out whether she really wanted to be rid of him, and the way she'd responded to his lovemaking had been very encouraging. She'd welcomed him and shared herself eagerly and willingly, until—

"Until she woke up," Jack muttered, depression quickly descending. "If you can keep her asleep you'll have a wonderful married life, absolutely top notch. If you can't, you'll be spending most of your time *defending* your life."

Jack blew out a breath in vexation at the memory of how he'd had to jump and run, but what choice had he had? The girl had been livid with anger, and she knew what she was doing far too well to play games with. If he'd tried, one of them would have gotten hurt, probably Amanda. It had been bad enough when he thought he'd hurt her accidently with lust; doing it on purpose with Chinese boxing was completely out of the question.

So rather than stand and fight he'd run, and now he was no better off than he had been, possibly even worse. Not only hadn't he been able to find out why she'd drugged him and then tried to get rid of him, he'd announced his intentions while she was furious with him. Now she was committed to actively opposing their marriage, while he was determined to see it happen. Well, he was the one who liked games, so he ought to be blissfully happy while he played one with her.

And he would be, as long as he won. But first he had to find some place dry to sleep. Tomorrow—that would be another day.

Chapter 16

Amanda awoke later than she intended to the next day, but it wasn't so late that the day was spent. She had investigating to do in the village, and then there were counter-marriage plans to be made. Jack Michaels had all but thrown down a gauntlet in challenge, and she intended to pick it up.

But first she had to find out something about the area, which she accomplished by taking a late breakfast in the kitchens once she was dressed. Luckily for Amanda, the local cook was a talkative woman, and one general question put between bites got Amanda more information than she needed. She also found out that the Duke and Duchess of Norland had arrived at their house a couple of days earlier. That house was only a short distance from the one they now sat in, and Amanda was certain she could do something with that information.

And she found out that Mr. Lichfield's relatives were also named Lichfield. The family consisted of the widow of Mr. Lichfield's late brother and her youngest daughter and son, the three older boys having gone off on their own years earlier. Additional details were freely added, so many, in fact, that Amanda finally had to excuse herself. She'd finished the meal, and Pei was undoubtedly waiting to walk to the village with her.

Amanda had put on her plainest day gown and a good pair of walking shoes, but she also took her bamboo staff. The neighborhood was supposed to be safe, but taking un-

necessary chances would be foolish. On a stone bench
under a tree, Pei sat reading in the warm sunshine.
Amanda started them walking away from the house, waiting until they were well free of any possible listeners, and
then she turned to her friend.

"So how did *your* night go?" she asked. "More quietly
than mine, I hope."

"Weren't you able to sleep?" Pei asked, immediate concern in her voice. "If you'd rather go back and save this
walk for another time, I don't mind in the least."

"No, this needs to be taken care of now, before Richard's man finds Mr. Lichfield's relatives and asks the
wrong questions." Amanda added a frown to her headshake, hoping the man hadn't already been there. "At this
point another investigator would only muddy the waters,
and there's a second consideration involved. I don't want
anyone to think I'm giving up my own investigation simply because I was told to."

"Told to?" Pei echoed, turning her head to stare at
Amanda. "Who could possibly have— No, don't tell me!
Is *that* what you meant by that comment about lack of
quiet? But, how—what—why—"

"He showed up last night, after I'd gone to bed,"
Amanda explained. "As a matter of fact I'd fallen asleep,
and at first I thought he was a dream. But I discovered
rather quickly that dreams do *not* do what he did. Somehow he found out about the Claws of the Tiger. Or, rather,
he's convinced that *something* was used on him, and he
came to return the favor."

"Oh, my," Pei breathed, her eyes wide. "He must have
been furious, and that's why he hurt you. But—"

"But he didn't hurt me," Amanda corrected her. "He
wasn't gentle and sweet, but the worst I can say about the
experience is that he took over completely—and tried to
keep on in that same vein once it was over."

"As applied to what besides your investigation?" Pei
asked, her brows still high. "I know you, Amanda, and
there's something you're not saying."

"He announced that he means to marry me," Amanda said grudgingly, wishing she could have avoided mentioning that. "Maybe I ought to say he announced it again, just as though half of London hadn't seen him chasing after that blonde hussy. I don't know why he's pursuing this, and I don't really care. I've made up my mind not to let him do it."

"Have I mentioned lately how glad I am that I'm not Occidental?" Pei commented, her expression pained. "Back home men are expected to be interested in more than one woman, and even to marry them. Here . . . Is that your only reason for refusing to marry him? That he involved himself with another woman?"

Amanda hesitated a very long moment before saying, "No, it isn't, but it's a good part of it. Back home men *are* expected to find interest in more than one woman, but this is *here*. In England it's shameful for a man to play around after asking a different woman to marry him, and it means only one thing: the man doesn't love the woman he proposed to. *That's* my main reason for refusing him, and you know why."

"Yes, I certainly do," Pei agreed with a sigh. "Better to live with a man you don't love than with one you do who doesn't love you back. But I thought Richard had agreed not to accept his suit. How does he expect to get around that?"

"I've been asking myself the same question," Amanda said, seeing the end of the private road a short way ahead. Running perpendicular to it was the public road, and the village lay to the right, about half a mile away. "He might be thinking about getting his father to speak for him, not in general but directly to Richard. If that happens Richard could well be so overwhelmed that he agrees, so I've got to take steps to be sure that doesn't happen."

"I see," Pei commented with a nod. "You're going to kidnap a duke to be certain he doesn't speak with your brother. That might work, and if it doesn't you'll have prison to think about rather than marriage. Or did you intend to lock up your brother? That might also work, but—"

"Pei, I think you're letting too much of this country rub off on you," Amanda interrupted with a sudden grin. "The best plan of action is the subtle one, and even very obvious actions can be subtle ones in disguise. Our cook told me Jack's mother and father are here, so I think I'll call on the duchess this afternoon."

"Uh-oh," Pei said with an answering grin. "I have no idea what your plan is, but I already feel sorry for the poor woman. How outrageous do you intend to be?"

"Not outrageous at all, if she's a reasonable woman," Amanda replied casually. "If she is receptive, I'll simply explain how—unacceptable—her son's behavior has been with me, and ask her the favor of having the duke speak sternly with his son. If she isn't agreeable, then that should make things even easier. An unreasonable woman won't hear of her son marrying a woman who has insulted and embarrassed her."

"Too true," Pei conceded with a smile. "Even the women back home have *some* say in a situation like that. But that's for this afternoon. What will we be doing in the village this morning? Simply speaking to Mr. Lichfield's relatives?"

"I think we'd be wise to do more listening than speaking," Amanda said, pulling a leaf from the low-hanging branch of a tree. "Our cook tells me the widow Lichfield used to take in washing to support herself and her children, but hasn't had to do that for a while now. Her three older sons went to London to find work, and apparently they've done well enough to send her money on a regular basis. Everyone in the village knows that because she tends to brag."

"You find that sinister or unreasonable?" Pei asked with raised brows. "To me it sounds perfectly natural."

"It would to me too," Amanda agreed, "except that the people in the village are surprised. It seems those three young men had less than wholesome reputations when they lived here, and no one expected them to find decent jobs. But since they did, it's apparently only to be expected that they would send money. They're a very close family, I'm told, and take family ties very seriously."

"I still don't see what interests you about all that," Pei said with a shake of her head. "What do you expect the woman to say?"

"I have no idea," Amanda admitted, looking at the leaf she held before throwing it away. "It just feels as if there's something in all that that I can use, and if I keep my ears open I'll find more. It could just be a matter of wishful thinking, but for some reason I don't believe it is."

"For your sake—and Mr. Lichfield's—I hope you're right," Pei said, and then, after a hesitation, added, "What do you think Mr. Michaels will do when he finds out you haven't stopped investigating? You did say he wasn't pleased about you continuing on your own?"

"Pleasure doesn't enter into it," Amanda returned sourly. "He just about ordered me not to go on alone, which proves he has more nerve than intelligence. Since I certainly won't be working with him again, how else will I proceed if not alone? With the only other option being to give up altogether, he was a fool to even mention it."

"It's almost as if he's become even more concerned about you," Pei said just as hesitantly as before. "If he really doesn't love you, why should that be?"

"Maybe it's himself he's concerned about," Amanda answered with a shrug. "I didn't learn much of anything working with him, so he doesn't want me to do better on my own and make him look bad. Or maybe he simply *is* concerned, worrying about a poor little female incapable of protecting herself. What you have to remember, Pei, is that you can be concerned about someone without actually loving them."

"I suppose so," Pei granted with a sigh. "Perhaps I'm trying to read things into his actions that simply aren't there. But if the subject comes up, please remember that you *aren't* doing this alone. I'm with you, which means you're perfectly safe."

Amanda was forced to chuckle at that, which was obviously Pei's reason for saying it. Pei was trying to raise her spirits, and the least Amanda could do was cooperate. It was a lovely day, after all, and lovely days that also offered the chance to learn something important should be fully appreciated.

So Amanda worked at feeling cheerful, and by the time they reached the village she had at least left depression behind. The village was a charming place, full of houses with gardens to either side of the road that became the village's main street. A short way down were shops and a smithy, as well as what looked like a tavern with rooms above. There were a good number of people about, most of them working near their houses or in their gardens, and she and Pei drew unconcealed glances of curiosity.

"Our cook said to turn right after the smithy, then go down two streets to a yew hedge," Amanda told Pei softly. "Beyond the yew hedge is a small yellow house, also on the right, and that's where the widow Lichfield lives."

Pei nodded calmly without speaking, which told Amanda that she was trying not to notice the stares. Amanda felt those stares were unfriendly and intrusive. She imagined how much worse it must be for Pei, since Amanda had experienced similar reactions from time to time in Po San, where she was the alien. But Pei had always told her not to pay attention to the ignorant, so Amanda didn't say anything. Instead she hooked her arm around Pei's to show exactly where she stood, and after exchanging warm smiles the two walked on.

The large green hedge wasn't hard to find, and neither was the yellow house beyond it. The house *was* small, but it looked carefully kept up and as well-tended as the garden around it. There was another tall hedge on the far side of the garden, and as Amanda led the way up the walk she couldn't help but think that the Lichfields seemed to like their privacy. Three well-swept steps led to the porch, and a moment later Amanda was knocking on the front door. It took another brief moment, and then a woman opened the door.

"Can I help you?" the woman asked with a pleasant smile, looking at Amanda with dark, friendly eyes. Of average height with dark but graying hair, the woman was on the heavy side without actually being fat. She wore homespun rather than any fancier fabric, but it was clean and reasonably new and not in the least shabby.

"I'm looking for Mrs. Lichfield," Amanda answered with her own smile. "My name is Amanda Edmunds, and Mr. Miles Lichfield was my father's secretary until my father passed away a few months ago."

"Edmunds? Why, yes, I know that name," the woman exclaimed, her accent that of an educated person and in no manner lower class. No wonder the people in the village liked to talk about her—she wasn't one of them, and probably made them feel uncomfortable. "The last I heard from Miles, he promised to come and visit. If you're looking for him, I'm afraid he hasn't yet arrived."

"I know that, Mrs. Lichfield," Amanda told her gently. "May we come in for a few moments?"

"Oh, why certainly," the woman said, beginning to look worried. "I didn't mean to keep you standing on the doorstep. Miss Edmunds, has anything happened to Miles? Please tell me quickly."

"Something has happened, but we aren't sure what," Amanda said, taking the woman's hand in an effort to lend strength. "I'm very worried about him, but I'm convinced he's still alive. I've come to ask your help in trying to find him."

"I'll do anything I can. Anything," the woman assured Amanda, then squeezed her hand before releasing it. "Please come in, and we can talk in the parlor."

She opened the door wider as she stepped back, and Amanda took that opportunity to say, "Mrs. Lichfield, this is my friend Miss Han Pei. She's been helping me in my search, since she and I have known—and cared for—Mr. Lichfield all our lives."

"Miss Han, it's a pleasure," Mrs. Lichfield said, then smiled at the startled expressions Amanda and Pei both undoubtedly wore. "As you can imagine, Miles wrote me quite a lot about China. I'll get you settled in the parlor, then fetch some tea."

The parlor was a small, pleasant room at the back of the house that didn't seem to be used much. Amanda and Pei sat in the chairs they were shown to, and it wasn't long before Mrs. Lichfield was back with a plain porcelain tea service.

"Now please tell me everything you can," she said as she began to pour tea for each of them. Although she looked shaken to Amanda, she appeared to have no intention of going to pieces.

Amanda told her everything she'd discovered, which was actually very little, then mentioned the clerk who had been killed. She pretended she'd been told that unofficially by someone in authority, and Mrs. Lichfield nodded knowingly. It was something they weren't supposed to have been told, so she'd been careful not to mention it to anyone else.

"That poor man," Mrs. Lichfield said with a sigh. "But now I understand why you believe Miles is still alive. If that clerk was killed so casually and simply left where he fell, there's no reason to think Miles would have been treated any differently. But where can he be?"

"I can't even begin to imagine," Amanda said with a shake of her head. "The only possibility that occurs to me is that Mr. Lichfield was attacked but escaped, and is now hiding out somewhere in fear of his life. Have you any idea where that place might be?"

"If anywhere, it should be here," Mrs. Lichfield said with her own headshake, her expression troubled. "Miles and I have always been good friends, he and I and his brother, my late husband Regis. We're a very close family, you see, and when, some years ago, my older sons chose the wrong man to work for, Miles helped Regis to straighten the matter out. He was home on holiday, and so naturally became involved. If he needed sanctuary, where else would he go but to family?"

"If the situation were dangerous, he might not want to jeopardize the safety of you and your children," Pei pointed out, the first words she'd spoken. "But that doesn't explain why he didn't go to Lord Pembroke. Surely your brother would have been able—and willing—to protect him, Amanda."

"Of course Richard would have protected him," Amanda agreed with a nod. "That suggests Mr. Lichfield wasn't able to go to Richard, possibly because of where he did find refuge. Now all we need to figure out is why he needed refuge to begin with—aside from the fact that he knew something he wasn't supposed to."

"*And* it had something to do with the clerk Reggie Nichols," Pei pointed out. "But he didn't know it before he went to the Registry Office, or he would have written it in that journal you told me about. So it was something he saw there, either in the clerk's office, or his friend's office."

"It probably has nothing to do with Mr. Melton," Amanda said with a shake of her head. "Mr. Lichfield was only there for a moment or two, and it was Reggie who refused to answer questions and who was subsequently killed. It has to have something to do with him."

"My goodness, that gave me a chill," Mrs. Lichfield said with a hand to her breast, literally shivering. "That poor Mr. Nichols—when you referred to him as 'Reggie,' for just an instant I thought about *my* Reggie. My eldest son and his two brothers have taken positions in London, and they're doing really well. I'm very proud of them, and I know Miles would also have been proud."

"I'm sure he would have," Amanda agreed soothingly. "Where do they work in London?"

"If you mean exactly where, I have no idea," Mrs. Lichfield answered with a smile. "I'm afraid I don't know

London very well, but I do know they're in private service
with some gentleman. He knows how good they are, and
pays them well enough to let them send money to me.
They're really good boys, and never fail to think of their
family first."

"When your family gives you love, support, and understanding, it isn't hard to give it back," Amanda said as she
reached over to pat the older woman's hand. "That's why
I won't rest until I've found Mr. Lichfield safe and sound.
If you should happen to hear from him, please let me
know immediately. I'm currently staying at my brother's
house, which isn't far from here."

"I thought you might have opened up your father's
house," Mrs. Lichfield said after nodding agreement to
Amanda's request. "The place hasn't been lived in in
years, and I would have offered to take you two young ladies in here rather than let you struggle with age-ruined
surroundings. But if you're at Lord Pembroke's house,
that's perfectly all right."

"You're very kind, Mrs. Lichfield," Amanda said, smiling warmly. "If we *were* on our own, we would have been
glad to accept your hospitality. I do plan to see my father's
house, but my brother would never hear of my staying
there."

They sat and chatted until the tea was gone, then left after Amanda gave her own promise to keep in touch. Mrs.
Lichfield had been fascinated with Amanda's bamboo
staff, and under other circumstances Amanda would have
given it to the lovely woman as a gift. With the situation
as it was, however, Amanda spun a tale about how the
large "walking stick" had been a gift from Mr. Lichfield
which she prized above all her other possessions. Mrs.
Lichfield smiled sadly, and didn't mention the staff again.

"You know, you didn't lie," Pei remarked once the
small yellow house was a short distance behind them. "Mr.
Lichfield *did* give you that staff in a way. He was the one
who provided the cash for you to pay Master Ma."

"That's certainly one way of looking at it . . . If only I

knew where Mr. Lichfield is," Amanda responded with a
sigh. "That woman probably won't sleep tonight."

"She is a wonderful person, and I feel very sorry for
her," Pei agreed, only glancing at the houses they passed.
"She doesn't seem to belong in this village, but if she had
to take in washing to support her family, I'll bet she did it
cheerfully. It bothered me when she became upset over the
name 'Reggie.' What a horrible coincidence, to have a son
with the same name as a murdered man."

"I just hope it was a coincidence," Amanda muttered, finally forcing herself to discuss the terrible idea she'd gotten. "You have to remember that Mr. Lichfield recognized
someone in the Registry Office. It may have happened
while he was in the Bureau of Vital Statistics, and that's
why Reggie Nichols refused to answer any questions. I'm
starting to believe it was Reggie Nichols himself that he
recognized."

"But Mrs. Lichfield said her sons are in service with
'some gentleman,' " Pei protested, with a shocked expression on her face. "If Reggie Nichols was really her son,
there would have been no need for him to lie to her.
There's nothing wrong with being a clerk in a government
office in this country, is there?"

"No, there isn't, which is exactly the point," Amanda
countered, glancing around to be sure no one was near
enough to overhear their conversation. "There's no shame
in being a clerk, and also no reason for someone named
Lichfield to call himself Nichols. Unless the man was
working there only because the gentleman he really
worked for wanted it that way. The thing I still can't figure
out is what anyone could hope to get from working in an
office that gathers information that's available to the public. Why put someone in there under a false name, when
simply walking in and asking to see their records would
accomplish the same thing?"

"The only possible answer to that is it would *not* accomplish the same thing," Pei responded slowly and
thoughtfully. "With that in mind, what could you learn

working there that you would miss by simply walking in and checking their records?"

"Bribes of some sort?" Amanda suggested, remembering how quickly Jack's silver was accepted. "Maybe a list of those who offered the bribes? If you're not paying money out to quicken the process, then maybe you're paying it to hide something."

"Like, register this quickly before someone notices that the birth or death or marriage isn't completely proper?" Pei suggested in turn, her tone doubtful. "But wouldn't that just bring attention to something you don't want anyone to notice?"

"I'd say so, but people can be very strange sometimes," Amanda said with a shake of her head that dismissed the entire subject. "At this point all we can do is guess, so let's think about it a while before we decide on something that's entirely wrong. Later we can talk about it again."

Pei agreed with a nod, and they left the village behind along with their discussion. Amanda had meant to look around in the shops while they were there, but the unfriendly stares had made her change her mind. If those people wanted nothing to do with her and Pei, she felt just the same in return.

The road turned, putting the village entirely out of sight, and once it did Amanda was relieved. But only for a matter of five minutes. That's how long it was before two men stepped out of the woods that stretched in all directions around them and grinned at them nastily from no more than five feet away.

"Well, now, hain't this nice," one of them said, first looking Amanda over and then doing the same with Pei. "Two tasty treats, an' they's all ourn. Whadda ya say, bucko? Let's share'n share alike, hey?"

And with that they started for Amanda and Pei.

When Jack left Amanda Edmunds, he decided against going to the inn on the far side of the village, and went to his father's house instead. He'd originally planned to stay at the inn until the next morning when people were awake at his father's house, but it hadn't taken long to realize he couldn't take the chance. Knowing Amanda Edmunds, she would probably be off on her own investigations at the crack of dawn despite his warning. Because of that, Jack knew he had to sleep in a place where he was certain he would be awakened when he needed to be.

It took time to wake up one of the servants in his father's house, more time before that man woke one of the servants who knew Jack, and even more time beyond that to settle him in rooms of his own. It wasn't early when he finally lay down, he wasn't able to fall asleep quickly, and once he did fall asleep his dreams were full of Amanda. In the dream she danced naked under a waterfall, turned to see him, then smiled as she called to him to join her. But the grass under his feet wrapped around his ankles to keep him from doing just that, and by the time he had freed himself and was ready to join her, a servant woke him to say it was dawn.

So it wasn't a very happy man who sat his horse in the woods, watching the house from which Amanda Edmunds would emerge, on her way to look for danger and trouble. When it was almost midmorning before the girl appeared, Jack felt the definite urge to throttle someone. If he'd known she was going to sleep late, he could have done the same.

"Instead of getting up early and now feeling as if a herd of very angry horses had run over me," Jack muttered to the surrounding trees as he watched Amanda and Miss Han walk toward the road. "She'd better be willing to share whatever it is she learns, or I'll probably lose my temper."

To say the least. Jack looked around again to be certain no one else was in sight, then he reluctantly dismounted and tied his horse to a nearby tree. There had been the chance that Amanda would ride or be driven to the village so he'd had to have the horse. Now being mounted would just make following two women on foot harder.

And the worst of it was, he could well be exerting himself for nothing. Jack managed to keep from muttering to himself as he walked, following them, but thinking dark thoughts was another matter entirely. There were no signs that the clerk's murderer was anywhere around, and if Amanda happened to trip over *him* while he was shadowing her, she would certainly make his life even more miserable. He couldn't claim he was performing his duty; following Amanda Edmunds around was completely his own choice.

And a choice he still couldn't entirely understand. There had been other women whose favors he'd enjoyed, and he hadn't thought twice about bowing and leaving when the idyll was over. Suddenly, though, he found it impossible to walk away, and the world looked different from this side of the fence. Especially considering the woman involved. He was in love with a dragon, disguised as a tempting woman, soft and sensual but with sharp teeth and claws just below the surface, a woman who didn't seem to be in love with him. Jack sighed as he moved as silently as possible through the edge of the woods, keeping the two women in sight. The uncertainty of Amanda's feelings for him was driving him mad. Was there a possibility that she might love him, or were his own desires making him see things that weren't really there?

Jack squared his shoulders, promising himself some definite answers before he decided he had no choice but to walk away. He would have enjoyed confronting her on the spot, but since he knew that would hardly weaken the Silken Dragon's resolve, he decided to bide his time playing invisible shadow.

When the girls reached the village he hesitated, unable to think of a way to continue following without being seen by someone. There was nothing for it but to wait until they came out again.

Jack retreated to the bend in the road and sat behind a large tree to wait, but the women took so long to come back that he actually started to doze. It was the sound of

voices that woke him, but not female voices. He got
quickly and quietly to his feet and peered around the tree,
just in time to see two men start for Amanda and Miss
Han in what had to be an attack. Jack cursed under his
breath and started to run out to help, but one step was as
far as he got before it was all over.

If Jack hadn't known what he was seeing, he probably
wouldn't have been *able* to see it. Everything happened
that fast, and the two men probably had no idea what hit
them. Jack had forgotten about the bamboo staff Amanda
was carrying, but she hadn't forgotten it. The two men,
who reached her almost together, each got an end of it in
the temple without either of them seeing it coming. When
they dropped like stones Jack slipped back behind his tree,
glad he hadn't been needed but also feeling frustrated. He
very much wanted to be a hero in the eyes of his lady
dragon, but she kept refusing to give him the chance!

"Well, *that* went easier than the last time," Jack heard
Miss Han say as she looked down at the two men. "If it
ever happens again, you'll have to try not to let them get
even that close."

"It was easier this time because there were only two
rather than three," Amanda returned with amusement in
her voice. "But as far as distance goes, I'm afraid you'll
have to accept this one until I get a longer staff. This walk
has worked up my appetite; let's go have lunch."

Miss Han agreed enthusiastically, so the two girls cir-
cled the bodies on the ground and walked off arm in arm.
They may have been amused, but Jack wasn't. He frowned
at what he'd heard, wondering, *What other time with three
men? Does she consider being attacked nothing more than
ordinary, everyday doings like brushing your hair or
dressing for dinner? This is ridiculous.*

It was more than ridiculous, but it was also one more
event that was clearly out of Jack's hands now. He went
back to following the women until they reached their own
front door, and then he was able to consider himself off
duty for a while. Since the church bell hadn't yet rung

noon and lunch was usually taken at half after, if he went straight back to his rooms he'd be able to lie down for an hour or two before resuming his watch post. He'd been hoping to be able to speak to his father, but this close to a meal wasn't the best of times. He'd have to catch him later, when they'd both have time to talk.

Jack took one last look at the closed front door of Lord Pembroke's house, then made his way back to where his horse was tied, mounted, and headed for his own house.

"It's still nearly an hour until lunch," Amanda told Pei after checking with a girl in the kitchens. "People take the meal at half after up here, but I don't feel like sitting around and waiting. I've told them to serve on time even if I'm not back, since I'll only be a few minutes late at most."

"Where are you going now?" Pei asked, beginning to rise from the chair she'd taken as soon as they were inside. "And why are you going? Don't you want to rest after that walk we had?"

"You can rest for both of us," Amanda said with amusement, pressing her back into the chair. "I'm not in the least tired, so I'm going to see if I can get an interview with the duchess. Whichever way it goes, I'll be happier with a short interview rather than a long one. Being interrupted by lunchtime will be the perfect excuse to get me out of there, so please remind our people to serve lunch as usual. I'll be back before you know it."

"Don't forget to take your staff," Pei said with a sigh, showing she had no intention of arguing. "If I'm not going to be there to protect you, you'll need something in case those two ruffians come back."

"Those two ruffians, assuming they're not still unconscious, are probably halfway to the next village," Amanda said with a snort. "And once they get there, they'll hopefully think twice before attacking supposedly helpless women. But I do intend to take the staff, so don't worry while you're resting. I'll be perfectly safe."

Pei's nod didn't look quite so sure, but that was only because she always worried about the people she cared for. Amanda smiled as she left the house again, the staff back in her hand. It was wonderful to have a friend like Pei, and when it came time for her to go home Amanda expected to be devastated. But for now she was still here, so Amanda concentrated on being glad instead.

The walk to Duke Edward's house wasn't long, as it lay on the other side of the public road just a little farther from the village. It was also a good deal larger than Richard's house, but Amanda spent no time admiring its size. She announced herself as the sister of Lord Pembroke to the servant who opened the door, and asked if she might see the duchess. When the servant went to find out, Amanda crossed her fingers to continue her good luck. At least the woman wasn't out or busy entertaining company, which would have entirely ruined Amanda's plans.

It wasn't long before the servant was back, and he bowed to Amanda before gesturing.

"Her Grace Duchess Katherine will see you in the library," he said. "Please follow me."

Amanda did so, and was shown to where the duchess was waiting. Jack's mother was a slender woman about Amanda's size, dark-haired and light-eyed and still beautiful despite no longer being young. Her morning gown was pale blue and gray and quite lovely, and the warm smile she wore lit up her face.

"Well, so *you're* the sister Lord Pembroke has been talking about these past months," Duchess Katherine said in a soft voice that matched her smile. "Welcome home, child, and do come in. We've all been looking forward to meeting you."

"Thank you, Your Grace," Amanda said with a curtsey, although she'd almost bowed Oriental style. Katherine, Duchess of Norland, had enough presence and regality to be a member of the Imperial Family—or the royal family.

"I'm delighted that you haven't waited on some silly protocol before coming to visit," Duchess Katherine went on, obviously meaning what she said. "You'll stay for lunch, of course, and until then we can chat. Please sit down."

"Thank you, Your Grace, but I'm afraid I'm expected back at Richard's house for lunch," Amanda said, taking the chair that had been offered to her. "I've—come to ask your help with something, and I really do apologize for burdening you with my problem, especially when this is our first meeting—"

Amanda's hesitant pauses weren't entirely acting. She'd liked this woman at first sight, and no longer considered dragging her into this mess to be the best of ideas. If only there was another way. . . .

"My dear girl, don't be silly," Duchess Katherine said earnestly, leaning forward in her own chair. "If you have a problem that I can help with, I'd be only too happy to do so. I knew your mother, after all, and even met your father once or twice. Tell me what's wrong."

"It's—your son," Amanda said, lowering her eyes from the older woman's gaze. Since she had no choice about going through with it, it might as well be done right. "The one who calls himself Jack Michaels. He has announced that he intends to marry me, but considering his behavior, I—that is, I would really prefer—"

Amanda stopped short, as though the properly delicate words refused to be found, and Duchess Katherine immediately got the point.

"Oh, dear, what *has* he done this time?" she asked, and Amanda looked up to see a pained expression on her beautiful face. "My son John sometimes takes things to extremes, and that despite the fact that he's basically good-hearted. However did he come to propose to you?"

"We met at a party shortly after my arrival in this country," Amanda said, still playing young and innocent. "I happened to mention that I was very worried about my late father's secretary, Mr. Lichfield, who seems to have disappeared after filing the information about my father's death. Mr. Michaels offered to help me look into the mat-

ter more fully, and of course I agreed. I was very grateful
for his assistance, especially when I was told he came
from an honorable family, but—"

Again Amanda broke off, giving the duchess time to say
something. When she didn't, Amanda took a deep breath
and plunged on.

"But he seemed to be acting oddly right from the very
first. My brother Richard noticed it as well, and when
Mr. Michaels suddenly asked for my hand, Richard refused. That was the night we all went to another party together, and—and after telling me about the proposal, Mr.
Michaels proceeded to ignore me completely while paying
all his attention to the other women there. Everyone noticed, of course, and I didn't feel so much humiliated as
truly hurt. I can't imagine a woman wanting to marry a
man who did that to her, and Richard quite agrees. The
only trouble is . . ."

"Yes?" Duchess Katherine encouraged gently when
Amanda stopped again. The older woman's expression had
turned sympathetic—as well as faintly outraged.

"The only trouble is he seems to have followed me up
here," Amanda said on a single breath, as though eager to
have the words spoken and behind her. "Richard let me
come up here early so that I might get away from Mr.
Michaels's proximity, but somehow your son discovered
where I'd gone. He came into my bedchamber last night
through the terrace doors after I'd gotten into bed, and—
and—said again that he meant to marry me. But I couldn't,
Your Grace, I really couldn't, and I told him that even
though I feared he might—insist. He refused to accept my
answer, and now—now I—"

"And now you're afraid of what he might do next," the
duchess finished for her, obviously thoroughly incensed. "I
can't imagine what could have gotten into the man, but I
assure you his father will see to it that it gets right out
again. A man who refuses to take no for an answer—and
has the audacity to invade a lady's bedchamber—is no
man *I* am willing to call a son. You have my word that this

will be seen to quickly and thoroughly, Miss Edmunds, so you must calm your fears completely. I've been told that John is here in the house now, so I'll speak to my husband at once."

"Thank you so much, Your Grace," Amanda said, letting real relief color the words. "You can't know how grateful I am, and I do apologize again for—"

"Nonsense, child, nonsense," the duchess interrupted warmly, standing again as Amanda did. "If a woman can't speak her fears to another woman, who *can* she tell them to? And you must promise to come to the house tonight, to join the small gathering we're having. I want you to meet my husband and some of the other neighbors we have in common. About eight?"

"That would be wonderful, Your Grace, but my companion, Miss Han Pei, has come up from London with me. It would be very ungracious of me to leave her sitting at home alone—"

"Nonsense again, child," Duchess Katherine interrupted a second time with a smile. "If you have a companion with you, she's certainly welcome as well. Miss Han, is it? My husband has a Mr. Soong Tao in his employ, who is thoroughly a gentleman despite his not being Occidental. Would you care for a cup of tea before you go?"

"No . . . thank you, no," Amanda said, giving up on trying excuses. "I really must be getting home."

The duchess made the proper sounds of disappointment and saw Amanda to the door, but the last sight Amanda had of her was the way she sailed determinedly toward another door off the entrance hall. The duchess was angry and meant to tell someone about the source of that anger, which made it seem to Amanda that her errand had been a success. As Amanda walked back toward the road she wished she also could have refused the invitation to that night's party, but being too firm would have ruined her earlier performance.

So she and Pei had another party to attend, but one that would go a good deal better than the last one. Richard would be pleased that she'd gone when he was told about it, and if the duke needed additional convincing in addition to what his wife meant to say, Amanda would be right there to do it. She'd have to repeat the official version of her experiences with Jack for Pei's sake, of course, but Pei could be counted on to say the right thing at the right time. Now, aside from wondering how Jack would respond to her gambit, all Amanda had to worry about was what to wear.

Chapter 17

"**M**r. Michaels, please wake up," Jack heard, the words dragging him out of a sound sleep. "Please, Mr. Michaels. His Grace would like to speak to you."

"What's going on?" Jack mumbled, forcing himself to sit up. He'd lain down fully dressed, so it wasn't surprising that he felt thoroughly rumpled. "Have two hours gone by *already?*"

"No, Mr. Michaels, it's barely been an hour," the servant answered, his tone painfully neutral. "Their Graces have just sat down to lunch, and His Grace your father asks that you join them. At once, sir."

That didn't sound good, but Jack couldn't imagine what might be wrong. Granted, his father had never summoned him so peremptorily before, but nothing *could* be wrong. Jack marked the feeling down to lack of sleep, threw some water in his face to help wake himself up the rest of the way, then he went down to the dining room.

Edward, Duke of Norland, sat at the head of the table as usual, but Jack's mother sat to his right rather than presiding over the other end of the table. That was, of course, because no guests were at the meal, only Soong Tao sitting to Jack's father's left. Tao had arrived, then, but Jack couldn't help noticing that his friend wore no revealing expression whatsoever. The feeling that something was wrong surfaced again.

"Father," Jack said with a bow once he'd entered, then

he turned to greet his mother with a kiss on the cheek and said, "Mother, lovely as always."

Jack's father seemed intent on the cheese he was just then tasting, and his mother made no effort to smile at his greeting as she usually did. Servants stood by ready to serve or fetch things away, and Jack felt totally bewildered.

"Father, you sent for me?" Jack tried the gentle reminder, swallowing the urge to get out while the getting was good. Something *had* to be wrong, but for the life of him he couldn't—

"Sit down over there, John," Duke Edward said in the tone he usually used only for matters of state, gesturing to the chair beside Tao's. "There's a matter that needs to be discussed without delay, so you will sit and lunch with us."

Jack, feeling ten years old again, silently took the chair pointed out to him. Both of his parents were now intent on their food, but Tao exchanged a glance with him that seemed to offer sympathy, at the same time shaking his head very slightly. He seemed to be telling Jack he wasn't responsible, but not responsible for *what?*

"John, your lady mother has come to me with a very disturbing tale," Duke Edward said, and Jack looked up to see his father's dark eyes directly on him. "I'll relate the details of this tale, and then I'll hear your side of it. I'm told that you've proposed marriage to a Miss Edmunds, sister to Richard Lavering, that both Lavering and Miss Edmunds have refused your suit, but you persist in following the young lady and insisting that she surrender to your demands. Is this true?"

"What?" Jack yelped, feeling as though the roof had fallen in on him. "How—where—"

"I'm waiting for a yes or a no, John," Duke Edward said in the hardest voice he'd ever used to Jack. "Is this true, or is it not?"

"Well, yes, it's true for the most part," Jack babbled, incapable of lying to his father. "But that's not—"

"So it's true," Duke Edward interrupted, those dark eyes pinning Jack where he sat. If his voice had seemed cold before, now it was mountain ice. "I'm also told that you were so dishonorably forward as to enter a lady's bed-chamber after she'd retired, a lady who had neither invited you nor welcomed your appearance. Is this true as well?"

"Father, you must believe me!" Jack protested, too well aware of all the ears listening to the conversation. "There's more to the matter than I'm able to discuss here, but if you'll just—"

"John," Duke Edward said in a voice of doom, drowning out the rest of Jack's pitiful request. "Is it true, or is it not?"

Jack, who had never lost a serious fight, knew he was beaten without anyone having launched a single blow. He'd been completely outmaneuvered again, not to mention wrapped, boxed, and shipped. His mother's outraged stare told him she was ready to have a switch cut for his father to use on him, but there was nothing he could say to make matters better; quite the reverse.

"Yes, sir, that's also true," Jack was finally forced to say, hearing the defeat in his voice. "But if you'll just give me a few private minutes of your time—"

"I think it would be best if we didn't speak privately, at least not today," Duke Edward said in a choked voice, back to giving his food most of his attention. "Tomorrow I may have sufficient control of myself again not to send for a horsewhip, but we'll just have to wait and see. For now I'll settle for seeing *your* embarrassment and mortification rather than that of an innocent young girl."

An innocent young girl! Jack suddenly wanted to murder that innocent young girl, preferably in the slowest and most painful way possible. It had to have been Amanda who had spoken to his mother, and if not her, then someone at her instigation. He'd told her last night that he *would* marry her, and this—this—*scene* with his parents was her answer to the challenge. Just wait till he got his hands on her. He'd—

"May I be excused now?" Jack forced himself to say, feeling more than ever like a naughty child who had had a dressing down. He would have simply gotten up and left, but after his father had specifically told him to take a place at the table, just walking out would have made things even worse. Although how they could be worse short of getting him hanged . . .

"You are *not* excused, John," his mother answered when his father remained silent, her tone as frosty as her stare. "You were told to take lunch with us, and so you shall. You will be served, and you will eat."

"And you will not, under any circumstances, approach that young lady again," Duke Edward added, raising his eyes to Jack's to emphasize his words. "Have I made myself clear?"

"Yes, sir, extremely clear," Jack muttered, leaning back to allow a servant to put a plate in front of him. "Most incredibly clear."

And those were the last words spoken during the meal, which at least gave Jack time to think. He wondered whether it was his mother's idea or his father's to dress him down in public, giving him the same humiliation he'd supposedly given an innocent. In an hour the word would be spread far and wide, that poor, innocent Miss Edmunds had been so desperate she'd needed his parents to intercede for her. She'd come out of it with sympathy for her plight and admiration for her courage in speaking out, while he—he'd have his public reputation reinforced almost to the point of scandal.

Just to be sure I can't turn over a new leaf even if I want to, Jack thought with a scowl while he forced down food that now tasted like straw. *If I'm trapped in my public character, I can't find a way to make her marry me. Hell and damnation, she's even made my* father *forget that I'm not really like that! If she mounts even one more campaign against me, I* will *end up hanged! But* I'm *the one who was first wronged here. I'm* the victim, *and that means I can't let her get away with it!*

Jack refused to let himself descend to brooding, but he certainly came close. When the meal was finally over he stood respectfully as his parents left the table, waited a brief moment, then headed for a side door out of the house. He was so intent on what he meant to do that he didn't realize he was being followed until a hand touched his arm just short of the door.

"Jack, calm down." Tao's voice followed his touch, reminding him of the other man's presence during the meal. "Making decisions while your blood is still up just guarantees they'll be the wrong decisions."

"What's so wrong about committing cold-blooded murder?" Jack asked, able to speak freely with no one else around. "Especially if it's done in hot blood? During the last hour the idea has become more and more attractive, and now I'm eagerly looking forward to it. That little brat mousetrapped me again, but this is the last time. When I'm through with her, she'll never play another game for the rest of her life."

"I was under the impression that you'd given your father your word to stay away from her," Tao said, somehow having moved himself to a position directly in front of the door. "Are you now prepared to also break your word?"

"My father asked if I understood that he wanted me to stay away from her, and I agreed that I understood," Jack pointed out, folding his arms. "That has nothing to do with giving my word to stay away from her, and I'm sure you know it. Are you going to step out of my way, or do we have to fight first?"

"I can't just step out of your way," Tao denied, and now faint frustration could be seen in his dark eyes. "His Grace has asked me to keep an eye on you to make sure you behave, and inviting me to the meal was his way of letting me know what was going on. If he'd mentioned the matter sooner, while we were alone . . . But he didn't, so I had no chance to speak on your behalf."

"As if that would have helped," Jack said sourly. "Right now the only thing that will help is for *her* to tell him the truth. If I'd had some warning I could have come up with a story to get them on *my* side, but apparently dragons attack *without* warning. I've never been able to lie to my father, and that simply iced the cake. But you still haven't answered my question: do you get out of my way, or do we fight?"

"I take it as a measure of your agitation that you're now willing to fight with me," Tao said, his calm voice faintly disturbed. "Once you came back from China you even refused to spar with me, which I took to mean that your skill had grown to the point of far surpassing mine. Now your anger changes that stance, and I'm forced to ask if you've moved forward—or backward."

"Tao, philosophy leading to self-recrimination doesn't have much of a chance with me right now," Jack answered with a sigh. "I've discovered that when you fall madly in love with a woman, all normal thoughts and feelings disappear as if they were never there. I have to talk to Amanda and get this mess straightened out, or my life will never be normal again. I mean to ask her straight out whether or not she loves me, and if the answer is no I'll walk away and never go near her again."

"A more worthy end than cold-blooded murder done in hot blood, but not a less dangerous one," Tao said, his frustration having increased. "I agree that you need to know the truth, but you seem to be overlooking the fact that you're leaving your back unguarded again. What if the young lady agrees she loves you, but for reasons of her own refuses to marry you? She'll then most certainly strike at you again, and will undoubtedly find an unshielded target."

"Unfortunately that's much too true," Jack muttered, rubbing at his face with one hand as his mind finally began to work rationally. "My biggest problem in all this is that I've been trying to behave honorably and as a gentleman, while my opponent has gleefully made up the rules as she went along. It's time to change that, and not only because I'm more than tired of losing. I have a stop to make before we go out."

Jack saw the way Tao raised his brows at the words "before *we* go out," but he refrained from commenting as he followed Jack back into the main part of the house. A servant told Jack that his mother was in her sewing room, so he made his way up there and rapped gently at the door. When he was told to come in he did so, but stopped just inside the room.

"Mother, I'd like to speak to you for a moment," he said quietly, trying to project an air of utter defeat. "If you'd rather not I'll understand and go, but . . ."

He let the words trail off, leaving it up to her, and the three house girls who were sewing with her sat utterly still. If the duchess let him stay, he hoped the girls would do the same. Having his version of the truth circulated, even in the form of gossip, could only help, but his mother still hadn't said a word. She stared at him silently for a moment, obviously trying to retain her anger, but she had always been too good-hearted to ignore her family when they needed her attention.

"Very well, John," she finally allowed. "But only for a minute. The girls and I must finish this gown before we can start on the gift I mean to make for your father."

"Thank you, Mother," Jack said, now projecting sadness as he went closer and sat himself at the edge of a chair, then clasped his hands contritely between his knees. "It's painful to know that you're angry with me, and I simply wanted to apologize. I have no idea how everything got so far out of hand, even with love involved. I can understand Richard Lavering refusing to take *my* word of honor, but also refusing to take Father's? Well, what's done is done, so I'll just repeat my apology and leave—"

"Just a moment, John," his mother interrupted as he began to stand, her frown exactly what Jack had been hoping to see. "What are you talking about? None of what you said makes any sense."

"That I know," Jack agreed with a sigh, settling back in

his chair. "Amanda and I love each other, Mother, and when I discovered that my feelings were returned I was the happiest man in the world. But Amanda won't marry without her brother's permission, which we assumed would be easy to get. I gave the man my word that I would change my life if he accepted my suit, and if my word wasn't good enough he could speak to Father. You know I would never let Father down once I pledged to do something, but Lavering refused to even consider it. I tried to find out why, but couldn't."

"But John, it was Miss Edmunds herself who came to see me," his mother protested, now looking upset. "She said not a single word about you two loving each other, only that you—that is, that you were—"

"I know, Mother," Jack responded, now showing a wry expression. "She made me sound like a villain, but she sees doing that as her duty. Her brother has refused my suit, so *she's* bound to reject me as well. I visited her bed-chamber last night in an effort to convince her not to compromise her heart, and she knows it. But she's also wonderfully clever, so she decided to use it against me. I have no idea what the two of us are going to do, but I find myself unable to stop loving her. When I told her that last night she cried, but also said she'd take care of it."

"Well, she's certainly made an excellent start," his mother commented with raised brows. "Frankly, John, I haven't the least idea of what to say. Or what it might be possible for you to do."

"That's the problem I'm working on right now, Mother," Jack said as he stood. "If anything comes to you I'd appreciate hearing about it, but I'm beginning to believe there *is* no solution. If that turns out to be true . . . Ah, well, no need to borrow agony beforetime."

He bowed politely and headed out of the room, leaving his mother with clear sympathy and sadness for him in her eyes—and the three house girls showing exactly the same expressions. Normally he wouldn't have enjoyed manipulating the woman he loved so dearly, but his mother was an incredibly strong and influential force that he needed on his side. He was fairly sure he now had her there, a feeling Tao confirmed as soon as Jack closed the door behind himself.

"Excellent work, Jack," Tao said with a grin. "Pitched just right and hopefully even covering the young lady's future efforts. What do you mean to do now?"

"Now I pay a visit to the innocent Miss Edmunds," Jack answered, squaring his shoulders. "There are a few questions I have to ask her, and who knows? What I said to Mother may turn out to be the absolute truth. But I want to hear it from *her.*"

Tao nodded and accompanied Jack, and this time they headed for the front door. As anxious as he was to see and speak to Amanda, he also felt faintly frightened. It was possible that he'd get the answer he *didn't* want to hear, but he had to take that chance. He *had* to know the truth, he simply had to.

"Well, how did it go?" Pei asked as soon as they were alone in Amanda's rooms. They'd also lunched alone, but with servants going in and out there hadn't been time to talk about Amanda's visit to Jack's mother. "Was she reasonable or otherwise?"

"More than reasonable," Amanda said over her shoulder as she continued on into her bedchamber. "She was like what I remember of my own mother, and by the time I was through she was furious with Jack. She's also invited the two of us to a small party tonight, to introduce us to our neighbors. I've already told the cook we'll be eating early."

"Is it wise to attend?" Pei asked, following Amanda into the bedchamber. "I mean, won't Mr. Michaels also be there? It *is* the house of his parents, after all."

"If they haven't thrown him out by then, I'll simply ignore him," Amanda said, reaching into a chest to pull out her *chih fu.* "I can't go into hiding for the rest of my life, after all, and wouldn't even if I could. Mr. Michaels ought to know by now that he'll be best off leaving me alone. Give me a hand getting out of these clothes, will you, Pei?"

"Are you changing into that uniform for a reason?" Pei asked as she came over to help Amanda. "I thought we were going to sit in the garden this afternoon and simply enjoy the beautiful day."

"You can stay here if you like," Amanda said through the folds of cloth she was in the process of taking off. "I want to have a look at my father's house, but I don't care to ruin a gown in the process. That house hasn't been lived in for almost twenty years, so it must be a real mess. Since I don't expect to find anything of value or interest, you certainly won't be missing anything by staying here."

"No, I'll come with you," Pei decided with a sigh as she put the gown aside. "I suppose I knew you weren't in the mood to sit around quietly, so I'm not in the mood for it any longer either. But after you change your clothes, I want to change mine. Neither one of us brought up enough clothes that we can afford to ruin something good."

Amanda smiled to show she was glad for the company, and once she was in the *chih fu* she went with Pei and waited while her friend changed. It didn't take long, and in only a few minutes they were on their way. Amanda's father's house was the next one over from Richard's, but it took longer to walk there than Amanda had been expecting. Her slippered feet were beginning to hurt by the time they reached the house, and she and Pei paused outside to look it over.

"It obviously needs to be scraped and painted, but other than that it's better than I expected," Pei remarked. "It's all on one floor the way a house is supposed to be, and the line around the roof looks enameled."

"Father had already visited China by the time Mother met him," Amanda said, also liking the house. Pulling a key from her belt, Amanda went on, "Richard knew I'd want to come here, so he gave me the key before we left. Let's see what the inside is like."

The lock resisted a little, but once Amanda had it open, the door itself was no problem. They walked into an entrance hall that was plainly and simply furnished, but the small tables and one painted wall were definitely flavored by the Orient.

"I think we may have changed our clothes for nothing," Pei said after walking to a wall and sliding a panel aside to make a doorway. "Everything is covered with dust, but I'd say this place is cleaned and repaired every few months at least. Did your brother say anything about that?"

"No," Amanda answered, sliding a panel aside in the opposite wall to discover a different room. "It looks like it's possible to go through this house without coming back to the entrance hall. I'll go this way and you go that, and we can meet in the room on the opposite side. Then we'll come back by taking each other's outward path."

Pei raised her brows at the suggestion, but apparently she knew Amanda well enough not to argue. What Amanda wanted was to be alone in her father's house for a while, to see if she was able to feel the spirits of her parents. They'd lived in that house for a while, and she'd been born there. Not that she remembered it, more's the pity. Amanda would have enjoyed remembering it, along with her parents.

Amanda went slowly from room to room, each of which had at least one window and a sliding panel that led to a central garden. There was wood rather than bamboo and rice paper, but it felt so much like China that Amanda began to feel homesick. If someone had appeared and told her she had to go back, she wouldn't have argued. The dream she'd had of finding a wonderful life in England wasn't turning out the way she'd hoped. She refused to let herself think about Jack, but if she had she would have been able to point to where her greatest dissatisfaction lay. If only she hadn't met him. . . .

Amanda heard the sound of a panel being slid aside in the next room, which meant Pei had gotten there before her. Well, she wasn't actually racing, and the next room might very well be the one her parents had used as a bed-chamber. The one she now stood in looked like a nursery, and amusingly enough there were tiny dragons painted on one wall. Brightly-colored dragons, flying around like carefree birds. . . .

A panel into the room was slid aside and slow footsteps approached, stopping just behind her. Amanda, still staring at the dragons, gestured to them.

"Apparently I was fated to be entwined with dragons right from the beginning," she commented to Pei softly. "Which one of those do you think is supposed to be me?"

"Definitely that blue one," came the answer, but not in Pei's voice. Amanda whirled around and there stood Jack Michaels.

"Where's Pei?" Amanda demanded, trying to see around Jack into the next room. "What have you done with her? If you've hurt her, I'll—"

"Hurt her?" Jack echoed, and suddenly he looked very angry. "I don't happen to make a habit of hurting women, but in your case I'm getting very close to making an exception."

"All right, you don't hurt women," Amanda granted, hating herself for even suggesting the idea. "But that doesn't answer my question. What have you done with her?"

"A friend of mine is keeping her company while you and I talk," he said, folding his arms as he looked down at her. "There are several things I'd like to discuss with you, and for that I wanted privacy."

"What sort of things?" Amanda inquired, wondering if he knew what she'd said to his mother. "I thought I'd made myself perfectly clear last night. I don't want to have anything more to do with you."

"But we still haven't found your friend Mr. Lichfield," he pointed out, although Amanda had the feeling he'd briefly meant to say something else instead. "That's some-thing I'm still involved with, since my people have specif-

ically asked me to look into the matter. I know you visited
Mr. Lichfield's relatives this morning, and I would appreciate it if you told me what was said."

Amanda hesitated, wondering if she should humor him
that much, but there was really no choice. If Mr. Lichfield
was going to be found, she needed to accept whatever help
was available.

"I spoke to the widow of Mr. Lichfield's brother, a really lovely woman," Amanda said after making up her
mind. "She told me that she hadn't yet heard from him,
and was very upset to hear he'd disappeared. She mentioned how close their family was, and how pleased Mr.
Lichfield would have been to learn that her three eldest
sons had good positions with a gentleman in London.
They earned enough to send money home on a regular basis, and the odd fact came up that one of her sons was
named Reggie. We agreed it was a terrible coincidence."

"Coincidence," Jack echoed, obviously seeing the point
at once. "Lichfield saw someone he knew before visiting
his friend, there's a Reggie in his family, and then a
Reggie is killed. If that's supposed to be a coincidence,
then I'm a cross-eyed cooper. You did very well without
me, possibly even better than with me."

"Does that mean you admit you were wrong when you
told me not to investigate alone?" Amanda asked.

"But I wasn't wrong," he disagreed after taking a deep
breath, his arms now at his sides. "Investigating alone
could have put you in serious danger, and for me nothing
is worth seeing you hurt. That's because I happen to be in
love with you."

He looked straight at her as he said that, obviously waiting for a response of some sort, but for the first minute or
two Amanda *couldn't* respond. Stunned shock kept her
standing there with her mouth open, but then an unpleasant memory broke her out of it.

"You say that with such sincerity and feeling that it's
hard to doubt you," she observed, now folding *her* arms.
"But if you don't mind, I'll do it anyway. Why don't you

try the line on that blonde woman you were dancing with at the Ashford's party? I'm sure *she* would believe you immediately."

"Her?" Jack blurted, at first looking bewildered, then he laughed. "I'm afraid she has more important things on her mind right now than confessions of love. Being under arrest for treason against the Crown tends to do that. Don't you remember I told you that I had to be at the party for official reasons? Did you really think I was lying because I danced with *one* other woman?"

Put that way her reasoning sounded ridiculous, and Amanda was tempted to feel very embarrassed. But her mind was shouting at her too loudly for anything as trivial as embarrassment to have a chance. Jack had said he loved her, and if the blonde woman *was* just business, he must have been telling the truth!

"Your mouth is open again," he teased with a grin as he stepped closer to put his arms around her. "I was very much afraid I'd hear you say you don't feel the same, but now I know you won't. If you had no feelings for me, you never would have felt betrayed. But *I've* said it out loud, and now I'd like to hear *you* say it. Do you love me?"

"I've loved you since the first day I saw you, all those years ago," Amanda admitted, ecstatic to be able to finally say it. Her hands rose to his face, caressing gently, and then they were kissing. It wasn't a sweet or fleeting kiss, it was filled with all the passion that burned within them both. Her arms around his neck crushed him as strongly as his arms around her, and it was a very long time before the kiss ended.

"I'm flattered that you wanted me so badly you used a drug on me," he murmured once the kiss was over. "You ought to know, however, that feeding me a drug to make love to you is like adding a cup of water to the ocean: completely unnecessary. And if you ever try it again, you have my word that you won't sit down for a sennight."

The look in his eyes told Amanda he was completely serious, but she was much too happy to do anything but laugh. Besides, chances were that if he ever did try to spank her, other considerations would divert him before he got very far. .

"I promise not to do that to you again—unless it becomes absolutely necessary," she responded with a laugh. "Does that make you feel better?"

"Considering who I'm dealing with, no it doesn't," he said, trying to look stern, but a grin broke through instead. "You are the most marvelous—if unscrupulous—girl I've ever met, and I can't wait until we're married. I'll also have to find a position where I can come home at lunchtimes, at least for the first ten or fifteen years. After that I may be able to wait until the end of the workday to hold you."

He lowered his head again, obviously intending to kiss her once more, but Amanda pulled back from him with a frown.

"What do you mean, you'll have to find a position?" she asked. "You already have one, doing a job that's absolutely necessary and one that you love. Why would you need to find something else?"

"Because I can't continue doing what I did and still be a respectable married man," he answered, all amusement suddenly gone. "Even if I changed my public character completely—which would then cause people to stop being careless around me—the hours I would have to keep would be completely erratic. You'd never know where I was or what I was doing or when I would be home. I flatly refuse to do that to you, my love, not to mention putting you in jeopardy because of my activities. No, finding something else to do is a much better idea. Like the idea I get looking at you in that *chih fu.*"

He began to run his hands over her, obviously trying to coax her into making love with him, but Amanda didn't need encouragement for that. She wanted Jack every time she saw him, but they had to get something else straight between them first.

"That's absolutely ridiculous," she stated, causing him

to break off with raised brows. "Your leaving government service, I mean," she clarified at once to erase the hurt look accompanying his surprise. "Why can't you just continue on as you've been doing, except for being married? As long as I know you love me, I *won't* wonder where you are or what you're doing. I'll already know, and I'll be there to greet you with a kiss whatever time you come home."

"Even after months or years of needing to put up with people's commiseration or ridicule over what a complete fool your husband is?" He asked the question quietly, but the pain in his eyes had increased. "I could never do that to you, or to myself. You'd grow to hate the sight of me, and I'd hate to face you and see it in your eyes. I do love my job, but not as much as I love you, and I've made my choice. It's the best one for both of us, and I'll never regret it."

"You say that now, but what about after those ten or fifteen years you mentioned?" Amanda returned just as quietly. "You'll look around at the deadly boring life you'd been forced to endure, and you'll know whose fault it was that you'd had to do it. The wise men say that the death of a dream can never be forgiven, and I'd be the one responsible for that death. It would end up coming between us more surely than any blonde ever could, and I refuse to play the lovesick child who sees nothing but the man she wants. I did that once, and it nearly ended in irreversible tragedy. If it isn't possible for you to continue on with your professional life, it also isn't possible for us to marry."

"Amanda, you're being ridiculously stubborn," he said with annoyance once the initial shock had passed. "We *are* going to be married, and I won't hear of you refusing. A job is just a job, but finding someone you love—"

"Finding someone you love means thinking of someone other than yourself," Amanda finished for him, raising her chin defiantly. "You can not hear what I've said all you please, but that won't change my mind. If you have to give up your work in order to marry me, then you won't be marrying me."

"But I've already handed in my resignation," he pounced, looking as if he'd found a point she couldn't argue. "If you refuse to marry me, I'll have nothing left at all."

"Are you trying to make me believe they won't take you back in an instant?" she countered, seeing the truth in his eyes as soon as the words were spoken. "Yes, I thought so. They want you as much as you want to be one of them, so I think we can forget about resignations and having nothing left."

"You are the most intractable, unreasonable—!" Words failed him then, but the way he glared at her was clear enough. Jack was very unhappy, but not as unhappy as he would be if she ever gave in and did as she so wanted to do. Her mother had once told her that her father had offered to give up his research if she would marry him, but she'd known better than to allow that. When a man is dedicated to what he does in life, it becomes a part of him. If you try to reject that part, you end up with none of him.

"So what are we supposed to do now?" Jack demanded testily. "Just forget about each other? I'm not about to accept that no matter how stubborn you are. Now that I know for certain that you love me, I *will* see us married."

"Not if you leave your position, you won't," Amanda returned, making sure her tone was just as determined as his. "And you don't have much time to come around to the side of reason. I'm not getting any younger, and I want to be married and out from under my brother's feet. If you don't find something both of us can accept rather quickly, I'll just have to marry someone else."

"You're blackmailing me again!" he stated in outrage, dark eyes flaming with anger. "You think you can push me into doing as you want, but you're wrong. This time it's going to be the way *I* want."

"And how do you expect to accomplish that?" Amanda asked calmly, challenging him. She knew her Golden

Devil would be able to find a way out of the current mess they were in, but only if he had a really good reason for doing it. "If you'll stop to remember for a moment," Amanda goaded, "you may recall that my brother Richard has already refused your suit at my urging, because I didn't believe you loved me. If you think he'll change his mind without my agreement, you still don't really know me."

"Oh, I know you, all right," he said darkly, then deliberately folded his arms. "I also know what you told my mother, but it won't do as much good as you're expecting. I told her something myself, and my father is an intelligent man. He'll soon realize there's more going on than he first thought, he'll remember who and what I am, and then he won't believe another word you say."

"But he did believe it to begin with," Amanda said, tickled that her plan had worked so well. "Even though he knows exactly what you're involved in. I hadn't expected that, and if the need arises I can do quite a lot with it. I'd say you'd better get cracking on finding a solution."

"Oh, I *will* find a solution," he growled, unfolding his arms to take hers and pull her slowly closer to him. "I *am* going to marry you, and once I do I'm going to teach you a good lesson every night. In fact, I may even start right now."

He looked down at her with all the ominous power natural to a big, capable, and angry man, but Amanda looked back up at him serenely. Her Golden Devil would never hurt her no matter how furious he got, and her confidence in that belief was unshakable. After a moment he saw that, but rather than grow angrier he slid his arms around her, and then they were entwined in another kiss.

Amanda slid her arms around him, under his coat, to caress his strongly muscled back. His lips were warm and soft, playing against the intense desire in his kiss and the incredible strength of his body. She wished his shirt and vest weren't there, so that she could feel all of him again without any clothes, but that couldn't be allowed to happen. The more she shared love with Jack Michaels the more she wanted him, and she couldn't afford to let her body betray her good sense. When his hands began to move on her in a way that showed the fire in his own blood, she forced herself to push away from him.

"I think it's time I looked at the rest of this house, then went back to Richard's," she said, trying not to sound breathless. "I still have things to do today, and I'm sure you do, too."

"Yes, I have to find someone who can teach me how *not* to be a gentleman," he said, his tone back to growling. "And I want to hear that you weren't serious about finding someone else to marry. You have to know I'd never allow that."

"Until you learn how *not* to be a gentleman, I think you'll have to," Amanda responded, working very hard to sound amused. "And let's not forget the matter of scandal. Your father may know who and what you are, but real, true scandal isn't something he'll be able to overlook. Do enjoy the rest of your day."

She moved around him then toward the open panel leading into the next room, and his now wordless growl followed her a moment before he did. Amanda took her time looking at the rest of the house, but with almost all of the furniture and decorations gone it was hard to picture anyone living there. The presence of a wordless, hulking shadow also helped to distract her, so it wasn't long before she was outside again and relocking the door.

Jack waited until she turned to leave before he stalked away. Amanda's eye caught sight of an Oriental man, dressed in European clothing, who quickly rose from the stone bench he'd been sharing with Pei and hurried after Jack. They disappeared into the woods in no time, and by then Pei had also left the bench to rejoin her.

"Amanda, what happened?" Pei demanded, the worry thick in her voice. "He looked so angry it's a wonder you weren't murdered."

"Right now the possibility of being murdered is the

least of my problems," Amanda answered. "Who was that man you were sitting with?"

"His name is Soong Tao, and he has a position with Duke Edward," Pei replied, somehow sounding odd. "He's also known Mr. Michaels for years, and although he didn't say so, I believe that they're friends. He mentioned that they found out where you'd gone from one of the girls at your brother's house."

"I'll have to think about it for a while before I decide whether I'm grateful to that girl or furious with her," Amanda said with a sigh. "He came to tell me he loves me, Pei, and made me admit that I feel the same. He wants to marry me, but I had to refuse him."

"Oh, Amanda, why in the world did you do *that?*" Pei demanded, actually showing exasperation. "If you love each other, why *shouldn't* you marry?"

"Because he'll have to give up something important to him," Amanda said, not about to discuss Jack's secret even with Pei. "If I let him do it then I'll be responsible for his loss, so I told him I won't marry him unless he can find a way to keep that valued possession as well. I also told him he'd better hurry, because I won't stop looking for an acceptable husband while I'm waiting. And I won't wait long, because I'm not getting any younger."

"I take back everything I said about that man," Pei stated, looking at Amanda the way she might have looked at a crazy person. "If he hasn't murdered you after *that,* he never will. Do you think he'll succeed, or will he just give up and walk away?"

"If he gives up and walks away, he doesn't love me as much as I love him," Amanda whispered, turning to stare at the place where Jack had disappeared. "I know what I'm risking, Pei, but I'm doing it to save what he and I can have together. The only other thing I can do is trust in him to save us. Shouldn't the hero of a woman's dreams be able to save the two of them?"

Pei didn't answer, and Amanda couldn't blame her. Dreams usually had happy endings, but sometimes they slid into nightmares. If that happened here . . . But she'd already started them on the path of destiny. She would simply have to continue on as she'd said she would, and pray that somewhere ahead their separate paths would merge.

Jack was already deep in the woods before Tao managed to catch up, and for a while Jack didn't trust himself to speak. But he could feel Tao's silent question waiting to be answered, and finally he felt able to do it.

"She loves me," Jack said, the words almost a snarl as he stomped through the woods. "More than I'd dared to hope, and at least as much as I love her."

"Then why do I have the feeling you're looking for something to mangle?" Tao asked, sounding as confused as Jack felt. "And would you mind slowing down at least until I understand what's going on?"

"I can't afford to slow down that long," Jack muttered, but he did ease the pace just a little. "I'm convinced that understanding women is beyond *all* men, but if you find I'm wrong don't hesitate to correct me. I told her I'd decided to give up my work with the government so I could marry her, because I couldn't marry her under my current situation. She came back with the decision that she won't marry me unless I *do* stay with the government, and I'd better hurry up and find a way to accomplish it. If I take too long looking for that solution, she'll marry someone else. Now go ahead and tell me that you understand what she's doing."

"Well, one thing she's doing is getting you into a state no one else has ever been able to accomplish," Tao commented, putting a calming hand on Jack's arm. "Dragons are talented that way, but if you lose control of yourself you'll never be able to hold your own. Now that I've said that, I can admit I'm just as confused as you are. I thought women were interested in nothing *but* marriage, so why does this one keep refusing you?"

"She said that at first she thought I didn't love her,"

Jack told him after blowing out a long, deep breath. "Now she thinks I'll eventually end up hating her for giving up a career I love. It doesn't seem to matter that I love her more than any job, or that I'm not likely to find the solution she wants. And if I don't find it, I'll lose her."

"If finding a solution to the problem is so impossible, maybe you'd be better off *letting* her marry someone else," Tao said in the bland way that was so familiar to Jack. "You two may love each other, but sometimes love isn't enough."

"I think it would be more accurate to say that sometimes love is too much," Jack countered, refusing to let his friend bait him. "Everything else becomes not enough. But all philosophy aside, if you think I'll let her marry another man, you're as crazy as she is. If it comes down to it, I'm not above kidnapping her and carrying her off."

"If it comes down to *that,* we'll all be in trouble," Tao said with a sigh, obviously knowing Jack wasn't joking or bluffing. "So what do you mean to do next?"

"The only thing I *can* do," Jack said, picking up their walking pace again. "I've got to tell my father exactly what's going on, so he'll be prepared for imminent scandal. And also so that he won't fall prey to another of her tricks. Unless I miss my guess she's already scheming, just to be certain I'm neutralized if I can't give her what she wants."

"Why does this sound more like a military campaign than a courtship?" Tao demanded, and for once he let his annoyance show. "I've never seen anything else like it, and I'm tempted to believe you two really are made for each other."

Since Jack already knew that, he didn't have to reply. He and Amanda *were* made for each other, but not necessarily fated to be together. Accomplishing that was *his* job, and he wouldn't have minded all that much . . . except that he had no idea where to begin.

Chapter 18

❦

"**. . . a**nd that's where it all stands now," Jack said, not as comfortable in the chair in his father's study as he was pretending to be. He hadn't been able to speak privately to his father until just a few minutes ago, only a short time before their party was due to begin. Jack was dressed for the party in clothes he kept in his father's house for exactly that sort of occasion, but his father had been staring through him for the last few minutes, as if Jack had turned invisible.

"This has to be the most bizarre situation I've heard of in my entire life," Duke Edward said at last, faint annoyance behind the words. "I was so busy being angry with you, John, that I never stopped to think the thing through. I feel like a fool, but I'm also reluctantly impressed. If you manage to marry her, your children could well conquer the world."

"Father, this isn't as funny as you've suddenly decided it is," Jack told him sourly after seeing the unmistakable gleam of laughter in his father's eyes. "I know how much you'd enjoy having grandchildren who conquered the world, but at this rate they'll never be born. Not unless I carry their mother off, which I'm seriously considering to be my best option. I'm telling you about it so you and Mother can brace for the scandal."

"The thought of scandal only shocks me in public, John," his father responded with a grin. "Or when your mother is around. I would have been perfectly willing to

278

carry *her* off, if her family hadn't fallen all over themselves accepting my suit. So the young lady was so mad about you that she took unscrupulous advantage, eh? It looks like everyone who has told me you'd come to a bad end was right. You played fast and loose one time too many, and now you've been ruined."

"Father, please!" Jack said with a groan. "It isn't a joke! If she were plotting against the British government rather than against me, we'd probably soon see a queen installed on the throne in place of the king. I haven't the faintest idea of what I can do to satisfy her demands, and I'm beginning to believe more and more that I'll be wasting my time trying. Which do you think would be better to carry her off to, a mountaintop or a cave?"

"Oh, definitely a cave," his father said, obviously trying to restrain his amusement. "Furnishing a cave is a good deal easier than doing a mountaintop. But you're right about the need to discuss this seriously, John, and the young lady is also right. You can't simply resign your position even if she changes her mind and agrees to accept your proposal. If you do, nothing will be remembered about you but your public character. How will you like having your children come across *that* when they're grown? And they *will* come across it—depend on that even if you depend on nothing else."

"I hadn't thought of that," Jack muttered with a frown, suddenly seeing himself trying to explain away something he would still not be able to tell the truth about. "Even if I become an absolute model citizen from now on, I'll have people's memories hanging over my head forever. Maybe I've been foolish thinking I could afford to marry at all, ever."

"This is the second time today I've wished you were a boy again," his father said, and now his smile was filled with sympathy and pain. "But just as I couldn't take a switch to your backside this afternoon, now I can't solve this problem for you. Being an adult and a man means you must solve your own problems, John, a statement which should also tell you that I haven't a clue about what your course should be. All I can do is thank God that the decision isn't mine to make, and wish to God it wasn't yours."

"But it *is* mine, so I'll have to make it," Jack said after taking a deep breath. "I've come to the belief that if we could somehow force these decisions on criminals, crime would virtually disappear in the empire."

"In the world," his father corrected with a bitter smile, and then he stood. "Our guests should be starting to arrive, so we'd better get ourselves to the salon before your mother has to come looking for us. And I think you ought to be warned: your Miss Edmunds and her friend Miss Han will be among the company. Your mother also asked Tao to attend to keep Miss Han from feeling too alone, and he agreed almost before she had the words out."

"Tao?" Jack said with raised brows as he also stood. "The man who has to be bound hand and foot and *dragged* to social occasions? But that's right, he spent the time I was arguing with Amanda talking to Miss Han. Do you think a spark could have been struck between them?"

"Either that or he's suddenly become addicted to parties," the duke responded dryly, adjusting the lace at his cuffs. "I warn you right now, John: if Miss Han carries him off with her back to China, I'll hold you personally responsible."

Jack was about to protest his innocence, but then it came to him that he *was* responsible. If he hadn't gotten involved with Amanda . . . But he had, and she would be at the party tonight. He didn't have to be told that he would be expected to stay away from her, and all things considered that might be the best idea in any event. If he was forced to decide that marriage to him would be unfair for Amanda under any circumstances, this would be the last time he'd be able to see her.

Following his father out of the study, Jack tried to remember what it felt like to look forward to a party. It seemed like forever since the last time he had. . . .

Amanda wearily approached the salon with Pei trailing on her heels. That was where the servant they were following had said the party was being held, which meant it wasn't a ball. Hopefully it also meant there would be fewer people, since Amanda wasn't much in the mood to be charmed or charming. If she'd had her choice, she would have stayed home to brood and worry.

But the duchess had all but demanded that she come, and she needed to find out what Jack had said to counter the story she'd told that morning. If she meant to continue thwarting him, she had to know what Jack was doing.

"Miss Edmunds and Miss Han," another servant announced as the first bowed them through a double doorway. There were already a few people in the room, and their hostess was right there to greet them.

"Ladies, how nice of you to come," Duchess Katherine said with a warm smile for each of them. "And how lovely you both look. Come and meet the others who have already arrived."

The duchess gestured to the other side of the large room, where several people were standing with drinks in their hands. A string quartet sat on a platform playing soft chamber music, and quiet servants stood here and there, ready to provide whatever a guest might want.

Amanda glanced at Pei as they followed the duchess, but Pei was too busy looking at the group they approached to notice. *Now, who could she be looking for?* Amanda wondered, but then she noticed Soong Tao standing on the fringes of the group, and his eyes had already found Pei. Amanda forgot her own troubles in her sudden delight for her friend.

"Gentlemen, allow me to present Miss Amanda Edmunds," Duchess Katherine said to the group once they reached it. "Miss Edmunds is the sister of Lord Pembroke, and she's currently staying in his house. My dear, this gentleman is Colonel Harwood Ebersham."

"I'm delighted to say that the young lady and I have already met," Colonel Ebersham said enthusiastically, while brandishing his ever-present walking stick in his left hand. "She and I were fellow passengers on the ship returning us to England, and I'm also acquainted with Miss Han. I thought surely we would never meet again, Miss Edmunds, but happily I was wrong."

"I'm afraid I've also met Miss Edmunds, Your Grace," another male voice said with amusement while Colonel Ebersham bent over her hand. Amanda looked up to see Robert Blake, Baron Delland, and had to forcibly keep herself from groaning.

"My presence, however, unlike Colonel Ebersham's, is no coincidence," Blake went on with a grin. "Lord Pembroke was kind enough to tell me where Miss Edmunds had run off to, so I came up here at once and opened my house. I've been convinced, you see, that it's been much too long since there was a lady of that house. A man does best with gentle companionship, after all, and his heart knows when the time comes for mourning to end."

"Well, the end of mourning is always welcome news," the duchess said while Blake took his turn bending over Amanda's hand. Her voice sounded odd to Amanda, as though her words had been nothing more than a formality, and then she turned to the last of the group. "This gentleman, my dear, is Mr. Soong Tao, my husband's most valued assistant. Mr. Soong, this is Miss Edmunds and Miss Han."

"Ladies," the man said with a bow, his bland expression disclaiming that they had already met. Amanda realized that so far Duchess Katherine had completely wasted her time with the introductions, and because of that Amanda had to swallow a smile. Pei simply performed her own bow to acknowledge the introduction, but Amanda felt something more was needed.

"The wise man knows when not to speak," Amanda said in Chinese as she also bowed. "What a pity all men cannot be wise."

"The man who knows himself for a fool is wise in his own way," Mr. Soong returned with the faintest of smiles.

"Beware such a man, for he will most often take you by surprise."

Hearing that, Amanda had a bigger smile to swallow. She hadn't mentioned Jack by name and neither had Mr. Soong, but both knew they were talking about no one else. The man seemed to be trying to warn Amanda, as if she didn't already know what a thin and unsteady line she walked.

"Why, how interesting," Duchess Katherine exclaimed, turning her smile on Amanda. "It hadn't occurred to me that you would naturally speak Chinese. Do tell us what was said."

"We merely exchanged polite greetings," Amanda told her, aware of Pei's amused expression. "Chinese is a beautiful language and quite intricate, so that the most usual of comments comes out sounding like poetry."

"Epic poetry," Robert Blake said pointedly, hinting that in his opinion the exchange had taken too long. He hadn't moved his gaze from Amanda's face, as if no one else stood in the room.

"Ah, new arrivals," Duchess Katherine said as a servant began to announce more guests. "Please excuse me."

All three of the men bowed as she walked away, obviously seeing nothing odd about the woman's behavior, but Amanda sensed something unusual. The duchess had seemed downright reluctant to leave, as though she felt that something unacceptable might happen without her there. It didn't take a genius to guess that her behavior had something to do with the story that Jack had told her, which meant she could now be considered to be working in her son's cause. Since most heroes won their ladies fair *without* the help of their mothers, Amanda decided that Jack shouldn't be allowed that assistance either and began her campaign to counter it.

"Colonel Ebersham, do tell me how you happened to be here," she said with a smile. "I was also under the impression that we'd never meet again."

"I ran into an old friend in London," the colonel said,

gesturing to a servant with a tray. "He and his wife have a house up here, and he insisted that I visit until we get caught up on each other's lives. We were all invited tonight, but my friend and his wife had a previous engagement that didn't include me. For that reason, I'm here all alone. Will you have a drink, Miss Edmunds?"

"Thank you, Colonel," Amanda replied, choosing a glass of fruit punch from the servant's tray. There were also glasses of champagne, but Amanda intended to have a clear head to face whatever the night happened to bring.

"I, too, am here all alone, but deliberately so," Robert Blake said after he and the colonel had helped themselves to champagne. "You don't seem at all impressed by that, Miss Edmunds, which probably means you're remembering my forward behavior when we met and are now holding it against me. If that's true, I apologize most sincerely. If it isn't, then possibly I can be forward a second time. With your permission, of course."

"You're asking my permission to be forward?" Amanda said, beginning to be amused in spite of herself. "Assuming I gave that permission, what would you be forward about?"

"Oh, I'd certainly think of *something,*" Blake returned with a grin, the expression in his green eyes clearly one of relief. "Possibly I might begin with how lovely you look tonight, and remark that I can't imagine you *not* looking lovely. Have *you* ever seen the lady looking less than lovely, Colonel?"

"Not in all the time we sailed together," Colonel Ebersham answered, his words showing not the least doubt. "But what impresses me most about her is her heart and wisdom. Most ladies tend to lack those qualities, but not Miss Edmunds. The man who wins her will be the most fortunate of men."

"The few times I tried gaming, fortune ignored me completely," Blake said with a sigh. "It occurred to me that my luck might be saving itself up for a special occasion, but I couldn't quite believe that—until just recently. Now

I'm hoping it's the truth, but I'm also trying very hard not to trip over my own feet. It would spoil the effect, I think."

Amanda chuckled while Colonel Ebersham simply smiled, and then the duchess was back with newcomers to perform introductions again. Happily only Blake knew Lord and Lady Tremaine, but Amanda still found the situation amusing. Lady Tremaine babbled while her husband spoke only in grunts, and Blake deftly directed the lady's attention to Colonel Ebersham. Amanda thought it was a mean trick, but couldn't help feeling grateful to Blake as he guided her out of the small crowd.

"That's the biggest problem with these small get-togethers," he said ruefully once they stood by themselves. "There are only so many victims for the enthusiastic talkers, so you're bound to be trapped at *some* time. The trick is to learn how to put that time off for as long as possible."

"Throwing someone else to the wolves doesn't strike me as the nicest way to accomplish that," Amanda responded, glancing around. "Quietly suggesting to the wolf that she's overdoing it might serve the same purpose, but the only one I know who's likely to do that is temporarily unavailable. And I think she might become annoyed if she's interrupted just to speak to a wolf."

"She and the gentleman both," Blake agreed, following her glance to where Pei and Mr. Soong stood talking. "They make a handsome pair, but not nearly as handsome as we would be. And imagine how my friends would envy me, having a lady on my arm whose companion speaks to wolves. Now *there's* something you don't see every day."

Amanda joined his laughter, and that was when two others appeared beside them. One of them was Jack, and the other a handsome older man with enough presence to suit a king.

"Duke Edward, how nice to see you again," Blake said while offering a bow, confirming Amanda's guess about the identity of the older man. "Has Miss Edmunds been introduced to you as yet?"

"No, as a matter of fact she hasn't," Jack's father said with a warm smile, taking Amanda's hand as she curtsied. "Welcome back to England, Miss Edmunds. The empire has need of ladies of your caliber."

"Thank you, Your Grace," Amanda murmured in answer, aware of the amusement in his eyes. She had no idea how much Jack had told him, but it must be quite a lot if he was amused rather than embarrassed over what Jack had supposedly done. She'd have to move with care around the duke, but it might still be possible to accomplish something.

"Blake, have you met my son?" the duke asked, and when Blake shook his head the duke continued, "Baron Delland, may I present my son John? He's up here visiting with us for a short time."

"An honor, sir," Blake responded with a small bow while Jack nodded with something of a flourish. The two men were very much alike physically: tall, broad-shouldered and handsome, even though Jack was dark, and Blake fair. The main difference between them was that Jack was clearly in his public character again, which definitely made him look foppish and foolish. If he had come over to prove a point to her, Amanda intended to make him regret it.

"In turn, allow me to present Miss Edmunds," Blake continued to Jack, but Amanda was ready.

"Mr. Michaels and I have already met," she interrupted calmly. "He even apologized once for being too bold, which was really quite silly. Mr. Michaels is obviously not the bold sort, are you, Mr. Michaels?"

Amanda watched Jack hesitate very briefly, clearly fighting his anger. He must have known that she didn't want him there, especially when she spoke to other men. Didn't he realize he made all other men lose by comparison? He'd deliberately come over to ruin things for her, so *she* had no qualms about forcing him to react in his public character.

"Why, dear me, no," he answered at last. "Boldness is for dashing men of action, not for the likes of me. But does your comment mean you *prefer* bold men, Miss Edmunds? Most of the ladies of my acquaintance prefer gentlemen such as I am. Boldness can become *such* a bore."

"I, too, prefer gentlemen, Mr. Michaels," Amanda replied with a faint smile, demurely meeting the eyes of none of the men. "But boldness also has its place, sir, as long as it's done with a lady's permission."

Blake, apparently remembering their previous conversation about forwardness, began to chuckle. Duke Edward seemed to be trying not to chuckle, and that left only Jack. He smiled and bowed to allow her the point, but to Amanda's eyes he'd had to force himself to do it. His father then came to his rescue.

"I see more of our guests have arrived," Duke Edward announced, as though only just having made the discovery. "I'll have to ask you to excuse me now, but we'll certainly speak again later. Come along, John, and I'll introduce you to those you haven't yet met."

Jack's bow to indicate his own leave-taking came almost immediately, but Amanda had caught the instant of hesitation. It seemed Mr. Michaels wasn't pleased with the idea of leaving her alone with Blake, but his father hadn't left him any choice. Amanda added a pleasant smile to the nod she gave father and son, and that hopefully made Jack grind his teeth as he walked away.

"Odd man, Michaels," Blake murmured once their host and his son were out of earshot. "He and I have never really met before, but I've certainly heard about him. Runs with a wild crowd and spends his time gaming and wenching, I'm told. Most are amazed at Duke Edward's patience with his son, but the rest consider him foolish for not disowning him. Personally, I admire the duke for his loyalty to his own flesh and blood. One day Michaels might surprise everyone by turning himself around."

"That's a really lovely thing to say," Amanda, looking up at Blake, couldn't help observing. "Not many people seem to realize that standing by your children may be difficult, but the eventual reward can be enormous. Do you have children of your own, Mr. Blake?"

"I would have had if my wife hadn't died," he answered with a sigh, then forced himself to smile. "One day I hope to have a houseful, which I'll probably live to regret. For now, why don't we go and see what nibbles our hosts have provided for us? I had dinner before I came, of course, but being with a beautiful woman always makes me hungry."

Amanda had to laugh at that, and it wasn't the last time they laughed together that night. Robert Blake was fun to be with, and she hoped they would stay friends even after she married Jack. If she did marry Jack. It was impossible not to notice that Jack had disappeared early and didn't return. Had he given up? Had she finally gone too far by baiting him in public? Amanda found his absence so distracting that she didn't realize Duchess Katherine had come up to her before the woman spoke.

"My dear, I hope you won't mind if I have a word with you," Jack's mother said. "Baron Delland has been roped into a business discussion, but he's certain to free himself again in a moment or two so I'll be brief. I know the truth about how matters stand between you and my son John."

"You do?" Amanda said, pretending there was only a single truth circulating about that very complex relationship. "And what might that be?"

"Oh, my dear, let's not pretend," the duchess said with great sympathy. "I know the two of you are in love, and only your brother's refusal to accept John's suit is keeping you apart. I would never council a young lady to disobey the brother who watches over her welfare, but surely there's a difference between disobedience and wholehearted cooperation."

"I would venture to say that most people would agree with that statement," Amanda granted warily. "There *is* a difference between disobedience and wholehearted cooperation, quite a large difference. May I ask what point you're trying to make, Your Grace?"

"I think the first point is how bad I am at beating around the bush," the duchess answered, clearly annoyed with herself. "I'd better speak straight to the point and forget about the niceties. Just because your brother turned John down, that doesn't mean you have to rush right out and immediately find someone Lord Pembroke won't turn down. You won't be disobeying him if you simply take your time and give my son and his father a chance to straighten matters out. I know Baron Delland is a lovely man, but so is my son."

"Oh, but, Your Grace, I'm afraid that won't do," Amanda said, finally understanding exactly what Jack had told his mother. Amanda was supposed to love Jack, but was refusing to disobey her brother's wishes . . . "If His Grace the duke speaks to my brother, and then Richard changes his mind, it will be as if my brother had been *forced* to accept Mr. Michaels. I could never consider that getting Richard's blessing, really I couldn't."

Amanda looked at the older woman wide-eyed, trying to show what an awkward position the duke's talking to Richard would put her in. Of course, awkward wasn't the word, but Duchess Katherine still got the message.

"Oh, dear, I suppose in a way you're right," the woman fretted, looking frustrated. "I don't agree, mind, but I *can* see your side of it. So what do *you* think ought to be done?"

"I really don't know," Amanda said with a sigh. "I suppose if Mr. Michaels performed some marvelous feat or other, possibly my brother would reconsider. Do you think that might happen?"

"That John will perform some marvelous feat?" The duchess shook her head with a sad smile. "I love my son

very much, but I'm afraid he isn't the sort to accomplish
that. Now I'm really at a loss."

Amanda sympathized, but she couldn't help feeling satisfied by what she'd learned. Jack's father might know all
about him, but his mother didn't. It could prove to be a
useful thing to know, but all revelations ended when Colonel Ebersham joined them.

"I hope you don't mind, Miss Edmunds, if *I* spend some
time in your company," the colonel said after bowing to
his hostess with one hand still on his walking stick. "Blake
may be younger than I am, but that doesn't give him the
right to monopolize your attention. Unless you prefer it
that way?"

"There are no agreements or promises between Baron
Delland and myself, Colonel," Amanda told him, enjoying
his blunt, military way of going straight to the heart of the
matter. "I would very much enjoy spending some time in
your company."

Amanda, having grown fond of the man, meant every
word she said, but the duchess brightened immediately.

"You see, my dear, that's exactly the sort of thing I
meant," she said with a broad smile when Amanda took
the colonel's arm. "Two men are a much better idea than
just one, and three or four would be better still. I'll look
about and see if there are any others. If you will excuse
me, Colonel?"

Colonel Ebersham bowed again, but his brows were
raised in a way that amused Amanda. He had no idea what
the duchess had meant, but Amanda understood perfectly.
Jack's mother thought she was playing the field in order to
give Jack time to "fix" things. That was almost what
Amanda was doing, but from a slightly different point of
view.

Her attention was the colonel's alone for another few
minutes, but then Blake came back. He'd been talking to
some people to whom Amanda had been introduced but
whose names she couldn't remember, and he seemed to be
annoyed. He muttered something about people who had no

idea what they were talking about, and then he set about trying to separate Amanda from Colonel Ebersham, which he didn't quite accomplish. Amanda spent the rest of her time at the party watching the two fence verbally and politely—and struggling *not* to think about Jack.

Chapter 19

The evening had been a diversion of sorts for Amanda, but she wasn't sorry when the time came to leave. She and Pei had been driven over in a light carriage by one of her brother's house men, and Duke Edward insisted that Mr. Soong accompany them back to their door. Pei didn't seem to mind, so Amanda thanked her host and accepted the protection. Braxton Meadows seemed to be a generally quiet area, but Amanda still hadn't neglected to put her staff in the carriage.

Mr. Soong waited until they were inside before having the driver take him back, and just inside the door Amanda's maid waited to help her get undressed. Since the short trip back had been pleasant but silent, Pei gave Amanda a glance that said Amanda would do well to come to her rooms as soon as the maid was gone. Amanda returned a brief nod and smile, assuring Pei she would be there.

Once she was into a nightgown and robe, and the maid had left her chambers, Amanda waited at the hall door until the girl was completely out of sight, then she silently crossed the hall to Pei's rooms. The candle she carried lit her way through the darkened sitting room, and a single knock got her into the bedchamber.

"Finally," Amanda said as she closed the door behind herself. "I thought we'd never be left alone to talk. So tell me quickly: are you in love with him?"

"How can I possibly know this soon?" Pei countered

with a laugh from where she sat on her bed. "We only met this afternoon, after all."

"But you do like him?" Amanda pressed, putting her candle on the nightstand next to the bed before sitting opposite Pei. "What is he like? What's he been saying to you?"

"Mostly we've been discussing you and Mr. Michaels," Pei answered with a rueful smile. "This afternoon we both thought you'd be together longer than you were, and tonight we decided you were both wrong. Mr. Michaels shouldn't have come over to you, and you shouldn't have said what you did."

"I only said what I did because he *did* come over," Amanda protested, trying not to sound defensive. "It's not my fault he ended up feeling foolish, not when he should know better than to play that silly game with me. He should have saved it for the people he's supposed to fool."

"He had no choice about acting that way, and it's possible his father insisted that he accompany him," Pei countered in Jack's defense. "You were just annoyed because he didn't jump to do as you'd told him to, so you thought you'd teach him a lesson. Mr. Soong tells me that Mr. Michaels isn't a man to jump to anyone's bidding, and chances are excellent that this time you've gone too far."

"What do you mean 'too far'?" Amanda asked, suddenly worried. "He hasn't changed his mind about marrying me . . . ?"

Amanda couldn't bring herself to go on, but Pei simply shook her head in annoyance.

"Mr. Soong tells me there's no chance of *that,* although why he's so persistent I can't imagine," she said. "If I were Mr. Michaels and a woman treated me the way you've been treating him . . . Well, that's his business and none of mine. I just think you've been horrid."

"And here I thought you wanted to talk to me because of Mr. Soong," Amanda said, trying not to react to the accusation. "Didn't you two discuss anything but me and the horrid way I've been treating poor, helpless Jack Michaels? Don't tell me you haven't even noticed if you like each other?"

"We discovered that there's a mutual attraction between us because we share knowledge of something that others of our people don't know about," Pei said coolly. "We not only speak the English language, we've both seen this country, although he's seen a good deal more of it than I have. Why don't you write a note of apology to Mr. Michaels? Mr. Soong is very discreet, and he'll be glad to give it to him as soon as—"

"What a shame I forgot to bring any paper or ink with me," Amanda said abruptly, getting off the bed to retrieve her candle. "Sleep well, Pei. I'll see you at breakfast."

Pei was so annoyed she let it show in her expression, but Amanda didn't care. She simply left Pei's rooms as quickly as possible, determined not to let the argument go any further. She was beginning to feel as though everyone was on Jack's side and no one on hers, maybe not even herself. She'd already been wondering if she might have gone too far even before Pei said anything. Now . . . now she was certain she hadn't, and not just because she was too stubborn to admit it. If Jack hadn't come to *her* she never would have done it, so it had clearly been Jack's fault.

Deciding that didn't make Amanda feel any better, not the way it should have. Morosely she reached her bedchamber and closed the door behind herself. She didn't feel like going to bed, but what else was there to do? Even if she'd had a Go board and the necessary markers, the only one who could have played the game was Pei, and Pei wasn't—

"How nice of you to come back so quickly," a voice interrupted her thoughts. "When you left immediately after changing your clothes, I thought I'd have something of a long wait."

The first words had made Amanda whirl around, to see Jack leaning against the wall near the shadows with his arms folded. He'd obviously been hidden in those shadows the whole time, simply waiting for her maid to leave. . . .

"What are you doing here?" she tried to demand, but his nearness shook her so thoroughly that her voice turned sultry. He'd stood there watching her undress, had seen her naked before she'd put on her nightgown, and knowing that began to raise her internal heat beyond control.

"I just stopped by to find out if you enjoyed yourself tonight," he remarked, unfolding his arms as he pushed away from the wall. "Did you have as much fun as you expected to, possibly even *more* than you expected? In all modesty I think *I* might have helped to make that happen, so I'm here to give you a chance to thank me."

Even in the dimness of the room, it wasn't hard for Amanda to see the anger in his eyes. When he got too close she began to back away, but not because she thought he might hurt her. On the contrary, she expected him to touch her gently, and that was something she couldn't afford to let happen. She wanted Jack very badly, but if she got him then he would get *her* as well. Men were notorious for working much harder to win something they'd been denied, everyone knew *that*. . . .

"Don't you *want* to thank me?" he pressed, slowly pursuing her across the floor. "But maybe *I* should be thanking *you* instead, for telling me so clearly that it's bold men whom you prefer. Most men are naturally bold, but out of deference to women's sensibilities they usually restrain themselves. You have no idea how pleased I am that I no longer have to restrain myself."

"If you'll remember, I *qualified* that statement about liking bold men," Amanda countered, trying to regain control of the situation even as she continued to back away. "A man is welcome to be bold with me only with my permission, and I haven't given you that. But that's beside the point, because you have no business being here at all. If it turns out that I have to marry someone else, it won't be fair to him if I—"

Jack's growl interrupted her and then he was coming toward her even faster, a hard look in his eyes. Amanda could have kicked herself for babbling instead of stopping to think, but that regret came much too late. Just as late as the realization that she'd stopped retreating and was in the midst of defending herself! She'd been trained to react without forethought, and the side kick she had already launched was just about to connect with the man coming toward her so fast.

But that wasn't simply a man, it was the Golden Devil. Without breaking stride Jack blocked her left-footed kick with his right forearm, using enough strength in the block to knock her off balance. Amanda tried to use a hand blow as she staggered backward, now willing to do anything to divert him until she regained her footing, but the Golden Devil was ready. He also blocked her hand blow as he slid behind her, and then her elbows were pulled together behind her back.

"It looks like you want to fight," he murmured in her ear as his right hand slid around to stroke her middle under the robe. "All right, go ahead and fight then."

"Jack, let go of me!" she snapped, finding it impossible to kick him or pull free. Her nightgown and robe were getting in the way of her feet, and her arms were being held too high. "I wasn't the one who started this, so you have no right to—"

"Ah, but you *are* the one who started this," he corrected, making no effort to do as she'd asked. "Or do you expect me to believe that that was me talking about you and other men? If you want me to turn you loose, you can apologize for trying to provoke me. It's a nasty habit you have, and one I won't put up with any longer."

"Stop trying to sound as if you're already my husband," Amanda gritted out through clenched teeth, hating the way her struggles were being ignored. And even through the yellow lawn of her nightgown, the touch of his hand was driving her mad! "Let me go this instant or I'll scream."

"Go ahead and scream," he offered, sounding completely unworried. "I happen to know how far away the servants' quarters are in this house, and it's also much too late for any of the staff to be wandering around in this part of the house. Now, are you going to apologize, or do I have to continue to be bold?"

"You're not being bold, you're being outrageous," she maintained, still trying to break free. "And if this is your idea of proper courting, then—oh!"

"Apparently you haven't noticed, but we've gone beyond courting," he told her dryly, pretending she hadn't yelped when he sat on the edge of a table and lifted her across his knees. It was now her wrists that were being held behind her back, but only in his left hand. His right was free to stroke her bottom, slowly and caressingly, making her want to moan as well as squirm.

"Courting is for those who are only just learning to know each other," he continued, now slowly beginning to lift her gown. "On first acquaintance it's necessary for a man to find out if the woman who has aroused his interest has any quirks or habits he'd find intolerable. You have a cartload of those, but for some mad reason I love you anyway. God knows I've tried to talk myself out of it, but since it hasn't worked I've had to come to terms with it. Once again: do I get that apology?"

By then her nightgown was up to her waist, and it was now her flesh his hand stroked. Amanda wanted to scream and curse over the way she was being tortured, but to do that she'd first have to admit how she felt. Jack knew she wanted him physically, but if he ever found out that the least touch of his hand turned her desperate for him. . . . No, that would do much more harm than good, so she'd *have* to apologize. If she didn't, and he spanked her before taking her to bed . . .

"All right, I'll apologize," Amanda hissed. "Do you want to tell me what to say, or shall I compose it myself?"

"Why don't you start off yourself," he decided, his hand still moving. "If I don't like what I hear or think it needs amendment, I'll be sure to let you know."

"Fine," Amanda said after clearing her throat, preparing

herself to be meek and obedient. He wasn't likely to accept anything less, blast his stubborn hide. "I—shouldn't have mentioned other men to you, and I apologize. It was extremely insensitive of me, considering your intentions. I'm sorry and I won't do it again."

"That was a fair beginning," he allowed, now running two fingers up the inside of her thigh. "Now say you were a very bad girl tonight who deserves to be soundly punished."

Amanda had almost choked trying not to gasp at what his toying was doing to her, but he probably hadn't noticed. The heavy swelling in his breeches under her left side told her his attention was almost certainly on other things.

"I—I was a very bad girl tonight," she managed to get out after licking her lips from a dry mouth. "Yes, very bad, and I deserve to be—be punished. May I get up now?"

"No," he answered distractedly, his fingers now toying with the nub of her womanhood. "Since we agree you ought to be punished, what do you think that punishment should consist of?"

Amanda was too busy trying to keep herself from fainting or going mad to answer immediately. She was desperate to touch Jack in the same way he was touching her, but he refused to allow it. She could almost remember him doing that once before, but her mind wasn't working well enough to let her remember when.

"Well?" Jack prodded with both his words and his fingers. "What do you think that punishment should be?"

"I . . . I don't . . . I can't . . . you can't mean you intend to force me to your pleasure." After a stumbling start, Amanda had been struck with inspiration: if she could make him believe she still didn't want him to make love to her, he might decide to punish her by doing the one thing she wanted most desperately. "Please, Jack, you can't put me through that humiliation again. It just isn't proper . . ."

"If it isn't proper, why did you start the game by doing it to me first?" he returned mildly. "You've long since forfeited any consideration in that area, and I believe I know what your punishment will be. Do you remember our once discussing the subject of concubines?"

"No, you can't mean it!" Amanda protested as she renewed her struggles, hopefully doing a believable job. "Please, Jack, you can't make me act the concubine with you!"

"Oh, but I can," he disagreed, and now there was a grin in his voice. "And not only can, but will. What's more, you'll be a very good little concubine, otherwise I'll tan your bottom and make you start over from the beginning. Do you understand me?"

"Yes, Jack, I understand you," Amanda answered meekly in a small voice. "I'll try very hard to please you."

"Then let's get to it," he said, finally putting her back on her feet and letting her go. "And if you try to fight me again, you'll start out with an aching bottom. Do you understand *that* as well?"

"Yes, Jack," Amanda repeated, keeping her eyes down and her voice very small. But if he didn't stop talking and start doing something soon . . .

"All right, the first thing you'll do is get out of that gown and robe," he ordered, leaving her to walk to the bed. "Just take them off and drop them right there."

A faint tremor tickled its way through Amanda, making her want to shiver. She'd never deliberately undressed in front of anyone who wasn't female, and the idea of doing it in front of the man she loved was turning the very air around her to raging flames. She wanted him to see her, wanted him to want her, but this latest game had to be played just right. If he found her out he could decide to leave, and that would be worse than anything else he might conceivably do.

So feigning reluctance was her only option, but there might be a way to hurry his intentions; Green Jade had once demonstrated the technique for Pei and herself.

Amanda took a deep breath and began, praying that she
could be even half as good as Green Jade had been. Her
robe closed at her throat with two tiny buttons, so Amanda
opened them slowly. She also kept her eyes down, as
though too embarrassed to look at Jack. When the robe
was open, she let it slide from her arms and down her
body to the floor.

"An excellent beginning," Jack's voice came from
where he lay on her bed. A glance showed Amanda that
he'd taken off his coat, leaving him only in plain shirt and
breeches. His finery from the party had been replaced with
ordinary clothes. "Now let the nightgown follow."

Still keeping her eyes down, Amanda slowly pulled her
left arm from its sleeve, did the same with the right just as
slowly, hesitated very briefly, then let the garment fall. It
slid down her body quite seductively, exposing first her
breasts, then her belly, and lastly her legs. Then she stood
there in the pool of yellow lawn, eyes and head down, but
body fully exposed.

And Jack's eyes directly on her! Amanda had no need
to look up to know that, not when her blood steamed from
his sound of appreciation. She longed to see him in the
same way, but she didn't expect that to happen for quite a
while, if at all.

"Lady mine, you are the most beautiful woman I've
ever seen," Jack murmured, so quietly that Amanda
thought she might not have been meant to hear it. But she
had heard, and the thrill that passed through her had nothing to do with physical desire. She loved Jack with every
single fiber of her being, more than she had ever dreamed
it was possible to do. Knowing that he returned her love
made it all so incredibly much better, so wonderfully magical that she was suddenly very ashamed of herself.

"Jack, I'm going to apologize again, but this time I'm
going to mean every word," she said, looking up to see the
surprise in his eyes. "You're the most wonderful man in
the world, and I treated you extraordinarily badly tonight.
If I were you I *would* punish me, but not by insisting I do

something I love the idea of doing for you. I'm very ashamed of myself, and although I know you'll forgive me, I also know I don't deserve it."

She forced herself to watch as his eyes grew wide with surprise, and then he left the bed and came over to her. She had no idea what he meant to say or do, but the time for games was over. She looked up at him, ready to accept anything he did, but was unprepared for the gentle hand he raised to her face.

"You *love* the idea of playing concubine for me?" he asked, brows raised in disbelief. "I can tell you're serious, but I don't understand how that can be true. You're the feistiest female I've ever encountered, so playing concubine ought to be humiliating. Why isn't it?"

"It's not humiliating because I love you," she answered simply with a smile, revelling in the touch of his hand on her face. "If anyone else had suggested the same, I would have laughed at them. Being a—'feisty female' means I know who and what I am, so pretending to be something else is only that—just a pretense. For you, though, if it gives you pleasure to see me acting like a concubine, then it gives me pleasure to do it—because I love you."

"And acting like something doesn't make you that something," he agreed with his own smile. "If anyone should know that, I'm the one. But that leaves me with a very large problem. We both agree you deserve to be punished, but now I'm out of ideas. Do you have any suggestions?"

"Yes," Amanda said firmly, surprising him again. "We're going to leave punishing me for another time. Tonight we'll be too busy giving you pleasure. You're due as much as you can handle, so let's see just how much that happens to be."

With that she put both hands flat on his chest and pushed, showing that she wanted him to back up. He did so with his brows high again, puzzled but not so dim that he even considered resisting. When he'd backed to the bed she pushed him down onto it, then she returned to the memory of Green Jade's lesson.

Amanda knelt at his feet to remove his shoes, then slowly and gently coaxed his hose off. With that out of her way she slid her hands up his legs to his thighs, across his thighs to his belly, and up his belly to his waist. Still kneeling, she pulled his shirt out of his breeches, and then she stood, gazing down at him. He caught her by the waist, pulled her close, and began to lick at her nipple before taking it in his mouth.

Amanda gasped at the tremors coursing through her. She wanted Jack to have pleasure, and if making her moan and writhe with his lips and tongue gave him pleasure, so be it. His hands stroked her bare body, and she had to grasp his shoulders in order to stay on her feet. Her knees trembled, and it took a moment before she was able to pry her fingers from the broad and solid bracing of his shoulders.

But when she did, she ran her hands down his upper body to the bottom of his shirt, then slowly pulled it off his body and arms. Tossing the shirt away gave her the chance to look down into Jack's eyes, and what she saw there nearly made her shiver with need. The man under her hands was currently accepting what she did to him, but that would last only as long as *he* wanted it to. As soon as he was ready he would take her, whether or not *she* thought she was through. Jack Michaels was a very strong, very dangerous man, the sort of man she'd always wanted, and she didn't fear him in the least. Whenever he was ready, she had no doubt she would be the same.

But right now there was more to do. Once again she pushed at his chest, and he obediently lay back on the bed. That let her climb onto the bed straddling him, and the next moment she began to lick and kiss the broad chest she'd exposed. His hands went to her thighs and closed around them as he gasped, holding on to her as she had to him, his eyes closed as he gave himself up to the sensations of pleasure.

Amanda kissed and licked her way slowly down to his breeches, and by then the bulge in them was all but screaming its demand to be released. He'd also had to let go of her thighs to keep from crushing them, so Amanda was able to turn around and straddle him backwards. Then she began to slowly unbutton his breeches, one button at a time, pushing aside his underpants as she kissed her way down. By the time she finished with the last of it Jack was breathing like a stallion run too hard, making Amanda certain he couldn't hold off much longer.

And he couldn't. She felt him move at the same time his arm went around her waist, and then she was on her back on the bed and he was kneeling between her thighs. His thrust into her was accomplished so quickly that she cried out with surprise, and then he had her wrapped in his arms while he devoured her lips and stroked deep and hard in the place she wanted him most. She moaned and held on to him, swept up helplessly by his storm, gladly accepting the ecstasy he brought. He climaxed quickly and violently, but that wasn't the end of it. His lips refused to leave hers, and in another moment he was stroking deeply again, this time obviously meaning to take his time.

Ages seemed to pass before it was over, and Amanda had no idea how many times Jack had brought her to release. They lay side by side across the bed for quite a while, and then Amanda heard Jack stir. The sound of rustling cloth whispered in her ear, and then his hands were on her again, stroking in the way that began to wake her blood again.

"That wasn't bad for firsts," he murmured, nuzzling her ear as his warm breath tickled it. "Now let's start all over again and see what we can accomplish the second time."

"So, for my punishment you've decided to kill me," Amanda said without opening her eyes, not sure she *could* open her eyes. "I know that's the way I *want* to die, but it's not easily accomplished when you can't move. Let's get some sleep first, and then——"

"Sleep is for old people and dandies," he interrupted,

now kissing her neck between words. "I've got to go back to London when I leave you, and I intend to have more than a few memories to take with me. If I'm going to find a way to satisfy your demands in order to marry you, I'll need lots of incentive."

Amanda wanted to ask why he had to return to London, but his kiss refused to allow for words. And his hands and lips and tongue and body . . . Before very long she ached for him again, and she gladly aroused him back to the point of being able to merge them. When it was over this second time exhaustion refused to be denied, and she was asleep even before he withdrew. Her dreams held the memory of a final kiss, and when she awoke, under her quilts and with sunshine flooding the room, Jack was long gone.

Chapter 20

I t was daylight before Jack reached London, but that was exactly the way he wanted it. He took the letters he'd written the night before while waiting for Amanda to leave the party, and delivered them to the people who would see that they reached their ultimate destination. Then he went home and went to bed, to dream about the marvelous wonder who was the woman he loved. It wasn't possible to even consider not marrying her any longer, no matter what had to be done to make it all work out. If he had to live without her, he'd rather not live.

His dreams were filled with Amanda: laughing with her, making love to her, seeing her again as she aroused him. How could he ever have considered her an innocent? There were famed paramours who couldn't have bettered her performance, possibly not even matched it. Some of what she did was on the awkward side, as though she had no real experience touching a man's body, but that just made it all the better for Jack. If it was practice she needed, she could practice on him forever.

Jack was chuckling as he slid out of sleep, roused by the knocking on his door. Withers was there to say a gentleman had come calling, and in any event it was the time Jack had asked to be awakened. Since Jack had slept in his clothes and even his boots, he only had to throw some water in his face before he was ready to go down.

Withers had put the newly-arrived Hughes in the study with a cup of tea, and Jack's breakfast was all ready to be served. Withers also clearly expected Jack to bathe, but even if there was definite need, there was no time. And where Jack planned to go, no one was likely to notice. He gave Withers the rest of the day off, and once his man was gone Jack stuck his head into the study.

"Bring your tea into the dining room, Hughes," he directed. "I want to eat while you tell me how things have gone."

"You look like you need sleep and cleaning up more than you need food," Hughes remarked as he followed Jack. "I thought you'd gone away to be on holiday."

"I did and I was, but something came up," Jack answered, sitting down and pouring his own cup of tea. "If I look tired it's only because I am, but I'll get over it. Have those men been located?"

"Without the least trouble," Hughes said with a nod, taking his own seat at the table. "Your description of the four was detailed enough so that the area constables and some of Magistrate Fielding's people had no difficulty in recognizing them. Sir Charles had the four arrested when they were found, but now everyone wants to know what to do with them."

"We're going to question them," Jack replied around a mouthful of eggs. "Those four tried to attack me in the park after Reggie Nichols refused to answer my questions. At first I thought the trail ended with Nichols's death, but then I remembered those four. If he sent them after me, which he most likely did, then *they* are the next section of trail I need to investigate."

Hughes shook his blond head in confusion, so Jack brought him up to date on Amanda's investigation, without mentioning that he'd originally been blackmailed into helping. If Hughes ever got hold of *that* tidbit, Jack would never live it down.

"So, if what Miss Edmunds and I suspect is true, there are still two of Reggie's brothers around," Jack finished up. "Those four thugs are the most likely ones to know where they are, because those four are probably the ones who kidnapped Lichfield. If Nichols *was* Lichfield's nephew, he and his brothers would never have stood still for his being murdered. They're a very close family, remember, and a body was never found."

"But why would Nichols be murdered and not Lichfield?" Hughes asked with a frown. "If the other two insisted on keeping their uncle alive, how could they possibly ignore their brother's death?"

"They may not know yet that he *is* dead," Jack said, pouring a last cup of tea for each of them. "They didn't live together, so they may not have seen each other all that often. And Lichfield was safely out of the way, while Nichols wasn't. Nichols could have been arrested and questioned at any time, and whatever he knew had to be deadly to his employer. He worked in the Bureau of Vital Statistics for *some* reason, and if that reason was legitimate or innocent he would still be alive."

"So you expect to get the answers from Lichfield when you find him," Hughes said after finishing his tea in one long swallow. "If so, let's get to it."

"I only expect to get *some* answers from Lichfield," Jack responded, staring down into his tea before following Hughes's example and finishing it. "The rest, I expect, will come from his two nephews, when they learn their brother was struck down like a dog. I just pray that Reggie's murderer didn't decide to make a clean sweep and finish *them* as well. If he did . . ."

"If he did, we'll still find him," Hughes said firmly when Jack's voice trailed off. "And we'll find out what he's up to. Sir Charles was very strong on that point especially, and I can't say I blame him. His Majesty would not care to learn that one of his public bureaus was being used against the very public it was established to help."

"Then let's not waste any more time," Jack said, getting to his feet. His current undertaking had nothing to do with solving the problem Amanda had set him, but it still had to be properly finished. After that he could drive himself crazy with a problem that might not *have* a solution, but first there was a murderer to catch. . . .

Amanda hadn't left any instructions to be awakened, so everyone had let her sleep. It was broad daylight when she awoke and Jack was long gone, but he'd put her under her quilts and had turned down the lamp.

Amanda lay still for a while, smiling and thinking about Jack, but hunger eventually drove her out of bed. Once dressed, she went downstairs for a late and solitary meal and spent the time trying to think of a way to apologize to Pei. It would not be as much fun as apologizing to Jack had been, but it was just as necessary. She and Pei were more than simply friends, a fact that had been underscored when Pei had told her how horridly she'd been behaving. Amanda *had* been behaving horridly, and it was something that needed to be admitted aloud.

Pei was out reading in the garden again, but she didn't look up as Amanda approached. Amanda knew Pei was aware of her presence, but it was up to her to plunge in first.

"If you'll put your book down, you'll enjoy my apology more," Amanda ventured, hoping things hadn't gone so far that all words were useless. "You were absolutely right in everything you said, but this situation here is *your* fault."

"*My* fault?" Pei echoed, laying the open book down in her lap while glaring indignantly at Amanda. "How do you justify *that?*"

"Well, you're the one silly enough to be my friend," Amanda answered sheepishly. "If you'd been smart enough to stay away from me, you wouldn't be furious with me now."

"You know, I hadn't thought of that," Pei granted with a slow and sober nod. "If you look at it that way, I suppose it is my fault. But I'm not furious, only very annoyed, and I'd like to know if I'm the only one to whom you intend to apologize."

"You're the only one left," Amanda said, glancing

around to make sure no one else was close enough to hear them. "You suggested a note, but Jack had an alternate suggestion we both enjoyed a good deal more."

"So *that's* why you were so late getting up!" Pei whispered excitedly, finally closing the book and setting it aside. "Come sit down and tell me all about it."

Pei made room for her on the bench, so Amanda sat down and told her best friend as much as she could. The way she felt when Jack touched her or she touched him, the harmony they shared when they were locked together—it wasn't possible to put those feelings into words, so she didn't even try. But memory of them brought a smile to her face she couldn't hide, and Pei got the idea.

"I can see you've grown really fond of him," Pei drawled, clearly teasing. "What will you do if you end up having to marry someone else? Keep Mr. Michaels as a pet?"

"If I end up having to marry someone else, I'll *kill* Mr. Michaels," Amanda grumbled, the smile suddenly gone. "And then I'll probably kill myself, which will certainly prove easier. Pei, do you think I was wrong to insist on what I did? If I have to marry someone other than Jack, I really won't want to live."

"The ancients say there's only one way to find out if a decision of yours is right or wrong," Pei said soothingly with a hand on Amanda's arm. "You have to wait and see what happens because of that decision, and then you know without confusion or doubt. But at least you'll have diversions until it's time to look around."

"What are you talking about?" Amanda asked, frowning. "What am I supposed to have to divert me?"

"Suitors," Pei returned with a sigh. "Another one added himself to the list this morning. Our friend and traveling companion Colonel Ebersham came calling, and was very disappointed to learn that you were still asleep. He told me to tell you he'd be back after lunch, and would be honored if you'd show him the gardens."

"I'd rather show him the door," Amanda said with her own sigh. "I knew he found me attractive, but I had no idea he would come courting. You know, Pei, there is one decision I made a mistake with, and I'll have to do something to change it as soon as possible. Being sweet and pleasant to men is no way to discourage them, and that's what my aim has to be right now. I can't very well end up married to another man if there *is* no other man who wants me."

"Oh, this should be fun!" Pei exclaimed softly, all but clapping her hands. "I intend to watch closely to see what you do, so don't be surprised to find me peeking around corners and doors. I'd like to know the technique if I should ever need it."

"Do you think Mr. Soong will enjoy having me give you lessons in discouragement?" Amanda asked, taking her own turn at teasing. "If he finds out, he may ask Jack to scold me."

"If he asked Mr. Michaels to do anything, it would not be to scold," Pei returned, a blush showing in her cheeks. "He was annoyed at the way you spoke to him at the party, and remarked that Mr. Michaels would do well to teach you the manners you should have learned from your father's hand. He also said he hoped I hadn't been too corrupted by you."

"Aha!" Amanda pounced with a grin. "So he *is* interested in you! If he wasn't, he would hardly care about you being corrupted. But you still haven't said how you feel about him."

"That's because I don't know *how* to feel," Pei said grudgingly, looking down at her hands. "Yesterday, when we spoke outside your father's house, I told him I had to go home eventually because my father expected it and would insist. All he did was nod, showing absolutely nothing of what he was feeling. He seems to have mastered the art of showing nothing, so how can I know how *I* should feel?"

"If you have the choice, you're fortunate," Amanda

said, patting Pei's hands in a return of comforting. "I had no choice at all about loving Jack, it was one of those at-first-sight things that just got stronger the longer it went on. I don't regret being in love with him, but life would have been a good deal easier if I could have smiled vaguely in his direction and just kept going. Ah well, where's the fun in life if things are easy?"

"I'm afraid too much of you *has* rubbed off on me," Pei said dryly. "Whatever my life turns out to be like, it certainly won't be easy."

"But that means it also won't be boring," Amanda countered with a laugh. "I want you to tell me everything Mr. Soong has said to you, so we can check together to see if he's given anything away. Then I'll outline some possible plans of discouragement, and you can criticize them for errors or omissions. If I miss something I want to know about it now, not later when it will be too late."

Pei agreed with another sigh, and they spent the rest of the morning talking and planning. When lunch was announced they went in to eat, and Amanda took the opportunity to do some thinking. There was nothing she could do to affect Jack's efforts one way or the other, so she'd do best by concentrating on her investigation of Mr. Lichfield's whereabouts. It might prove profitable to find out more about his nephews, like what kind of trouble they'd gotten into and at whose request. Once she'd thought of that, her course became clear. She'd see to it that very afternoon, as soon as she'd discouraged Colonel Ebersham.

The Fates, however, had other plans. Not long after lunch was over, a servant came to tell her that Colonel Ebersham had sent his regrets. It seemed he'd had an accident on his way back to the house he was staying at that morning, so he would not be calling on her that afternoon after all. Amanda's first reaction was relief, but then she got curious about the "accident." Her best sources of information were in the kitchens, so she went there and asked a few questions, then she returned to Pei.

"Something's going on, but I'm not sure what it means," she told Pei, sitting down in a chair in the otherwise uninhabited withdrawing room. "Colonel Ebersham's accident was no such thing."

"How can that be?" Pei asked with a frown, once again putting aside her book. "The man is lame, after all, and needs a walking stick to get around. Maybe whatever happened to him *was* an accident, and he's just too embarrassed to admit it."

"If you're right, then we almost had the same accident yesterday," Amanda countered with a headshake. "I'm told that two ruffians attacked him on the road, and might have beaten him to death if some farmer and his sons in their wagon hadn't come along on their way home from Taring Poole village. The ruffians ran off when the farmers went after them, so they took Colonel Ebersham back to the house where he's staying. He'd insisted on 'strolling' over, probably to show that he wasn't quite as lame as all that, and the ruffians apparently did a good enough job on him that he won't be going anywhere for several days."

"I suppose a description of the ruffians circulated with the rest of the story, and that's why you believe it was the same men who attacked *us.*" Pei waited for Amanda's nod, and then she shook her head. "But that doesn't mean there's anything going on. Obviously those ruffians prefer helpless victims, and that's why they chose us first and then the colonel. If they attacked someone who seemed able to defend himself, then I'd be suspicious."

"But that's the whole point," Amanda insisted, leaning forward. "If you were the sort who preferred helpless victims and got what they got from me yesterday, would you go after someone else carrying a stick as your second victim? And Colonel Ebersham *was* the second victim, or we would have heard about others."

"When you put it like that, it doesn't make much sense," Pei agreed with a frown. "After yesterday, the colonel should have been their last choice in victims. What do you think it means?"

"I have no idea," Amanda admitted. "But it still worries me. If those two came from somewhere else looking for easy pickings, they ought to be long gone to a safer neighborhood by now. But they're not gone, and the colonel was only their second victim. What have they been up to since yesterday? Where have they stayed? And if they aren't simply passing ruffians, why attack us first and then the colonel? It simply makes no sense."

Pei contributed nothing more than her own headshake, and then they were interrupted by one of the servants.

"Baron Delland has come calling, Miss Edmunds," the man said with a bow. "Are you at home to callers?"

Amanda was tempted to ask the servant to say she was out or busy, but there was no sense in putting off what had to be done.

"Please tell the baron I'll be right there," Amanda said, then turned to Pei again when the servant was gone. "I thought I'd be using my discouragement tactics on the colonel first, but it looks like Robert Blake will have the honors. It's really a shame because I like the man, but self-preservation is more important than keeping a friendship Jack probably won't like anyway. And now I'll have to put off my investigation of Mr. Lichfield's nephews. Bother! Maybe I can get rid of him fast."

Pei wished her luck as she left the room, but luck became conspicuous by its absence. Robert Blake was delighted to see her, and invited her out for a drive. When she insisted on walking in the gardens instead, he was perfectly happy to change his plans. He tried to draw her into another amusing and teasing conversation, but when she pretended to be bored and uninterested, he talked about flowers instead. When she ignored him and his conversation and observations in the hope of insulting him, he just went blithely on as though she were participating with enthusiasm.

Amanda had no choice but to invite him to stay for tea. She couldn't make her intentions too obvious, or Richard might hear about them and decide she was misguided. But

she *was* able to include Pei in their company, and then refused to let Blake exclude her friend again. He didn't
leave until it was time to dress for dinner, but once he was
gone Amanda turned to Pei.

"So what do you think?" she asked anxiously. "Has he
become less enchanted than he's been until now?"

"Well, he definitely wasn't happy," Pei said, considering
her words carefully. "He pretended to notice nothing but
your adorable little self, but every time you looked away
from him there was anger and frustration in his eyes. He
may have acted as if nothing has changed between you,
but he certainly knows better."

"I sincerely hope you're right," Amanda said as she led
the way to the stairs, feeling somewhat better. "I'll know
for sure if he doesn't come around again, but if he does
I'll just have to keep it up. Richard will be up here in just
a few more days, so Mr. Blake has to be sufficiently discouraged before then."

Pei agreed and they separated to dress for dinner. The
meal was, as expected, delicious, and afterward Amanda
spent some time speculating, along with Pei, about the
supposed ruffians. Neither of them had been visited with
inspiration since that afternoon, so they gave up wasting
their time and went to their rooms.

Amanda read for a while after undressing, but her mind
kept going off on tangents. Was Jack all right? Did he go
back to London for a reason she ought to know about?
Should she have told him about the attackers that morning? She had the strongest feeling that everything tied in
with her search for Mr. Lichfield, but she couldn't imagine
how. There *were* no ties between the colonel and Mr.
Lichfield, and between her and the colonel the lines were
faint at best.

She fought for at least two hours to pay attention to her
book, but finally Amanda had to admit defeat. She'd read
the same page over at least a dozen times, and she still had
no idea what it said. Putting the book aside, she stood up.
She needed to tire herself out, and then maybe she could

dismiss this endless speculation for a time. And on top of that, practicing a few forms might be a really good idea. The next time those ruffians showed up, she might not have her staff with her.

It wasn't long before Amanda was in her *chih fu,* and after a few stretching exercises she began to do forms. She had gone through three and had just begun the fourth when she heard a sound outside. With her balcony doors open the sound came to her clearly, but she couldn't identify it. She stopped to listen in case it came again, taking the opportunity to blot at the light sheen of sweat on her forehead, but the sound wasn't repeated. The thought came that it was probably a wild animal of some sort. . . .

But maybe not. With all the strange things that had been happening, Amanda knew she'd never be able to close her eyes when she went to bed if she didn't check first. Just a quick trip downstairs to make sure all the doors and windows were closed, and then she'd be able to finish the forms in peace.

Amanda thought about taking a candle, but quickly dismissed the idea. She knew the house well enough by now to make her way through it in the dark, and that way no one would be accidently disturbed. Or warned, if it came to that. Besides, not taking a candle meant she'd have both hands free for her staff.

It took only a few moments for Amanda's eyes to adjust to the dark in the sitting room, and then she was able to slip out into the hall. Using the wall to guide her through the darkness, she found the stairs and stepped down lightly. The dark wasn't quite so intense on the ground floor, but that meant there were more pockets of deep shadow which could hide anything. It was a nerve-wracking business, this sneaking around in the dark, but Amanda just swallowed hard and continued on.

When she reached the terrace doors directly beneath her bedchamber windows, Amanda was glad she'd taken care to move as quietly as possible. The sound she'd heard had been the doors being forced open, and no wild animal was likely to have done *that*. Whoever had come in might well still be there, so she'd have to rouse the servants for a room to room search. Simply assuming they were gone would be stupid, and—

Amanda heard a faint sound in the hall behind her and was immediately alert. If the intruders were taken care of before she roused the servants, there would be a good deal less of a fuss. She glided back to the doors leading out of the room and looked into the hall. A shadow form moved about, doing something Amanda couldn't make out, but that didn't matter. She could see well enough to take the man, and that was all that counted. For an instant she wondered why her instincts told her there was more than one intruder but the question was a waste of time. If there were several, she and the staff would find them. But until they could search . . .

She began to move out into the hall silently, the staff held in both hands before her—but then there was the scuff of a foot *behind* her and something painful hit her head . . . she tried to turn . . . tried to bring the staff up . . . but the something hit her again . . . turning everything black—

Chapter 21

"**I**t looks like a perfectly ordinary house," Hughes commented, then Jack saw self-annoyance flash across the man's face. "That didn't come out the way I meant it. I wanted to say that such an ordinary house in such an ordinary neighborhood—"

"You're trying to say that the house of plotters, kidnappers and possible murderers should have something to mark it as unusual," Jack said, coming to his associate's assistance. "This whole neighborhood is as dull as dishwater, so the residents of the houses ought to match. Only in this instance they don't, and we never would have found it without the help of those four bully boys."

"Even if it did take three hours before they got the first word out of them," Hughes grumbled. "*You* spent the time in an empty cell, catching up on your sleep—and now I know why you didn't bother to bathe—but *I* had to sit around twiddling my thumbs. I know Sir Charles thinks you've stumbled across something important because you've done it so often before, but I'm still not convinced we aren't wasting our time. I hope you and Sir Charles turn out to be the ones who are right."

Jack did too, but although he had that familiar feeling telling him there was more involved than met the eye, he didn't know if he'd be able to prove it.

"There's the signal," Hughes commented, referring to the man who had stepped out from behind the house they were strolling toward and had waved his hand. "That means everyone is in position, so it's our turn."

Jack nodded as they both quickened their pace, and a moment later they were at the front door of the house. Hughes would have put his shoulder to the wood, but Jack slammed in a side kick that sent the door flying open. The two men entered almost at the same time, others of their force coming to guard the door from the outside behind them. They heard the sound of running footsteps, interrupted by the breaking in of the back door, and then there were shouts and scuffling. By the time Jack and Hughes got there it was all over, and four men stood sullenly in custody.

"Good work, lads," Hughes said to their men, some of whom were constables or Magistrate's people. "Now let's take a look around this place."

Jack silently joined the three who were supposed to make the search, knowing Sir Charles would be unhappy but ignoring the point. Sir Charles had wanted Jack on the sidelines again, but this time Jack had flatly refused. He was even prepared to break into the house alone if it came to that, and *that* was the reason he hadn't bathed or changed his clothes. If he'd had to do something illegal, he'd also need to look the part. But Sir Charles had grudgingly agreed to let Jack go along, but he was adamant that Hughes run the show.

Jack, if he wanted to be there officially, had no choice but to cooperate. Still, Sir Charles wasn't here at the moment, so Jack took his part of the search upstairs. If you're going to hold someone a prisoner, keeping him on the ground floor didn't make much sense. An older man like Lichfield would have trouble getting out of an upper-story window even if he managed to free himself from whatever restraints they were using. If he was there at all, Jack would wager he'd be upstairs or possibly down in the cellar.

Jack was gambling that the Lichfield nephews would not put their uncle in a damp cellar, and he quickly proved himself right. The third-floor attic door was locked, but another kick quickly remedied that. Inside it was dim, the only light coming from hooded ventilation slits, but the man the room held wasn't hard to see.

An older man, in shabby clothing, sat on a wooden cot, one leg held by the long shackle attached to the heavy wood of the wall. He peered at Jack uncertainly, as though trying to recognize him, and Jack was finally able to take a deep breath of relief. If he'd ever had to tell Amanda that her beloved Mr. Lichfield was dead, it would have crushed her. Now . . .

"You *are* Mr. Lichfield, I hope," Jack said with a smile as he walked closer to the man. "A lot of people have been looking for you."

"If they had asked, I would have told them I was right here," the man responded, and then, suddenly, tears were running down his face. "Is this a dream? Please, tell me if I'm just imagining you. I've waited and prayed so *long* . . . !"

"I'm no dream," Jack quickly reassured him, taking the man's hand in a firm grip to prove it as he crouched in front of him. "Are you all right? Do you need a physician?"

"The only thing I need is to be let out of *this* vile place," Lichfield responded in an unsteady voice, trying to smile as he held onto Jack's hand with a death grip. "May I ask who you are, and how you came to be searching for me?"

"My name is Jack Michaels, and I'm here on behalf of a very determined young lady named Miss Amanda Edmunds," Jack told him, returning his smile. "She's turned my life upside down in her efforts to find you, so I'm here purely out of self-defense."

"Beloved *Ssu Te Lung,*" Lichfield murmured, eyes shining even through the tears. "I had no idea how you would accomplish it, but somehow I knew you would. . . . Mr. Michaels, is Amanda all right? I wasn't given the opportunity to arrange her passage here, and I worried that she would do something foolish on her own. . . ."

"Her brother Richard Lavering made all the necessary arrangements," Jack said, his smile turning wry. "But you certainly do know her, and I need to ask you about other things you might know. Just a moment, and I'll see about getting you unlocked from that shackle."

Jack went back to the door and called downstairs that the prisoners needed to produce a key, and then he went back and stayed with Lichfield until the key was brought. The older man wasn't very steady on his feet, but despite his need for assistance going down the stairs, he insisted on walking alone whenever he could. Jack escorted him to a comfortable chair in the ground-floor parlor, had one of the men bring in tea, and then it was time for some answers.

"Yes, it was my nephew Reginald I saw in the Bureau of Vital Statistics," Lichfield confirmed when Jack put the question to him. "I was delighted that he'd found himself such a responsible position, but for some reason he seemed shocked and upset at seeing me. I was on my way back to my rooms through the park when I was accosted by four ruffians, and they forced me to go with them to this house. William and Geoffrey, Reginald's brothers, were here, but rather than releasing me they chained me in that attic. I still have no idea why."

"Didn't Reginald tell you?" Jack asked, simply holding his own teacup. "Reginald did come by to see you, didn't he?"

"Oh, yes, and he admitted that I'd been kidnapped at his instigation," Lichfield concurred with a nod. "But that's all he told me, along with the fact that he didn't yet know what he would do with me. For some reason releasing me was out of the question, but he refused to consider the alternative of killing me. We are a rather close family, but the whole thing seemed so bizarre. . . ."

"Did Reginald come here on a regular basis?" Jack

asked next. "If so, do you know when he's due here again?"

"In two days," Lichfield answered promptly after drinking some of his tea. "Reginald comes once a week like clockwork, and he always visits with me. But the odd thing is that this time William and Geoffrey expect some sort of trouble. When they brought my tray yesterday, they took the opportunity to discuss between themselves the two men who had just moved into the house with them. They didn't like or trust the two new men, and felt certain that Reginald would not be pleased with their presence. I overheard them say that the shackle had always proven enough to hold me when they'd had to be away doing research—research on what subject, I have no idea—so why did the arrangement suddenly have to be changed?"

"You seem to be telling me that someone else was in authority above Reginald and his brothers," Jack pointed out carefully. "After all, if one of them had been in charge, they would hardly be complaining about arrangements they didn't like."

"That thought occurred to me as well, but no names whatsoever were mentioned," Lichfield responded with a sigh. "It was fairly obvious the boys were mixed up in something unpleasant again, but they took pains not to discuss the matter in my presence. I'm sure the authorities will question them now, but they're extremely loyal young men, even if that loyalty is to the wrong cause. The chances are excellent that they won't speak a word."

"I think that this time they will," Jack disagreed as he got to his feet. "Something's happened that neither you nor they know about as yet, and that should make all the difference. Tell me, you mentioned that your nephews were involved in something unpleasant *again*. Did they just happen to get themselves in trouble the first time, or were they doing something on someone else's behalf?"

"Oh, definitely on someone else's behalf," Lichfield said with a grimace. "I never did care for that man, and certainly didn't believe him when he said the boys had acted on their own. The boys remained loyal and insisted they *had* come up with the idea themselves, but I didn't believe it for a moment, and neither did my brother."

"Excuse me," Hughes said just as Jack was about to ask who the man involved was. Hughes had just stepped into the parlor, past the constable standing in the hall. "May I speak to you for a moment, Mr. Michaels? We've just learned something you might like to know."

Jack really didn't want to be disturbed at this particular time, but Hughes wore an expression that said the matter was important. He excused himself from Lichfield and stepped out into the hall with Hughes, where he found a surprise waiting. The man Sir Charles used most often as a courier stood there holding an envelope, and for an instant Jack had the ridiculous thought that it had to be a reprimand for his having taken part in the search.

"I've already seen it," Hughes murmured, obviously referring to the message. "It's an identification of the device you saw on the coach of Nichols's murderer. You didn't recognize it because it's French, rather old and all but forgotten. The old story of a once-proud house turned penniless and powerless."

Jack nodded and took the report, scanning the precisely neat handwriting of the researcher who had done the work. The last member of the family who owned that crest was British rather than French, the man having been raised on his father's estates in England rather than in his mother's native France. Both parents were now dead, and the man's name was—

"Good lord," Jack breathed, touched by a chill. "Robert Blake, Baron Delland. But Blake is at Braxton Meadows now, paying court to Amanda! It can't be him."

"That's the name," Lichfield's voice came, making Jack turn. "Robert Blake, Baron Delland. There had been a rash of thefts from the big houses in the Meadows, and Delland had made himself popular with his peers by supposedly buying back the stolen items from the thieves through a middleman. He always hinted he'd paid out quite a lot of

gold to reclaim the items, and those people the things belonged to insisted on reimbursing him. He usually tried to
refuse the money, but somehow he always found himself
talked into accepting it.

"One day my nephews were caught trying to walk off
with a small but valuable item from one of the houses they
did odd jobs at, and they nearly ended up thrown into a
cell to be hanged. Delland came forward to speak for
them, saying the boys probably got the idea from hearing
stories of the thefts. He said he knew for a fact that the
real thieves were grown men, but they'd no longer be taking things from the houses of Braxton Meadows. He'd
paid them one last time, telling them it *was* the last time,
so they might as well move on."

"And did they?" Jack asked. "Move on, I mean."

"Everyone thought so when there weren't any more
thefts," Lichfield answered with a grimace. "My brother
and I were certain we knew differently, but it wasn't possible to pursue the matter. Assuming we managed to make
the boys confess, we would have proven nothing but that
they *were* the thieves. No one would have believed that
Blake put them up to it to play the hero and collect gold,
not on the word of three village boys with less than perfect
reputations."

"Well, I believe it," Jack growled, then he looked
around. "Where did you put the two brothers, Hughes? I
need the final answers from them, and then I'm going
back to the Meadows. I'm sure Amanda—Miss
Edmunds—is perfectly all right, but I'll still feel better if
I'm up there with her. So far there's nothing concrete
against Blake, but—"

"Excuse me, Mr. Michaels, but I'm forced to point out
that you have no official standing in this matter," Hughes
interrupted in a very deliberate way. "We allowed you to
accompany us out of deference to Duke Edward, but letting you take over goes much too far beyond the proper
limits. If there's something you'd like our prisoners to be

asked, you'll have to tell *me* about it and I'll see to getting the answers."

Jack felt the urge to grind his teeth, or maybe even to bite someone. The speech Hughes had just made showed that Sir Charles had had some instructions for Hughes, the primary one being to keep Jack's true position a secret. Jack very much wanted the truth to be known, but he hadn't *earned* that and now probably never would. Only doing his job well enough to merit official thanks and reward would have freed him from the reputation he'd built up, but now . . .

"You're quite right, Mr. Hughes, and I apologize," he said after the briefest hesitation, fighting to sound properly chastised. "If you'll step into this corner with me for a moment, I'll explain what I'd like to know."

Hughes followed him to the end of the hall, just short of the stairway up to the right, with the closed doors leading to the rest of the ground floor to the left. No one could see or hear them easily from there, but they still kept their backs to the people at the other end of the hall.

"Sorry about that, Jack," Hughes murmured as soon as they'd stopped. "Sir Charles promised to skin me alive and then roll me in salt if I let you take over where everyone could see it. He's not going to let you wreck things for yourself, old son, even if you *want* them wrecked. He said to tell you that everything will work out just right if only you'll have a little patience."

"I have plenty of patience," Jack returned sourly. "What I don't have is an equal amount of time, but trying to explain that to Sir Charles would be useless."

"It seems to me that what you need is a good night's sleep," Hughes suggested sympathetically. "Problems look huge when you're tired, but once you've rested up they get cut down to size. Now, what are those questions you want me to ask the brothers?"

"First you have to tell them a few things," Jack said as he rubbed the back of his neck. Hughes was right about his being tired, so he'd probably stay the night in London and head back up to the Meadows in the morning. "The first thing they'll need to know is that their brother Reggie won't be coming for his regular weekly visit in two days. Reggie Nichols *was* really Reginald Lichfield, their brother, and I'm positive they don't know he's dead."

"How can you be so sure?" Hughes asked, eyeing Jack curiously. "Isn't it possible they were told, but are too afraid of their employer or too uncaring about someone already dead to make a fuss?"

"If family loyalty wasn't more important to them than their own safety, their uncle would be long dead," Jack countered with a headshake. "They don't know their brother was murdered by the man who employs them, but they were bound to find out about it in two days, when he failed to show up. That has to be why those other two were sent here, as nothing else makes sense. Those other men were supposed to see how they took the news, and if they took it too hard that would have been the end of them *and* their uncle. Just make sure they understand that."

"And *Blake* is the one behind all this?" Hughes asked, his frown close to disbelieving. "I've met the man, and he may be terrible with business matters but aside from that he seems perfectly decent and likable. But if he considered them enough of a threat to send men prepared to kill them, why didn't he order it done immediately? Why take the chance of waiting to see what they did when they found out?"

"I can make a guess about that," Jack told him, hating the coldbloodedness of it all. "Finding men to commit murder is easy, but finding ones who can pose as clerks in a governmental office is a good deal harder. With Reggie dead, Blake probably needs one of the remaining brothers to take over Reggie's post with the bureau. They may come from a relatively poor home, but they were most likely better educated than any of the other children in the village. Their uncle is a well-educated man, and from the way he speaks of his brother, their father was probably the same. And don't forget that the very fact that Reggie had the job meant he was able to do it. If he couldn't, he would have been promptly sacked."

"That makes more sense than I can argue against," Hughes said with a sigh. "And if Blake did kill Reggie himself, it was probably because he had to make sure the job was done right. If it wasn't, the clerk would then have been able—and willing—to testify against him. So what do I ask the brothers once I've passed on all this information?"

"First get them to name their employer, and then find out why he had Reggie working in the Bureau of Vital Statistics," Jack directed. "Those are the two things we most need to know, along with anything else the brothers are willing to volunteer. And then be sure to follow up with the constables to be certain that the brothers are protected. We'll want living witnesses against Blake, not second-hand testimony because the brothers have been killed."

"An excellent point," Hughes agreed, now looking grim. "I'll be sure to take care of it. Do you intend to wait around for your answers, or do you want me to bring them to your house as soon as I have them?"

"I still have to tell Lichfield that his nephew is dead," Jack said, rubbing his eyes. "It will probably take a while for him to pull himself together afterward, and by then you should have the answers. When I leave, I intend to take Lichfield home with me. Withers will need something to do while I'm up at Braxton Meadows, and Lichfield could do with some pampering. Once he's back on his feet, he can take up his own life again."

Hughes nodded and turned to the door that probably led to where the brothers were being held under guard, and Jack turned back up the hall to Lichfield. He wasn't looking forward to passing on the bad news, but he *was* looking forward to going home. It might still be early afternoon, but Jack intended to bathe and then fall into bed. By tomorrow morning he ought to be feeling human again, and then he'd be able to put his mind to his most important problem.

After all, he wasn't likely to be able to continue finding reasons to arrest Amanda's suitors. . . .

Amanda's head throbbed, and she had to force her eyes to open. Very briefly she thought she was back in Master Ma's school, but one glance around told her she wasn't. This place looked like part of a small house, the room bare of all furniture but the wide wooden cot on which she lay. The cot stood in a corner of the room opposite the wall containing the only door.

Sitting up was only slightly painful and briefly dizzying, but it didn't accomplish anything. Amanda looked around at the room a second time, but the lamplight showed nothing but dust and emptiness. The windows were either shuttered or boarded over from the outside, and Amanda was certain she'd never seen the place before. How in the name of sanity had she gotten there?

Standing up and walking back and forth returned the strength to Amanda's legs, but when it also brought back the memory of what had happened she stopped short. She'd been right to think there'd been more than one intruder, but she should have thought to look behind her for the second one. He'd obviously hit her over the head with something, and then the two of them had carried her off. But to where, and for what reason?

Amanda did a few stretching exercises to get the kinks out of her neck and back, and by the time she finished, the headache had also faded back to a manageable size. If she'd been kidnapped, they probably expected her brother to pay a ransom to get her back. Richard was certain to agree no matter what price they asked, but that whole situation still felt wrong. There was more involved than a simple kidnapping, but the details weren't something Amanda was yet able to see.

Almost the first thing she'd done was try the door to see if it would open, but whatever lock was on the outside had to be in better condition than the rest of that rundown place. The heavy door hadn't budged, but suddenly the sound of unlocking came, and then it swung wide. Two men stood there in the doorway, the dimness of another, unlit room behind them, and Amanda's suspicions flared even higher. They were the two men who had tried to attack Pei and herself on the road, the two who had reportedly beaten up Colonel Ebersham.

"An' there she be," one of the men said with a grin as he stepped into the room. "Pretty'r 'n gold in them foreign silk things, ready t' treat us nice as y'please."

"Without no stick," the second pointed out with his own grin. "Owe 'er good f'r bashin' us, we do, an' now she gets t'collect. Gold'll be paid over 'fore they know as whuts been done, an' then it won't matter t'none 'cept 'er."

"An' us," the first corrected with a small laugh. "You 'n me'll 'ave 'er sugar, steada one a th' gentry. Never 'ad me a pretty lady afore, but sure gonna 'ave me one now."

With that said, the two of them advanced on her slowly, obviously wanting her to be good and frightened before they began to have their way with her. Amanda *was* frightened, just as anyone short of Master Ma himself would be, but she refused to let the fear paralyze her. Fear was a weapon like any other, Master Ma had once told her privately, a weapon to be used by the attacked as well as the attacker. Fear under control added strength to a fighter, and even sometimes blocked the awareness of pain. Those two intended to rape Amanda and they just might succeed, but not because she simply stood there and let it happen.

As the two took their first steps, Amanda shifted automatically into fighting stance. They were both big men and her staff was gone, but she could see that they were completely untrained. She would have fought even if she'd known she would lose, but nothing in a fight is guaranteed beforehand. One of Master Ma's instructors had once gotten a broken arm from a relative beginner, simply because he'd faced the beginner with overconfidence. *We most often defeat ourselves,* Master Ma had been fond of saying. . . .

But overconfidence wasn't Amanda's problem. Creeping terror was, with its threat to send her screaming and cowering into a corner. She didn't *want* to have to fight two big men all by herself, but Jack wasn't there to do it for her and he'd be terribly disappointed if she didn't at least try to do it herself. You can't ever be blamed for not winning, but not trying is another matter entirely . . .

The first man was a step ahead of the other, so he reached out first to grab Amanda's left arm with his right hand. Amanda let him get his grip before covering his hand with her own right hand, and then she kicked out hard at the second man. Since he hadn't expected to be attacked he was wide open, and the front kick with all her body weight behind it landed squarely on his groin. He tried to scream at the excruciating pain, but only managed to choke before he collapsed.

The first man was startled and distracted by the attack on his companion, and that became *his* fatal blunder. The kick had taken no more than seconds, and while the first man was still in shock over the speed of the attack on his partner, he became the next victim. Amanda used her right hand and left arm to twist *his* right arm, and his body twisted right after it. In that position the outer side of his elbow was presented to her, so she used her left knee to kick hard into it. The man's arm snapped like a rotten twig, and he did manage to scream before fainting from the pain.

Amanda, her heart thundering and her body trembling, stepped back as her second attacker collapsed at her feet. She'd never had a *serious* hand-to-hand fight before, and it was horribly nerve-wracking. But she'd still managed to win, and the door to her prison now stood open. All she had to do was walk through it, and she'd be—

"I wonder why it's so hard to find competent help these days," a voice drawled, and then Robert Blake was blocking the doorway with two other men behind him. "That's the second time you've done for those fools, and I suppose I should have known better than to give them another chance. Real men wouldn't have been bested in the first place."

"Those two are yours?" Amanda asked with a disbelieving frown. "But that doesn't make any sense. You were courting me, so why would you send them to attack me?"

"To give me the chance to come riding to the rescue, of course," he answered with his most charming grin. "The first time they approached you I was lurking in the woods, intending to wait until they began to rip your clothes off before I jumped out and frightened them away. You would then have been so grateful that I would have become your knight rescuer, and when your brother heard about it my suit would have been instantly accepted."

"But it didn't work out that way," Amanda said, wondering how she could have ever considered this man attractive. "I took care of the matter myself and didn't need to be rescued."

"I took that for the purest luck," he returned with a shrug. "It hadn't occurred to me that *everyone* raised in that heathen place you come from is trained the way that Soong commoner was. I disliked his airs when he simply guarded the duke, but now that he's been promoted above himself he's completely intolerable. But that's beside the point now, just something to be seen to when an opportunity arises. The matter presently under discussion is you."

"Well, in case you were wondering, I decline your offer of marriage," Amanda said dryly, forcing herself to show nothing of her true fear. All she wanted was to be safely out of there, but that didn't seem likely to happen.

"Now, now, let's not be so quick to make decisions," he scolded mildly, waving a finger at her. "You may think you've ruined my second plan to have you as my wife, but I'm nothing if not creative and adaptable. With a few minor changes, this plan will still serve."

"And what plan is that?" Amanda asked, wondering if sudden attack would get her through the three men in her path to freedom. A flying two-footed kick would certainly knock Blake backward, but the biggest problem was the two men directly behind his shoulders. She didn't have enough body weight—or skill—to send three big men sprawling, and if even one of them delayed her long enough for the others to grab hold . . .

"My plan is quite simple but utterly brilliant, even if I do say so myself." Blake's grin had widened, and he really looked as though he were enjoying himself. "Those two on the floor were sent to kidnap you from your brother's house. Everyone in the neighborhood knows by now that you're staying there alone with only a skeleton staff, so they'd naturally be unsurprised to learn that ruffians had taken advantage of the fact."

"Ruffians who had already shown their presence by attacking Colonel Ebersham," Amanda interrupted. "Was that why you ordered it done, to prepare the way for *this* plan?"

"Not at all," Blake denied amiably. "I had the fool beaten for his presumption in trying to court a woman I had already chosen. And who had already accepted me, or so I thought. Imagine my surprise and dismay when I came calling, and you treated me like a foul-smelling chimney sweep. I had no idea what had turned you against my suit, but I decided not to risk the possibility that you had enough influence with your brother to have me completely dismissed."

So Pei had been right when she said he was angry and unhappy, Amanda realized. Too bad they hadn't known just *how* angry and unhappy.

"And so I devised another little game," Blake continued. "My two servants there were ordered to kidnap and ravish you, their supposed plan being to collect your ransom despite having despoiled you. They were to have used this abandoned caretaker's cottage on my property without my knowledge, but I was to discover you here and rescue you from them. I would know, of course, that you'd been despoiled, but would have shared the knowledge of that only with your brother. He would then have known that any other match was completely out of the question, and would have immediately accepted my generous offer to marry you despite your shame. I would have admitted my love, you see, and love will make a man overlook many things."

"Love," Amanda echoed flatly, more than disgusted. "You don't know the meaning of the word. What is it you really want from me?"

"Why, your inheritance, of course," he replied with brows high. "Oh, but that's right, no one realizes yet how valuable an inheritance you actually have. They think your late father left you no more than a modest private income and a worthless old house. Eventually they'll get around to noticing how much property comes with that worthless old house, but by then it will already be mine."

"And you want to divide it up and sell each piece for a fortune to those people desperate to have a house up here," Amanda said with sudden revelation, remembering what Richard had told her. "There's no more available and suitable land for sale, except for my father's property. But how did you know about it and me, and why would you bother in the first place? Everyone thinks of you as a very wealthy man."

"I *was* a very wealthy man," he corrected, his amusement fading. "My first wife's inheritance was extremely large, a good deal greater than most believed, which was why I had no trouble gaining her hand. That, along with a private enterprise I've developed, kept me rather nicely— until my so-called peers began to cheat me in business deals. They claimed the losses were my own fault and nothing that they had done, but considering who I am that's patently ridiculous. I am the offspring of true nobility, from a family much older than any of theirs, so how could the losses be my fault?"

By now Blake had turned furious, and Amanda knew better than to comment or interrupt. The man was seriously unbalanced, and the realization chilled her all the way through.

"I knew those people were lying to me, but there was

nothing I could do about it," Blake went on almost in a mutter. "To accuse them publicly would have ostracized me from the group to which *I* had the greatest right to belong. And then my wife chose to take her own life rather than perform her wifely duties any longer, but her method of suicide—drowning herself in our lake—could be called an accident once I saw to the disposal of the letter she'd left. That was when I expanded my enterprise against those pitiful fools who consider me their friend and victim, and I began to make them pay for what they'd stolen."

He'd been staring down at the floor during his bitter denunciation, but now he looked up at Amanda again and smiled.

"I doubt if you're capable of knowing the true worth of the family you're about to marry into, but I'll make an effort to explain. My father was a mere baron in this country, but his wealth allowed him the incredible opportunity of marrying my mother. She was the last of her line, her father and grandfather having been victimized by the newcomers pretending to gentility even more than their fathers before them. But it was their blood that counted. They hadn't a sou but they were the crème de la crème of France, the most aristocratic family ever to be ennobled there. My father was a pig and a fool, thinking *he* did *her* a favor by marrying her and paying off the debts of her family.

"He accepted her because she was so beautiful, of course, and he vented his lust upon her at every opportunity. She accepted being defiled only so that she might produce *me,* a male heir to carry on the best of bloodlines. She raised me to know exactly who and what I was, and my father hated that so he had her sent away. He claimed she'd gone mad, but of course that was a lie. He'd simply tired of her, as though she were nothing but an ordinary woman. You won't be allowed to bear my children, however, no more than my first wife was allowed the honor, but you *will* serve my pleasure. It's only fitting that I be served, don't you agree?"

"As long as I get to decide what sort of serving's to be done," Amanda answered, finally refusing to encourage his fantasies any longer. "I don't know who you think you're playing with, but in any event your game is about to be over. I'm *not* going to be marrying you, so you can just continue to save yourself for the princess royal I'm sure you think is the only one fit to bear your children. The only choice you have now is to get out of my way or kill me, but whichever you decide on, stop wasting my time and get on with it."

Amanda succeeded in keeping her voice steady to the end of her speech, but her blood raced again and this time the terror reaching out for her was stronger. Robert Blake was a madman, but if she could get him away from the doorway and those other two men . . . Her taunting had been aimed at getting him to attack alone, and if he did she would do her best to kill him. For a long moment the furious anger he showed gave her the hope that she'd succeeded, but then the anger disappeared and he laughed.

"I do believe I'm going to enjoy myself quite a lot with you," he said, suddenly the charming gentleman again. "Sweet, obedient women are very much overrated as perfect mates, a fact I learned with my first wife. It was so easy to terrify her that it was scarcely worth the effort, but I can see you won't be the same at all."

"You must be hard of hearing," Amanda said, desperately trying again. "I said I won't be marrying you, and that's a solemn promise."

"Dear girl, of course you'll be marrying me," he countered with a grin. "You see, when I finally discover you here after the ruffians who kidnapped you also violate you, you'll be so terrified and hysterical from your ordeal that you'll confuse *me* with the beasts who had their way with you. I'll be devastated when I discuss the matter with your brother, and then I'll ask the very great favor of being allowed to marry you. Only with you as my wife will I ever be able to banish your confusion, and prove that I will never touch you in any way but lovingly. The rest will

go as I've already outlined, and our nuptials will be cele-
brated as soon as humanly possible."

"I can think of any number of ways to counter that
story," Amanda said, hating the way he now looked at
her—and the way her voice had begun to tremble. "It
won't work the way you want it to, especially since—"

"Yes?" Blake encouraged with a wider grin when her
words abruptly ended. "Were you about to add 'especially
since you *haven't* been put to brutal men's pleasure'? How
clever of you to have noticed the fallacy in that argument,
dear girl, and with no more than a hint from me. Those
two on the floor won't be taking pleasure from anything
but unconsciousness for quite some time, but we three
here—ah, that's another story entirely. What say we celebrate the new day just dawning outside, eh?"

And with that he began to walk toward Amanda, but not
in anger and not alone. All three of them came at once,
and the men behind Blake had knives at their belts. One
threatening move from her and those knives would be in
their fists. . . . It was going to happen . . . they were going
to . . . *No!*

Chapter 22

❧ ∽◯◯∽ ❧

Jack called Withers back from his day off, and Withers took over without breaking stride. He got Lichfield settled in after putting up bath water to heat, fed them both while the water was heating, then got Jack bathed and into bed almost before he knew it. Withers had talked Jack into taking the first bath by saying Lichfield would want to soak for a while, and the man even sent a boy out to buy new clothes for their houseguest. Jack thought the money for it must have come out of Withers's household allowance, but it didn't matter. He went to bed knowing Lichfield was in the best of hands, and sleep came almost before he closed his eyes.

When he opened his eyes again it was dark out, and very few sounds could be heard through the open window from the street below. It had to be late, then, but *something* had disturbed Jack's sleep. He lay there listening, expecting to drop off again, but instead came even wider awake. It hadn't been a noise that had awakened him but a nightmare, and Amanda had been in it. He couldn't quite remember the details, but it hadn't been pleasant.

When sleep refused to return, Jack got up and put on his robe, then went downstairs to make a cup of tea. He needed something to warm his insides anyway, since thoughts of what Blake had been doing had turned him cold and angry. Who would have believed that so many secrets would be hidden in plain sight of the Bureau of Vital Statistics? Or so many opportunities to cause mischief

336

or make a killing? Blake hàd been raking the coin in hand over fist, and no one had any idea he was the one behind all the heartache and loss.

Jack sat down to wait for the tea water to boil, remembering one of the incidents that he'd witnessed personally. Lord Haringer's eldest son had just won some trophy or award or something, the latest in a long line of.them. The boy was the only one of the Haringer sons to excel at all, not to mention on a regular basis, so his father never bothered to mention his other children. Only the eldest, his pride and joy, and that day Lord Haringer was in the club and bragging—as usual. Haringer had had business interests all over Europe, and had some sort of diplomatic post as well. He wasn't well-liked among his peers, but no one could argue his success in life.

But they *could* resent and envy it. That day in the club had seemed about to go like so many before it—Haringer bragging, most of the others forcing themselves to congratulate him—until Sir Kenneth Wilford ambled over. Wilford and Haringer were rivals of long standing, both immensely wealthy, influential—and hated each other thoroughly. Wilford had handed Haringer two pieces of paper, the small smile he wore filled with a great deal of eager anticipation. Haringer had looked at the papers one at a time, his frown of confusion clear, and then he had gone pale. The next moment he'd crumpled the papers and thrown them away, and then he'd fled the club.

Since Wilford had simply laughed and gone on his own way without trying to retrieve the papers, someone else had picked them up and looked at them. One of the papers had been a copy of Haringer's son's record of birth, day, month and year, and the other had been copies of newspaper articles about Haringer's business and diplomatic travels, his departures and arrivals back home. His comings and goings had been many in the year his first son had been born, so it was easy to see why no one had noticed sooner—but he'd been traveling back and forth between France and Spain for six months, and six months after his return his prized first son had been born. The dates were clear, and with him traveling and his wife remaining at home . . . It was no longer a mystery as to what sort of thing the other Lichfield nephews were researching.

Jack sighed as he got up to take the kettle off. The newspaper articles had had to be researched, but the boy's birth certificate had been on file in the Bureau of Vital Statistics. It had been much too late to claim that the date had been copied down wrong, and Haringer hadn't even bothered. He'd simply gone home, killed his wife, and then himself. The resultant chaos hadn't died down for months, and it had all come about because of Blake. He'd had one of his men offer the information to Wilford, and after checking to be certain it was true, Wilford had paid handsomely.

As Jack set the tea to steeping, he wondered how many scandals and tragedies Blake had been responsible for altogether. There was that girl he'd married, the one who had died accidentally. She'd been left orphaned by a boating accident that had claimed not only her parents but her aunts and uncles as well. The girl had ended up inheriting from all of them, since none of the others had had offspring, but there had been a delay in issuing copies of the various death certificates. Because of that the estates had been delayed in being settled, and by then Blake had slipped in and married the very plain girl. Everyone else had thought she was nearly penniless, and without even the spur of beauty he'd had nothing in the way of competition. What he *had* had was someone to tell him about the situation beforehand, and then delay the paperwork to let him take advantage of the knowledge.

"I was hoping I was the only one who couldn't sleep," a voice came, and then Lichfield had joined him in the kitchen. "The young do need their rest, you know."

"I'm not *that* young," Jack returned with as much of a smile as he could manage. "Would you like to join me for a cup of tea?"

"I'm tempted to ask for something stronger, but tea will

be better in the long run," Lichfield answered with a sigh as he took a chair at the table. "You never did tell me, and I was too upset to ask earlier, but—do they have any idea why my nephews chose to kidnap me?"

"Because of Amanda—Miss Edmunds," Jack told him, running a hand through his hair. "Blake decided that he wanted to marry her when he first learned that her father was dead. He already knew, from having had your other nephews research the point, that the only property available in the Meadows belonged to her father, and that it came to her at his death. Maybe Lavering mentioned the death when *he* first found out, and Blake happened to be nearby. Whatever, Blake decided he wanted her, but then *you* turned up to file the death certificate. Your nephew Reginald realized immediately that Blake would order you killed; after all, you not only knew about your nephews' previous illicit relations with Blake, but now had discovered one of them working in the Bureau of Vital Statistics. When Blake came courting you would certainly voice your disapproval, and might even put two and two together. So Reginald had his small gang of toughs kidnap you, and that put you safely out of the way."

"A pity he couldn't do the same for himself," Lichfield said with another sigh. "But then he should have been bright enough to stay away from Blake entirely. When you see Amanda, please tell her that her search for me was not what caused Reginald's death. Reginald has always been greedy and rather foolish, refusing to understand that if he put as much effort into a proper job of work as he did into trying to avoid work— Why, Mr. Michaels, where are you going?"

"Back up to Braxton Meadows," Jack answered, pausing at the stairs after abruptly leaving the table. "I know Amanda is all right, but as long as Blake is still running around loose up there I'll be happier if I'm up there as well. Withers will be here in the morning, and he'll help you to return to yourself."

"I'll be fine, Mr. Michaels, don't waste a moment of

thought on me," Lichfield said with an understanding
smile. "You're a very lucky man, but you still have my
most sincere sympathy."

Jack ran upstairs to dress, wondering what Lichfield had
meant, but after only a few minutes it came to him.
Lichfield had realized that Jack was in love with Amanda,
and assuming that Amanda felt the same he'd called Jack
a very lucky man. Lichfield obviously knew the girl he'd
all but raised himself, which was why he had extended his
sympathy as well. Being involved with Amanda meant
Jack was going to need it.

By the time Jack got his horse, it was about one in the
morning. He no longer felt as tired as he had been, but the
ride up to Braxton Meadows would take care of that. He'd
be ready to crawl back into bed by then, but this time it
would not be his father's house to which he went. He'd be
careful not to wake Amanda, but he needed to be beside
her if he meant to get any sleep. He wanted to know she
was safe, even if there wasn't much that could harm her.
For her sake he ought to forget about marrying and forget
about *her,* but that choice had become absolutely impossible. He'd sooner forget about wanting his heart to beat. . . .

The ride was as long and tiring as Jack had known it
would be, but at least it wasn't raining. The closer he got
the more he looked forward to climbing under the quilts
with the woman he loved, which made that part of the ride
extremely uncomfortable. Jack was in the midst of cursing
his vivid imagination when he saw something that banished all other thoughts and sent a chill down his spine.
The Lavering house was all lit up both inside and out, the
wall torches bright in the predawn darkness.

It seemed to take longer to reach the house from the
road than it had to ride up from London. Almost before his
horse had come to a stop, Jack was dismounted and running up to the door, a door that stood ominously ajar. Inside, all was a bedlam, with some people running back and
forth, others standing about wringing their hands, and still
others crying. In the midst of it all was a no-longer-calm

Soong Tao, with Miss Han standing beside him. Tao was coldly but vehemently dressing down some men, while Miss Han stood there silently looking very ill.

". . . couldn't have *flown* away, so there *must* be tracks *somewhere,*" Tao was saying as Jack strode up. "Use the torches and fan out from the house, covering every inch of ground until you find either a track or where a track has been brushed away. There has to be—"

"Tao, what's going on?" Jack demanded, shouldering his way through the swarm of men. "What's happened here?"

"Miss Edmunds is missing," Tao told him grimly, wasting no time on their usual game of affected dislike. "His Grace suggested I have some of my men check on the house during the night, to be certain the ladies were all right here alone. One of them discovered that the terrace doors had been broken open, and he roused the servants and then came and told me. By the time I got here they'd discovered that Miss Edmunds was missing, and had in fact never gotten to bed or turned down her lamp. Apparently someone has abducted her."

"Her staff was on the floor of the room that had been broken into," Miss Han added, turning Jack's blood to ice. "The broken door is right below her rooms, and her own balcony doors were open. If she heard the sound of breaking glass . . ."

"She probably went down to investigate," Jack finished furiously when Miss Han's words trailed off. "Without rousing any of the men in the house to go with her. If she's still alive when we find her, I'll kill her with my bare hands. Tao, get your men together and let's go. I'm certain I know who has her, and if she isn't being held in his house, he'll know where she *is* being held. Come on."

Jack turned and all but ran for the door, aware that Tao and his men were following. He'd *known* it was a mistake to put off sending people to arrest Blake, but those in authority had wanted sworn statements and documented details before initiating anything. They worried about having

a clear-cut case, not about what Blake might do while they
were getting it. If he hadn't been so tired he might have
argued. . . .

Since no one else was mounted, Jack led the way to
Blake's house on foot at a trot. The house wasn't all that
far away, so they'd be there in a matter of minutes. Jack
kept telling himself that Blake wanted to marry Amanda,
so she would be fine. It was almost dawn; they would be
there in plenty of time to keep anything beyond minor discomfort from happening to her. They would . . . they
would . . . !

Refusing to consider the question of why Amanda had
been kidnapped if Blake planned to marry her, Jack simply
kept going. In a little while he realized that only Tao was
keeping up with him, but that didn't make him slow down.
The sense of urgency inside him refused to believe all the
comforting assurances he'd been telling himself; when
Amanda was safely back where she belonged, *then* he'd
stop worrying.

"Is *that* where we're going?" Tao asked as the fence and
gate of Blake's property came into view. "You do know
the place belongs to Baron Delland?"

"I know," Jack agreed, glancing over his shoulder. The
others were far enough behind that he could add, "Baron
Delland is about to be arrested for murder, and we're just
lucky he made that mistake. There don't seem to be any
laws against the rest of what he's done, even though there
should be."

"But didn't you tell me at some point that you didn't actually see the man who killed the clerk?" Tao asked, worry
suddenly in his voice. "If the only proof you have is a carriage with a device you must have traced back to him . . ."

Tao didn't finish the thought, but it wasn't necessary.
Even Lichfield's kidnapping had been his nephew's idea
rather than Blake's, and neither of the two surviving brothers had ever committed murder at Blake's orders. Reggie
must have been the one with all the necessary dirty details,
and that was why Reggie had been put out of the way. The

other two men arrested at the house where Lichfield had been held had refused to speak a single word. No wonder they'd been so concerned with building a "clear-cut" case. As it stood, they had nothing but a coach *anyone* could have used.

"But he *is* involved in Amanda's kidnapping," Jack muttered, once again trying to convince himself. "Somehow, some way I'll prove that. . . ."

By then they were up to the gate, where three big men stood guard. The guards seemed prepared to refuse entrance to Jack and Tao, but there was no need to fight their way in as Jack was ready to do. Tao demanded entrance in the name of Duke Edward, and the large group of men who came running up helped to convince the guards. They opened the gate, and once again Jack led the way.

They were about halfway up the long drive, heading toward the house, when Jack noticed lamplight off in the woods to the right. At another time he might have ignored the oddity, but right now his mind refused to dismiss *anything* unusual. Rather than continuing up the drive he headed off into the woods, and in a moment he saw a small house. Dawn began to make itself known just then, but Jack didn't stop to admire the beauty of it. If Amanda was in that house he would get her out, and if not he would continue on to the main house and choke her location out of Blake.

"No!" Amanda said sharply as the three men began to walk toward her. She knew better than to show any fear to those three predators, but it was a near thing. "I won't let you touch me. If you try, I'll make you kill me, and then your plans will really be ruined."

There was amusement on Blake's face and he seemed ready to point out that with three of them they wouldn't *have* to kill her, something she already knew. Unless she got very, very lucky she would lose this last fight badly, but before any words were spoken there was noise in the other room. It was the noise of a number of people coming into the house, and Blake and his men turned quickly to see who it was. Amanda thanked God for the distraction and was about to attack when—

"Isn't it rather early for a party?" Jack's voice came, harder than Amanda had ever heard it in public, but sweeter than birdsong to her ears. She'd been sure he was still in London and had no idea how he'd found her, but the flood of relief his presence brought was dizzying. When he saw her he pushed past Blake and the others to hurry over and take her in his arms. "Are you all right?" he asked, dark eyes filled with worry looking down at her.

"Of course she's all right," Blake said blandly, only glancing at the men who had followed Jack inside and now stood in the other room. "Those ruffians who kidnapped her were fools to believe they could hide her here without my knowing of it, and my men took great pleasure in dealing with them. We were just about to escort Miss Edmunds home."

"That's a lie," Amanda said immediately, appalled at how quickly Blake had adapted to the changed situation. *"He's* the one responsible for having me kidnapped, and if you hadn't gotten here when you did he would have violated me."

"Please, Miss Edmunds, not again," Blake said with weary kindness as Jack stiffened, fury burning in his eyes. "You've had a terrible shock, I know, but as I've already told you, you're confused. It was the men who kidnapped you who meant to violate you, not *me.* Why in the world would I do such a thing, when I mean to ask your brother for your hand?"

"So that no one else would want me," Amanda returned, not about to let him get away with it. "That way Richard would agree to our marriage without question, and you would end up controlling my father's property. But there's an easy answer for that now. I'll simply ask Richard to dispose of the property, and—"

"Of course, dear girl, just as you like," Blake said soothingly when Amanda's words suddenly broke off, the laughter in his eyes showing he knew what had stopped her. It was the realization that selling her father's property would simply substitute gold for land, since Richard would never consider just handing it away for a pittance. It would be her dowry, after all, and *his* duty to see it as large as possible. . . .

"As I kept trying to tell you, I care only about you," Blake went on, still sounding extremely sincere. "I know well enough that people will believe you *were* violated before we were able to rescue you, no matter that it isn't so, but I don't care. I will still insist on marrying you, and I'm certain your brother will agree."

Amanda parted her lips to argue, but for the first time in her life she was trapped. Blake had been right about what people would believe, and Richard would know how impossible actually proving the truth would be. She hadn't been completely virginal even before she drugged Jack; if no more than a hint of scandal would be enough to make the men from the best families lose interest, her inability to pass a physical examination would ruin things completely.

"But you won't be the only man willing and eager to marry her," Jack said to Blake, his arms tightening around her. "*I'm* still here, and I'm not gotten rid of as easily as some gullible clerk."

For an instant Blake's eyes blazed with hatred, which shocked Amanda even though it shouldn't have.

"My dear Michaels, you must be joking," Blake said, and now the hatred had been replaced once again with that damnable amusement. "As I understand it, Lavering has already refused your suit. I'm the only one left who might be accepted, and if I'm not I'll certainly have to make a fuss about the wild accusations Miss Edmunds has been making. After all, a man must think about his reputation. And with that in mind, I'd appreciate if it you would release my future wife. Now."

Jack stiffened again at the command, but once again Amanda knew Blake had spoken the truth. Thanks to her

Jack *had* been refused, and that made her absolutely desperate. The men in the next room were shuffling their feet and muttering to one another, but it wasn't Blake they were glancing at with embarrassment. They believed Blake, just as everyone else would, and when Jack actually let her go her desperation found one last ploy.

"But you can't become my husband," Amanda said to Blake, fighting harder than ever before to keep her voice steady—and as filled with amusement as his had been. "I very much want to have children, you see, and you aren't able to *give* a woman children."

A shocked silence fell on everyone in the house as Blake literally froze where he stood. No part of him moved as he stared at her with soulless blue eyes. Amanda was making a wild guess in the hope of reaching the madman within, and now that she'd begun there was no turning back.

"I mean, it was perfectly obvious from what you told me," she continued, just as though he'd raised his brows in confusion. "You said you would not *permit* me to have your children, any more than you had permitted your first wife to have them. But a decision like that is in God's hands rather than yours, and I'd say God seems rather eager to be rid of that wonderfully noble bloodline of yours. After all, your very special mother was only able to have *you*, and you haven't managed even that much. Saying you *won't* have children when the truth is that you can't. How very amusing."

Amanda had been trying to make the man show his true colors, but her plan worked better than her wildest expectations. There was a moment of deep silence, and then Robert Blake threw his head back and screamed. The sound was the vocalization of madness, surely chilling everyone who heard it with the touch of terror, and then Blake proved he had snapped completely. Even as he screamed a second time a knife appeared in his hand, and then he was charging at *her* with murder in his eyes.

Amanda wanted to do nothing more than turn and run,

but she couldn't desert Jack, who still stood beside her. If she got out of the way the madman could very well turn on the man she loved, and she couldn't allow that to happen. So instead of running she went into fighting stance, and that was an even bigger mistake than triggering Blake's madness. Jack must have expected her to back away and give him fighting room, not to stand there properly balanced. When he tried to jump into Blake's path he collided with her, and the collision momentarily put Jack off balance.

Which Blake tried to take advantage of. He almost seemed to be foaming at the mouth as he slashed at her underhanded, paying no mind to the fact that Jack was in the way. She couldn't block the attack because Jack *was* in the way, but she could and did jump back to avoid the blade. But Jack was too far off balance to do the same or even to manage a block, and the knife caught him instead.

"No!" Amanda screamed, cursing her reflexes for taking her out of reach. *She* was the one who should have been hurt, not Jack! She began to launch herself at Blake, intending to kill him even if he killed her at the same time, but two arms wrapped themselves around her from behind and pulled her well to one side.

"Stop struggling and stay out of the way!" Soong Tao's voice whispered harshly in her ear. "If you throw Jack off again, that crazy man could kill him!"

Amanda didn't want to listen to Soong, but what he'd said was the truth. Despite being wounded, Jack had managed to get Blake's attention. The madman now stalked Jack as Jack backed slowly away, one hand to his side. He was hurt, but he still clearly meant to fight.

"Then *you* help him!" Amanda hissed at Soong, terrified that Jack would be killed. "He's hurt and can't do it alone, so you help him!"

"He not only *can* do it alone, he wants to," Soong disgreed, still keeping steel-hard fingers wrapped around her arms from behind. "That mad dog nearly stole his woman, and then he nearly killed her. Do you think Jack will let *anyone* else have him?"

Amanda looked at Jack's expression and eyes and knew at once that Soong was right. Jack meant to have Blake's heart for what he'd done, and he wasn't about to give up the privilege or even to share it. *Men!* Amanda thought, silently adding the worst curses she knew. *Why do they have to be so pigheadedly unreasonable? Why will they refuse help even when they're hurt?*

The only answer to that was simply because they were men, stubborn fools born to give women grief because of their irrationality. Amanda tried to make herself angry over that, but she couldn't even manage indignation. Jack was leading Blake to the other side of the room, far enough away from her so that she'd remain safe no matter what happened.

And what would happen was no foregone victory for Jack. The way he held himself said he was in pain, and now his blood could be seen staining his shirt in an ugly, spreading flood. Blake jumped forward and stabbed at him, trying to stop his retreat permanently, but Jack managed to avoid the lunge—barely. Amanda realized that he must be hurt worse than she'd thought, and then—

And then Blake made the mistake Jack had been trying to lure him into. He grabbed Jack's coat with his left hand in an effort to hold his victim still, and stabbed forward again with the knife in his right fist. He would have added to the wound Jack had on that side, but Blake's intended victim had only been trying to bring him in close in order to hide what he did. With his back to the watching men, Jack grabbed the wrist of his assailant with his left hand while punching once, hard, at Blake's throat with his right fist. The movement was so fast and over such a short distance, that most of the watchers must have missed it or thought it was a feeble attempt to fight back. In reality it was a very harsh and effective death blow, and if others missed it, Blake didn't.

Blake choked, his eyes undoubtedly bulging as he

fought to bury that knife in Jack even as he struggled to breathe through a crushed windpipe. But neither effort was successful, and after an unbearably long moment Blake dropped the knife and collapsed. He twitched briefly on the filthy floor before all movement was finally done for good, and only then was Amanda able to take a deep breath of relief. It was over at last, and Jack was—

"Catch him!" Soong ordered sharply, but there was no one close enough to Jack to keep him from collapsing next to the man who'd tried to kill him. Amanda didn't consciously notice crossing the distance between them, but one moment she stood staring with terror in her heart, and the next she knelt beside Jack with his head in her lap. He wasn't dead at least, thank God for that, but it took a minute before he was able to look at her and know who he was seeing.

"Lady mine," he whispered, trying to raise his hand to her face but stopped short by pain. "I've failed you."

"No, Jack, you didn't fail, you won," she whispered back, tears forcing her voice to break. "And now you're going to be perfectly fine, so that we can marry and—"

"No," he interrupted sadly, his words still a whisper as he found her hand instead. "I wasn't able to find your answer, and now . . . now . . . I love you . . ."

And then there weren't any more words, and his eyes didn't see her because they were closed. Amanda cried as she never had before, sobbing out her grief as she held to Jack's hand with all her strength, and then Soong was beside her with an arm around her shoulders.

"He isn't dead, Miss Edmunds, only unconscious," Soong told her gently. "We're putting a litter together to carry him back to his father's house, and one of the men is running to bring a physician there. Jack is strong and his wound isn't all that serious. You have my word that he'll be fine."

Amanda had already guessed as much, but she was still reluctant to let go of Jack's hand. She finally moved out of the way so that Jack could be transferred onto the impro-

vised litter, which had been constructed from two long
branches from the woods, hastily trimmed before a blanket
was tied between them.

Amanda watched them lift him gently and put him on
the blanket, and then shuddered helplessly as the two men
on each pole stood up together. Wracked with guilt,
Amanda thought of all she'd done to this good man, and
all because she'd thought she was so clever. She'd given
him an impossible task to perform, and had encouraged
other men, before his eyes, just in case he failed. How
could she have been so coldblooded and heartless? He
must have thought he was dying just now; he was the most
marvelous man in the whole world, and he could have
died thinking himself a failure.

And it was all her fault. Amanda followed Jack's pro-
cession slowly, paying no attention to the two men Soong
assigned to accompany her back to her brother's house.
Now she knew she should have worked with Jack to find
an answer to their problem that they both could have lived
with, not sent him out to find a solution alone. That way
they still could have announced their betrothal after she
had a talk with Richard, and Blake's plans would have
been frustrated before things went this far.

But she'd been too clever to do anything so intelligent,
and now everything was lost. Blake had been right in saying people would believe she had been violated, and she
couldn't do anything to disprove the lie. If Jack tried to
marry her now, it would only serve to embroil his family
in scandal. Even if his father did know the truth about him
he might be forced to disown Jack, and that was one tragedy Amanda would not allow to happen.

Outside the day was well begun, but it was a gray day
threatening rain. *How fitting,* Amanda thought as she
walked numbly through it. *A gray day for the death of a
blackguard and the death of dreams.* She wanted nothing
more out of life than a man named Jack Michaels, but that
was the one thing she couldn't have. The pain of losing
her would be easier for him to bear than what would come

from losing his family, and he'd even be able to continue on with his work. She'd made up her mind, and that was the way it was going to be.

But she would never get over *him*, not if she lived forever. And without the man she loved, no matter how long or short a time she lived it would seem like forever.

Chapter 23

Jack awoke in his bedchamber in his father's house to find Tao sitting in a chair, watching him. He felt rested and strong and hungry, and only when he tried to sit up did the pain in his side remind him about what had happened.

"That slice won't heal very fast if you don't take it a little easy," Tao said, getting out of the chair to stand beside Jack's bed. "The physician told us that you seemed to be suffering more from exhaustion than from the wound, and the loss of blood simply pushed you over the edge. Are you hungry? You need to restore the strength you lost."

"I'm starving," Jack said, examining his bandaged side as best he could. "My father's kitchens will probably be empty by the time I'm done 'restoring my strength.' How long was I asleep?"

"First unconscious and *then* asleep," Tao corrected firmly. "If you try to forget about the unconscious part, you'll be too likely to do something to make it happen again. And it's been almost a day and a half."

"A day and a half!" Jack echoed with a frown. "Someone should have awakened me no matter what the physician said. Amanda must be worried sick, so forget about that food you just rang for. Unless she's in the next room, I'm getting dressed to go over and see her."

"You're not going anywhere," Tao disagreed, using a hand to his chest to press Jack down onto the bed again. "His Grace knew you would try to leap out of bed as soon as your eyes opened, and that's why *I'm* here. If you try to get up before the physician says you can, we'll finally find out which one of us is the better fighter. And besides that, Sir Charles Kerry is here to see you."

"Why is *he* here?" Jack muttered, eyeing Tao as he rubbed his chest. Jack knew he was a better fighter than his friend, but after a day and a half in bed and with a wound in his side, he wasn't likely to be able to prove it. "No, let me rephrase that: I don't *care* why Sir Charles is here, not while Amanda is still worrying about me. If she's here in the house, then send for her. If she's gone back to her brother's house, send someone to tell her that I'm awake and dying to see her."

"His Grace made sure she was told yesterday that the physician expected you to recover completely," Tao answered, suddenly looking uncomfortable. "Why don't you wait until you *are* recovered, and then you can go and speak to her. By then maybe something will have—changed."

"What do you mean, changed?" Jack demanded, his insides suddenly hollow from more than the lack of food. "Tao, there's something you're not telling me. The Amanda I know ought to be *here,* waiting to see for herself that I'm all right. She would have gone back to her brother's house to change clothes, but for nothing more. Tell me what's wrong."

Tao stared at him expressionlessly for a moment, then took a deep breath.

"I didn't plan to tell you this yet, but you're giving me no choice," he said heavily. "I—spoke to Miss Han last night for quite some time, and she was nearly in tears. It seems Miss Edmunds told her what happened, but also told her about a decision she's made. Do you remember what Blake said, about how everyone would believe she *had* been violated no matter how firmly it was denied?"

Jack nodded, now feeling a good deal worse. *He* knew those two ruffians hadn't stood a chance against Amanda, but anyone who didn't know of her abilities would be hard-pressed to believe the same. And because she'd loved him so much that she'd drugged him into using her body, it would be impossible for her to claim her innocence.

"Well, unfortunately Blake was right, may his soul rot for all eternity," Tao continued bitterly. "Miss Edmunds realized that fact, and also realized that the scandal would force your father to disown you if you married her anyway. So she's decided not to marry you under any circumstances, and doesn't even want to see you again."

Jack was so devastated, he just sat there staring at Tao. He couldn't believe he'd lost the light of his life, and all because of a dead man's malicious plans. If Blake had still been alive Jack would have killed him again, but slowly enough this time to exact some small measure of the agony *he* now faced. But he couldn't just accept it all, even if the scandal touched the British government as well as his father. Amanda was his *life*, and it wasn't in him to simply give up his life. . . .

"I'll get that," Tao said, bringing Jack back to the moment at hand. He'd heard the knock, but his mind had been too busy searching for a way out of that horror to pay attention.

"Well, Jack, it's good to see you awake and alert again," Sir Charles said pleasantly as he entered. "When Mr. Soong rang for food for you I was informed immediately, because I have something to show you. It's guaranteed to make you heal twice as fast, but I do need to see you alone. If Mr. Soong would be so kind as to wait outside for a few moments . . . ?"

Tao bowed silently in answer to the request, then left the room. Jack couldn't imagine anything that would heal the wound he'd received a moment earlier, but he decided he might as well listen to Sir Charles. He had nothing better to do, since his appetite had disappeared like a bursting soap bubble.

"This is what I wanted to show you," Sir Charles said, handing over a folded piece of paper. "It's only a copy, you'll notice, but the real thing will be given to you after the ceremony. It won't be *entirely* official until then, but you can take it as an accomplished fact on my authority."

Jack was listening with half an ear while he glanced through what was written on the paper, but suddenly a phrase caught his eye. He went back and read it again, this time skipping nothing, and by the time he was through his jaw had dropped in astonishment.

"I've been working on that for quite some time," Sir Charles told him with a chuckle. "It wasn't that they hesitated to give it to you because they didn't think you'd earned it. They knew you had, but giving it to you would have meant losing the very services for which they were rewarding you. When your father sent his man to me in London yesterday to let me know what had happened, I took that resignation you'd given me and paid those people a visit. I told them they were about to lose you anyway, then pointed out that they now had the perfect opportunity to do what they wanted to and what was right. I also mentioned that if they rewarded you as you deserved, they would *not* be losing you."

"How can that possibly be?" Jack asked, his head now swirling dizzily. "Once people find out about this . . ."

"What they'll find out about is the great service you've done for king and country," Sir Charles interrupted smoothly. "Miss Edmunds enlisted your help to find her late father's missing secretary, and you not only accomplished that but uncovered a malicious rogue at the same time. In addition you put your own life in danger in order to save that of Miss Edmunds, and against all odds prevailed over the villain. His Majesty's public bureau will no longer be used against His Majesty's loyal subjects, and that's what you're being rewarded for. What else you've done will never be mentioned, but having risked yourself so greatly and having been wounded should be adequate reason for you to change your public image. Your new position will all but demand *that.*"

"New position?" Jack echoed, still half-believing he was in the middle of a pleasant dream. It was exactly what he needed and wanted, and his own efforts had made it happen. But—

"The position as my second-in-command, who will eventually take my place as the head of His Majesty's agency for discreet investigations," Sir Charles said with a great deal of satisfaction. "As my wife keeps reminding me, I'm not as young as I used to be. I need someone who *is* young to handle the middle-of-the-night emergencies, and to go trotting all over the city to be certain that whatever task our agents are in the midst of is going as smoothly as possible. You'll need to pretend to be respectable, of course, which means no more jumping into the middle of things unless someone's life is at stake, but that won't ruin it for you *completely,* will it?"

Sir Charles was actually teasing him, but the euphoria Jack should have been feeling was being dissipated by depression. He now had exactly what Amanda had felt was needed, but he didn't have *her*. The threat of scandal would still keep them apart at her insistence, unless . . . what was that thought he'd had earlier?

"Sir Charles, I need your help," Jack said slowly. "I have something to tell you, which will explain why I'm not in the middle of thanking you as enthusiastically as you deserve. After that I need you to do something for me, something I can't do myself without getting my head jumped on by that oversized nanny waiting out in my sitting room. Will you help me?"

"Of course, Jack," Sir Charles said at once. "What do you need me to do?"

Jack started his explanation, and it wasn't long before Sir Charles's eyes began to gleam. But not as much as when Jack started to outline his plan. . . .

Amanda sat in the gardens, staring at the lovely trees and shrubs and flowers without seeing them. The house was too busy now that Richard and Claire and the rest of the servants had arrived, and Amanda wasn't in the mood for it. She hadn't been in the mood for more than being alone since she'd returned from Blake's house, five days ago now.

One of the servants had gone back to London that same day to tell Richard what had happened, and the very next day Richard and Claire had come up. Their first concern had been for her safety, but once she'd reassured them she'd also asked to speak to Richard alone. The first thing she'd done was confess that she was in love with Jack Michaels, and had turned Richard against him because she had believed Jack wasn't in love with *her*.

Richard hadn't been too displeased to hear that, not considering how good a "catch" Jack was, but then had come the hard part. She first explained what people would think even though it wasn't true, and happily didn't have to explain why she couldn't disprove it. Claire had spoken to Richard about Amanda's physical situation from her Chinese boxing exercises as she'd promised to do, and he understood only too well.

That was when she'd begged Richard not to accept Jack's proposal under any circumstances. It was even possible that Jack might get his father to intercede for him, but she'd die if she was the cause of letting dishonor and humiliation touch any of those people. She'd rather live out her life as a lonely old maid than do that, and she swore not to be a burden to her brother. Her father's property could be sold, and whatever it brought would be enough to keep her in a small cottage of her own.

Richard had actually cried, but he'd agreed to do as she'd asked. He would *not* find her a lonely cottage until all hope of any sort of marriage was gone, but other than that she would have his complete cooperation. Amanda had also cried, and it hadn't even helped when Mr. Lichfield appeared at the door the next day. After they'd hugged he'd asked about her young man, that delightful Mr. Michaels who had helped to free him. Amanda had run sobbing to her rooms, leaving Richard to make any explanation he chose.

She'd also been avoiding Pei, after telling her about

what had happened and what she planned to do. Pei had
cried, but she hadn't kept trying to talk to Amanda. As a
matter of fact she hadn't even seen Pei, except at meal-
times. Her friend had watched her pick at her food, but
still hadn't tried to encourage her to eat more. As if she
knew Amanda would never really want to eat again. . . .

"Excuse me, Miss Edmunds, but Lord Pembroke would
like to see you in his study," a servant said, one Amanda
hadn't seen approach. "If you're free, he would like it to
be immediately."

If she was free. At another time Amanda would have
laughed at the suggestion that sitting and staring at nothing
could be considered being busy. Now she just nodded wearily, and went inside to Richard's study. He stood when
she entered and closed the door behind her, then he gestured to a chair in front of his desk.

"Sit down and have a cup of tea with me, sister," he
said in his usual kindly way. "There are some things you
have to be told, and now is as good a time as any."

Amanda sat and accepted the cup of tea, then waited for
Richard to tell her whatever he had to.

"It breaks my heart that I haven't seen you smile even
once since I got up here," Richard said after a moment. "I
wish I had news to change that, but I'm afraid I don't. You
may be aware of the fact that Duke Edward paid me a visit
this morning. I don't feel it necessary to go into the details
of what we discussed, but you ought to know that there is
now not the slightest chance that you'll ever marry a man
named Jack Michaels."

Amanda was vastly relieved that she would never bring
shame to Jack and his family, but beyond that she was des-
olate. Even knowing it could be no other way did nothing
to ease the pain, but she hadn't expected it to be eased.
She nodded to Richard—knowing the tightness in her
throat would never let her speak—to tell him she'd heard
him and appreciated his efforts on her behalf.

"The next thing you need to be told is that someone
representing Sir John Blackburn has made a proposal or

Sir John's behalf," Richard continued. "A Colonel Harwood Ebersham spoke on his own behalf, and both asked for your hand in marriage."

"Colonel Ebersham is a dear," Amanda said after clearing her throat. "It was nothing but pure luck that he survived the attack Blake sent against him, and he's just being gallant. He deserves better than to marry a woman who no longer has any sort of heart, and he would be miserable with me. As for Sir John Blackburn, I've never heard of him. If we ever met at any time I can't remember the occasion, but I'm sure he'll change his mind once he hears the stories. Was there anything else, Richard?"

"Amanda, my dear, I wasn't telling you about the proposals in order to get your opinion as to why they should be refused," Richard said, faint reproof in his tone. "Acceptance or rejection is mine to do, but I happen to agree that Colonel Ebersham is unsuitable. He seems to be a fine gentleman with a strong sense of honor who is genuinely fond of you, but that very fondness would make him too indulgent. A woman of spirit needs a man with a firm hand to keep her in check, which is why I accepted the Blackburn proposal."

"You *accepted* it?" Amanda was stunned as well as shocked, completely unprepared for news like that. "But Richard, I don't even *know* the man! Not to mention the fact that he'll withdraw the proposal as soon as he hears about what happened! How can you think that he won't?"

"Not everyone listens to or cares about idle gossip," Richard soothed her, leaning back in his chair. "I happen to feel that Blackburn is the perfect man for you, which you'll discover for yourself when you meet him. But speaking about meeting people, there's someone Duke Edward would like you to meet with. He's spoken to the man himself, but hasn't made the least impression. Others have also tried, but the man remains unconvinced."

"Who are you talking about?" Amanda asked, partially distracted from the appalling prospect of marrying a man she'd never love. "Who could possibly refuse to believe Duke Edward, and what was he disbelieved *about?*"

"The man is some official from London, possibly one of Magistrate Fielding's people," Richard said, pulling thoughtfully on his lip. "Frankly, I can't imagine anyone having the nerve to doubt Duke Edward either, but apparently the man is rather stiff-necked. He's investigating Robert Blake's death, and has found what he considers a highly suspicious inconsistency in some of the statements about the incident. Because of those suspicions, he thinks Michaels may be guilty of murder rather than simply having defended himself."

"What?" Amanda growled, sitting up straighter and ridding herself of the teacup. "Is the man crazy, or simply looking to make trouble? Jack could have been *killed,* and would have been if he hadn't put Blake down first!"

"Amanda, *I'm* not the one who doubts that," Richard said, obviously trying to calm her. "The difficulty comes from the fact that Blake said *his* men had overpowered those two ruffians, and Michaels and Soong gave statements saying *you* were the one who did it. Blake's claim was included in the statements from the other witnesses, and surely you must realize that the idea of a woman besting two large men is rather ludicrous. The man from London believes Michaels and Soong may have murdered Blake together, but didn't rehearse the stories of the other men beyond what they were to say about the supposed fight. That, he claims, is why there's an inconsistency."

"But that's ridiculous," Amanda protested, really beginning to be annoyed. "How can a difference of opinion— which happens to be *right*—show anything to suggest murder? It makes no sense at all."

"So Duke Edward maintained, but the man disagreed," Richard said with a sigh. "His Grace wonders if *you* might talk to the man, in an effort to convince him that Michaels and Soong weren't simply trying to play some incomprehensible game to cover up a murder. I told His Grace that I would see if you were up to it."

"I'm up to it," Amanda stated flatly, in point of fact eager to meet the man who was trying to harm Jack. So it was ludicrous to believe a woman could disable two big men? They'd see what the man thought after Amanda showed him just how possible it was. "How soon can His Grace get the man here?"

"We've arranged for them to come by after dinner tonight," Richard answered, finishing his cup of tea. "If you hadn't been willing I would have cancelled the appointment, but I do think it best that you do whatever you can to set the matter straight."

"I guarantee you, Richard, that I *will* do whatever I can," Amanda said with grim satisfaction before rising from her chair. "If you'll excuse me now, I'll see you at dinner."

Richard nodded good-naturedly, so she left his study and went to her rooms. Once there she struggled out of her day gown and the rest of her clothes, then began doing every stretching exercise she knew. The man might *walk* in for the appointment tonight, but if he wasn't exceptionally lucky he would end up being *carried* out. After all, the only thing bothering him seemed to be his belief that a woman couldn't fight. Wasn't it her duty to prove to him how wrong he was? Once she did prove it, Jack would be safe. That was all that mattered, that Jack be safe . . . even if she never *could* see him again.

Chapter 24

The rest of the afternoon disappeared so quickly that Amanda barely noticed it. She didn't go down for tea, and she didn't spend any time fretting over being betrothed to a stranger. Jack was in trouble and needed her help, and that was all that mattered now. Unimportant things like unwanted marriages could wait until she had the time to worry about them.

Amanda bathed and dressed for dinner, then ate well but carefully. She didn't want to be weak from hunger, but she also couldn't afford to stuff herself. Conversation at the table was rather sparse, but it had been the same for days now. She neither noticed nor cared, not with Jack's well-being at stake. All her thoughts revolved around what she would say and do to the man when he arrived, and she intended to be ready. After asking to be called when their guests got there, she excused herself and went back to her rooms to change.

Once she was in her *chih fu*, Amanda sat down to wait. She'd had to change her clothes a number of extra times today, but that was nothing compared to the effort she was prepared to make. Jack would not be accused of murder if *she* had anything to say about it, but it did seem strange that anyone would make an accusation based on so odd a point. And the way Richard had been acting was strange as well, so calm and agreeable about it all. Well, Richard *was* calm and agreeable by nature, but—

A knock at her door ended all extraneous thoughts, especially when Amanda opened it to a servant who said she was wanted downstairs. She followed the servant down without saying anything, and found Richard and his guests in the front hall. There were three men she didn't recognize, but two were dressed like lower-class retainers of some sort. The third was dressed like a gentleman and was tall and blond, which made things a good deal easier. Blake had been blond, and because of him Amanda had developed a definite distaste for blondness. Although *this* blonde somehow looked faintly familiar. . . .

"Amanda, how good of you to join us so quickly," Richard said when she reached the bottom of the stairs. "You know His Grace Duke Edward, of course."

Duke Edward smiled and seemed prepared to take her hand, but she stopped short of the group and bowed. It was a perfectly acceptable way to greet someone who deserved respect, and dressed as she was a curtsey would have looked silly. Duke Edward blinked at her bow and returned it in European fashion, but made no comment in words.

"And this gentleman is Mr. Hughes," Richard continued, gesturing to the stranger. "He's here looking into Robert Blake's death."

The blond Mr. Hughes had been eyeing her *chih fu* with very little approval, and when Amanda simply nodded her head after the introduction he was even less pleased. He seemed to be unhappy with everything about her, and she hadn't even done anything yet. The two other men stood silently behind him, but they, apparently, weren't there to be introduced.

"I've agreed to discuss a ridiculous contention with you, Miss Edmunds," Hughes said in a voice filled with annoyance. "I expected the discussion, at least, to be serious, but now that you've appeared in that—that—outlandish costume, I'm beginning to believe that *nothing* about this matter can be taken seriously."

"If I were you, Mr. Hughes, I would take *everything* about this seriously," Amanda said coolly, locking gazes with the man. "This is what I wore when I bested those two ruffians Blake had sent to attack me, and I thought you should see it. Surely you didn't believe I was wearing a gown at the time?"

"Frankly, Miss Edmunds, I fail to see what clothing can possibly have to do with the matter," Hughes returned stiffly, his gaze flickering away from hers. "Obviously Michaels and Soong hoped to use a preposterous story to divert attention from what they'd done, but when Michaels was wounded they became flustered and failed to brief their men properly. Just as obviously—"

"Just as obviously, you need to reconsider your conclusions," Amanda retorted. "Would Mr. Michaels and Mr. Soong have prepared a story for their own men to tell when four of Blake's men were also there? Granted two of them were unconscious during the time under discussion, but *they* can say who stopped them and the other two can tell about what actually happened."

"None of the four has been willing to speak to us," Hughes came back after the briefest hesitation, almost as if he'd had to stop to think. "And with their employer dead and no longer able to protect them, they'll consider their necks and likely say what they think we want to hear when they do speak. I have no interest in speculation and prevarication, Miss Edmunds, only in fact."

"But there's one fact you still haven't touched on, Mr. Hughes," Amanda said very softly, fighting to keep anger from taking control. "This entire disagreement centers around—"

"Allow me to interrupt for a moment, sister," Richard said suddenly, putting a hand to her arm. "I should have considered privacy when this conversation began, but it isn't too late to rectify the oversight. Let's step into the ballroom, and then the entire house needn't be party to affairs that don't concern them."

Everyone else agreed to that immediately, so Amanda had no choice but to agree as well. In point of fact, the interruption might have come at a most useful time. Amanda had come very close to losing her temper, and that was far from helpful at the best of times. Right now it could be downright harmful, especially for that Mr. Hughes. She wanted the man to know the truth, but hadn't planned on making it the last thing he ever learned.

They all entered the ballroom, whose double doors had been standing open. Some of the servants must have been working in there, as there were lamps and candles lit along the walls to the left and right. It seemed to Amanda an odd time for servants to be working, but maybe they'd been there to take down the heavy drapes covering the entire far wall of terrace doors. She could have sworn the drapes *had* been taken down, but she must have been mistaken. But now that she thought about it, why hadn't Richard taken them all into his study . . . ?

"Now then," Hughes said as soon as they reached the center of the large room, turning to face her belligerently. "What was that nonsense you were in the middle of spouting?"

"Nonsense?" Amanda echoed, all the anger she'd pushed away returning immediately. "You have the nerve to call what *I* say nonsense? I know it's usually a waste of effort to try to teach the ignorant, Mr. Hughes, but this is probably one of the times it will work. If what Mr. Michaels and Mr. Soong said is so preposterous, why don't *you* try attacking me? If your half-witted theories are right, I won't be able to stop you."

Amanda had used the sort of taunting tone of voice that usually got the person you were talking to angry enough to start a fight. That, along with what she'd said, made Hughes's jaw tighten and put an angry glint in his eyes. For an instant Amanda thought he *would* be stupid enough to attack, but something seemed to be holding him back.

"I'm not in the habit of attacking women," he growled, for all the world sounding as if he wished he could say something else. "But I'm also not in the habit of denying their requests. If it's attack you want, you shall have it. Teach the—*lady*—a lesson, men."

The two retainers who hadn't been introduced grinned at the order as Hughes stepped back, giving them the room to do as he'd demanded. They were almost exactly the same size as the two who had kidnapped her, and Amanda was in fighting stance even before they took their first steps forward. She would have to take them fast, before Richard or Duke Edward tried to interfere, but she still meant to wait for *them* to make the first move. Strange that the other two men hadn't already tried to interfere . . .

And then Amanda had time to think about nothing but the men coming at her. The first, to her left, came forward fast with his fist cocked, apparently intending to smash her face in. Amanda leaned back and side-kicked him in the groin, but somehow he managed to twist so that most of the kick was absorbed by his thigh. So she followed through with a jumping axe-kick, the top arc of which came across like the axe it was named after and caught the man in the face. He hadn't been able to twist away from *that* one, which meant he dropped flat and didn't get up again.

But that still left the other one to consider. He yelled as he charged at her, obviously expecting to freeze her with fright, but that hadn't ever happened. Amanda sidestepped and tripped him as he stumbled past, then helped him on his way with a one-footed flying kick in his back. When he went down Amanda expected him to get up again and try a second time, so she was ready. But not only didn't he do it, there was suddenly a great deal of noise that sounded like applause, and Richard and Duke Edward were laughing and congratulating her. . . .

"Excellent job, dear girl, really an excellent job of work," Richard said as he laughed and hugged her.

"You were even more magnificent than we expected, child," Duke Edward enthused as he patted her hand.

Amanda wanted to tell them how close they'd come to joining those two men on the floor, but instead simply accepted their congratulations without speaking. One did *not* come over to hug or pat a fighter in the middle of a fight . . . But there was all that noise to consider, and when she turned around it seemed that every person she'd met at the duke and duchess's party was stepping out from behind those drapes that she'd thought had been taken down. All of *them* were laughing as well, not to mention applauding. Mr. Soong appeared from somewhere and bent to the man who sat on the floor, and when he got a nod from the man he continued on to crouch beside the one who was still stretched out. He put a hand to the man's throat pulse, waited a moment, then gently began to try to rouse him.

But the biggest surprise was the man named Hughes. He stood there grinning just like everyone else, obviously de-lighted with the way things had worked out. Amanda de-cided they had all gone mad, but she might as well give them the chance to come up with an alternate explanation.

"What in the world is happening here?" she demanded, looking from her brother to the duke and back again. "I know you two are responsible, so tell me *now!*"

"My dear, we had no choice," Richard said, his smile softening as everyone came close to make a thick circle around them. "We knew that no matter what anyone *said* about your supposed violation, there would still be enough people about to disbelieve it and cause you grief. After all, everyone *knows* how helpless well-bred ladies are, and you are clearly a well-bred lady."

"So we needed to coax out the dragon that had done such a good job settling the bacon of those two ruffians," Duke Edward said, taking up the narrative. "We couldn't tell you what we were doing, not when it was necessary for everyone to see how you reacted without being certain of your safety beforehand. Some people are extremely ca-pable when they believe everything around them is under control, but tend to fall apart when that control is absent. Our neighbors happily agreed to help us prove you were not that sort, and now they'll be able to tell everyone what they saw with their own eyes. Isn't that so, my lords and ladies?"

"It most certainly is," one heavyset man growled emphatically while everyone else commented or applauded again. "Thought it was pure rubbish, m'self, now I'm pleased to say it ain't. Never saw anything like it, and I'm damned pleased it wasn't *me* going for her."

Everyone laughed at that even while they agreed, and Amanda had the time to notice Claire and Duchess Katherine among those in the crowd. Then Richard held his hands up to quiet the enthusiasm.

"Refreshments have already been put out in the salon, so let's not keep them waiting," he announced. "I'm sure my sister would like to rest and refresh herself, and then she'll certainly dress and join us. Just follow me."

His guests agreed with even more enthusiasm, and then they were all strolling out after Richard while still talking excitedly with each other. Amanda wasn't sure *how* she should feel, and before she could decide the man Hughes was in front of her.

"Since the safest thing I can do is apologize to you for the way I behaved, I'm taking this very first opportunity to do so," he said with a grin. "My instructions were to get you angry, but I nearly did too good a job of it. If you'd done to me what you did to *those* two poor chaps, I wouldn't have been able to handle it nearly as well."

"Oh, good lord, I forgot about that," Amanda gasped, suddenly mortified. "If none of this was serious, then what I did to those poor men—!"

"Was entirely expected," Mr. Soong interrupted to finish for her while he watched the second man helping the now conscious first man toward the door. "Those are two of *my* men, ones I trained and who volunteered for this. They were warned to be very careful and to protect themselves against serious response, but the nobility aren't the only ones who consider a well-bred lady helpless. They were certain they had nothing to fear from you, and they're very fortunate you treated them more gently than you did your kidnappers."

"And I have to admit that *I* almost joined them," Hughes said, looking abashed. "I was warned that under no circumstances was I to make an aggressive move toward you, but you got me so angry that I nearly forgot. It's a good thing I didn't refuse to take his orders *this* time."

"*His* orders?" Amanda echoed, feeling as though she were missing something. "Who are you talking about?"

"He means me," another voice said, one she'd thought she'd never hear again. "Hughes is a friend of mine, and he agreed to do this as a favor to me. Although if he'd gotten bashed, I'd never have heard the end of it."

Amanda turned to see Jack standing there, Pei not far from him. She tried to make herself turn back, leave the room, run as far and as fast as she could, but it simply wasn't possible. She'd missed him so much and had been so worried about him, even when everyone had assured her he would be fine. And he did look fine, dressed in royal blue brocade with white ruffles and gold buckles. All at once Amanda ran to him, and being folded in his arms was what reaching heaven must be like.

"Are you really all right?" she whispered, looking up into his beautiful face. "The last time I saw you—"

"The last time you saw me I was wounded as well as having overdone it *much* too much," he said after silencing her with a brief kiss. "Thanks to Tao's sitting on me for the last few days, I'm just about good as new. And you're even better. You're not only completely unhurt, your good name has been cleared. That bunch will spread the word all over London, and laugh down anyone who tries to voice a different opinion. I wish I could have seen you do it."

"But—I thought you were right there with everyone else," Amanda protested, trying not to think about what he'd said. Her good name had now been cleared. . . . "If you were there, how could you not see it?"

"I couldn't see it because I had to turn away," he answered with a laugh. "I know well enough how good you are, otherwise I never would have suggested all this. But the day will never come that I'll be able to simply stand there and watch while *anyone* attacks you. If I hadn't turned away, I would have ruined everything by jumping out and defending you."

The three other people in the room laughed at that, but Amanda was too depressed to join in the merriment. She let Jack go and stepped back from him, ready now to leave the room.

"Amanda, what's wrong?" Jack asked at once, his hand coming to her arm to stop her. "You weren't upset by what I said—?"

"Jack, I'm betrothed," she blurted, knowing of no other way to say it than straight out. "If my good name has been cleared then he'll *never* change his mind, so we just can't see each other again. It would be dishonorable and unfair, and I know you're neither. I wish I could be, but I've given my word to Richard and can't take it back. Please, let me go . . ."

"I think we need to talk," Jack said without releasing his grip. "Miss Han, Tao, Hughes—if you please?"

Pei looked as if she were considering refusing to leave, but Mr. Soong spoke softly to her and then escorted her out. She held to his arm the way Amanda wished *she* could hold to Jack, and Hughes followed them to close the doors behind himself.

"Speaking of being betrothed, Tao has told Miss Han that he means to return to China and ask her father for her," Jack said conversationally. "He has you and me to thank for being able to do that, since we're the ones who found and freed your Mr. Lichfield. As soon as my father discovered that the man was available to accept a position, he hired him immediately. He's regretted letting your father beat him to hiring Lichfield all those years ago, and now he finally has him. Which also lets *me* off the hook."

"About what?" Amanda couldn't help asking, even though she didn't turn to look at him. "Are you in some kind of trouble with your father?"

"Not anymore," he replied with a chuckle. "My father said he'd hold me responsible if Tao left him to follow Miss Han home, but with Lichfield to take care of business matters in the office, Tao is free to travel anywhere he pleases. He'll be taking some trading offers from my father with him when he goes to see Miss Han's father, which will hopefully make him a more attractive prospective bridegroom. If everything works out, the happy couple will spend time both here and in China, at least until Tao sets up a business of his own. They'll decide together where to make their permanent home."

After that he fell silent, but Amanda knew what he meant to say and she had no intentions of listening to it.

"No, Jack," she said, answering the question before he asked it. "We can't make love one more time before saying good-bye. It would be vile, and there's been enough vileness already."

"Even if I assured you that your intended husband wouldn't mind?" Jack asked, sounding not in the least bothered. "I happen to know him rather well, and I can give you my word that he won't find it in the least vile."

"Why are you doing this?" she demanded, finally turning to look straight at him. "Because you think I'm lying about being betrothed? If you don't believe me, ask Richard for yourself. Because you think you're entitled to a reward for devising a way to restore my reputation? I think you're due that reward, too, but you and I are in the minority. I've been promised to another man, and to betray that promise is beyond me. Isn't it enough that he'll eventually learn I can never love him? That my heart belongs to a man I'll never see again—?"

Amanda's throat closed up so tightly that she couldn't say another word, but when she tried to turn and run Jack pulled her into his arms.

"*Ssu Te Lung,* don't cry," he crooned, rocking her like a child. "Everything isn't lost, it's all been found. I only meant to tease you for a moment, I swear it, but I never stopped to realize how hurt you would be. It isn't another man you're betrothed to, Amanda, it's me. When my father was here this morning arranging for tonight, he arranged our betrothal as well."

Jack's hand tried to stroke the tension out of her back, but he was wasting his time. No matter how much Amanda wanted to believe what he'd said, she knew it wasn't so.

"Why do I have the feeling you don't believe me?" he asked after a moment, much of the gladness gone from his voice. "I'm telling the God's honest truth, and you can ask your brother and my father together if you like. I'm so excited I can hardly wait, and it's all I can do not to carry you off to the village church right this minute."

"Is *that* what your plan is?" Amanda asked, ignoring the tightening of his arms that made her want him more than she wanted her next breath. "You think that if you convince me we're betrothed, I'll run off with you for a secret early ceremony? Only later it will turn out that we weren't betrothed at all, but by then it will be far too late to undo the marriage. Don't you see that that would be the worst thing we could do, Jack? It would make us end up hating each other just as much as—"

"Wait a moment, wait just a moment," Jack interrupted, holding her at arm's length to look down at her. "I'm telling you as plainly as I can, Amanda: you and I *are* betrothed. I'm not trying to steal you from the man who has rightfully claimed you, *I'm* that man. What can I say to convince you?"

"Nothing," Amanda told him sadly. "I love you with all my heart, Jack, but Richard told me this afternoon that as of right then there wasn't the slightest chance that I would ever marry you. You don't expect me to believe that my brother lied?"

"Of course not, and I don't believe it either," Jack said, now looking frustrated. "He isn't a man to lie, especially not to the sister he loves. But we *are* betrothed, so how could he possibly say we're not? . . . Wait, now. Have you told me his exact words? Think back, and try to repeat them just as he said them."

"I already have," Amanda protested wearily with a sigh. "He said something like, 'As of this moment, there isn't the slightest chance that you will ever marry a man named Jack Michaels.' How could I possibly have misinterpreted *that*, Jack? He also told me the name of the man I was betrothed to, and it wasn't you."

"What name was it?" Jack asked, his brows low and drawn together.

"It was Sir John Blackburn," Amanda replied, then immediately regretted having said it. What if Jack lost his head and called the man out? What if he—?

"Oh, that devil," Jack exclaimed, but suddenly he was grinning rather than looking disturbed. "I had no idea he had it in him, but my father might have instigated part of this confusion. He was amused over what happened between him and me because of that story of yours, but he doesn't believe in letting naughty children get away with being naughty. And I'd venture to guess you told Richard how you'd been playing him along where I was concerned. It would have been kinder of him to warm your bottom for it, but for a man to give back what he's been getting is a good deal safer when dealing with a woman like you."

"Jack, what *are* you talking about?" Amanda demanded, wondering if the shock hadn't been too much for the man. "Yes, I did tell Richard about what I'd done, but I don't understand the rest of what you said. And do you know this Blackburn? I can't remember ever having met him."

"In a manner of speaking you haven't, not formally," Jack answered, his grin softening. "Your brother told you the absolute truth, love, but there are one or two things he knows that you obviously don't. For instance, I have some marvelous news that I meant to tell you much sooner. My superiors have decided that they've finally found the perfect excuse for rewarding my efforts on behalf of the empire. You furnished that excuse by forcing me to help you look for Lichfield, which led to uncovering the late Baron Delland's schemes, so the reward is one you deserve to share with me. And it will let me change my public character, so I never have to act the fool again. People will get used to the new me, and forget all about the silly fop."

"Oh, Jack, that's wonderful!" Amanda said with a laugh, delighted for him even if she would not, as he hoped, be sharing that reward with him. "I'm so happy for you! And you'll still be keeping your present position?"

"They're giving me a new position," he said with a smile, his arms having found their way around her again. "One of those changes I mentioned is a promotion, as I'll be working with my immediate superior to prepare me to succeed him when he retires. That's where not having to act the fool again comes in."

"It sounds like the answer to our former prayers," Amanda said, trying not to ruin his justified pleasure by letting free the tears demanding to be released. "Now you'll be able to live a normal life, and . . . and . . ."

"Amanda, my reward was a knighthood," he said quickly before she could pull away again. "Doesn't knowing that make you look at what your brother said in an entirely different way? Haven't you any idea what my family name is?"

Amanda almost said of course she did, it was Michaels, but then she realized that was wrong. Michaels was a use name, supposedly because he'd been forbidden to use his real family name. But that could mean . . . it was really possible that . . .

"That's right, my real name is Blackburn, and Jack is the familiar form of John," he said, obviously reading her expression. "His Majesty won't get around to knighting me for another sennight or so, but that's certainly soon enough for you to marry Sir John Blackburn."

"Which means I never *will* marry a man named Jack Michaels," Amanda finished, practically open-mouthed. But she *would* marry her heart's love, and now, finally, she did believe. The relief was exhilarating, but then she thought of what it also meant. "That Richard! If he hadn't distracted me with needing to protect you from someone trying to prove you a murderer, I would have been sick about the whole thing! But I'll get even, just give me a little while to think!"

"There's only one thing you'll be thinking about for a while, and that's me," Jack said, suddenly bending and lifting her in his arms. "Besides, Richard was just getting even for what *you'd* done, and I know exactly how he felt. Do you really want to do something else to him, and possibly cause him to delay the wedding in retaliation? He can do that, you know."

"I suppose I knew, but it hadn't occurred to me," Amanda muttered, her arms already wrapped around Jack's neck. "All right, I won't try to get even, at least not until after the wedding."

"Not even then," Jack murmured in her ear, then began to kiss her face and neck. "You'll be Lady Blackburn, and I won't have a wife of mine acting like a hellion. Or like a dragon, which is almost the same thing. Have I mentioned how glad I am that you're wearing your *chih fu?* That means much less clothing to remove, and we'll need the time. We'll have to join the party soon, so they can announce our betrothal."

"Where are you taking me?" Amanda asked, aware that Jack had been walking, but not knowing where. She'd been nibbling and licking his ear, and his breathing had grown satisfyingly heavier. She wanted to get at the rest of him, but it wasn't possible there in the ballroom . . .

"Right here," Jack answered, pushing open the door to one of the retiring rooms with his shoulder. "Knowing the party would be in the salon rather than in the ballroom let me make certain preparations. There's an adorable young lady I've been dying to tumble, you see, and I knew if I just kept trying I'd eventually get her."

"Do you mean the same young lady who first tumbled *you?*" Amanda asked innocently, getting a glimpse of comfortably arranged blankets before Jack turned again to close the door. "That had better be who you mean, because if it isn't, you're destined to know an adorably *flattened* young lady."

"Temper, temper," Jack said with a grin, going to one knee to set her down on the blankets. "Once word spreads about what you can do, I won't *ever* be bothered with unwanted female advances. Which suits me perfectly, since I've somehow acquired an insatiable taste for *dragon* advances. Men who haven't learned the difference don't know what they're missing."

And then he kissed her, lying beside her in order to take her in his arms. She already held him as tightly as was humanly possible, loving him so much she thought she would burst. She'd set her hero an impossible task, and not only had he come back with a solution, he'd even managed to save her in the bargain. And now he really was her knight. She'd wanted a Golden Devil and had gotten him, even if the devil now had to be hidden beneath the shining plate armor of respectability. Her devil would still be there for *her,* which was all that really mattered.

"I'd better get out of these clothes now," Jack murmured when he grudgingly ended their kiss. "We still have that fool party to go to once you're dressed. I don't want the servants tossing me out because I'm so rumpled I've turned into looking like a beggar."

"Let me help," Amanda said at once, but not because the state of his clothes worried her. She just wanted him out of them as soon as possible, so that they could love each other. It seemed like years since the last time they'd been together, and she still wasn't completely over thinking he was lost to her forever. It would take a long while before she did get over it, but with the passage of enough time and loving . . .

Jack pulled his clothes off and Amanda folded them neatly, trying not to grin over feeling like a maid. It was ridiculous to have to worry about clothes when what she really wanted to do was rip them off him, but if she tried it Jack wasn't likely to be amused. But sometime she'd have to, sometime after they were married, just to see what he would do. . . .

"All ready," Jack announced, reaching for her. "Now it's your turn."

"Jack, wait!" she said, suddenly noticing his bandaged side. "I forgot about your wound. If I let you do this it might hurt you."

"If you *don't* let me do this, it will definitely hurt me more," he countered, picking her up again and taking her down to the blankets with him. "Because either way I still mean to do it, even if you pound me to pulp. Go ahead, pound me to pulp."

By then he'd removed her belt and had opened the ties of her *chih fu*, and his lips had gone right to her breast. She gasped at the feel of them and tried to squirm free, but he refused to let her do that. He held her gently but firmly, and the only way she'd get loose was if she *did* pound him to pulp.

Only that wasn't possible either, and not simply because she loved him too much to hurt him. One of his hands had undone the tie of her trousers, and now stroked between her thighs with the same dragon-flame he brought to her breast. Both things together had immediately stolen her strength, leaving her a writhing mass incapable of speech. It wasn't quite fair that he was able to do that, especially since it also robbed her of the chance to touch *him*.

And then, like magic, he seemed to read her mind again. His lips came back up to hers, and they shared a kiss full of all the relief they both felt. He also used the time to pull her *chih fu* off completely, and then *his* body was made as available to her as hers was to him. Their kiss merged souls as their hands spoke their love, touching and stroking everywhere. Amanda reached to Jack's desire and rubbed it against her own, driving them both wild with need.

When Jack finally let her lie flat she was more than ready, greeting him with an eagerness that matched his own. She moaned when he thrust into her, then locked her legs around his waist to make sure he couldn't escape. She was his captive and he was hers, and his strong, deep thrusts were met by the frenzied movement of her hips. They shared their blending for an endless time, the pleasure beyond description, and when it was finally done they lay wrapped in each other's arms. After lovemaking love should be left, and with her and Jack it certainly was.

"My own Golden Devil," Amanda murmured, as she snuggled even closer to Jack, thrilling to the idea much more than to the words. "And he actually loves me as much as I love him."

"Lady mine," Jack whispered just before kissing her again. "Your Golden Devil always will."

And Amanda knew he would, from now through the rest of forever.